FAKE SHOT

Boston Rebels Series
Book 2

JULIA CONNORS

*To the women who have built up walls to protect themselves,
and to the men who prove it's safe to take them down.*

Author's Note

Fake Shot deals with topics that may be sensitive for some readers, including anxiety and panic attacks, parental abandonment and death of a parent, and past cheating. For a full list of content warnings, please visit my website: juliaconnors.com/fake-shot

Chapter One

JULES

Six Years Ago
Las Vegas, NV

From my spot at the edge of the craps table, I take another sip of my whiskey sour. I should have picked a sweeter drink, because then I'd be able to tell if it's the drink turning my stomach, or if it's the way the woman in the barely-there pink dress is hanging all over Colt.

"She's a less pretty version of you," Brock Lester says as he leans into my side. Clearly, I'm failing in my attempt not to stare at Colt and tonight's *woman du jour*.

She can't be much older than me, and while her hair is light brown with blond highlights and not a shiny blond like mine, there's enough of a resemblance for a comparison. And it's that fact that hurts.

All those excuses I've made for years—that I'm too young for him or that I'm not his type—to explain why he's not interested in me, they're all lies in the wake of tonight's evidence. It's not my age or that I'm not his type. It's just me. Whatever the reason, he's just not into me, and he never will be.

I know I need to accept that . . . probably should have accepted it years ago, but I can barely remember a time when I didn't love Colt. From the time I was old enough to be interested in boys, my brother's best friend and teammate was the only one I had eyes for. It didn't matter that he was eight years older than me or that he's always treated me like a little sister. I've been too stubborn to quit on my feelings for him, because I'm entirely certain we could be perfect together if only he'd open his eyes and *see me.*

Tilting the drink against my lips, I drain the glass before I turn toward Brock. "I'm not sure what you're talking about."

"Sure you're not," he says, a low chuckle following his words. "But if you want to make him jealous, you just let me know."

I narrow my eyes at him, telling myself it's because I'm trying to make sense of his meaning rather than because my vision is getting the slightest bit unfocused.

"And why would I do that?" I attempt to keep my voice indifferent, the way I have all night as the NHL's resident bad boy has shamelessly flirted with me. But my disinterest only seems to have increased his dedication to getting my attention.

"Because we could have a lot of fun together." The backs of his knuckles trail along the outside of my thigh, and even though he's not my type, it sends a shiver of excitement up my back. Around us, the large and now very drunk group of hockey players who have congregated in Las Vegas for All-

Star Weekend, along with their wives and girlfriends and a fair number of puck bunnies, are loud and laughing and paying us no mind.

I'm fairly certain I'm not cool enough to be here.

Audrey and I convinced our brother, Jameson, to bring us to All-Star Weekend with him—even though we'd each be missing a couple of days of our college classes—so we could enjoy a weekend of sun and relaxation, and attend the game. As an agent, he represents several of the players, including Colt, who's a goalie for the Boston Rebels, a young center named Alex Ivanov, who's having a stellar second year in New York, and a defenseman from Ottawa named Tom Bonovono.

When the players headed out tonight after the post-game dinner, Audrey went back to the hotel because she's very pregnant and always exhausted. And even though I could have hung out with her in the hotel room, watching movies and raiding the snacks in the mini bar like we'd done the last two nights, I felt like going out.

The funny thing about being a freshman in college is that you get used to making your own decisions about how you spend your nights, and I'd forgotten what it was like to need to ask my brother's permission. Luckily, he didn't put up a fight about me coming out with them, even though, at nineteen, I'm not technically old enough to be at the gaming tables, and I'm definitely not supposed to be drinking.

Like I suspected, no one has asked for my ID because I put on some makeup and a slinky dress with high heels, and I walked in with a group of the best players in professional hockey. As we moved through the doors of the casino earlier, Colt slung his arm over my shoulder to usher me in with the group, making sure I didn't get left behind. That moment had given me all kinds of hope.

But that was hours ago, before that woman in the pink dress started hanging all over him. He hasn't looked at me since.

Except when—about an hour ago—Jameson told him he was going with a few of the players to a strip club. He claimed it was to "make sure no one got in trouble," and while I believe him, it also feels like these are grown men who should be responsible for themselves. Then he asked Colt to "keep an eye on me."

Unlike his players, I don't need a fucking babysitter.

"Are you thinking it over?" Brock asks, and it's only then that I realize I've been completely lost in my thoughts about how I'll never be anything more than a kid in Colt's eyes—someone he needs to take care of when my big brother isn't around.

He's never going to see you as more.

"Yeah, I'm considering it . . ." I bite my lip as I flag down the waitress assigned to our private VIP area. Then I order another whiskey sour because I'm afraid to change my drink order. I've never been drunk before, but I've heard horror stories about mixing alcohols, and sticking with the same drink feels safe.

He leans in again. "You're way too beautiful and sweet to be spending this weekend alone, Jules." My name is a caress coming off his tongue, and his warm breath glides along my bare shoulder, wrapping me in the promise of companionship.

I've dated here and there just to see what all the fuss is about, but I've never had a boyfriend because I've held on to this stupid childhood crush way past its expiration date. I've also never had sex, nor drank too much, nor made a single bad decision.

And suddenly, three drinks in, all these rites of passage that other people my age have typically experienced make me feel like I need to grow up. And moving on from this ridiculous crush, with someone who is *not* Colt, feels like the first monumental step toward actual adulthood.

"What did you have in mind?" I ask. Notching my index finger behind his belt buckle, I relish his sharp intake of breath and the way he half closes his eyelids as he looks down at me.

And then I let Brock wrap his arm along my lower back, grip my hip, and pull me against him, whispering promises about all the dirty things he wants to do to me. I'm seriously considering his suggestions because, hell, someone needs to take my virginity. I have an incredibly good-looking, highly attentive man standing right here, offering to spend this weekend making sure I have "fun." And he's rebuffed every other woman who's tried to talk to him tonight, focusing all his energy on me because, unlike Colt, he's clearly into me. Would I be a fool to turn him down?

Before I can agree, Colt's next to us, one hand on my shoulder and one hand on the neck of Brock's button down as he pulls him away and tells him to mind his fucking manners with "Flynn's baby sister."

Of course he has to go and make me feel and sound like a goddamn child—I don't know why I'm just now realizing that this is how he views me. I'm so pissed off I could cry, but I have years of experience hiding my anger and frustration and so instead, I stand taller and square my shoulders as I turn to face him.

"I can make my own decisions about whose company I keep."

"I told Jameson I'd be responsible for you tonight," he says, looking down at me, "and I'm headed to my room. So I'll take you to yours on my way."

"I'm fine here for now. I can find my way back to my own room," I tell him. In the dim light of the casino, it's impossible to tell what time it is. It could be ten at night or three in the morning, I have no idea. But I do know that I'm not tired, and I want to stay out longer. Mostly, though, I want him to stop treating me like a child.

Colt reaches out, gripping my elbow in a way that's not painful, but is definitely meant to show me he's not playing. "Let's go."

"I'm fine here, *Dad*." I spit the word at him, hating how much I sound like a little brat. But who the hell does he think he is?

He leans in close, and I force myself not to notice the way he smells tangy and spicy, or the way his hard chest feels pressed up against my arm and shoulder as he says, "We can do this the easy way or the hard way. Either way, I'm seeing you back to your room like I promised your brother I would. Should I throw you over my shoulder, or can you walk out of here like a good girl?"

I grind my teeth together in frustration. Of all the times I've imagined words of affirmation like that coming from his mouth, it was never in a situation like this.

"I'll see myself up to my own room," I say, turning to walk away without even saying goodbye to Brock. I don't want him to notice the anger creeping up my skin, leaving my chest, neck, and face flushed, or my eyes watering from the embarrassment.

Colt's on my heels as I speed through the lobby of the hotel and approach the elevator. After hitting the button, I turn to tell him he doesn't need to follow me, and I'm completely blindsided by the puck bunny in the pink dress standing there under his arm.

There's no way Colt doesn't know I've had a crush on him for years. And the fact that he's standing here with another woman, taking her up to his room—not an ounce of subtlety or shame, not even having her follow a few minutes later to spare my feelings in this situation—tells me what I've suspected all night.

He doesn't give a shit about me, except as his best friend's baby sister. And given how I feel about him, that's utterly heartbreaking.

We ride the elevator in silence, my eyes on the floor the whole time. I don't want to see how he's looking at her or what he's doing that's making her giggle. When we hit the sixteenth floor and the doors open, I zoom out of the elevator like I'm turbo charged.

I'm sliding the key card into my door and pushing it open—hoping I can make it inside before he sees the tears that have started falling—when he passes behind me on the way to his room a few doors down. "'Night, Tink."

I slip into the dark room almost silently, determined not to wake Audrey up, and slide my back down the door as I crumple to the floor, completely and totally crushed.

And that's when my phone lights up with a text. When I tap on it, there's a photo of Brock, his lips wrapped around the straw sticking out of a whiskey sour, one of his light brown eyebrows raised as his hair falls across his forehead. He's stupidly attractive. Whereas Colt's all muscle with fair skin and a chiseled square jaw, Brock's thinner with darker skin and a more refined bone structure that showcases his cheekbones and his slightly pointed chin.

BROCK

This whiskey sour isn't going to drink itself.

I'm about to respond and ask him how he got my number when I remember that he put contact info in my phone when he first started flirting with me, saying, "in case you ever need it." I glance up at the top of the screen, and what I didn't realize at the time was that he also sent himself a text from my phone that says, simply: *Jules Flynn.*

I press my lips together to hold back the smile, not that there's anyone to see it. Audrey's consistent breathing is a sure sign she's dead asleep in her bed on the other side of the bathroom wall.

I should go put my pajamas on and climb into my bed and let myself have a good cry through the heartbreak that was inevitable. There was never a world where Colt was going to feel the same way about me. I knew it, and I held on anyway.

Or . . . I could go into the bathroom, wipe these tears away, and go out and have fun.

And as the image of that woman wrapped around Colt filters back into my mind, I don't feel sad. I feel angry.

I deserve to move on, with someone who *is* interested in me. Colt doesn't deserve the love I've been saving for him. Neither does Brock, but I can go back down there with no expectations that there will be any feelings involved—we're just having fun. And isn't that what a nineteen-year-old college freshman should be doing?

Slipping into the bathroom, I shut the door as quietly as possible, wetting a washcloth, and wiping away the evidence of how hard this night has been on my heart.

JULES

I'll be back down in ten minutes.

BROCK

I was hoping you'd say that.

JULES

Enjoy my drink, and order me another.

Brock sends another selfie of him smiling and holding up an already empty glass.

BROCK

I just ordered us both another. Get your cute ass back here quickly or I might have to drink both of them too.

As I smile, it feels like it might be the first time in too long. I'm serious by nature, and because I've loved Colt for as long as I can remember, I never really flirt with other guys. But this—the attention and the longing—feels good.

I leave the hotel room hoping that by the time I get back downstairs, the red stain of embarrassment and tears from earlier will no longer be visible through the concealer I just reapplied. And as the elevator descends, I make myself a promise: *Those were the last tears I'll ever cry for Mathieu Coltier. Any feelings I had for him are officially dead.*

It's time to move on.

Chapter Two

COLT

Present Day

"You need another?" Tiana asks as she glances up and sees me standing at the entrance to the galley in the back of the plane. Her voice is soft in the silence, but I don't miss the notes of sympathy—and there's nothing I hate more than someone feeling bad for me. I'm no one's charity case.

"Please." Even though I'm known for being the loud and crazy one, I keep my voice quiet. Behind me, the airplane is dark, and my teammates are still sleeping on our overnight flight back to Boston after tonight's win in our last regular-season game. We clinched our playoff spot a while ago, and I can't wait to have the next week off from games and travel before the first round starts.

As she turns and pulls out one of the sleek metal storage drawers, I stand here gritting my teeth. There was a time when I loved being on the road—the flights with my team-mates, the hotel stays in different cities every night, and the endless stream of women. But maybe I really am the old man my teammates jokingly accuse me of becoming because, lately, the week-long road trips have me questioning how much longer I can do this.

For now, the perks of being the longest-running goalie in the NHL still outweigh the drawbacks. But I find myself wondering more and more often what it would be like to not be on the road for half the year. To eat meals at home, and sleep in my own bed every night. *Lonely. It would be fucking lonely.*

But the allure of my brand-new bed—in all its expensive, advanced-technology memory foam glory—is all I can think about as Tiana hands me two fresh bags of ice. Literally all I want in the world is to get home and crawl into bed.

I make my way back to my seat, rest the bags of ice on my knees, then recline until I'm lying almost vertical. I used to be able to sleep on these overnight flights, no problem. I'd be so exhausted coming out of those games, I could just close my eyes and drift off in these big, comfortable chairs the minute they dimmed the lights. But that was before every-thing hurt . . . before I started feeling way older than my age.

"You need to see the fucking trainer about your knees, not the flight attendant," Drew mumbles from beside me.

Turning my head toward my seat mate, I find that he's no longer asleep. "Most judges wear robes."

"Dude, it's not a judgment, it's a fact. We're about to start fighting for the Cup. You need to be in the best shape you've ever been in."

I love it when these younger players talk to me like they know shit. Drew Jenkins has been in the league for six years, but it's his first year with the Boston Rebels. For some players who come to the NHL out of college, like Drew did, six years can be an entire career. The conventional wisdom used to be that by thirty, you were on your way to retiring. Even though Drew's career is finally taking off, he should know his place.

"Please, regale me with your knowledge about winning the Cup." He rolls his eyes in response to my dry tone, but I continue. "Once you've won two, like I have, I might listen. And once you've been in the league for over a decade, you can tell me how to take care of myself. But for now, it's past your bedtime. Go back to sleep."

I don't know why it brings me such joy to give him shit. Maybe I really am the overgrown child that my best friend and agent's youngest sister, Jules, constantly accuses me of being. I can't seem to stop antagonizing her either. To be fair, I'm only like this with people I care about.

If I don't like you, you don't exist. Period.

And as if the universe is trying to fuck with me, a text from my brother immediately follows that thought.

GABRIEL

I need to know if you're coming. It's Mom and Dad's 50th anniversary. Please tell me you'll be there.

It's been fifteen years. You have to be over this by now.

It's five in the morning, which means we'll be landing in

Boston soon, and somewhere outside of Montreal, Gabriel probably just finished a shift at the hospital. He's an ER doctor, because of course he is.

I stop pucks from going into a net, and he saves lives.

I power off my phone so I won't be inundated with his messages—once he gets started, the texts just roll in. Drew's watching me with interest, but this isn't a conversation I want to have. So I close my eyes and turn my head away from him. Maybe I can catch a few minutes of sleep before we land.

———

"You sure you don't want to come to breakfast with us?" Zach Reid asks as we're wheeling our suitcases across the tarmac toward the parking lot at the private airport we flew into.

"Yeah," I say. "Positive. The only thing I want to do right now is sleep."

"You didn't sleep at all on the plane, did you?" Drew asks.

"Not a wink."

"You're too old to pull all-nighters," Ronan McCabe, our team captain, says.

"No shit, Cap." I glance over at McCabe, and his lips are pressed into a thin line. I know he worries about how many years I have left in me. We've played together for a decade already, but I've got five years on him. I've never played anywhere but Boston, and I count myself lucky.

There are guys like Drew who have moved around at the end of every contract—though Boston just signed him for another six years, so he should be here for a while. Which is good, since he lives with and has a kid with Jameson's other sister, Audrey.

"Don't fucking call me that," McCabe says. As always, his voice is a low growl.

This is an old argument, so I say the same thing I do every time. "Why? You're our captain."

He side-eyes me. "So are you."

I'm not technically a captain, because the NHL's rules don't allow goaltenders to hold that role for logistical reasons—there would be too many delays if the goalie had to leave the crease every time he wanted to talk to the refs about a call.

So instead, McCabe took on that distinction, while I settled for the very unofficial title of "off-ice captain." Sure, the guys generally look up to me because I've been here longer than anyone else, but McCabe is the one whose grumpy ass gets to lead this team officially.

He never treats me as anything less than an equal, but it still sucks sometimes knowing that I'll never see that "C" on my jersey. Of all the things I've accomplished in my years in the league, I'm not sure anything would mean more than knowing my teammates, coaching staff, and the organization felt I was worthy of the title.

I roll my eyes and press the button on my key fob to open the trunk of my Porsche Cayenne. It's rained while we've been gone, and my baby needs to be washed. I'll drop her off with the valet in my building when I get home so she can get detailed.

Once I sling my suitcase into the trunk, I shut the liftgate and say goodbye to my teammates. As good as breakfast sounds right now, I need sleep more than anything.

Fifteen minutes later, I'm exiting the tunnel onto the surface roads leading to the Seaport, having navigated what would normally be a much longer drive in a short time thanks to the early Sunday morning lack of traffic. And that's when I realize I never turned my phone back on. While waiting for a light, I power it up and set it on the charger. As it syncs up with my car, I see that I have 42 text notifications and 2 missed calls, which is not normal for 7 a.m. on a Sunday morning.

Most of the texts are from my brother, so I ignore those for now. But both calls are from the head of maintenance at my building, and that can't be good.

———

"How could it possibly be this bad?" I ask Andy as I walk down the hallway from my front door toward my living room.

On the right, the entire ceiling above my kitchen has collapsed—drywall, plaster, insulation, and water cover every surface. Through what used to be a ceiling, you can see broken, soaked wood flooring, and the corner of either my washing machine or dryer is poking through, but is held in place by the splintered floor and the steel beams that support it. The walls of the kitchen are soaking wet, and the top cabinets look like they might fall off at any moment. As it is, we're standing in at least an inch of water that's spread down the hallway.

"It's hard to know how long the water ran after the washing machine hose burst. But based on the damage, it seems like maybe it's been running for days."

We stop walking when we reach the wide stairs that lead to my sunken living room, which appears to have served as a waterfall area for the water to collect there. My couches are soaked, and the wooden table that normally sits between them is floating like a boat in several inches of water.

"Is it even safe to be standing here?" I ask him. "Given that the ceiling of my second floor collapsed, what's stopping this area from collapsing into the condo below us?"

"Luckily, not enough water has soaked through this floor to cause that kind of collapse," he says as he stands next to me in the blue uniform of our building's maintenance crew.

"Just enough for my downstairs neighbor to notice water leaking?"

"Exactly. Thankfully, they noticed when they did, or it could have been a whole lot worse. We probably should get out of here," he says. "I just wanted you to see what we're into. The power's off indefinitely, and the cleanup crew is on their way here. But . . ."

"But what?" I ask when he doesn't finish the sentence.

"When I've seen damage this extensive before, it takes a long time to repair."

"How long?"

"Months, probably."

"Months?" I practically yell the question. What the hell? All I wanted was to come home, go to sleep, and enjoy this next week of no travel before we start our road to the Cup—because this year, this team . . . we have a serious shot at this. I don't have time for this shit.

"Yeah. Everything the water touched will need to be ripped out. It takes time to dry things out so you don't have a mold problem. Your electrical in all these rooms will probably need to be rewired. You'll need new studs, walls, floors, ceilings, insulation . . . new everything, really. It'll be more like a rebuild than a remodel."

"How could one burst washing machine hose cause this much damage?"

"It wasn't a slow leak, Colt. Water was coming out of that thing for at least a day or two. Think how quickly your washing machine fills up when you turn it on, and now imagine all that water running out of a hose for that long." He nods his chin toward my front door, and I follow him to my entryway and out into the hallway.

"How far did the damage spread? Am I going to be repairing my neighbors' places too?"

"It seems like we caught it before it got too far. Aside from the Millers below you, no one else has mentioned any damage. But you should call your insurance company because they'll need to come in and do an estimate. They always try to low-ball you, so you might want to have a contractor here with you when they come in."

I tilt my head all the way back and exhale, trying to release some of the tension in my neck and shoulders.

"Should I stick around for when the cleanup crew gets here?"

"You can. Or I can just have them take pictures of everything they have to dispose of, if you don't want to wait around."

"I haven't slept in over twenty-four hours, so if I can get out of here and come back later, I'd appreciate it."

"Sure. I'll take care of it. Just text or call if you need me."

"Thanks, Andy," I say as I turn toward the elevator, rolling my suitcase behind me. I'm almost too tired to think, so I dial the one person who I've trusted to think for me over the past decade.

Two rings, and then Jameson growls, "It's seven o'clock on Sunday morning."

"Yeah, and I need a huge favor."

Chapter Three

JULES

"You seriously slayed," Audrey whispers as she leans toward me. We're standing together at the front of the room, with the heads of four other nonprofits who are all looking for start-up funding.

"I didn't do that alone. You were awesome too."

"All I did," she says quietly, tucking a piece of her long dark hair behind her ear while we wait for the applause to die down, "was talk a bit about the financials. It was your passion for this program that's going to get us some funding."

She might be right, but I couldn't do this without her. I tell her as much as I loop my arm behind her back and squeeze her to my side in a quick hug.

The host thanks all of us for presenting and then welcomes each nonprofit to take a seat at the tables around the room. While the first half of the evening was a typical pitch fest where we had to sell the work of our nonprofit, the second half of the evening is an opportunity for potential donors to stop by and chat with us over drinks and hors d'oeuvres if they're interested.

There's an excited energy coursing through me as we take our seats. I don't get nervous, and when it comes to my work, I almost never second-guess myself. I have an acute sixth sense about what's going to succeed in our business, and this nonprofit that we've started as a spin-off of our company is no different. When I meet the right donor, I'll know.

The first two people who come talk to us both express interest in investing in Our House, the all-female design and construction company we've built together over the past few years.

"It's so weird," I say to Audrey as the second man leaves. "We were perfectly clear about what we were looking for in terms of donors, and at no point did we indicate that we were looking for investors for Our House. This whole event is for nonprofits."

Her response is practically a snort. "They must know a good business opportunity when they see one. But do they really think we'd turn over ownership of *any* portion of our company to a man, when the whole basis for our company is that we're entirely female owned and operated?"

"Maybe . . ." I bite the corner of my lip. "I don't know, maybe the purpose of our nonprofit would be clearer if we could get a video testimonial from someone like Rosie?"

"Think she'd say yes if you asked her again?"

"I'm not sure." I shrug, thinking about the first woman I mentored. I met her when our friend, Morgan, who now runs all our business's social media, suggested partnering with trade schools to help develop a pipeline of qualified female contractors to work with us.

Even though we're the same age, Rosie's life experience makes me feel like a damn baby. She's had it hard and risen above it—going to electrical school as soon as her daughter was old enough for kindergarten—because she's determined to break past cycles of abuse and poverty to provide a better life for her child. As soon as she finished trade school, I hired her and arranged for her to complete her required hours of work experience with our master electrician, Jessica, so she could earn her journeyman license.

Rosie was the first person I mentored, back at the beginning of our program, which we're now trying to turn into a full-fledged nonprofit so we can help even more people.

"She might be more open to it now than she was when I first asked her," I say.

"Maybe you can try. Because if we can show that kind of first-hand testimonial, those success stories, I think it'll be even more clear how this work has the potential to change lives."

I start to respond, but a man I recognize as the third donor we were hoping to talk to strides up and takes a seat at the high-top table we're sitting at. "You're looking for a large-scale donation, is that right?"

"We like to think of it as an investment in women, and an opportunity to improve their job options," Audrey says.

"So then . . ." His voice has the hard edge of someone used to talking about money, but his face is full of interest. He's handsome in that way older men often are—when they've grown comfortable with who they've become and are confident in their own skin—but our age difference doesn't intimidate me. The fact that I've accomplished so much by my mid-twenties makes me that much more sure of myself. " . . . tell me more about how this enriches lives."

"Trade jobs offer steady and dependable work, and yet there's a shortage of qualified people in almost every construction-related skilled trade. Women make up less than 10% of people in these industries. Our goal is to help bridge that gap—to make sure that there are enough skilled trades-people by helping to get more women into these professions."

His eyes slide down my body and then back up to my face. He's most likely sizing me up, rather than checking me out, but either way, it gives off a slimy vibe that makes me question if he's the type of person I want to work with.

"I'm intrigued. I want to know more about the success rate of people you've mentored and what my role would be as a donor. I have a few hundred grand I'd be interested in donating to the right nonprofit as long as my input is considered in how the money is used. I'd like to talk more about this." He glances at his watch, which I'm fairly certain costs more than my brand-new truck. "But I'm supposed to be on a flight to Ireland in like forty minutes."

"Shouldn't you already be at the airport, then?" Audrey asks, and he coughs out a laugh.

"I just have to get to the helipad a few blocks away, and it'll take me straight to the jet. Don't worry about me," he says. I'm so focused on not cringing at his condescending tone that I almost don't notice when he turns his attention back to me. "I'll be back at the end of the week. Maybe we can meet for lunch on Saturday to discuss this further?"

"We already have plans during the day," I say pleasantly as

I gesture between Audrey and me, trying to remind him that she's part of the conversation. The way he keeps his eyes trained on me makes me think he's missing my cues.

"Dinner it is, then."

"I don't—" I start, ready to tell him dinner won't work for us because I know Audrey's going to be busy that night, but it's a surprise I can't ruin for her.

"Dinner is perfect." She smiles brightly as she hands him our business card. "Feel free to email or text the details. We appreciate your time."

Once he's gone, I turn toward Audrey. "What the hell? We don't want him involved in this."

"Are you sure?" she asks. "Because he said the magic words: a few hundred grand."

"He's too pompous for my taste."

"He's got three hundred grand he's willing to sign away, and you're surprised he's pompous? Who cares, as long as he's also interested in giving us money to further a mission we care about deeply? Let's hear what he has to say, and then we can decide."

"Fine," I say, having accepted long ago that I'm incapable of saying no to my siblings. Since I'm the only person who knows the surprise Drew has up his sleeve, I know full-well there is no *we* when it comes to this dinner meeting—I'll go alone.

The event wraps up quickly after that, and when Audrey and I part on the sidewalk, we say the same thing we always say: "Text me when you're home."

She heads toward the Back Bay condo she now shares with Drew and their son, Graham, and I head toward our family brownstone in the South End that, until recently, I shared with both my siblings and my nephew. But Jameson moved in with his fiancée, Lauren, and her two kids a year ago, and Audrey and Graham moved in with Drew five months ago.

As if he knew I was just thinking about him, my phone rings and Jameson's name pops up on the screen. "Hey," I say as I make my way into Copley Square, headed toward the bridge over the Mass Pike that will take me into the South End.

"Hey, I thought you'd be home."

"Audrey and I just gave a pitch to some potential donors—"

"For the nonprofit?" Jameson's question cuts me off. He's technically a silent owner of Our House, and even though he remains 100% uninvolved in the day-to-day, he does like to know what's going on.

"Yes, for the nonprofit, not the business."

"Remind me why I can't be your investor in that?" he says. He's been an agent for several of the NHL's best players for many years. Given how many players he represents, he makes more than the highest paid players in the league. And he's nothing if not generous, but Audrey and I want this program to stand on its own merit, not because our brother invested in it.

"We don't need to have this conversation again. Anyway, I'm on my way home now," I say, coming to a stop at one of the crosswalks in Copley Square. "Are you there?"

"Yeah. See you in a few minutes."

The traffic light changes, and I start to move with the after-work crowd across the crosswalk. Once I hit the tree-lined streets of the South End, some of the noise of the city fades away. I inhale the early-spring scent—the trees, with their leaves finally blossoming, and the tulips and daffodils that line people's small planting areas in front of the brick row houses. The days are finally getting longer and warmer, and I already can't wait for the first really nice day.

Audrey's text that she's arrived home safely comes right as I take the steps to our row house, so I let her know I'm home too. And when I shut the heavy wood and glass front door behind me, all I can see of Jameson is his dark dress pants and his crisp light blue button down, because his head is shoved into my refrigerator.

"Why are there no leftovers?" he calls out, standing fully and turning toward me.

"I haven't felt like cooking lately." I shrug out of my long cardigan and hang it on the hook by the door.

"Life not stressful enough?" he teases.

It's always been the joke in our family that you can tell if I've had a stressful day by how much I cook that night. But the truth is, cooking is my love language, and without my family around to enjoy the food, there's far less pleasure in it. I still cook for our weekly family dinners, but I find myself making something simple or ordering out more often than not on the weekdays.

"What's the point, if there's no one here to eat it?" Setting my bag on the counter, I reach up to grab a glass off the open shelf above it. I spent so long talking tonight that I'm parched.

"I might have a solution for that," Jameson says as he shuts the refrigerator door.

My face scrunches up in confusion as I try to figure out what he's talking about. "A solution to what?"

"To not having anyone here to eat your cooking."

Pausing mid-step on my way toward the water dispenser, I turn my head slowly and look at my brother. "What are you talking about?"

Oh god, please don't let something be wrong with him and Lauren. I send the plea up to the universe, even though the thought is ridiculous. But he's standing in my kitchen asking about leftovers instead of going home after work to her . . . so for the briefest moment I'm worried he means he's moving back into his old apartment on our third floor. But no . . . I've never known him to be this happy, and Lauren has the quiet confidence of knowing he'd do anything for her or her daughters. They're solid.

"I need a favor."

"The last time you asked me for a favor, I ended up remodeling Lauren's entire house." I place the empty glass on the counter and fold my arms across my chest, a small smile on my lips.

"And look how that turned out," he says.

Our lives all changed for the better when Lauren moved back to Boston. Not only is she now one of my closest friends and my future sister-in-law, but I also gained her sister, Paige, and her cousin, Morgan, as close friends. Combined with Audrey, we have a very tight-knit circle—they're part of the family we've built in the aftermath of losing both our parents. "I don't need any more friends, Jameson. What's the favor?"

"I . . ." He pauses and then shoves his hands in his pockets as the next words come tumbling out in a jumbled rush that's entirely unlike my brother's normal air of calm confidence.

". . . told Colt he could stay in my old apartment for a couple months."

"You . . . what?" My heart races as the reality of the situation settles like lead in my stomach.

No. No, no, no. This isn't happening. This can't be happening.

"His entire condo flooded. He came home yesterday to a partially collapsed second floor and six inches of water in his first floor. It's totally uninhabitable. He needs a place to stay while his condo is fully gutted and remodeled."

"How about he rents something?" That man is the highest paid player on the team, and he's had lucrative endorsement deals since I was a kid. It's not like he can't afford it.

"He's about to start the playoffs, Jules. Finding a place to rent, furnishing it . . . he doesn't have time for that shit. He just needs a place to stay when he's not traveling for hockey."

"So find him a furnished apartment to rent for a couple of months."

Distance is what makes our relationship work. Having him in my space, where I can't avoid him, is a no-go.

"I *have* a furnished apartment he can stay in. Why would we go through the trouble of looking for other places? Neither of us has time for that. Colt's in New York today and tomorrow filming a commercial for one of his brand endorsements. We have Drew and Audrey's party this weekend, and then Lauren and I are heading up to Blackstone with the kids for a few days next week to visit Jackson," he says, referring to one of Lauren's best friends who owns a ski mountain in New Hampshire with her husband, Nate. "I told him I'd help him move in on Wednesday once he's back."

Closing my eyes, I take a deep breath, trying not to let my

thoughts escape my mouth. My family always accuses me of not having a filter. *If only they knew the things I* don't *say.*

"You can't just offer up that apartment like that, Jameson. It's not like it's separate from this house."

After our mom died and our father left a note under an empty bottle of scotch saying he "couldn't do this anymore," Jameson retired from the NHL to become a sports agent, and to serve as Audrey's and my guardian. He raised us in our family's brownstone, trying to give us as much stability as possible after a few years of hell.

And then when we were both in college, he remodeled our house and created a one-bedroom apartment for himself on the third floor. But to get to it, you have to come in through our entryway, which with our open floor plan basically means you walk into our living room and kitchen, and then go up two flights on the central staircase, right past the second-floor bedrooms. This wasn't a problem when it was my brother living on the third floor, and Audrey, Graham, and me living on the first two floors.

"It's just Colt." Jameson says it dismissively, and my nostrils flare as I try not to react to that statement.

Just Colt.

To Jameson, Colt is family. He has no idea about my complex emotions around the man—how I went from idolizing him when I was younger, to a terrible crush that just about ruined me, to doing everything I can to avoid him. Since Vegas, I've used sarcasm as a defense mechanism. But there isn't enough sarcasm in the world for me to be willing to be around him without my entire family there to serve as a buffer.

"No." I pick my glass up off the counter and walk around the table to the sink.

"Jules, I need you to be okay with this," he says from behind me, his voice placating like he's talking to an unreasonable teenager. I stare out the window above the sink, looking at the back of the brownstone across the alley behind our house.

How do I tell him I can't live with Colt, without also telling him that everything that happened in Vegas was a result of feelings I had for him back then?

"Why? This is Colt's problem to deal with, not mine."

"I don't see why it's a big deal," he says, exasperation creeping into his tone.

I can't tell him the truth, so instead I say, "He's a grown man. He can find his own damn accommodations. Stop babying him."

Colt's got the kind of golden retriever energy that draws people to him, makes them want to do things for him. He and Jameson were best friends as teammates, and since Jameson became his agent, he's basically managed Colt's life —gotten him out of trouble, made him a fortune with endorsement deals, and brought him into our family since he doesn't seem to have much of a relationship with his own back in Canada.

"I'm not babying him, Jules. He's a grown-ass adult. But like I said before, he doesn't have time to find a place. He's leaving next week for his first playoff games, and I can't risk *anything* taking his focus away from hockey right now," Jameson says.

I hold in my questions about whether Colt could spend

less time being a man-whore and use that time to find his own place instead—because I do have a filter, even if no one believes it.

"There's too much on the line," Jameson says when the dubious look on my face must speak for me, "for his career, and for the whole team."

Well, fuck. Even as much as I hate hockey—or have said I do since the All-Star Game in Vegas—I don't want to be responsible for this screwing with his focus and the Rebels ending an amazing season at the beginning of the playoffs. I know how important this is.

"Just until playoffs are over, then." I sigh. A few weeks. *I can manage that, right?* "After that, if his condo isn't inhabitable, he needs to find his own place."

Jameson reaches out and squeezes my arm. "Thank you, Jules."

"Tell him to stay out of my way. I don't want him in my space." *Can't* have him in my space is more like it.

"I'll mention that."

"Jameson, make sure he *understands* it. He can stay in your apartment, but aside from coming in and out, I don't want him around." My words are practically a desperate plea, and he eyes me like he's trying to figure out what's going through my head.

For the past six years, Colt and I have bantered as he tries to antagonize me, but I've never indicated that I don't want him around. It's always been easier to keep him at a distance, pretend like he's just another older brother to me. I don't want to think about how the truth would change things between him and Jameson. I can't be responsible for that.

"I will. And I'll make this up to you," he says.

I sigh again, thinking about everything my brother has sacrificed for me in the past, and how in comparison, this is a small ask. There's nothing I wouldn't do for him.

"You already have."

Chapter Four

COLT

"You couldn't have hired a fucking moving company for this?" Jameson says through clenched teeth as we carry my mattress across the gleaming black marble entryway of the high rise that houses my condo.

"We're moving a bed and some suitcases. We don't need a moving company." I readjust my grip because this king-size mattress is heavy as hell. "Or are you too weak in your old age to carry heavy shit?"

"Fuck you," he spits out.

We met during our rookie year on the Rebels together, but he's a few years older than me because he came to the NHL after college, whereas I came up directly through the Canadian league. And I never let him live down the age difference.

"Really, though," I say, as we walk slowly across the lobby, "if you need me to get someone else to help, just let me know. I should have asked Jules. She's probably stronger than you, old man."

Jameson leans forward on the mattress, pressing it into my chest so that I almost stumble backward and lose my balance. Almost.

I just laugh and then ask, "Can we carry this outside now, or do you need to whine some more?"

"Is this how you say thank you for fixing your problems?" Jameson's voice is low and raspy in his annoyance, which only fuels my desire to piss him off.

"Save that tone for your family, asshat. I'm immune."

"I don't know why I still put up with you," he mutters as we continue moving across the lobby. The doorman rushes to prop open the glass doors, and he follows us out to the truck so he can open the back like he did when we brought my suitcases out. Once we load the mattress in, I tip the doorman and we're on our way.

"I can't believe how much damage there was from a busted hose," Jameson says, shaking his head before he looks over his shoulder and pulls out into traffic.

My entire first floor was already gutted by the restoration company, and it was pretty shocking to walk into. The glass doors to my balcony were wide open and fans were placed strategically around the space to dry everything out. It smelled faintly dank, like moisture without mildew. Thank God. The upstairs was significantly better, with the bedrooms at least being mostly unaffected. Some water had seeped through the doorways and caused damage to the floors, but the walls and all the furniture were fine. I was able to pack up most of my clothes and my personal belongings from my bedroom and bring my brand-new bed with me.

"Yeah, the insurance guy is coming by this week to take a look at everything and let me know what they'll cover."

"Did you find a contractor yet?"

"I was going to ask Jules and Audrey," I tell him, even though that should be obvious.

He gives a dismissive snort. "Good luck with that."

"Why? I'm practically family," I say. There's no one else I'd trust like I trust them.

"That's why Jules won't do it," he says. "She doesn't work with friends and family."

"Bullshit. Isn't she renovating Drew's mom's house right now?" Drew's practically married to their sister, Audrey, so he's both a friend and a family member.

"Yeah, but that was a favor to Audrey."

"Okay, well, she renovated Lauren's house last year—"

"That was a favor to me." He and Lauren weren't even dating yet when they started the remodel on her house, but I'm pretty sure he'd been secretly pining over her for years before she moved back to Boston.

Slowing the moving truck down, he waits to make a left turn that will take us out of the Seaport.

"So you can ask Jules to renovate my place as a favor too."

"I'm fresh out of favors with her," he says. "Letting you stay in my old apartment has already exceeded her good will."

"Why?" I ask, pulling a pack of Hot Tamales out of the bag that sits on the bench seat between Jameson and me. "I'm awesome. She'll love having me around."

The sound that comes from the back of his throat is practically a snort. "I don't think she sees it that way." He glances at me with one eyebrow raised before looking back at the road and then making the turn.

What the hell? People love spending time with me.

"How does she see it, then?" I toss some of the cinnamon candies into my mouth. I'd offer him some, but I know he hates them.

"Jules is a very private person," he says cautiously.

Of his two sisters, I think she's the one he's always worried about. Audrey got pregnant in college and didn't tell anyone who the father was, then finished architecture school and started Our House with Jules—but he didn't seem to worry about her. Audrey is a straight shooter; you always know where you stand with her.

Jules, on the other hand, is much harder to read. She's brazen and comes across as a bit brash. She seems kind of like a badass, but I think there's a lot more below the surface —especially because she's got a complicated past that she never wants to talk about.

"I've known her since she was, like, ten," I remind him. It's funny to think that when I met her, she was all long, gangly limbs, and perpetually covered in construction dust. All she wanted to do was build shit.

"That doesn't mean you *know* her." Jameson's words give me pause, because when you think of someone like family, you think you know them. It makes me wonder what I *don't* know.

"Okay, so she's a private person," I say, suddenly feeling tentative. I'm not used to being told to get lost. Quite the opposite. Women, especially, seem to love me. "I can stay out of her hair if that's what she wants, or needs, or whatever."

"Can you, though?" Jameson asks.

"Of course I can. I'm not used to having people around constantly, either." I've lived by myself since I moved to Boston when I was nineteen. In that time, I haven't had a roommate or even a serious girlfriend. I'm used to having my own space, too.

"And you can't parade a different woman through there every fucking night. You know that, right?"

"Won't be a problem." Why does it bother me that he's judging my reputation? It's not like everyone else doesn't do the exact same thing. "Also, you're judgy as fuck now that you've settled down into a serious relationship."

"You came by your reputation honestly, Colt. Don't make this about me. I'm just making sure you're not going to make Jules uncomfortable by having a string of different women there every night."

"Scout's honor," I say sarcastically, holding three fingers in the air.

Jameson barks out a laugh. "I've never met anyone who was less of a Boy Scout."

"Just because you were always better at hiding your womanizing doesn't make you a Boy Scout either."

"No, but the difference is, I understand the meaning of discretion."

"You sure it wasn't because you lived with your little sisters, so it wasn't like you could bring women home all the time?"

"Speaking of, I have a feeling my old space is going to feel small for you pretty quickly."

It's true that the one-bedroom apartment is significantly smaller than anywhere I've lived as an adult. It's smaller than his old place too—the sleek apartment he had downtown before he retired to move back into his family home and essentially be a parent for his sisters. But I'll only be there for a couple of months.

"And," he continues, "I told Jules that you'd only stay until the playoffs are over. After that, if you can't move back into your place while they finish the remodel, I told her you'd find a different arrangement."

"The fuck?" I groan. The thought of having to look for a place once playoffs are over feels kind of overwhelming. Then again, if we go all the way, maybe they'll be done with my condo by the time it's over. Or done enough that I can live through the finishing touches?

"Sorry. But it's her place, and she's doing you a favor letting you stay there."

"Don't *you* own that house?"

Jameson releases a deep sigh as he turns the van onto a side street. "Technically."

"And you don't feel like you can let your best friend stay there for a few more weeks after the playoffs are over."

I glance over in time to see his jaw flex like he's biting back his words. "We'll see what happens. Maybe you'll play like shit and be out after the first round."

"Asshole," I mutter. He just broke the first rule of playoff superstition. There's no *if.* We only talk about the Cup like we're going to win it.

"But if you go all the way, and there's only a short time before your place is ready, then we'll see."

"Maybe Jules will love having me around," I suggest, but he only snorts in response, his eyes sliding to the side to look at me like I'm an idiot.

———

We got my bed moved into Jameson's old apartment and carried all my suitcases and my few boxes upstairs. It's freaking hot out, as our unusually warm spring has taken an even warmer turn, so now there's sweat trickling down my back. I adjust the thermostat so the air-conditioning comes on before we carry his old bed downstairs.

"Graham's old room should be totally empty, and we can store it in there," he tells me as we move the mattress from the third floor down to the second, where Audrey and Graham used to live. It was only a few months ago that I was helping carry their boxes and Graham's bedroom furniture out when we moved them in with Drew. "Jules moved up here to Audrey's old room."

She'd lived in the bedroom on the first floor since she moved home from college, which makes me realize how much has changed for her in the last year with Jameson moving out, and Audrey and Graham leaving shortly after.

Setting the mattress down as we stop in front of Graham's closed bedroom, Jameson reaches out to open it, but it's locked.

"That's weird," he says. "Hold on, there's a Jack and Jill bathroom between the two bedrooms, so I'll go through Jules's room and open the door."

A few seconds later, a loud, "What the hell?" comes from the other side of the door.

"What's wrong?" I call out.

Jameson opens the door, and behind him is what can only be described as a Kardashian-level closet. There's a chandelier made up of some sort of flat, shiny shells hanging from the high ceiling. The walls and ceiling are a deep gray, and the floor-to-ceiling built-ins are painted to match. Natural light floods the room through the sheer floor-length curtains hanging in front of the windows, bathing the enormous island with a shiny wooden countertop in the middle of the room in a soft, glowing light. Between the windows on the far side of the room is a tall floor mirror, trimmed in ornate gold and leaning back against the wall.

"Is this . . . Jules's closet?" I ask.

"I have no fucking idea. Last time I saw this room was when we moved Audrey and Graham into Drew's place," Jameson says. "It was barren, and still the same pale blue we painted it before Graham was born."

My eyes scan the room again, and I can't reconcile this space with what I know of Jules. I've rarely seen her in anything besides jeans, T-shirts, and flannels, or leggings and sweatshirts. And while there are obviously portions of this closet dedicated to those essential parts of her wardrobe, there are also a lot of really nice items hanging up here. There are entire shelves of handbags, sunglasses, and necklaces, half a wall of shoes that are far from her typical work boots, and tons of built-in drawers that I can only imagine house more items.

"This is a pretty big change," I say, and it feels like a huge understatement.

"I got bored and needed a project." Jules's voice comes from the hallway behind me, and both Jameson and I jump before turning to face her. She has a distinctly annoyed look on her face, and I feel like she's caught us snooping through her underwear drawer or something. "And it's not like this space was being used for anything else."

She crosses her arms under her chest and leans back against the exposed brick wall at the top of the stairs, but her mouth twists to one side, and Jameson's words from the truck come back to me: *Jules is a very private person.* Her raised eyebrow and the way she tilts her chin as she looks at us asks the question without her having to say it.

"We thought this room was empty, and we were going to store Jameson's old bed in here," I say. "We didn't mean to pry."

"It's just a closet, Jules," Jameson adds, and I can tell it was the wrong thing to say by the way her eyes narrow in on him.

"Usually, when doors are locked, that means you shouldn't enter." Her gaze sweeps from her brother to me before she points at the ceiling of the second floor. "Your space is up there. Do I need to build you a special exterior staircase up the back of the house so you can find your way?" Her tone is sarcastic, and I want to believe she's teasing, but it feels like there's more to it than that.

"Jesus, Jules," Jameson mutters, and it's a phrase I've heard him use a lot when she says something out of pocket.

"Nah, it's fine." I shrug it off. "It's her house, and Jules made it clear that she wants her personal space. No big deal."

I'm not sure if this really is no big deal, or if I'm just acting like it is. There's something under the surface of her comments—some hostility that I didn't expect and wasn't prepared for.

"Is there somewhere else we can put the bed for now?" Jameson asks.

"How about in the storage room in the basement?" she asks.

"It won't be in your way?"

Jules converted the walkout basement into a sleek office for Our House, and the back part was a playroom for Graham. I've only been down there a handful of times, but I remember that storage room off the playroom being pretty small, and this is a king-size bed.

"If it is, I'll put it on the floor in the playroom and let the kids jump on it like it's a trampoline every time they're over."

"Don't you dare," Jameson says, and I'm guessing he doesn't want the twins getting any ideas about jumping on beds since they just moved into regular twin beds recently.

Jules rolls her eyes. "If it's in my way, I'll just move it. It's only for a few weeks."

Chapter Five

JULES

"I can't really explain why, but I just don't think he's the right person for this," I tell Audrey.

She scrunches her eyebrows together, forming the worry line between them that I used to tease her would become a permanent feature. But she's a lighter, happier person now that Drew's in her life, so I see that look a lot less these days.

"You have to have a reason," she says. "You can't just cancel the dinner and kiss three hundred thousand dollars goodbye because your spidey sense is tingling."

The laugh rips out of me so quickly it's practically a bark. It's not like I think there's some imminent danger, but as I glance at my phone where it sits between us on our kitchen table, his text with the restaurant details for Saturday night still lighting it up, something is telling me that Jerome Waters is not a man I want to be heavily involved in a project I care so much about. No matter how much money he has.

"He seemed like he's the kind of guy who'd try to throw

his money and his weight around," I say, "and I don't have the time or energy to deal with some guy's ego. Working with him just doesn't *feel* right."

"Business is about more than feelings, Jules. You know that. Speaking of feelings, how's it going living with Colt?"

A deep sigh rattles around in my throat and comes out sounding like a growl, but I'm secretly glad she's changed the subject. I've been so paranoid I'll let it slip that she's not going to make it to dinner Saturday night.

"It's fine, I guess. I mean, he just moved in today, so I haven't really seen him." Except for the closet debacle, but I haven't told Audrey that I redid the closet because . . . I don't know why, really. She knows I've updated her bedroom, adding decorative molding and paint, before I moved into it, but I've kept the closet just for myself . . . my own secret little safe space that I can retreat to.

"Are you . . . sure you're okay having him here?"

"Audrey, it's fine," I insist, halfway regretting that I told my sister everything. But we made a pact when our dad left that we'd always be 100% honest with each other. She's shared her biggest secrets with me, and I tell her (almost) everything too. "I made it clear that he needs to stay in his own space upstairs. Besides, he'll be gone soon enough."

"Hmmm." The skepticism rolls around in the back of her throat, and that worry line appears between her eyebrows again. I know exactly where her mind is.

"It's going to be fine. I promise."

"It's just . . . you haven't spent any time with him alone since—"

"I know," I say, not wanting to talk about Vegas right now. Or ever, really. "Bad decisions were made, but I was in a different place then. Yes, my crush on him back then led me to make stupid choices, but that was a long time ago. I'm not going to lose control or be reckless."

"I'm not worried about your decision-making abilities." She gives me a sad smile. She should be, though. Because the only place in my life where I feel reckless and out of control is when I'm around Colt. Even now. Even though it's been years since I had feelings for him. "I'm worried about your heart."

"What heart?" I joke, but her smile doesn't brighten. "Audrey, I have zero feelings for him and total control over my emotions. It's going to be fine."

I've set up my entire life so that I can avoid the kind of terrible choices I made in Vegas, when my jealousy and heartbreak, combined with too much alcohol, led me straight into the arms of someone who, as it turns out, I should *not* have trusted.

"I worry about you, you know. Especially with how closed-off you've made yourself since—"

"There's no need to worry," I remind her. "I am who I am, and I'm fine with it. I don't *want* to date. I don't *want* a relationship. I don't ever again want to feel like I've lost control."

"I know . . ." she trails off when her phone buzzes, and she glances down at it on our kitchen table. We've been sitting here for half an hour, having a post-work debrief after I got home late from a job site and she finished up some house plans she was working on downstairs in the Our House office.

I watch her read the message, then she says, "Alright, I have to run. Graham's baseball practice is wrapping up, and I told Drew I'd pick up dinner before they got home." Now that it's spring, Graham has hung up his skates for the season and is trying a new sport.

"Oh! You said you'd send me his game schedule. Don't forget, okay?"

"Are you just asking because I told you how hot his coach is?" she asks, a hopeful glint in her eyes. I'm not sure she and my friends will ever stop suggesting guys to me, even though they know I don't date.

"No." I drag the word out. "But I've gone to almost every practice and scrimmage for Graham's hockey team over the last two years he's played. Of course I'm going to his baseball games as well."

Audrey's smile is practically a smirk. "Uh huh." She says it like she's trying to put ideas in my head, even though we both know it won't work.

"Since I don't want kids, the whole hot single-dad thing doesn't really hold any appeal."

"You might feel differently when you see him," she teases.

"He'll still have a kid."

"Hey, you're great with kids."

"I'm an amazing aunt. That doesn't mean I want my own children. But don't worry, I'll enjoy the eye candy during the games," I promise her.

Audrey laughs as she slides her phone into her back pocket before carrying her coffee mug to the sink.

"Just leave it," I say. "The dishwasher's full of clean dishes, so I'll add it in after I've put them away."

"Alright. Thanks again for being open to this dinner with Jerome. We'll find the right donors, but to do so, we have to consider *all* our options."

Once I say goodbye to my sister, I realize that I'm starving. I haven't eaten anything since midday when I sat out on the lawn of Drew's mom's house, enjoying the lovely streak of warm spring weather and eating my sub. We're almost done with the renovations that will allow her to continue living at home safely and comfortably as her Parkinson's disease progresses, and then we'll be starting a new project next week.

I turn to the fridge and start pulling out ingredients that I think will make a decent pasta dish. Half an hour later, I've got a bowl big enough to feed a family. I don't know why I can't make anything in portion sizes appropriate for one person. After years of cooking for Jameson, Audrey, and Graham, I guess I'm still figuring it out. At least this way, I'll have leftovers for the next few days . . . or until Jameson stops by again.

I'm grating some fresh parmesan over the bowl of pasta with Italian sausage, artichoke hearts, sun-dried tomatoes, and baby spinach in a white wine, garlic, and butter sauce, when the front door opens and my head snaps up.

For some reason, I'm expecting to see Audrey, even though she already texted me that she arrived home safely. It's like my brain still hasn't quite accepted that she doesn't live here anymore. Instead, Colt walks through the door—and despite my earlier conversation with my sister, my brain definitely hasn't registered the fact that he *does* live here now.

Across the kitchen and entryway, our eyes meet. Then he looks away, his short-sleeve shirt stretching across the wide expanse of his upper back as he turns to lock the door behind him. It's one of those fancy T-shirts that probably cost $200 on Newbury Street, whereas I'm standing here in the leggings and old Our House T-shirt I changed into after I got home from the job site.

"What smells so good?" he asks.

"Just some pasta I whipped up."

"Hmm." Turning to face me, that smirk he's so famous for graces his lips. It's the one he flashes for fans and photographs, the one that so easily gets him into women's pants. Colt's got the easy-going attitude of someone who always gets what he wants in life. "That's an awfully big bowl of pasta. You having company over?"

I suspect he knows I don't have anyone coming over and is teasing me so he can offer to help me eat it. But that question rubs at me in a way that makes me feel kind of raw. As much of my life as I spent wishing I had some privacy—which I never had with Jameson and Audrey, and eventually Graham, always around—I wasn't prepared for how it would feel to live in this big house all alone once they each moved out. Moved on.

It makes me feel like I'm stagnant, while everyone else is growing.

Which doesn't even make sense, because I'm *happy* with my life. I've got great friends, an amazing family, and a job I love. It's exactly the life I wanted to create for myself, and it's perfect for me. Safe and stable, just how I like things.

"Maybe . . ." I say, a heavy dose of sarcasm in my voice, "I just have a really big appetite."

He looks me up and down, like he doubts I could eat half this much. His lips curve back into a small smile when he says, "Maybe you're just really stubborn."

"You *know* I'm stubborn, Colt," I say as I fold my arms

across my chest, hugging my T-shirt to me and wishing I had better armor against his charm. "This isn't news."

"Listen," he says, shoving his hands into the front pocket of his jeans like he knows how awkward this is for me. "I'm sorry Jameson and I went into your closet earlier today. We thought it was just an empty room at this point. We didn't know you'd made it into part of your living space." He swallows, his throat bobbing in a way that makes him look guilty.

It shouldn't be a big deal if he went into my closet . . . but if he started poking around, he'd find things I most definitely wouldn't want him to see.

"It's fine, Colt. You didn't know. Just . . . stay out of there now that you do, okay?"

"Sure thing, Tink."

Grinding my teeth together, I try not to let the old nickname from my childhood grate on me. No one ever calls me that anymore, except him—and I'm pretty sure he does it to piss me off.

I was a pre-teen when Colt and Jameson started playing together on the Rebels. Being eight years older than me, he's always treated me like his kid sister. He teased me mercilessly, probably because I was so easy to get a rise out of, but I secretly basked in the attention.

Then I hit puberty, and as I morphed into a teenager— growing six inches and adding some curves—he continued to treat me like I was a little kid, when all I wanted was for him to see that I was growing up.

"You can stop calling me that any day now," I say, hugging my arms even tighter across my chest.

To his credit, while he still teases me, he no longer treats me like I'm a kid. Which is good, because I operate power tools and boss people around for a living. I'm not inclined to take crap from someone whose only purpose in life is to prevent rubber pucks from going into a net.

"Nah," he says with a shrug, "you'll always be Tinker Bell to me—a tiny blonde spitfire with a temper when she doesn't get her way." His smile is affectionate, like he's remembering how tenacious I was as a kid. Telling me no, or that something was too hard, or that I needed to be older to do something, in my mind that only meant that I needed to try harder. Giving up wasn't in my vernacular. Still isn't.

"I'm hardly tiny, Colt." I'm five feet nine inches tall, and muscular. Most guys are intimidated by my height and the fact that I can usually lift more than they can. Not Colt, though. He's got at least six inches on me, and I probably couldn't even lift his warm-up weight.

He steps a little closer so that I have to tilt my head back to see him. If it weren't Colt, I would be intimidated as hell by a guy this large hulking over me like this.

"You're still kind of tiny to me." His voice is low and gravelly in a way that has butterflies shooting through my abdomen. I don't even recognize his tone . . . it's like he's talking to someone else. Someone he most definitely doesn't see as a little sister.

"Sit down," I say with an exaggerated sigh as I briefly consider all the bad decisions someone could easily make with a guy like Colt. I lightly push against his chest with one hand while stepping back and moving toward the counter where I set the huge bowl of food. "I need help eating all this pasta."

What I really need is for him to be farther from me, like

at the far end of the table, so I can forget the way I felt just now with him that close. How I could barely breathe because of the proximity. How I wanted him to take one step closer, even while I assured myself I did not want that.

It's just Colt, I repeat Jameson's words in my head.

And if Colt is known for anything besides playing hockey, it's the constant rotation of puck bunnies in and out of his life. It's like he can't help but talk to women like he's trying to get them into his bed. I'm about to tell him to cut that shit out—because we antagonize each other, we don't flirt—when he interrupts my thoughts by asking, "Can I get us some drinks? What do you want?"

"Just water," I tell him.

"Water it is," he says as he moves to grab two glasses from the shelf.

"There's some beer in the fridge if you want it," I tell him.

He gives me a look I can't quite read but wish I could, and then he says, "Water's fine."

I take two large flat bowls and dish heaping piles of pasta into both, then grate some extra parmesan onto each while he fills our water glasses.

"So, you guys aren't practicing this week?" I ask as we sit across from each other at the farmhouse table that takes up the middle of my kitchen. I get up early for work and basically want to know if he might be meandering through my space in the mornings. Do I need to put clothes on after my shower when I go downstairs to get my coffee, or can I go wrapped in my towel like normal?

"Coach gave us a few days off so we could rest and gear up for the playoffs, but yeah, we're back to practicing tomorrow."

"What time do you guys practice? Early morning?" For someone whose brother played in the NHL, I know shockingly little about how it all works. Jameson had his own place when he was playing for the Boston Rebels, so I have no idea what his schedule was like back then. By the time our mom died, our dad left us, and Jameson moved home, he had retired from the NHL.

"Nah, we usually don't take the ice until around ten. So I get there about two hours before to get ready."

"Of course it takes you two hours to get ready, pretty boy." I roll my eyes as I fall into the pattern of teasing him that's become our norm. We never have real conversations; we just needle each other, which is exactly how I like it.

Digging his fork into the pasta, he looks up at me with a grin, one eyebrow cocked as he opens his mouth to respond, and then his phone vibrates on the table next to him. He glances down, then back up at me quickly before declining the call.

When he looks up again, his easy-going demeanor has been replaced with the hard lines of a clenched jaw and narrowed eyes staring off past me.

"Everything okay?" I ask, when he doesn't say anything.

He shakes his head. "Yeah, just a phone call I've been avoiding."

Oh, I know all about those, I think to myself. It's been over two months since my dad reached out, which means I'm due. These longer stretches with no contact are both a relief, and also incredibly anxiety inducing—like knowing something bad will happen, but not knowing when, or how, or where.

I'm not sure how to respond to Colt's comment, but I guess I don't need to because that devil-may-care grin is back, and he says, "So, to get ready for practice . . ." And then he's off on a tear, explaining the ins and outs of what he brings to the rink, the protein-packed breakfast he eats once he gets there, and the warmup exercises and pre-practice workout he completes.

But I'm only half listening, because inside, my mind is playing back the way I watched his face go from easy-going, to hardened and angry, back to the cocky player I've always known him to be. And all I keep hearing, over and over, is the way my therapist assured me that we all wear masks. *The hard part*, she said, *is knowing when we're safe to take them off.*

Chapter Six

COLT

"I'll get you my estimate for the actual construction, and Colt will get you the costs for replacing the furniture and decor that was ruined," Jules says, her voice all-business in the way that leaves no room for argument as she walks the insurance adjuster to the door.

I'm relieved that when I'd told her the adjuster was coming, she'd insisted I have a contractor with me. And since I haven't hired one, she agreed to come with me so that I didn't get fleeced.

Luckily, she's totally taken charge and been such a boss the whole time the adjuster has been here. I have a newfound respect for her as I watch her in her element.

"I'll take that into account when I put together the estimate," the guy says in response. I can tell that he doesn't like having to justify his numbers with Jules, but she's not putting up with any bullshit when it comes to the lowball offer he wanted to give me for what it would cost to fix all the damage in my condo.

"I'm sure we'll make it work," Jules says, but the subtext is clear: *I'm sure I'll get my way.*

She shuts the door behind him, and turns to face me, opening her mouth, but I cut her off with, "Thank God you were here. For real, Jules, I don't know what I would have done without you. When he started talking numbers and materials . . . " I huff out a laugh as I shrug, because it really was all above my head. I've never even *thought* about shit like this, much less had to answer questions about the type of kitchen countertop I had—who the fuck knows? They were black?—or the myriad of other details he asked me about.

"You were completely useless," she says with a laugh. "How could anyone know so little about their own house?"

"Again, it's just a place to live. It's not like this condo holds sentimental value," I tell her as she walks over to the wall of sliding doors and stops where they open onto the balcony, with Boston Harbor stretching out in the background.

She releases a deep sigh. "But with a view like this . . ."

"The view is literally why I bought it," I say as I walk over behind her. "Can you see that tiny white speck on the island out in the Harbor?" I stretch my arm out over her shoulder and past her head so she can follow where I'm pointing.

"Umm hum." The sound emanates from her rib cage, and I feel the rattle against my chest because I'm way too close to her. I quickly step back half a foot.

"That's Boston Light. It's the oldest continuously used lighthouse in the country. From here, you can see it lit up at night. Apparently, it's like a normal hundred-watt light bulb, but it can be seen twenty-five miles out to sea."

She looks up at me over my shoulder, and I ignore the way the smooth skin of her cheeks is faintly pink and the way her lips shine like she just licked them. *Fuck, why am I noticing her like this? She's my best friend's little sister and my roommate. Not that she's so little now, but I would never go there.*

"How do you know that?" she asks, her voice low and breathy.

"My real estate agent told me when I came to see the place before signing the papers."

She clears her throat. "Karen sure got lucky with you. You must have been the easiest client she ever made half a million dollars off."

"How do you know what she made?"

"Because when I called her to see if she had any photos, she sent me the original listing with the sales price. I work with real estate agents all the time; I know what their commission is."

Jules was a champ when we arrived. As soon as she saw the condition of the place, she called my real estate agent herself, asking for the original listing with all the written details about the condo, including all the pictures. She had it in her inbox before the insurance adjuster even got here.

"Hmm. Seems like you're more interested in this property than you're letting on. You *sure* you don't want this project?" I ask, even though I know she's going to turn me down.

"Working for friends is never a good idea."

"You remodeled Lauren's entire house, and she's one of your best friends."

She crosses her arms under her chest, which she does a

lot—almost like she's giving herself a little supportive hug. But standing over her shoulder, I can't help but notice the way it pushes her cleavage up into the scoop neckline of the clean T-shirt she changed into when she got home from work. She turns her head back toward the windows and stares out at the view. "Lauren's renovation was different."

"How so?"

"Because first, we weren't friends when I started that project—it's how I met her. And second, Jameson called in the only favor that would convince me to take on that job."

"What favor could you have owed him that equated to remodeling an entire house?"

Her shoulders stiffen, and her neck elongates, making her seem even taller than she is. "He said the one word that would get me to do anything for him . . ." She stops speaking, and I wait her out, wondering if she's going to admit whatever it is to me. ". . . Vegas."

"Shit, Jules," I mutter, dropping my head so low it almost touches her shoulder. I want to wrap her in my arms as I repeat what I told her that morning in Vegas. But I don't touch her. I can't. "That wasn't your fault."

"Oh yeah?" Her voice is tight. "Then whose was it?"

I'm about to say "Mine" to admit to the guilt I've been carrying around for years, but my damn phone rings, the sound piercing the silence. Jules jumps, and I step back, cursing as I glance down at the screen in my hand and wishing I'd turned off the ringer after the inspector called to tell me he was here.

Or maybe I just need to block this number?

"Fuck, I'm sorry, I have to answer this." I don't want to talk to my brother, but I usually end up answering the phone in case he's calling to tell me something's wrong with my parents. After not answering last night, I can't let the call go again.

"No problem. I'll just . . . check out the view from out there."

"Hey." My voice is clipped while watching her walk through the open glass doors and across the large balcony. I turn and walk farther into my condo, hoping the noise of the fans still circulating air inside will drown out my conversation.

"So are you coming, or not?"

My nostrils flare and my chest expands as I take a deep breath, standing there leaning against the door frame, wondering why my brother just can't let this damn trip go.

"I told you," I say, my voice flat, "I don't know."

"It's two weeks away. If you want to come, I need to reserve one of the rooms at the bed-and-breakfast for you.

"I don't know. The league makes the schedule; I have no control over it."

"Well, it looks like even if you win your first series, you'd have that weekend off before advancing to the next round."

I watch Jules as she stares out at the horizon, and I think about what Jameson said about her being an incredibly private person. I wonder if I'm making her uncomfortable right now—having this conversation with my brother while she's trying not to listen. I guess I could have shut the doors behind her, but that felt even more rude. "Even if we're not playing that weekend, it doesn't mean I can come up."

"Just decide, Mathieu. You don't have to be so wishy-washy all the time."

"Listen, you're asking me to make a decision about something that I can't make a decision about yet. I don't know what our practice or travel schedule will be. It will depend on whether we win the series early, or go all seven games. So when I know, I'll let you know."

This conversation is already taking longer than I'd planned on allowing.

"It's been fifteen years—"

"Yeah," I cut him off, my voice heavy on the sarcasm, "you don't need to keep reminding me. For the last time—if I can come up, I will. I'll talk to you later."

I hang up the phone, then close my eyes and take a deep, slow breath—the kind my Zenned-out teammate Zach is always encouraging me to use as a calming mechanism. When I open my eyes, Jules is leaning with her back against the railing, her cool blue eyes assessing me in a way that makes me wonder what she sees.

"Sorry about that," I say.

"There's nothing to apologize for," she says. I can tell she's curious while trying not to be nosey, and she confirms it when she asks, "Want to talk about it?"

My gaze stays locked on her, and I say nothing for a moment, then I clear my throat. "Nah, it's fine."

"Okay." She raises those perfectly arched eyebrows. "But I'm here if you change your mind."

I'm oddly touched that she cares enough to offer, but simultaneously terrified to open up to anyone about my brother. "We should go." I nod my chin toward the glass doors, then turn to head back into my condo.

Adrenaline has me already across the now-dry plywood subfloor of the living room and taking the few steps up to the dining room when I hear her shut and lock the doors to the balcony. I pause, trying to get a handle on my emotions before turning to face her. I know I don't owe her an explanation, but for some reason, I feel like I should give her one all the same. "I don't normally get worked up like this. My brother's just . . . an asshole."

She freezes. "You have a brother?" Her eyebrows dip with the question, like she's trying to figure out how she's known me since she was ten years old and didn't know I had a brother.

I'm a very public person—somewhat showy, always smiling, happy to raise a ruckus. But there's a whole other part of my life that almost no one knows about. As time went on and my status rose to one of the best players in the league, I often worried that my past would resurface. And I'm not sure how it hasn't. Someone could have sold this story to the tabloids and made a small fortune, except obviously the small town I grew up in is protecting one of their own.

"Yeah. We . . . don't get along well." I try not to think about how he used to be my best friend. He was the role model I looked up to before he double-crossed me.

"Do you see him much?"

"I haven't seen him in almost fifteen years."

Her mouth drops open. "What about when you go home to visit your family?"

I never talk about this. I don't *want* to talk about this. But somehow, as she walks across my barren living room, with her look of concern, those big blue eyes boring into me and her light blond ponytail falling over one shoulder, I want to talk to *her* about it.

"I . . ." I struggle over the words, because I don't even know how to explain everything that went down after I left for the NHL. I don't want to revisit this, but I'm also so damn tired of it living rent free in my head. And it makes me wonder if talking about it would help me stop thinking about it? "I had a big falling out with my brother after I moved to Boston. There was . . . a lot of drama, and I haven't been home since."

"So when do you see your parents?" Her voice is casual as she comes to a stop in front of me, but I can tell by the way she squints her eyes at me that she recognizes the significance of this conversation.

"They come down to Boston a couple times a year," I tell her. And now it's my turn to try to decipher the look that passes over her face. "What's that look?"

She glances up at me, and now that she's only feet away, I can see that her eyes are glassy. Holy shit, did I say something?

"It's nothing," she says, shaking her head and moving to walk past me. "So tell me more about your brother."

I grab her wrist, gently enough that she could break free and keep walking if she wanted to, but instead she freezes.

"Not until you tell me why you just had that look on your face," I say, instantly regretting it—because if she tells me, I'm not sure I'm prepared to say anything more about Gabriel in return.

"It's nothing, Colt." She glances away again, and her throat bobs as she swallows.

It's not nothing, and my voice indicates that I know she's lying about this. "Jules."

She looks back at me. "I was just thinking about my own parents, and that feels shitty because here you are telling me about your situation and I'm bringing my own experiences into the conversation when it's not even relevant."

"Of course it's relevant. There's nothing wrong with you bringing up your parents when we're talking about family relationships. What were you thinking about, exactly?"

Her words are quiet when she says, "I was thinking about what I wouldn't give to see my mom again or have my dad back in my life . . . if he could be the person he was before she got sick."

I barely knew Jules and Audrey before their mom died and it wasn't too long afterward that their dad left. But once Jameson retired to stay home with his half-sisters, I spent a lot more time with them. Jules was probably twelve or thirteen then, and she was way more torn up about their dad leaving than either Audrey or Jameson were.

Jules was always his favorite. Jameson used to say how she'd follow him around on job sites, with her pink steel-toed work boots and tool belt, and everyone called her Tinker Bell because with her light blond hair, it was like Tink following Peter Pan around. At the time, I didn't realize how apt the Peter Pan analogy was.

"What was he like, before she got sick?" I ask. Jameson never talks about his father. I only know him as the asshole who walked out on his two teenage daughters, and from what I can gather, he wasn't much of a father to any of them before that. Jameson was much closer to his stepmom and his two younger half-sisters than to his dad.

"He was . . ." Jules sighs and looks at the ceiling. "He was always kind of a hard-ass. Like, he was this salty old Irish guy who worked long, physical hours and came home to unwind with too much alcohol. But he was also sweet in his own way. He'd pick up a charm bracelet for me because it had a hammer on it, or bring me saltwater taffy if he saw it in a candy store. And he loved that I wanted to learn how to do what he did. Carpentry has always been second nature to me. I always knew I wanted to be able to create things with my hands, and he ate that up. He loved showing me how to do things." She pulls her lower lip between her teeth quickly, her eyes getting a sad, distant look, and says, "I guess I loved that he paid attention to me."

She's all piss and vinegar most of the time, but I get the sense that Jules could use a good hug and a shoulder to cry on—not that she'd want me to fill that role.

Honestly, she has always been a bit of an enigma. As a kid, she loved any moment of my attention, but as an adult, she's always kept me at a distance. She's endlessly sarcastic and clearly disapproves of my reputation, but . . . I don't know. I like that she doesn't give a shit what people think of her. It's something we have in common.

"Anyway," she says before I have a chance to respond, "this isn't about me and my issues. So, tell me about your brother."

Fuck.

I glance down then, realizing that I'm still holding her wrist. Clinging to it is more like it. I let it go so quickly it's almost like I push her away. She takes it in stride, though, sliding her hand into her back pocket, her elbow jutting out to the side where it's bent. In the light filtering through the floor-to-ceiling windows behind her, I can see the little pieces of her arm hair standing on end, like she's cold—but with the power turned off and no air-conditioning, it's sticky-hot in here.

"My brother . . ." The pause stretches indefinitely as I run through the million ways I could finish that sentence. But I don't want to share everything and I sure as hell don't want to talk about Cheri. "We were really close growing up. But after I left for the NHL, he did something that broke my trust and forever ruined our relationship."

She searches my face, looking for clues, and it's a relief when she gives me a quick nod, like she understands I don't want to give any specifics about what he did. "Forever is a really long time."

"Yeah . . . I know." I'm a pretty open and trusting guy. I generally try to see the best in people. But if you fuck with me—if you break my trust or go back on your promises—I'm not big on giving second chances.

I know the old adage is, *fool me once, shame on you; fool me twice, shame on me.* But I've never understood why you'd give someone a chance to fool you a second time. I'd rather live by the philosophy, *when people show you who they really are, believe them.* And Gabriel showed me who he really was.

"I'm not saying that you should forgive someone who broke your trust." She says the words slowly, with a caution that tells me she's really thinking about how to say this. It's so at odds with the 'Jules has no filter' refrain I often hear from her siblings. "But . . . couldn't you still go home to see your parents, and just not see your brother?"

My parents didn't side with Gabriel. But they also didn't side with me. And I didn't make them choose, as I imagine that choosing between your own children is the kind of thing that would break a person. I know they spoke to us individually, letting me know that what happened wasn't my fault, and letting him know that what he did wasn't okay.

But as soon as their grandson came along, it sure seemed like all was forgiven. How could it not be? And how could I expect that they'd cut Gabriel and Cheri out of their lives when there was a child involved? Even if, for a very brief time, I thought that growing baby was mine.

"My parents and I have worked out a system for seeing each other. It's fine." I even see my nephew occasionally, when they bring him down to Boston with them for a game. He might be the reason I lost my girlfriend and my brother in one fell swoop, but he's blameless. I don't think he even knows the history, which is for the best. "But now my brother wants me to come home for my parents' fiftieth wedding anniversary."

"Fiftieth?" Her jaw drops open.

"Yeah, they got married right out of high school, then struggled to have kids. Gabriel wasn't born until they were married for almost ten years, and they had me four years later."

"*Fifty years*, and you're not sure if you're going up for that?" She sounds like she's trying to comprehend why I would miss it.

"My parents are the *only* people in my hometown I want to see. And I do see them. I don't want to go to some big party."

"I get that," she says, then takes a deep breath. "I really do. But half of life is showing up, Colt. Sometimes you have to be there for the people you love. Even when it's hard. Even when you don't want to . . . even when it hurts." Her eyes are glassy again, and I wonder about all the ways she's sacrificed and shown up for the people she loved in the past.

"I don't know what happened between you and your

brother," she continues, "and I'm not trying to diminish how big of a deal it was. But think about what it would mean to your parents to have you there for this special occasion."

I know she's right.

This shouldn't still affect me this much, because I've moved on. But in my mind, part of moving on meant never having to see that backstabbing asshole again.

I created the space I needed to heal from what Gabriel and Cheri did, and today, they no longer mean anything to me. And yet, I continue to let them influence my decisions about what I do now, fifteen years after the fact.

It would mean the world to my parents to have me there. *Why can't I be the bigger person and just show up? It's only for one night.*

"I'll think about it," I say.

"You don't have to forgive in order to forget, Colt." She studies me intently. "You just make the choice to move on."

"Yeah," I say, nodding my chin toward the entryway to indicate we should go. "Maybe."

Chapter Seven

JULES

I come downstairs wearing the dark blue sundress I bought for today and Colt side-eyes me when I walk into the kitchen to grab my keys and purse.

"What?" I ask, wondering why I still let his teasing comments and disapproving looks get to me.

"Nothing," he says with a roll of his eyes. "You just seem . . . dressed up."

"I'm literally wearing a sundress, which is what people do when it's eighty degrees and they're going to a party."

"You never wear dresses." His voice is tight, like he's annoyed or upset.

I look him up and down, noticing how his tight polo clings to every muscle in his upper body and how his belt and khakis rest on his hips, his pants showing every curve of his muscular thighs. He's not going to this party super casual, so why is he making it sound like I'm overdressed?

"Are you . . ." I'm about to ask him if he's mad for some reason, but when I fold my arms under my chest, his eyes slide from my face down my body. *Ohhh.* The realization that he's checking me out does thrilling and terrifying things to my body. ". . . *bothered* that I'm wearing a dress?"

"Nope." He pops the 'p' at the end of the word, and then reaches for the back door and holds it open for me. "I loaded all the food into the backseat of your truck."

"Thank you. I could have helped. You didn't have to do it when I was changing." I'd spent most of the morning in the kitchen, and he'd helped me get all the food packed into insulated carrying bags we were going to load into my car on our way out.

"I didn't mind." He follows me down the steps, then reaches past me to open the rear door of my truck so I can see the food he's carefully set up. "I still don't understand why you did all the cooking for Drew and Audrey's party, though. Couldn't they just have had it catered?"

"I like to cook, so I offered." Even from where he stands behind me, I can feel his head turn toward me, assessing. It's like his eyes are boring into the side of my head and I don't dare turn to look at him because our faces would be too close. I'm always aware of his proximity, always trying to keep some distance between us. It's better for me that way.

"What is it that you like about cooking?" Colt asks, his voice soft and curious.

I don't know how to answer that question—it's so innocent, and so deeply personal at the same time. I don't know how to explain that I like feeling needed. That in a time when everything in our lives was so volatile, cooking was the thing I could do to contribute to our new little family once it was just Jameson, Audrey, and me. It was the way I could show my older siblings I loved them and wanted to take care of them like they were taking care of me. The bigger the meal, the more it forced us to slow down, to spend quality time together while enjoying the food I'd prepared.

"I don't know," I say, standing there awkwardly, because there's no way to move from the space between him and the truck door without coming much closer to him. "I've just always liked it."

"I never really learned how to cook," he admits.

"What do you do for food then?" I ask.

"I eat out a lot. And I'm remarkably good at making grilled cheese sandwiches."

I snort out a laugh and, without thinking, I look up at him over my shoulder. Just like I expected, our faces are way too close. His breath softly skims my skin as he exhales in surprise. And yet, he doesn't step back; he keeps me trapped here, looking down at me like I'm a stranger and he's trying to figure out how he knows me.

"Grilled cheese? Really?" I tease, trying to distract from the way my whole body flushes under his gaze.

"Yeah," he says, and clears his throat. "I can make, like, 50 different variations."

"Now that I'd like to see."

"Anytime," he says. "You've cooked for me lots of times. I'm happy to make grilled cheese for you."

It's such a small gesture, but with his eyes on mine, it feels like he's offering up something that he's never given anyone. And it makes me wonder, once again, if maybe all I've seen of him until now is what he wanted me to see . . . the same version of himself that he shows everyone else.

And then I realize that this is just wishful thinking—just me romanticizing Colt the way I used to do when I was a teenager—so I force my thoughts away from that possibility and, instead, I glance at the backseat of my car again and tell him, "I like grilled cheese."

"Noted. Ready to go?"

"Yep." I slip under his arm, trying to ignore the way he smells as I squeeze past him—that combination of something tangy like orange, with deep, spicy notes of clove and cinnamon. The scent is so familiar it threatens to make me forget why, for years, I've made sure to keep my distance.

But as I walk around to the driver's side of the car, I take a deep breath of the heavy city air and promise myself I won't let my thoughts drift in that direction again. I'm stronger than that now.

The first thing Colt says when he hops into the passenger seat is, "I'll be in charge of music." Without even asking, he plugs his phone in and taps the "Connect" option on the screen, which overrides my phone's wireless sync and brings his apps up on my dashboard.

"We'll be there in, like, ten minutes," I say. "We could have just listened to the radio."

"You have crap taste in music, Jules. No thanks."

"What's wrong with country and classic rock?" I ask as I wait for him to buckle his seatbelt. This is an old argument, and I'm pretty sure *he's* the one with terrible taste in music. I don't understand how he listens to pop all the time. He also likes those crazy remixes by "famous" DJs I've never heard of, but it all sounds pretty much the same to me.

"I'll play Taylor," he says.

"Her old stuff?" I ask, hopeful. Country Taylor I can get into.

He scoffs and taps the screen to start one of his playlists. And as the music fills the space, I have to admit that I don't hate this new song. But I won't give him the satisfaction of telling him that.

We listen in silence as we pull out onto the city streets, but traffic is heavy for a Saturday midday. It's like the warm weather has brought every person in Boston outside, and they're all walking across the streets whenever and wherever they feel like, instead of only at the crosswalks. As a result, we're inching our way across Copley Square instead of actually driving, and it's taking us three times as long as if we'd walked. Which we couldn't do with all this food . . . but it's still frustrating.

We're finally pulling onto Drew and Audrey's street when a text notification pops up on my screen. Figuring it's Audrey, who said she'd text me when they were back from taking Graham for a bike ride, I instinctively reach up and tap the notification.

But the minute the robotic sound of my car reading the text fills the space, I realize my mistake. *Hey big guy, I'm in town tonight. My hotel bed is going to feel very lonely if you're not in it.*

"Fuck." Colt exhales the word. "What the hell, Jules?"

"I'm sorry." Even if I could look over at him while driving, I wouldn't. I'd be afraid of what he'd see on my face—some combination of embarrassment at hearing the contents of that text, and disappointment that this is who he is when he could be such a better person. *You gave up hoping he'd change long ago,* I remind myself. "I was waiting for a text from Audrey, and I forgot your phone was synced up, not mine."

Another text notification pops up on the screen, and I glance at it long enough to catch the sender's name. *Bambi San Francisco Mile High Club.* A laugh bursts out of me.

"Do you even know her last name, or is that how you keep track of the women you've slept with?" I'm careful to keep my tone amused. He clears his throat but doesn't say anything. "I'd love to see your contacts sometime," I say with another forced laugh. "I bet the women all follow the same formula: first name, a location, and something notable about the sex."

His lack of response tells me I hit the nail on the head. Finally, once I'm parked and have turned off the car, he opens his mouth to respond. But I'm suddenly deeply uncomfortable—wishing I didn't know this about him and hoping that I didn't go too far with the teasing—so I pick my phone up off the charging station and say, "Alright, I'm going to let Audrey know we're here with the food."

———

"So . . ." Lauren says, her voice dragging out the vowel like it's a mile long as she gives me a conspiratorial look. "How's it going living with Colt?"

"It's fine." I roll my eyes, hating that I have to keep having this conversation. At least she and Morgan don't know about my past feelings for Colt, as I've only ever shared that with Audrey. So I tell them the same thing I told my sister. "I haven't seen him that much."

"Doesn't he live in your house?" Morgan asks, then eyes Lauren like maybe her cousin misinformed her.

I glance around the party to make sure no one else is within earshot. I don't need my brother or any of Colt's teammates listening in. "Yeah, but he's in Jameson's old apartment on the third floor, so aside from him coming and going, I don't really see him. Except when we had dinner together the first night he moved in, and when I went to his condo to check out the damage. And he helped me pack up the food for this party and bring it over. But other than that . . ."

"So in the last four days, you've hung out three times?" Lauren laughs.

"We haven't *hung out*. I fed him because, as always, I made too much food. Then I helped make sure the insurance adjuster didn't screw him over, and he helped me carry some stuff here."

"Sounds like you two are becoming *friends*," Morgan says, tapping her finger on my forearm, like she's trying to get me to admit we're besties now. *Never going to happen.*

She must see something in the look that crosses my face, because Lauren follows up with, "Or is he still trying to rile you up every chance he gets?"

"He's still Colt." I shrug. "And tigers don't change their stripes." Though to be fair, he hasn't been needling me *quite* as much, but maybe that's just because he's living in my house and doesn't want to bite the hand that feeds him, sometimes literally.

"Well, if you ever need to get away from him, you're always welcome at my place," Morgan tells me. She lives in a top-floor condo on Newbury Street that her dad bought a long time ago, around the same time my dad bought our place in the South End, before real estate in Boston was as insane as it is now. "And also, you need to get out more. *We* should go out more, now that we're the only single ones."

"Paige is still single," I say, referring to Lauren's sister. "Isn't she?"

"Paige is married to her job. Where is she today, anyway?" Morgan asks Lauren as she pulls her strawberry blonde hair behind her shoulders. It's warm in here, even with the air-conditioning on—probably because there are a lot of us in Drew and Audrey's home, and many of the people here are huge hockey players who probably run hot because of their muscle mass.

And speaking of muscle, Colt walks past us just then, his biceps curled as he holds two drinks in each of his massive hands. "Ladies." He dips his chin at us. "And Jules."

And there he is . . . Forget the Colt who shared secrets about his brother and checked me out because I was wearing a dress. No, the Colt who lives to piss me off is back.

I roll my eyes and, not waiting for Lauren's answer about Paige's whereabouts, I say to my friends, "I'm going to go find Audrey."

The party's in full swing and yet I haven't seen my sister since she went to "take a quick shower" right when Colt and I arrived. I approach the kitchen island, intending to ask Drew where Audrey is, when Jameson asks him the same question.

"Still getting ready," Drew tells him right as the buzzer rings, signaling even more people are arriving. He seems entirely unbothered by the fact that she's still in her bedroom despite the fact that most of his team and both our families are already here. Colt ambles up next to me and starts handing out drinks.

"I'm going to go check on her," I tell Drew and turn toward the hallway that leads to their bedroom. I'm only a couple of steps into the hallway when Graham runs up to me.

"Auntie Jules," he says with a big smile, "are you excited?"

I bend down and ruffle his hair, giving him a kiss on his forehead and inhaling his scent, noting that he's losing that little kid smell he's always had. I hate how fast he's growing up, and I miss having him and Audrey in my house. Everything is changing too fast.

"I'm so excited," I tell him. "And you're doing such a good job at keeping this a secret. I can't wait to see your mom's reaction. Just keep your sweatshirt on for a couple more minutes, and I'll make sure your mom gets out here so you can take it off and surprise her."

He gives me a nod and another giddy smile, and then he heads back to the party as I continue down the hall. Two quick knocks on their bedroom door and Audrey calls, "Come in."

I push open the door to find their huge king-size bed littered with several outfits she must have tried on and discarded. Now, she stands in front of the floor-length mirror in a black sundress with tiny satin straps over her shoulders. Her hair is down in loose, dark waves and her skin is glowing. I can't help but smile as I watch her looking at her reflection, happy with what she sees.

Audrey was already a badass single mom before Drew came back into her life, but one of the best changes since they got together is that not only is she happy in their relationship, but she's also more confident in herself as well.

"Hey," I say, "you almost ready? Everyone's already here, so I just wanted to check and see how you were doing?"

In the mirror, Audrey's big blue eyes meet mine and she sighs. "I'm being a terrible host, aren't I?" She lets out a little laugh. "I was so sweaty after our walk on the Esplanade with Graham earlier, I had to shower. And then of course it took me forever to dry my hair. And now I feel like I'm sweaty again from the heat of the hairdryer."

I smile at her. "You look gorgeous—like you're glowing. You're not sweaty at all."

"Thank you," she tells me. "I know I can always count on you for an honest opinion, so I appreciate that."

I laugh a little to myself. As if I would tell Audrey she looked sweaty—even if it were true, which it isn't—when I know Drew is about to propose to her!

"Alright," I say, "so are we going out to the party now?"

"Yeah," she says, fluffing her hair one last time. "I just need to make sure I turned my curling iron off."

"I'll do it for you so you can head out and say hi to everyone."

As soon as she leaves the bedroom, I rush into her bathroom to unplug the curling iron, because I'm determined not to miss the moment. And as I come back down the hallway to the kitchen, Drew is kissing Audrey's forehead and then turning her away from him. Beyond them, Graham already has his sweatshirt off and is walking around in a t-shirt that says, *Dad wants to know if you'll marry him.* He's adorable with his shoulders back and head held high, like he wants to make sure the whole shirt is exposed so no one misses the message. I pull my phone out and snap a few quick pictures, because I know Audrey will love being able to see this later.

Audrey wanders from Drew over to some of his and Colt's teammates, and is chatting with them, completely oblivious to the fact that her son is walking around with a proposal on his chest.

I come up beside Drew where he stands leaning against the kitchen island and ask him quietly, "How long do you think it'll take her to notice?"

"No idea," he says with a small laugh, "but I probably should stick close to her, so I'm there when she does notice."

"Probably a good idea."

"I'll be shocked if someone doesn't accidentally spoil it," he says.

"Nah, everyone's going to love it so much, they wouldn't dare ruin the surprise."

"You didn't tell Colt, did you?" he asks, but his eyes focus in on Audrey as she chats with his sister and his mom.

"I told you I wouldn't tell anyone," I remind him. I had to lie to Colt this morning when he flat out asked if there was something special about this party, and if I thought Drew was going to propose to Audrey.

"Well, you do live with the man," he says with a shrug of his shoulder while his eyes search the room for Graham.

I snort. "Not by choice. And it doesn't mean I swap secrets with him."

His words are low and quiet when he says, "I don't need to know anything about what you two are swapping."

I slap his arm hard as the earlier text message from Bambi flashes through my mind. "Ew, stop it," I say through a laugh. "That's so gross."

Teenage me would have been thrilled that someone thought Colt might be interested in me like that. Adult me knows better. Not only is Colt the most notorious playboy in the NHL—as that earlier text message from Bambi reminded me—he has major Peter Pan syndrome. And the last thing I need in my life is another man who refuses to grow up.

"Let's just hope he knows how to keep it cool when he sees Graham's shirt," Drew says.

"Your message in the group chat was *very* clear. You've got a surprise planned, and when people realize what it is, they need to not act suspicious. I'm sure most people have guessed." I nudge him in the side as I watch Graham approaching Audrey where she stands talking to Jameson. "Go on, get your girl."

Holding up my phone, I try to be as discreet as possible, filming him walking over toward Audrey. This scene has me all up in my feelings. I'm so happy for my sister—that Drew found his way back into her life, that she was willing to trust him, that he's such an amazing dad to Graham. And I watch as other people at the party start to notice Graham's shirt. Lauren's hand flies to her mouth, which has Morgan swiveling her head to see what she's looking at.

And then I'm looking for Colt. When I find him, his eyes are wide and he's looking at me like he's amused *and* half wants to murder me. His lips move silently as he mouths, "Liar."

Oh, if only you knew half the things I haven't told you.

And then my eyes are back on my phone, making sure it's still focused on Audrey as we're all waiting for her to notice, waiting to see her happier than she's ever been before. She deserves this. She deserves the family she's always wanted after six years of being a single mom.

Graham seems to get tired of Audrey not noticing his shirt, so he walks up right behind her and asks her to tie his shoe for him. As she turns and looks down at him, her gasp fills the room because her eyes have finally landed on her son's shirt. She spins around looking for Drew and he drops to one knee directly behind her, the ring box already out in his hand.

My eyes fill with tears as my sister's hand flies to her chest, her own eyes filling with tears as she stares down at her future husband. I know she's shocked, because even though Drew has been saying for months that he's going to marry her, I suspect she thought that it would be a more private proposal. I suspect she would have *wanted* it to be.

But from his knee, Drew explains his rationale for proposing in a room full of people, telling her that we have all been there for them as they found their way back to each other. And then he's pouring his heart out, telling her all about the life he envisions for them. "Because none of it, from the happiest moments to the most difficult, would mean anything if you weren't by my side. And when I finally watch you walk down the aisle to me, and when we grow our family, and when I'm too old to play hockey and you're exhausted from all our kids . . . we're still going to be surrounded by the people who are in this room right now."

My sister says yes to Drew, and then he stands and is pulling her into a hug and whispering something in her ear. And when I glance down at Graham, he has the biggest smile on his face as he watches his parents commit themselves to each other. He's so happy, but he also looks proud that he's had a role in not only bringing them back together, but also in this proposal. That's when I see how intentional Drew's choice really was. He couldn't propose to Audrey without Graham being involved, without all of us here, because he's right—we're all so completely wrapped up in each other's lives, it wouldn't have been right if we weren't all present for this moment.

Chapter Eight

COLT

Most of my teammates have gone home already. It's basically just family left at this point, and I glance around, looking for Jules so I can tell her I'm going to walk home. It feels like it would be rude to leave without letting her know since we drove over together, but I don't want to cut her time with her family short.

She's standing in the dining room talking to her sister and friends. The late afternoon sun is getting lower on the horizon and shining right through the windows of Drew's fifth-floor Back Bay condo. Golden light reflects off her skin like she's being illuminated by a spotlight, her collarbones and the swell of her breasts appear almost bronze. Her ash blond hair is lit up like a halo framing her pretty face, and her blue eyes are more intense. It's nearly impossible to look away from her.

An entirely unexpected wave of longing pools in my groin and spreads from there, making my stomach flip over and my dick start to harden. It catches me so off guard that I'm rooted to my spot in the living room.

It takes everything I have to remind myself that not only am I *not* attracted to Jules—who is objectively gorgeous but is like a little sister to me—but I don't even like blondes. And besides, I wouldn't do that to my best friend. That's an unforgivable line I'm *never* crossing.

I close my eyes while I stand rooted in place, trying to wash away her image and forget the way it felt just now when my eyes landed on her. I need to stop noticing her like this.

But when I open my eyes again, her gaze locks on mine and she's looking at me with her eyebrows raised. Her lips part and her chest swells—I can't tell if she's going to say something or is just taking a breath. Then Morgan turns to her, grabbing her forearm as she speaks, and Jules looks over at her, breaking the moment.

Holy shit, what was that?

I pull at the buttons on my polo, because suddenly the neckline of this shirt feels entirely too tight, but they're already unbuttoned. So, why does it feel like I can't quite breathe, then?

I need to get out of here, so I head straight to Jules to say goodbye.

"Hey," I say as I approach. "I'm going to walk home. I'll see you later."

"Wait," she says, "I need to get going too. I'll give you a ride."

"You don't want to stay and hang out with your family?" I ask, as if putting the suggestion out there will change her mind. I *need* it to change her mind, because now that she's only a foot away, that feeling of not being able to breathe is back in full force.

"I have a business dinner I need to get ready for," she says.

"On a Saturday?"

"Oh my god," Audrey gasps from the other side of the table. "In all the excitement, I totally forgot about the dinner. Alright." She exhales with a quick sigh. "I'm sure Drew will be okay with me slipping away for a few hours tonight . . ."

Jules laughs, but it's a tight, uncomfortable sound that's nothing like her usual laugh. "You are *not* going to this dinner, Audrey. You never were. It's fine, I always knew I was going alone."

I'm trying to track what they're talking about and having marginal success.

"You *knew* this was happening? Is that why you didn't want to schedule dinner for tonight? Because you knew I wouldn't be able to come with you?"

Okay, this is making a little more sense. But Jules is tough, so the fact that she doesn't want to go to this dinner alone has me on edge. There must be a reason.

"It's fine," Jules says. "I'm sure he won't bite."

"*Who* won't bite?" I don't intend the question to come out like a protective growl, but I guess that's what happens when you're trying to get the words out through a clenched jaw. What the hell is wrong with me?

"We were supposed to meet with a potential donor for our nonprofit tonight," Audrey tells me. "And now Jules is going to have to go alone because obviously . . ." she trails off, her cheeks getting pink.

"Obviously, she needs to stay so she and Drew can *celebrate* once Graham goes to bed." Jules snickers, and normally

I'd be laughing too, but I'm still focused on how uneasy she seems. The way goosebumps spread across her chest and arms when she said it was fine, and that she was sure this asshole wouldn't bite.

"Is it a problem . . . you going alone?" I ask, taking half a step closer so I'm standing right next to her.

"No. He just makes me a little uncomfortable."

My chin tilts down as I look at her, trying to force her to make eye contact so I can get a sense of what she's feeling, but she doesn't look up. "And why are you meeting with him on a Saturday night?" I ask again. Most men I know don't take a woman out on a Saturday night because they want to talk business.

She sweeps her hand through the air. "Something about traveling for work, and this was the first available time when he was back in town."

"Sounds like a date to me."

"He probably hopes it is," Audrey teases.

I don't think she notices the way Jules tenses up again, but from where I stand, looking down at her, I see the way her shoulder muscles stiffen and her jaw clenches before she relaxes enough to say, "Don't be ridiculous. It's a business meeting."

"Let me know if you need someone to go with you." My words are quiet, so low I don't think Audrey can hear them from a few feet away, and Morgan's already turned and is talking to Lauren and Jameson.

Jules finally glances up at me. "It's. Fine." There's barely any sound as the words leave her lips, and I understand that she's asking me to drop this. She probably doesn't want Audrey to feel bad about not going.

I give her a curt nod before saying, "Okay, so you want to head out?"

"Yeah, can you just help me carry what's left of the food down?"

"Sure," I say. "I'll take care of it so you can say goodbye to everyone." In my experience, the Flynns take freaking forever to say goodbye when they're leaving a party—they've obviously never heard of an "Irish goodbye." Which is fine, because it will give me a little physical distance and a few minutes to process why I'm so keyed up about Jules going to this dinner.

"You want to help me carry the food?" I ask Jameson as I leave the dining room.

"Sure," he says, giving Lauren a quick kiss on her forehead before he turns to follow me to the kitchen island that divides the two rooms.

We grab two of the insulated food carriers, and as I trudge down the stairs in front of Jameson, he asks, "So, how's it going living with Jules?"

The skin on the back of my neck prickles as I pray he isn't asking because he noticed how I was looking at her a minute ago. "She hasn't killed me yet, so I think we're good so far."

His low rumble of laughter sets me at ease. "She'll warm up to you being around. Just don't piss her off."

"I've been pissing her off for over a decade; it's kind of my thing."

"Nah, trust me. If you actually pissed her off, you'd know it."

As we reach the bottom of the first floor, I look over my shoulder and am about to respond to his comment, when we hear Drew's voice from above us. "Why didn't you idiots take the elevator?"

"It's not like we're carrying furniture," I say, the sarcasm heavy in my voice. We look up and watch Drew as he comes down a flight of stairs, around the landing on the third floor, and down the next flight of stairs, carrying one of the insulated food bags we must have missed.

"I just thought with your old knees, you might need to take the lift down."

"The lift? Are you fucking British now?" Jameson says.

I half-listen as they give each other shit while we walk a block over to where Jules parked her truck, but I'm mostly in my own head about why I'm suddenly noticing Jules in a very non-sisterly way. When we get to the truck, I realize that I didn't get the keys from her. I set the bag on the sidewalk and pull out my phone to call her, but then she's sidling up next to me, the blue fabric of her sundress flowing around her muscular thighs.

"God, you guys walk fast," she says, her chest heaving in a way that makes it impossible for me not to notice the swell of her breasts above the low neckline of her dress—again. I glance up quickly and Drew's smirking at me. He clearly just caught me checking her out, but thankfully, Jameson doesn't seem to have noticed.

Shit. What the hell is wrong with me? This is not who I am. She's my best friend's little sister, for Christ's sake. Maybe it's just been too long since I had sex? I wasn't planning on calling Bambi in response to that text she sent earlier, but . . . maybe I should? Maybe then I wouldn't be keyed up and noticing Jules like this?

I busy myself loading the bags as she says goodbye to her

brother and future brother-in-law, and then we hop into her truck to head home.

Needing some air so I'm not surrounded by her sweet scent—she smells like vanilla or a cupcake or something—I roll down the window. The car is quiet as we drive, both of us seemingly lost in thought, until her phone rings. She glances at the screen briefly, her eyebrows raising when she sees the name Rosie Perot.

"I have to answer this," she says before accepting the call. "Hey, Rosie! What's up?"

"I got your text."

"The one I sent almost a week ago?" Jules teases.

"Yeah, I needed to think about it."

"And . . . ?"

"I think I'm ready to do this. What did you have in mind?" Rosie's voice is nervous, like she's trying to be brave, and I'm wondering who this woman is and what the hell is going on.

I listen for a bit as Jules describes filming a video testimonial for the mentoring program she and Audrey started, and how she's hoping Rosie will share how the mentoring impacted her personally and professionally.

"Do you think . . ." Rosie pauses, and Jules turns the steering wheel, guiding us home as she waits patiently for her to continue. ". . . could we maybe film it from my good side?"

I'm curious what she means about her "good side." The fact that Jules is quick to agree makes me think it's something that's really important to Rosie.

"We can do whatever makes you most comfortable," Jules says. "Your story is so powerful. *You* are such a badass and you deserve recognition for everything you've been through and the choices you're making now and how far you've come as a result. But I know how hard it's going to be for you to tell this story, and I want you to know how proud I am that you're doing this. You're going to be helping so many other women."

"I'm doing this to help *you*," Rosie says, "so that you can help more people, like you helped me. This testimonial isn't going to be about me. It's going to be about you and everything you've done to change my life."

Jules sighs. "I wish you could see how your strength is what got you where you are. I just helped smooth out the path a bit. That's what the mentoring program is all about." Her voice has the hoarse quality of someone who's close to tears.

Even though I knew she and Audrey had started this mentoring program, I didn't know much about the impact it had until now. By the sound of it, the experience has changed Rosie's life.

"Well, I was considering dropping out of electrical school before I met you, because I just couldn't see a place in the industry for myself." Rosie's response is full of gratitude as it carries through the speakers in Jules's truck. "You're the one who made me believe it was possible. So if you're uncomfortable being the hero in my story, maybe we shouldn't record it."

Jules swallows audibly, as Rosie waits for her reply. And for the first time ever, I realize that maybe Jules isn't comfortable with people's attention on her. It makes me wonder if maybe her sassy and sarcastic personality is just a deflection technique that covers up for . . . I don't even know? Some insecurity?

She's always taking care of others—helping Audrey raise Graham, cooking for her family, remodeling Lauren's house as a favor to her brother, even coming to my condo when the adjuster was there so I didn't get taken to the cleaners with the cost of renovations. I never recognized this side of her before, but it's so damn clear now, as I listen to the way this woman practically idolizes her for the help she's provided and how Jules is hesitant for Rosie to talk about that aspect of the program.

"I think we should record it and see how it goes," Jules says finally. "Just remember that it's the mentoring program that should be in the spotlight, not me."

Because I can't seem to take my eyes off her, I notice the pink creeping into her cheeks.

"Girl, you *are* the mentoring program," Rosie insists. "This thing wouldn't exist without you. Audrey's incredible, and the women you partner us with on job sites are wonderful . . . but without you? None of this would have happened."

"It wasn't even my idea," Jules insists. "My friend, Morgan, suggested it."

"Doesn't matter. You ran with it and built it into what it is, and you deserve recognition for that, too."

Jules forces another deep swallow, like her throat is thick from being choked up.

"Thanks, babe," she says. "I'll be in touch with more details when we're ready to record."

They say their goodbyes, and when she disconnects the call, I ask, "Is this the reason you're going to this dinner tonight? Because more donations will help people like Rosie?"

"Yeah, that and because I told Audrey I would."

"But if you're not comfortable around this guy, why go?"

"I'm not *uncomfortable* around him. He's just . . ." She sighs. "Have you ever met someone who was so focused on you that they ignored everyone else around you?"

"You just described every woman I've ever met." I'm half-teasing, but also . . . not.

She huffs out a laugh and her hand flies to the base of her throat. "Oh my god, Colt, I can't breathe. There isn't enough oxygen in here for me *and* your ego."

"My ego's not the only thing about me that's huge." She shakes her head, her eyes staying on the road, but she's smiling. "Anyway, I *do* know a thing or two about unwanted attention. Is that what you're getting from this guy?"

"Sort of? I hated the way he was so focused on me during our conversation that he basically dismissed Audrey, like she wasn't there or didn't matter."

"Did she notice this?"

"I don't think so. It's not a big deal. I'm going to go meet with him tonight because it's important to her that we at least hear what he has to offer. Besides, the food at La Gallina is amazing, so at least I'll enjoy my dinner, even if it's a terrible conversation."

It's like a rock is sitting on my stomach, pressing it down and making me sick. She's doing this because it's what she thinks Audrey needs her to do. I wonder if there's anything she wouldn't do for her siblings.

"I don't think Audrey would want you to go to this meeting if she knew how much you were dreading it."

"I'm not dreading it," she says as she pulls into the alley and slips into the parking spot near the back door before turning toward me. Her lips spread across her bright white teeth in a tight smile. "It'll be fine. So anyway, what are your plans tonight?"

"I'm meeting a friend for drinks," I tell her, the idea forming in my mind as the words come out of my mouth.

"Oh? Where are you going?" The question is asked like an afterthought as she reaches for the door handle.

"La Gallina."

She freezes, then looks over at me. "Colt." My name is spoken like a warning to not get involved. "I don't need you there to protect me, or whatever ridiculous notion you have in your head right now."

Like hell she doesn't. My mom raised me better than to let a woman walk into a situation where she's clearly not comfortable, without some sort of backup. *This is just about protecting her,* I assure myself.

"It's just drinks, Jules. Don't read too much into it."

Chapter Nine

JULES

I'm halfway through my appetizer when Colt walks into La Gallina with Zach Reid, one of the team's new defensemen. Zach does not look pleased to be at this upscale tapas restaurant, and it makes me wonder where he'd rather be instead. Probably home with his new girlfriend.

My eyes follow them as they walk over to the bar, which isn't as packed now with the dinner crowd as it'll be later tonight when the bar fully fills in. Colt pulls out his seat and angles it so his side is to the bar and he's facing Zach, with me right in his line of sight.

The way he sits there looking all broody with his eyes narrowed in on our table has me feeling quite flustered. It has nothing to do with the way his black shirt clings to his muscular chest beneath the open lapels of his tan tailored suit, or the way he's styled his dark blonde hair, and how his beard is neatly trimmed close to his face. No, it's the way his eyebrows form a straight line above each of those dark eyes as he scowls in my direction.

I don't know why he's bothered to come here and act all pissed off about it. It's not like I want him to witness what's sure to be an awkward dinner. In fact, as we headed into my house earlier, I specifically asked him *not* to come. There are at least thirty other restaurants on Newbury Street where he could have met Zach for a drink.

My eyes must have lingered on Colt for too long, because Jerome Waters casually glances over his shoulder.

"Oh, look," he says as he turns back toward me. "The most overpaid player in professional hockey is here."

I can't hold back my laugh, both because it's something I'd say myself, and because the disdain comes out sounding more like jealousy.

"Not a Rebels fan?" I ask.

"Lifelong Rebels fan, actually." Taking his napkin off his lap, he dabs the corner of his mouth. And that's when I realize he hasn't done his homework, because if he had, he'd know I was related to Jameson Flynn, and every Rebels fan knows he's a retired player and Colt's best friend. "I just happen to think we could take the nine million dollars a year that's currently going to pay that man's salary and signing bonuses and spend it on newer players, instead of wasting it financing the end of his career."

I don't know where the overwhelming desire to defend Colt comes from, but it rears up in me, coursing through my blood like lava. I'm about to open my mouth and start spewing statistics about Colt's save percentage (best in the league) and number of shutouts this season (second highest in the league).

He might be nearing the end of his career, I want to tell Jerome, *but he's performing better than almost any other goalie.* I catch myself just in time.

"Well, now," I say, my voice thick as I force myself to sound friendly and professional, even though I'm not feeling it. "Since we're not here to talk hockey, tell me more about what interests you in our nonprofit."

"I think you have this backward." He gives me a sly smile, almost a smirk, as he rests his elbows on the table in front of him, steepling his fingertips as he peers over them at me, his dark eyes narrowed. "I think *you're* supposed to be telling *me* why I should be interested in donating to your cause."

There's a teasing quality to his voice, but it feels disingenuous. I can't shake the feeling that no matter what I say, he'll want a harder sell. That he won't be happy until I'm *begging* him to donate, which is the last thing in the world I'm likely to do. I'd eat my own vomit before I'd pander to a man like that.

"I told you when we met," I say, "we have an amazing program for mentoring females who are entering the trades, but the need far outpaces what we can provide, and we require additional funds to grow the program."

"I guess I still don't understand why women need this special mentoring that men don't get."

"Workplace studies on underrepresented populations—which, in construction, women are—all show the same thing. Access to more experienced people who have had similar work experiences, and can answer questions and guide them, improves the way people feel about their jobs and increases the likelihood of them staying in the profession."

I wish I could tell him the types of questions we've

gotten, like, "How do I hide a used tampon in a portable toilet so every guy on the job site doesn't know I'm on my period?" or "What do I say to a co-worker who says my ass looks cute in my jeans?" or "How do I handle it when the guys joke about me being a diversity hire because I'm the only woman?"

Maybe *then* he'd better understand how those small things, time and time again, make working in this field particularly challenging. It's why women need the support and guidance of other women. Not because they're less qualified or less capable, but because they're an underrepresented population trying to carve out a spot without feeling marginalized.

Instead, I continue, "Men have plenty of opportunities for that type of unofficial mentorship in their field. Everywhere they look, they have role models, other people who have walked a similar path in their profession and can help guide them. It's not the same for women. Since they make up roughly ten percent of the construction-related industry, it is very possible they may not even *work* with another woman. So, it's much harder for them to find mentors who can help guide them through the unique experience of being a female in a male-dominated industry. Intentional mentorship will help attract and retain females in this profession, which is needed."

He leans in, an eyebrow raised as his gaze slides from my blond hair in its loose bun on top of my head, down my face, and then down to my blazer. "Did you have female mentors like that when you went through trade school or first started in construction?"

"I didn't go to trade school. I learned pretty much everything I know from my father, and then passed the test and got my license as soon as I was old enough. I was lucky that way, I guess."

There was nothing lucky about working with my dad. He made sure I learned every lesson the hard way, so I'd always remember *why* things needed to be done a certain way. There were a lot of things in life Jimmy Flynn wasn't good at —being a husband and a father chief among them. But if there was any area in his life where he gave nothing less than his best, it was his work. Until the alcoholism fully consumed him, anyway.

"But many of the women I work with," I tell him, hoping he can understand that this isn't about me at all; it's about opening up opportunities for women in general and making sure there are enough qualified people in the trades, "really struggled to get to where they are now, and I want to help smooth that road out as much as I can for women who are just getting into the profession."

"Here's the thing. The real world," Jerome says his voice harsh, "isn't always woman-friendly, and I'm not sure we're doing women any favors, especially in this industry, if we try to make the schooling or training process less rigorous—"

"I didn't say anything about making it less rigorous," I interrupt him, my voice equally forceful and my words slow so he can absorb their meaning. "I said that we needed mentoring to make sure that women feel supported as they join this male-dominated industry."

"When I was at MIT a few decades ago"—he leans forward again in what I can only describe as an antago-nistic stance—"women said the same thing about being outnumbered by men. And you know what? They developed a thicker skin and they're all extremely successful now."

"Well, when I was at MIT a few years ago, that wasn't my experience. Male and female enrollment is almost equal now, and I didn't feel the need to develop a thicker skin because of . . . I don't even know what you're describing? Institutionalized sexism? And yet, I've still managed to be extremely successful in a male-dominated industry."

My mom used to say, "You fight with a pig and you both get dirty, but the pig likes it." And that's exactly how this conversation feels. Like he's baiting me into an argument I don't even want to be part of, but I feel the need to fight anyway.

I watch as his eyes slide to my ringless right hand. "You went to MIT?"

"I graduated *summa cum laude* with a degree in structural engineering. And before you ask, I don't wear my brass rat," I say, referring to the custom class ring MIT students get at a ceremony in the spring of their sophomore year, "because I work with my hands all day."

Not to mention, the ring is kind of gaudy and masculine, and I don't have the insecurity that would make me feel the need to flaunt my degree to gain credibility.

He sits back in his chair, relaxing as a small smile plays on his lips. I feel like I just passed a test, but instead of feeling victorious, I feel dirty—because I just rolled around in the mud with a pig.

My gaze flicks over to Colt again, and though he's talking to Zach, his eyes are still on me. I can feel the flush creeping back into my cheeks as he catches me looking at him for the third time in the past ten minutes, so I quickly look back at

Jerome, who's eyeing me with what I assume is newfound respect.

"So," I say, giving him a broad smile. "Let's talk a bit more about that donation."

His eyes track from my face down my body, and I don't miss how they linger on my breasts even while I'm wearing an oversized blazer with a full-coverage tank top beneath. Some people might bask in this kind of open admiration, but I hate every second of this man's attention on me. I want people's opinions of me to be based on my accomplishments, not on my looks. And Jerome Waters can't seem to tell the difference.

He glances around the restaurant, where it's getting more crowded. His lips curve up to one side as he leans closer. "How about we get our dinner to go, take it back to my place, and figure out how you're going to"—he raises an eyebrow—"spend my money?"

I take a deep breath and focus on not throwing up the bile that's traveling into my esophagus or delivering my fist straight into his jaw. Boston's a small city where word travels fast, so I know I need to keep it professional.

"I'd say it was nice doing business with you, Jerome," I say as I stand, my chair pushing back across the tile floor in a way that leads other nearby diners to glance over at the noise. I keep my voice as pleasant as possible when I say, "But we both know that isn't true."

"C'mon," he says, his tone feigning friendliness as he quickly stands and steps toward me. He drops his voice low, his words come out like an angry growl. "You're making a scene, and I don't do scenes. So here's what you're going to do—fucking smile while I throw some money on the table to cover our bill, and we'll walk out of here together so neither of us looks like an asshole."

Tilting my chin up, I lock my eyes on his as I slide my tongue along the back of my teeth.

"I don't think so."

His hand grasps my wrist before I can step away, and his grip is so painfully tight it brings tears to my eyes. "Alright, bitch—"

Colt's voice is deadly, and not the least bit quiet, as he appears out of nowhere. "Take your hand off my fiancée, or I'll remove it from your fucking body."

We both spin toward him in surprise, and Jerome lets go of my wrist. Colt pulls me under his arm and into his side so he's wrapped protectively around me.

"Let's go, Tink." And then he guides me out of the restaurant.

I'm fairly sure my mouth is hanging open in shock as we walk out that door together. *What the fuck just happened?*

Chapter Ten

COLT

Jules has her head tucked into me, like she's trying to hide her face in my side as I steer her toward the doors of the restaurant. I can feel her shaking against me, so I glance over my shoulder, and that asshole she was with is pulling his wallet out like he's in a rush to pay so he can follow us.

I have no intention of letting him talk to Jules. Ever. So the minute we hit the warm outdoor air, I'm steering her around the corner of the building and into the narrow alley that runs alongside the restaurant.

When I guide her to the brick wall, she leans her shoulders back against it. Her chest is rising and falling quickly, her breath coming out in short pants like she can't quite get oxygen as she looks up at me with glassy eyes.

"Breathe, Tink."

Being as gentle as I can, I take the wrist that asshole grabbed and turn it over between my fingers, searching for any signs of an injury. Aside from some redness in the area, which will probably turn to a bruise tomorrow, she looks like she's okay. My eyes skim along her upper body on the way to her face. Her chest is no longer rising and falling rapidly. In fact, it's like she's not breathing at all.

"What's wrong?" I ask. Is this fear? Is she hurt? Is she pissed at me?

Her full pink lips part, but no sound comes out, and she's still not breathing. I plant one hand on the brick wall behind her and lean down so we're face to face. I'm trying to ignore the way her porcelain skin is glowing from the floodlights above us, the way her high cheekbones are edged in pink above her sharp jawline, the way her incredibly full lips are glossy like she just licked them, and the way her head, tilted back against the brick, leaves the long column of her neck exposed. She smells and looks like dessert.

"Hey, I'm going to need you to take a breath before you pass out."

Nothing. No inhale, no sigh, no sign that she even heard me except for the way her eyes widen as she gazes up at my face.

Just then, I hear her name being called from the street. Her breath is a sharp gasp—*at least she's fucking breathing now*—as we both turn our heads in the direction of the sound. The asshat from the restaurant hasn't seen us yet, so I bring my hand up to the side of her face and guide her head back so she's looking at me.

"I'm about to do something we're both going to regret," I tell her, "but it's the only way he's not going to try to talk to you right now and the only thing that will prevent me from killing him. Try to sell it, okay?"

Then my mouth is descending on hers, and to my surprise there's only the briefest moment of hesitation on her part before she's wrapping her arms around my neck and opening her lips for me, pulling my lower lip between her teeth, and sucking it into her mouth.

My body presses forward, anchoring her between me and that brick wall, and the low groan that slips out of her throat reverberates between us. It should be the wake-up call I need —the warning signal that I'm about to cross a line I can't come back from. Instead, it's the spark that lights a fire I have no desire to put out.

Because Jules Flynn isn't kissing me, she's devouring me —fucking my mouth so thoroughly that I'm pretty sure I'll never again want to kiss anyone but her.

My fingers dig into her hips, pulling her toward me even as my body pushes her into that wall, and then I'm sliding both my hands around her, cupping her ass and lifting. She tightens her arms around my neck, bringing her legs up and wrapping them around my hips, pulling me tight against her center. And the feel of my cock pressed between us has me hard and aching for her, my hips instinctively moving forward to create the friction we both need.

Her hum of approval reverberates through us both, fueling that fire. I'm acting on instinct rather than logic as I stand in this alley with Jules wrapped around me, practically dry humping her up against a wall. And I have no intention of stopping.

I bring one hand up to her face, tracing the line of her jaw with my thumb as my fingers work their way into the hair at the base of her head. Until now, I've never felt like I'm not in charge when it comes to sex. But there is no doubt in my mind that, in this moment, Jules owns me, and I'd gladly give her anything she wanted.

Legs tightening around my waist, she slides her center along me. My fingers tighten on her ass in response, and more than anything in the world, I want to remove the clothes that stand between us.

And then I hear, "Put the fucking phone away," and I pull back from Jules, glancing over to the street as Zach stands there waving his arms in front of three people who were just watching me making out with my roommate. My best friend's little sister. The one person I absolutely should not *ever* even *think* about touching.

And I just did so much more than think about it.

I rest my forehead against hers. "Fuck. Jules, I'm so sorry. I didn't mean to . . . It didn't mean anything."

I can't figure out exactly what the sound she makes is, but then she's dropping her feet to the ground and turning her head away, tucking her chin against her shoulder so she can't be seen from the street, or so that I can't see her face. It worries me that I can't tell which.

"Moving right along," Zach says, his arms spread wide as he ushers the three kids away, putting the corner of the building in between us and them. Thank God they weren't close enough to see my face or tell who I was.

"Hey, aren't you a hockey player?" one of them asks Zach, and I can tell he is drawing them farther away because their conversation fades. He's giving us the space to get out of here unseen, and I owe him, big time.

I look down at Jules, but that's a mistake. She's looking at the ground, and from this angle, all I see are the pink apples of her cheeks. I don't know if she's angry or embarrassed, but either way, I know I stepped over the line and fucked up.

Her chest is heaving as she takes big gulps of air, and I'm halfway afraid she's going to break down again if we don't get moving. I nod toward the entrance to the alley. "Let's go."

When we get to the street, I place my hand on her lower back to guide her to the inside of the sidewalk, leading her away from the restaurant in the opposite direction as Zach headed with those kids.

We walk in silence for a few blocks; the easy banter we normally fall into is gone and so is the heat from the alley. Instead, she looks straight ahead, shoulders squared, never once glancing at me as I walk next to her trying to figure out what to say.

We're all the way back to the South End before I get the nerve to ask her if she's okay.

"I'm fine." The words are clipped, and I know she's not fine, because if she was, she'd have a snarky comeback.

"Can we talk about what just happened?" I ask, glancing over to gauge how she's feeling.

"Let's not," she mutters. "In fact, let's never speak of it again."

"Jules." Her name is an apology and a plea. There aren't many people in this world whose opinion of me I truly value, but hers has become one of them. Over the past few days, I've opened up to her in ways I've never opened up to anyone else. And I don't want to lose that. I don't want to go back to exchanging nothing but snarky comments—though the longer she's silent, the more I'd be willing to accept even a return to that.

When we arrive at the tall stone steps of her brownstone, she says, "I'm going up to change. I'll see you tomorrow."

"Jules, can't we talk—"

"No."

I think about what Jameson said earlier today, about how if I'd really pissed Jules off, I'd know it. Her icy demeanor and sharp refusal to have a conversation about this is all the confirmation that I need: *I've stepped over a line, made her uncomfortable, and screwed this all up.*

My friendship with Jules is going to be forever strained, and my living situation is about to get really complicated. What felt like the right thing to do, especially with the way she'd reacted the minute our lips touched, was obviously the wrong thing in the end.

I stand on the sidewalk, trying not to focus on the way her skin-tight pants hug her muscular calves as she walks up those stairs to the front door. I don't want to crowd her, or for her to feel like I'm invading her space, so I hang back. Watching the door click behind her, I take a seat on the stone steps, still warm from today's heat, and pull my phone out of my pocket.

I sit there scrolling through social media for so long I lose track of time. Finally, I'm about to get up and go inside, when my screen lights up with a text.

ZACH

Call me.

Chapter Eleven

JULES

I lock my bedroom door behind me, then rush into my bathroom, shutting that door as well. When I finally make it through the bathroom and into my closet, I rest my hands on the big wooden countertop of the island in the middle of the room, hang my head, and let the tears fall.

How could I let that happen?

After literal years spent crafting a life where I was in total control, where I wouldn't be tempted to do anything reckless —living in the same house as my siblings, owning my own business, not dating or drinking or doing anything even remotely risky—I had to go and lose control. And worst of all . . . with Colt.

I can't even trust myself.

Being around Colt is *always* a mistake. I become reckless. I promised myself six years ago I'd never again have feelings for him or let him influence any of my decisions, and less than a week of living in the same house as him and I'm wrapping myself around him in an alley, practically dry humping the man!

And afterward, he looked at me with regret lining every feature of his face, his eyes panicked and his brow furrowed . . . and he fucking apologized and said it didn't mean anything. I was just some mistake he hadn't meant to make and wanted to forget about as quickly as possible.

Because that's what happens when I lose control—I become someone else's mistake.

I let the sobs rack my body, my fingers gripping the countertop and my shoulders shaking with the force of letting out my frustration and remorse. Then I glance over at the space that used to house the door from this room to the hallway— the doorway I'd found my brother and Colt standing in just a few days ago. That door's now locked, and covered with a layer of soundproof insulation, a piece of plywood, a piece of drywall, and some decorative trim.

I'd installed and painted that the next day, determined that Colt not walk by and hear anything that I wouldn't want him to hear coming from this room—which right now is the sound of my sobbing.

Taking a deep breath, I force myself to straighten up, and wipe the tears and snot from my face. I will not let another man make me question my sense of self-worth. I've been down this slippery slope before, and it's the whole reason I don't date. It's the reason I don't let myself have feelings for anyone but my family and closest girlfriends. It's the reason I started an all-female construction company. I'm a badass on my own, and make completely stupid, reckless decisions when men are involved.

My life is much, much better this way.

I suck in another deep breath, wipe away the remaining tears, then strip off my suit and throw it over the chair near the windows. Slipping on my favorite sweatpants—which are so soft and worn they are no longer fuzzy, making them perfect for this warm evening—I tuck my tank top into the front of the waistband, and head back into the bathroom to clean up my face.

When I look in the mirror, it's worse than I expected. My bun is loose from Colt running his fingertips along my neck and digging them into my scalp. I ignore the shiver that wracks my body as I remember the feel of his huge, warm hands on me. My lip gloss is smeared all around my mouth, and my mascara has pooled beneath my eyes, leaving sunken black circles and a dark trail down my cheeks. I look like I could be trying to pass for Harley Quinn on Halloween.

I scrub my face, wishing I could wash away the memory of the regret I saw in Colt's eyes after he pulled away from me in that alley. But it's still there. No matter how hard I scrub, the vision lingers just behind my lids each time I close my eyes.

The reason adult me has always held Colt at such a distance—every snarky barb pushing him further away—is that he's the only person who's ever driven me to be so damn reckless I almost ruined my own life.

Never. Again.

I promised myself that six years ago. Everything I've done since then was meant to ensure I never go on a bender like I did in Vegas. And tonight, I almost forgot.

I close my eyes, making sure I feel all the shame and regret and frustration so I can remind myself: *never again.*

And then, determined to distract myself from the shitshow that was tonight, I head back into my closet. There, I open the low door on the far side of the island and pull out the lift-up table inside the base cabinet that holds my sewing machine. I slide the foot petal out and set it on the floor, before opening one of the wide drawers that holds my fabric.

A few months ago, I went down an internet research rabbit hole trying to find myself a new bra that I could wear for work or lounging around the house—something that was supportive and soft, but didn't look like a typical sports bra, or like a grandma would wear it. Apparently, supportive, soft, *and* cute couldn't all exist together. And supportive, soft, and sexy? Forget it, not a chance.

So I got out my mom's old sewing machine—the one I'd learned on, but had only used a few times since she passed away. I'd ordered a variety of types of fabric in pretty prints and played around with different styles until I found something I really loved.

And it turned out that what I *really* loved was my ability to create something beautiful and functional. This probably should not have come as such a surprise given my line of work, but I've spent my whole life working with wood and power tools, so the fact that I also loved creating something delicate like a bra actually *did* surprise me.

Sewing has become a bit of an addiction, and my new form of stress relief at the end of a long day now that I no longer have a whole family around to cook for. Which, now that I think about it, was also probably a creative outlet for me since I rarely followed a recipe and was always trying new combinations of ingredients.

I pull out the softest knit lace fabric I've ever found and

pin the pieces of the paper pattern to it. It's one of the patterns I've created based on what I deemed most supportive while still retaining a little feminine sex appeal. And as I cut out the pieces that will form the bra, the feelings fade away.

I'm not thinking about Colt, or what happened between us in that alley, or how uncomfortable everything will be now that we crossed that line—I'm lost in the feel of the fabric, in the visions of what it will become, in the little decisions I'm making about what type of stitch I'll use to bind it together, and whether I should use black ribbon as straps to match the delicacy of the black lace, and if I want to try making a front closure on this one.

I'm so lost in what I'm doing as I arrange the cut pieces of fabric on the table in front of me, pinning them together where I need to create seams in preparation for sewing, that I don't notice the knock until it's become a loud pounding, followed by the sound of Colt's voice saying, "Jules, open the door."

I rush out of my closet, shutting the door behind me, back through the bathroom, shutting that door for good measure, and open the door to my bedroom.

Colt's eyes are a bit panicked, but I don't miss the way they change as he looks at me—the way they soften at the edges, and how the golden flecks in his light brown eyes practically disappear as his pupils grow.

I've read enough romance novels that I've heard phrases like "his eyes darkened with longing," but I never understood what that looked like until now. And I wish I hadn't seen that, because it'll just be another Colt-related thing for me to hyper-focus on—some other piece to add to the "Who is

Mathieu Coltier?" puzzle I've been putting together in my mind for years.

I fold my arms under my chest. *Never again*, I remind myself.

"Did you get lost on your way up to your place?"

He reaches out, gently running his thumb under my eye. "You've been crying?"

Shit. My eyes water again at the concern in his voice, and the gentle way he's touching me. I take a small step back and his hand falls away. "It's allergies. My eyes have been itchy, so I've been rubbing them."

He swallows like he's trying to stop himself from commenting on how my eyes weren't red and swollen in the alley—he was certainly close enough to have noticed. But he gives me some grace and doesn't comment on that. Instead, he says, "We have a problem."

I'm so tempted to make a flippant, deflective remark, but I refrain because he does actually sound worried.

"And what's that?"

He turns his phone to show me a text from Zach Reid. And as I click on the picture of an online news article to enlarge it, I think I might throw up.

Boston Rebels Goalie Engaged! the sizable headline screams. There's a photo of the back of us, Colt's arm wrapped around my shoulders as we leave the restaurant. And then the article begins below it.

Mathieu Coltier, long-time goalie for the Boston Rebels hockey team, is well known around town for the frequency of his late-night partying and the string of broken hearts he leaves behind. But he's apparently a changed man because tonight at the tapas restaurant La Gallina, a well-known hot spot on Newbury Street, he interrupted what appeared to be an altercation between a beautiful blonde and an older businessman. Loudly telling the man to "Take your hand off my fiancée, or I'll remove it from your . . . body," Colt then left the restaurant with the woman in question tucked under his arm.

The screenshot cuts off whatever the rest of the article might say, but this is enough to know the situation is bad. Like really, really bad.

I stare at the phone for longer than necessary, afraid to look up at Colt. Afraid to acknowledge that we'll have to figure out what to do about this. Afraid that we'll need to talk about what happened in order to work through this.

"How long do you think it'll take them to figure out who I am?" I ask, staring down at the way my fingers are gripping Colt's phone like it might jump out of my hand and attack me if I let go.

"I guess it will depend on whether there are better pictures than the one they've currently got in the article. But honestly, I expect they'll be able to figure it out tonight."

My shoulders sag as I sigh.

"We need to decide what to do here," he says.

"Can we rewind time and go back to that restaurant so you can *not* say I'm your fiancée? What the fuck, Colt?" I finally meet his eyes. "Where did that even come from?"

He shakes his head, his lips pressed together. "I have no idea. I was just so . . ." He looks beyond me, toward the bathroom, like he's searching for the right word, and the possibilities fly through my mind. *Angry, worried, pissed, frustrated, jealous . . .* but none feel quite right, especially the last one. Though why else would he act in such a possessive way, like

Jerome was touching something that was *his*, if he wasn't jealous? ". . . pissed off about how he was treating you."

"And that led to you calling me your fiancée, how exactly?"

"I don't know." He releases his own huge sigh. "Probably because I felt like I needed a reason to explain the insane rage I was feeling and it needed to be something that would convince him to get his hands off you, and because we'd just been at Drew and Audrey's engagement party, so . . . I don't know. I guess maybe the whole 'engaged' thing was just in my head? Honestly, I'm not sure why I said that."

He gives me a shrug and a sheepish smile, both of which are just so quintessentially Colt that it pisses me off. His happy-go-lucky, no-one-can-stay-mad-at-me-because-I'm-just-so-damn-likable routine has no place in this situation.

"You didn't need to step in, and I wish you hadn't. I had that situation fully handled."

He steps closer, and I tilt my head back to look up at him. "Did you, though? Because you might have been standing your ground, but the look on your face was . . . I don't even know. It looked like you were terrified."

Did it really? God, I hate it when I lose control of my own emotions. I can rein them in 98% of the time, but when I can't, I *really* can't.

"What happened?" he asks.

I don't say anything for a moment, wondering how to explain why I froze up like that in the restaurant, and why I couldn't breathe in that alley. I don't want to get too personal, but he also deserves an explanation. If I hadn't reacted that way, he may not have felt the need to step in and we might not be in this situation. Or maybe we still would be. It's impossible to know.

"I'm terrified when I'm not in control," I say, my voice weak and quiet.

"Tink." He grinds out the nickname like the thought of me being scared is pure anguish for him, then he cups my cheeks in his hands and tilts my face up so I have to look at him. "Why?"

I can't tell him the truth. He'll feel guilty, and it's not his fault that he didn't have feelings for me and that I handled the realization so badly.

That's on me.

"I just hate the feeling of not being in control."

His thumbs sweep across my cheeks softly. "Is that why you almost had a panic attack in the alley."

Fuck. He is way too perceptive. And with his eyebrows lowered as he gazes down at me, studying me, he doesn't look like he regrets what happened between us at all. In fact, he looks like he's about to make it happen again.

I step back quickly. "I wasn't having a panic attack."

He steps forward just as quickly. "Bullshit."

"Colt, *I'm fine.* I was just"—I shake my head, trying to quantify how I was feeling an hour ago so I can convince him he saw something other than what we both know he really saw—"frustrated about what happened. I was mad at myself for how I froze when he grabbed my wrist, instead of fighting back."

"You weren't breathing." He takes another step toward me, and I step back. But it doesn't stop him from advancing. "In fact, I don't think you started breathing again until I kissed you."

I take another step back. "Colt," my voice warns. He looks like he might try it again, and I don't know if I'd have the willpower to resist him if he did.

"Yeah, Tink?" His voice is low and seductive, and I force myself to think about that text from earlier today. The one that reminded me he'll never change—just another man in my life who refuses to grow up.

"You should probably go call Bambi back."

His head rears back like I threw cold water on him, but then he focuses those eyes back on me again. "Can't. I'm busy."

"Busy doing what?"

"Busy trying to figure out why you're wound so tight you're about to explode."

Oh, I'm wound tight alright. A shiver of desire snakes its way through my body, from my tailbone, up my spine, and to my shoulders, radiating forward so my core and my nipples feel the ripples of longing.

No. Never again.

I don't understand why my body doesn't remember that we're not doing the whole *longing for Colt* thing anymore, we're doing the *protect Jules at all costs* thing—and the two are entirely incompatible. My mind will just have to keep reminding my body.

When I take another step back, my ass hits my dresser, and there's nowhere for me to go as he comes closer.

"I thought we agreed that you were going to stay out of my space?" I say, raising an eyebrow as he stops inches from me.

"I'm not so sure I can do that," he says.

"And why not?"

"Because I'm worried about you."

His pupils have almost taken over his irises and his eyebrows dip low over his eyes as he gazes down at me. "You don't look worried."

He looks like I always envisioned he would if he wanted me.

"Trust me, I'm worried." And then he takes the last, tiny step so his body is flush with mine, wraps his hands around my hips, and lifts me onto the top of the dresser. Planting his hands on either side of me, he leans down so his face is directly in front of mine, and says, "Now, tell me what the fuck is going on."

Chapter Twelve

COLT

She stares at me, her teeth clenched so tight that her jaw ticks and her cute little nose flares as she takes a deep breath. The way she doesn't exhale has me worried she's going into panic attack mode again.

"When did they start?" I ask.

"When did *what* start?" Her reply is flippant as she rests the heels of her hands slightly behind her so she can lean back. I wish she wouldn't have done that, though, because it pushes her chest out toward me and now all I can think about is how stacked she is. God, I need to get my damn attraction to her under control.

"The panic attacks."

She sighs, deflating backward as her shoulders sag. Bringing her hand up to the necklace she always wears, she rubs the small gold disc between her thumb and forefinger. Audrey has a matching necklace, and I've seen her do the same.

"It's not like it happens a lot, Colt."

"When did they start?"

Another deep sigh, followed by, "A few months ago."

"What brings them on?"

"I don't know, the same thing that always causes panic attacks, I guess"—her voice is all sarcasm and sass—"an overactive limbic system combined with a trigger."

I bring one hand up to her neck, wanting to feel her pulse, but the way my fingers look wrapped under her jaw has my dick going hard instantly. Beneath my fingertips, her blood pumps faster, and she moves her hand from her necklace to my wrist, resting it there without pulling my hand away.

"And what are your triggers?" If it's assholes putting their hands on her, I'm going to hunt down that suit from the restaurant and beat him to a bloody pulp.

She swallows, her neck bobbing beneath my hand, and I run my thumb across her jawline. "Feeling scared, or like I'm not in control."

I run the tip of my nose along the bridge of hers. I can't stop myself. I know this is a bad idea. Maybe the worst I've ever had. She's my best friend's little sister. I've known her since she was ten, and until now I've been able to convince myself that she was like a kid sister to me, too.

But somewhere along the line, Jules grew up, and there is absolutely *nothing* sibling-like about the way my body craves hers. I know I can't do anything to act on the way I want her —can't cross that line again—so I'm just torturing myself by letting our bodies get this close.

And the fact that she's not pushing me away? That she's leaning into my touch and gripping my wrist like she's desperate for me to keep my hand on her neck? Yeah, I'll have to think about what that means later.

"Maybe you need to learn some new ways to let off steam," I suggest. It comes out sounding highly suggestive, which is not my intention.

"Should I follow the 'Mathieu Coltier method' and fuck every guy I meet?"

Normally, I'd take this as her teasing me, and I'd make a sarcastic remark about how I never fuck guys, but there's a hard edge to the question.

Plus, the thought of her fucking anyone who isn't me? It's wrong that I hate that idea, but I do. I really, really hate it. I can't have her, but I don't want anyone else to, either.

"I'm sure we can find you some healthier ways."

"Such as?" Her eyebrow raises, like she's trying to point out that I should take my own advice.

"I mean, my job is basically a way to blow off steam. But if having pucks shot at you at 90 miles per hour isn't your thing, I'm sure we could find other ways. I think you may need to put yourself in some new situations, though, to see that you can overcome them without going into panic mode. Maybe that would help when you're presented with something triggering?"

"You sound like my therapist."

"Believe me," I say with a self-deprecating laugh, "I am the *last* person you want to provide you with therapy."

"Believe me," she responds, "you're the *last* person I'd open up to."

I pull back so I can see her more fully. Maybe if I can read her body language, I'll be able to figure out what the fuck she means by that. Because every once in a while, Jules says something that makes me think she low-key hates me, and this was a perfect example.

As I move my hand from her neck to her shoulder, I notice the way her hand falls back to the top of the dresser, and she inhales sharply in response to my touch. But I can't tell if it's the kind of quick, surprised breath that comes from enjoying the contact, or if I'm about to send her into a panic.

"Did I do something to make you not trust me, Jules?"

She scoffs out a laugh, but it sounds forced. "No. I just meant because you're my brother's best friend. I'm not likely to tell you all my secrets."

"Who do you tell all your secrets to?"

"My sister, of course. And my therapist. What about you?"

"I'm an open book." I shrug. "No secrets here."

"Sure, you are," she says, shaking her head.

"What? I am. With me, what you see is what you get." I'm the good-time goalie. The one the guys all want to hang out with, and the ladies want to go home with. I know who I am, and I embrace it. It's easier that way.

Her big blue eyes narrow as her gaze locks onto my face. "That might be the biggest lie you've ever told. And the sad thing is, I think you might even believe it."

———

"Here you go. One Italian grilled cheese," I say as I slide the plate in front of her. The fresh mozzarella is oozing out of the lightly toasted sourdough, but the basil and fresh tomato have stayed between the bread.

She picks it up, blowing on the corner where I cut the sandwich at an angle, before taking a bite. "Holy shit," she groans. "You weren't kidding."

"I told you. Grilled cheese master right here." I point at my chest, and she rolls her eyes.

This is exactly the lightness I was hoping for after our heavy conversation in her bedroom. Her last comment made me feel so exposed—because for a moment there, I'd forgotten that she'd seen me on the phone with my brother and that I'd told her a bit about the situation. She knows I have secrets; she just doesn't know quite how big they are.

Luckily, I know she's always hungry and had only eaten an appetizer before that dinner ended, so I bribed her by offering to make her my specialty (aka the only thing I can cook). Down here in her kitchen, with me narrating my process for making grilled cheese sandwiches and her inserting her snarky comments, things feel more normal.

Which is why it comes as a shock when she says, "We need to talk about that article."

I've been so focused on her panic attacks and whether I want to let her in on any of my secrets, that I kind of forgot about the article that sent me straight to her bedroom door half an hour ago.

Grabbing the plate with my sandwich on it, I bring it to the table. She's sitting at the end, so I take the first seat on her left, setting my plate on the placemat and my phone right next to it.

When we sat here a few nights ago, she put me at the opposite end of the table, as far away from her as possible. But fuck that. We need to have a real conversation and I need to be able to see her reactions to things—it's the little things like the way her shoulders tense up or whether she's taking shallow breaths that will let me know how she's really feeling, and you can't see things like that from eight feet away.

"What do you want to talk about, Tink?"

The question is barely out of my mouth before my phone rings, which doesn't even make sense because I know I put it on silent. I look down and it's a video call.

"Shit," I mutter, then look at Jules. I don't understand why half of our conversations have been interrupted by calls from my family, but I'm over it. This one, though, I can't ignore. "It's my mom. And she never video calls me like this. Something must be wrong."

She nods her chin toward the phone. "You better take it, then. Do you want privacy?"

"No, it's fine." *Just shit timing.* I pick up the phone, angling it so there's no way Jules will be in the video. "Hey, Mom, what's up?"

"YOU'RE ENGAGED?" Her voice is equal parts excited and outraged. "You better be bringing her up here in two weeks for our anniversary party. I can't believe I had to learn about this from anyone other than you!"

I gulp as my eyes rise above the phone to look at Jules, who stares back at me in horror. But her face is also laced with amusement, like she's looking forward to seeing me get myself out of this.

I wish I hadn't answered this call. I wish we'd had time to talk about this first. Because bringing Jules up there with me, pretending she's my fiancée so that everyone knows I've finally moved on, feels like the perfect solution to my problems. But I'm pretty sure she wouldn't be amenable to that.

"How *did* you hear about this, exactly?"

"It's all over the internet. Some of my friends posted the article to The Facebook." It will never not be funny that my mom refers to it as The Facebook like it's 1999. "They were congratulating me and your dad. Mathieu, really? You couldn't have told me ahead of time? You couldn't have let me meet her first?"

"Are you mad?" I ask.

"And thrilled. I'm so happy for you," she gushes, one hand on her heart as she pushes the red-framed reading glasses she's always wearing these days up the bridge of her nose with her other hand. "I need details!"

"Mom . . ." I glance above the screen at Jules.

"Oh my god! She's there, isn't she? Mathieu, I need to meet her right now!"

Jules's eyes are huge, and she shakes her head vehemently.

"No, she's not here right now, Mom."

"Hmmm . . ." The disbelieving sound rattles around in my mom's throat as she gathers her pale gray hair back in a clip. Then her eyes focus on the screen. "Wait, where are you, anyway?"

Shit. "So, there was a flood at my condo earlier this week. I'm living in Jameson's old apartment. But Mom, I'm on my way out the door right now. I'm so sorry, I have to go."

"Okay, but promise me you'll bring her up to meet us? And call me when you have time to talk. I need to hear more about the engagement and meet . . ." She lets her voice carry off there, waiting for me to fill in the name of my elusive fiancée.

"Sounds good, I'll call you soon. Love you!" I hang up quickly, then slump back against the chair, tilt my head back so I'm looking at the ceiling, and groan out, "Fuuuuuccccck."

Jules's laugh fills the space. "Oh my god," she says as I take my phone and start searching for that article that Zach sent me a screenshot of. "You should have seen your face as she started asking you for details. And I'm sorry, but her excitement is obviously clouding her judgment. I mean, who would even believe *you* were engaged?"

I stare down at the article, completely dumbstruck. It's posted on one of those sports fan websites that has a very social media-feel to it. "Uh, apparently 1.5 million people."

"What?" Jules practically shouts as she snatches my phone from my hand. Her eyes scan the screen, probably noting the same 1.5 million likes that I saw, then she taps on something. Her face drains of color, and she looks like she's seen a ghost. I'm about to ask her what's wrong when she looks up at me, the same terror in her eyes that I saw in that restaurant, and says, "They figured out who I am. Already. And someone posted the video from the alley."

Chapter Thirteen

JULES

Colt hops out of his chair, turns mine toward him, and rests himself on both knees between my legs. He grips my hips in his hands, forcefully enough that I look up at him.

"Jules, it's going to be okay."

That feeling is starting again. The restlessness that makes me want to crawl out of my skin, the sensation that someone is sitting on my chest and making it impossible to breathe. My fingers twitch, and I clench them into my palms, making a tight fist and hoping I can stop this before it happens.

I take a breath through my nose, trying to get as much air in as possible, but it feels like my lungs aren't expanding all the way, which only increases the panic. If I don't get more air than this, I'm going to pass out.

Colt cups my face in his hands like he did in my bedroom earlier, and it soothes something inside me even though it shouldn't—there's no one in the world I'm *less* safe with than Colt. Not because he's any danger to me physically, but because not keeping my distance from him is dangerous to my mental and emotional well-being.

"You're going to need to breathe, or I'm going to start giving you CPR."

Letting out a small laugh, I relax enough to tilt my head forward to fully rest it in his hands. His humor had the intended effect, and I take a deep breath and exhale slowly, relieved as my heartbeat slows to a more regulated pace.

"Sounds like a sad excuse to kiss me again," I tease.

"Believe me, if I thought you wanted me to kiss you again, I wouldn't need to make excuses."

What does that even mean? Does he *want* to kiss me again?

"Well, I don't. Want you to, I mean," I tell him. Because even if Colt did want to kiss me, it still wouldn't mean anything to him. And the only thing that would hurt worse that Colt not wanting me at all, is him only wanting me for a random hookup and then letting me go afterward. And he's still my brother's best friend. He's practically part of our family. I'll still have to see him all the time.

Distance, Jules, I remind myself. *Keep your distance.*

He just chuckles—a low, deep sound that I feel in my gut —and says, "I know you don't."

"Do you even know CPR?" I ask, just to have something to say.

"Nah, but I was willing to bet you'd start breathing again if I tried it on you. It worked in the alley."

I can't hold in the snort. "That wasn't CPR, Colt."

He shrugs. "Whatever it was, it got you breathing again."

There's a split second when I think, *It's too bad he can't be around to kiss me every time I feel a panic attack coming on.* But that's a horrible idea for all the obvious reasons and makes me think about what my therapist said about pushing myself out of my comfort zone in order to learn that I don't always have to be in control—or shut down when I don't. And Colt's suggestion from earlier is still rattling around in my head.

"What did you have in mind, when you said that I need to find healthy ways to 'let off some steam.'"

"I don't know," he says, dropping his hands and sitting back on his heels. I appreciate that he's not right up in my face now—it makes it easier to remember that I'm supposed to be indifferent toward him. "Make a list of things that scare you, and do them? Challenge yourself physically? Learn how to meditate?"

I can tell he's just spitballing ideas, but I appreciate how he's trying to help me.

"I'll think about it," I say, and he nods. But then my anxiety spikes as I remember why we started this conversation in the first place. "In the meantime, what the hell are we going to do about this whole fiancée situation?"

"I was originally thinking we could just say that I saw you in a clearly uncomfortable situation and said you were my fiancée to get you out of it," he says. "But now that video . . ."

I'm glad he's at as much of a loss as I am.

"Yeah, even though it would have made me look like an idiot, that could have worked. But now . . ." I look away, staring off at the cabinets with the open shelving above them. "If that was the case, why would we be on top of each other in an alley afterward like two hormone-charged teenagers if you were just pretending to be my fiancée? People I work with are going to see that video. Oh my god, my clients and even potential donors are going to see that video! At best, I come off looking impulsive and unprofessional . . ."

"And I come off looking like I took advantage of you." His words are grim.

"You didn't take advantage of me." My response is instantaneous, because he warned me he was going to do something we'd both regret—though little did we know how much—and I didn't stop him. In fact, I jumped in wholeheartedly, which was the biggest mistake of all. "You were trying to help. But Colt, who's going to want to hire me now? Who's going to want to donate to our nonprofit or believe that I'm the kind of person who should be mentoring young women if I'm seen making out in an alley with a random hockey player?" I can hear the panic creeping into my voice the same way I can feel it moving under my skin again, little pinpricks of anxiety attacking my nervous system.

"Ouch." When I look at him for clarification, he cocks an eyebrow at me. "So now I'm just some random hockey player?"

"You know what I mean—the optics are bad no matter how we spin this."

"Yeah, unless . . . " He pauses, and I'm almost afraid of what he's going to say next. How could we spin this in any way that we don't tarnish both our reputations?

"Unless?"

"Unless we pretend that we actually are engaged. It would explain my reaction in the restaurant, and then you don't look like you're making out with 'some random hockey player.'" The way he repeats my words back to me sounds a little bitter, but he's got to understand that this is how people would see it. He's got a reputation and a list of past hookups that would probably stretch from here to the West Coast.

"Colt," I say as I stand. "That's the most ridiculous idea I've ever heard." Who gets fake engaged? That's not a thing that happens in real life.

"Why?" he asks, rising from his knees so he's towering over me.

"Because first off, no one is going to believe it. Anyone who knows us is going to know it's not true. Anyone who's ever *seen me* is going to know there's no way I'm engaged to you."

"What are you even talking about?" he asks.

"Colt, you have this . . . energy . . ."

He slides his hands into the pocket of his dress pants, all casual-like, but there's nothing casual about the timbre of his voice when he asks, "Oh yeah? What kind of energy is that?"

He knows exactly the kind of big dick energy he exudes as he swaggers through life, and I'm not planning to give him the satisfaction of telling him I've noticed.

"I think you know," I say breezily as I try to walk past him and out of the kitchen. But his big hand is around my wrist, pulling me to him.

When we're toe-to-toe, he straightens up to his full height, and I'm forced to tilt my head all the way back just to see him. "I want to hear you say it."

He wants to hear me say that he's got the kind of energy that has women dropping their panties before he even has to ask. Meanwhile, I've never even let a guy into mine? I look away. No way in hell is he hearing that admission from me.

"No."

His palm slides across my throat and he uses his splayed

thumb and fingers to cup my jaw, turning my head back toward him. I like the feel of his hand around my throat way more than I should.

"What's wrong, Jules? Can't back up your claim?"

"More like, I don't need to because we both know it's true."

"What's true?" he asks again.

I note the way his hand is gripping my neck possessively, how his gaze bores into my face with an intensity I can't muster, how his whole body practically vibrates with dominance. "That I don't match your energy."

"Maybe that's because you exceed it?"

A laugh bursts out of me. What in the actual hell is this man talking about? "Yeah, Colt. Sure."

"How do you not see what everyone else does?"

Yeah, I know what I look like. But my energy must scream *Stay away!* because that's exactly what guys do the minute they get to know me.

I step back and he lets me go, but he plants his hands on his hips like he's creating a barrier between the exit from the kitchen and me.

"Can we go back to talking about why you think it's a good idea to pretend we're engaged, and how in the world you think anyone would believe that for even a second?"

"Sure," he says as he shrugs his shoulders. "I think it's a good idea because it gives us both something we want. And I think the only people who aren't going to believe it are your family, and we can tell them the truth. Everyone else will believe it."

I don't even know where to start with that, so I circle

back to the first thing he said. "How does this give each of us what we want?"

"It gives me an excuse for why I haven't been with a woman in at least six months—"

"What?" The question bursts out of me with an incredulous laugh. There's no way that's possible. Being a manwhore is kind of his brand.

"Why is that so unbelievable?"

"It . . ." I don't want to admit that I've spent any time at all thinking about him or his sex life, so instead, I say, ". . . just isn't what I expected. So, you'd get fake engaged to explain away a dry spell?"

"No. No one even knows about that. I'm just saying that it's not like there would be women saying 'You can't be engaged, you were in my bed last weekend.' I wouldn't put you in that position, just so you know." He runs a hand through his short hair. "But mostly, what I get out of this is that you could come with me to my parents' anniversary party. My parents would be thrilled, and you could be a buffer between me and my brother."

"How do you think your parents would feel when they found out this was all fake? Or when we 'break up,'" I say, using air quotes. "Wouldn't that just hurt them in the long run?"

"They'd be okay. It's not like you guys are going to bond in a weekend. And we can make it an amicable split in the end, don't you think?"

The look on his face is as doubtful as my thoughts.

"And what do I get out of this, exactly?"

"I'll help you find *healthy* ways to overcome your fear of losing control. And you have a plausible reason for why you were making out with me in an alley. I don't think anyone would have any trouble believing I'd have you up against a brick wall at the first chance I got."

"Yeah." I bark out a laugh. "That's *exactly* the part I think no one is going to believe."

"You just gotta trust me on this one. No one's going to question it. And no one is going to think less of you because someone caught you on camera kissing your fiancé."

"There's a zero percent chance that anyone who knows me is going to believe this." Why am I even entertaining this idea?

"Besides Jameson, Audrey, and Lauren, who else isn't going to believe it?"

"Morgan. Drew."

"Okay, so we tell the five of them the truth." Colt shrugs like this is no big deal. "If they can keep their mouths shut, this will work. And then down the road, when all the news about this has passed, my parents' anniversary party is over, and the playoffs are done . . ."

"We fake break up?"

"Sure. But I have one condition."

"You're the one trying to sell *me* on this," I remind him. "And *you're* setting conditions?"

"Just one. You have to be the one to break it off with me." He shoves his hands back in his pockets, and it has the rolled-up sleeves of his dress shirt pulling higher and revealing his inked-up forearms. I don't even like tattoos, so why do I like them on him?

"Why? So I come off looking like the asshole?"

"No. So you don't look like another woman I slept with and discarded."

"I thought you said it'd be an amicable separation."

"Maybe. But if anyone needs to do the breaking up for any reason, I want it to be you. I don't care if I come off looking bad here. I do care if you do."

I tug on the engraved star on the gold disk hanging at the base of my throat as my eyebrows dip and I assess his motives. "Why are you trying to protect my reputation here?"

"Because it was my impulsiveness that got us in this situation in the first place. And I don't want you to have any negative consequences as a result."

That's a way more responsible and empathetic reason than I'd have expected him to come up with.

"I still don't think this is a good idea."

"Do you have a better one?" he asks.

"I might be able to come up with something if I had a little more time," I say, and that's when my phone vibrates in the pocket of my sweatpants. I pull it out and see Lauren's name on the screen. Given the important conversation we're having, I'd normally ignore the call. But Lauren usually texts unless something's wrong.

"Hey, Laur, what's up?"

"This is your courtesy warning that your brother is on the way to your house right now. And if Colt wants to live, he should probably not be there when Jameson arrives."

Shit. Without traffic, it's a fifteen-minute drive. Less if you hit the lights right.

"Oh shit, you guys saw the article already?"

"The articles," she says, emphasizing the plural nature of the word. "And the video."

Of course Jameson's seen them, he's Colt's agent. He

probably has all kinds of Google alerts set up for just this type of occasion . . . they just don't normally involve his sister.

"And," Lauren continues, and I swear I hear a smile in her voice, "then he called Colt, like, five times and there was no answer, so he decided to head over. He may have said something about castration on his way out the door? I can't be sure, though. I was distracted by the way his head looked like it was going to explode."

"You sound like you're finding this all quite funny."

"I sure am. Sometimes he forgets that you and Audrey are full-grown women, and he doesn't need to go into papa bear mode like you're still teenagers."

"It's funny now. Wait until Ivy and Iris are that age and you have to run interference."

Lauren groans, as she's probably picturing Jameson parenting their twins in a decade. "Call me if you need backup. You can put me on speakerphone."

"We won't need backup, but thank you for the offer."

"Okay, but once he leaves, will you *please* call me and explain what the hell is going on? Because I could have told you that Colt was interested in you, but I fully believed you hated him."

Wait, what?

"Uhhh," I stutter, my eyes flying to where Colt stands a couple of feet from me. But I don't have to question whether he heard her; the way his chest shakes with laughter is all the proof I need. "Okay, I'll talk to you later. Thanks!"

As soon as I disconnect the call, I tell Colt, "Alright, you better get your ass out of here before Jameson gets here. I'll explain the situation to him."

"Like hell I'm leaving you."

"This explanation doesn't require both of us, and he's much more likely to stay calm if the man who pushed his sister up against a wall in an alley isn't standing in front of him. *I'm* the one who needs to explain this to Jameson," I insist.

"You can do the explaining," Colt says, taking a step toward me and planting his hands on my shoulders, "but there's no way I'm not standing next to you while you do."

Chapter Fourteen

COLT

When Jameson pulls into the spot behind the back door, Jules and I are standing in the kitchen waiting for him.

"I need a minute," I say, reaching for the doorknob.

"What? No." She grasps my forearm as if she could stop me from going out there. "You said I could do the explaining here."

"And you can. But I need a minute with him first."

"Colt . . ." She drags my name out like a warning, and I'm tempted to tell her it turns me on when she does that. But even I know that now isn't the time.

"He's been my best friend for the last fifteen years, and I just had his little sister wrapped around me up against a wall in an alley. Trust me when I say, I need a minute with him so that he doesn't kill us both."

She sighs, but lets go of my arm. Shutting the door behind me, I meet him on the stairs.

"What. The. Fuck?" His words are low and slow, laced with an anger I've never seen from him.

I put both hands out in front of me, hoping it helps him slow his roll a bit. "Jules wants to explain the whole situation to you," I tell him. "But I just need you to know that she was in danger, and I did what I needed to do to protect her."

That has his head snapping back. "What?"

"You heard me."

"Who was trying to hurt her?" There's fire in his eyes, and I'm glad his anger is no longer directed at me.

"She'll explain. But I just need you to go in there and be reasonable. Don't lose your shit on her. Don't make her feel bad," I say. His eyes narrow, like he's trying to assess why I care about her feelings when all I've ever done is try to annoy her. But before he can ask any questions, I say, "Let's do this," and open the back door so he'll follow me inside.

Five minutes later, Jules has told him the whole story. His response is classic Jameson: "Tell me who this asshole is so I can fucking bury him."

"No."

He looks at her like he must have misheard her. "No?"

"No. Boston is a small city. I don't need you overreacting and doing something that's going to tarnish my professional reputation."

"I'm discreet as hell."

"Uh huh."

"Well, anyway," he says, like he knows there's no point in pushing because she'll lock up like a damn vault. "This engagement is the most asinine idea I've ever heard."

"Do you have a better one?" she asks, and my chest shakes with silent laughter. It's the *exact* question I asked her when she said it was a stupid idea. Now, it feels like we're on the same team. Us against everyone.

Jameson sighs. "It's not ideal, but in the circumstances . . . I don't know. Maybe it *is* the best move? It'll certainly help *your* less-than-stellar reputation"—he looks at me—"and possibly protect yours," he adds as he looks at Jules.

"Exactly," she and I say in unison.

"But I'm still not convinced that people are going to believe it, what with you sleeping with a new woman in every city," Jameson says. "Won't that just make my sister look like a fool?"

I hate that I have to defend myself to my best friend. I earned my reputation fair and square, but it's been a long time since I've acted like that. Everyone just assumes that nothing's changed because I continue to let them believe it. I play into it even, because it's always been my armor—the way I keep women from getting too close while showing everyone back home that I've moved on.

I tell him the same thing I told Jules earlier, and he folds his arms across his chest. "And you think your teammates are going to believe this?"

"There hasn't been another woman all season, and no one on the team could claim otherwise. So yeah, I think it'll be pretty easy to explain that the reason no one's seen me take a woman back to my hotel room, or leave a bar or a club with someone, is because I've secretly been dating Jules this whole time."

His jaw ticks as he grinds his teeth together. "But just to be clear, you haven't been? Right?"

"You already know the answer to that," I say, folding my arms across my chest.

"AJ wants to meet with you first thing tomorrow morning," he tells me. It's never a good thing when your general manager calls you into a meeting on a Sunday.

"Shit. Do you think I need to tell her the truth?" I ask.

His lips press together—it's his classic thinking face, the one I've seen countless times over the years as he's negotiated contracts and endorsement deals on my behalf. "Yeah. I don't know if she'll agree with what you're doing, but I think you should tell her. Because if somehow it comes out that you two lied about this, she will never, *ever* trust you again and your career with the Rebels will be over. Maybe even before the end of this contract."

I'm not sure how many more years I've got left in me anyway, but I don't want to piss off my GM or risk ending my career prematurely. I want to go out on my own terms.

"Alright. Should Jules come with me for this meeting?"

"What?" Jules squeaks out. "No way. She's low-key terrifying."

Jameson's laugh is a low rumble. "AJ doesn't take shit from anyone, but she's not terrifying. She's one of Lauren's best friends, plus, she'd probably really like you. You two are a lot alike, actually." He pauses, his eyebrows dipping, before he says, "Yeah, I think you should take Jules with you."

"Nope." Jules shakes her head adamantly, like a child who's trying to get out of taking medicine. "Sorry, I can't. I have plans."

"Oh yeah?" I ask, thinking about how freaking adorable she is when she's not getting her way, and how much I love to see her squirm. "What will you be doing?"

"Sleeping. I'm not a morning person."

Ironic, given her line of work. If the last two days are any indication, she leaves the house before I even wake up. "Come on, Jules. I need you to help me save my career."

"Just play better and AJ wouldn't dare get rid of you," Jules says.

Jameson and I lock eyes and we both laugh. I'm arguably still the best goalie in the league, despite my age. "That's not how AJ operates," Jameson says.

Then I add, "She's all about building a team of responsible, respectful men—"

"And she lets *you* play for the Rebels?" Jules asks, covering her mouth in mock horror.

"Exactly, so I need you to help me show her how responsible and respectful I am. Come on, Jules. Don't make me get on my knees and beg in front of your brother."

She knows I'm teasing, but Jameson practically growls and says, "Don't make me throat punch you in front of my sister."

I roll my eyes in his direction and turn back to Jules. "Please, Jules?"

"Alright, fine," she sighs, like she's being deeply inconvenienced. "But only because we need this to work. Though, sometime, I *would* like to see you beg."

"Fucking enough!" Jameson grinds out the words like he's in pain. "Save your flirting and innuendos for when you're trying to sell this fake engagement. And preferably not in front of me."

I try not to take offense to the way he visibly shudders, like the thought of me tainting his sister is enough to make him want to vomit.

"This is how we've always talked to each other," Jules says.

"Yeah, well, it has a whole new layer now that I've had to watch you two make out." He turns his head toward me. "You're my best friend, so I'll tell you this once and once only. When you're not out in public trying to convince people you're actually engaged, keep your fucking hands off my sister."

"Woah," Jules says before I can even respond. "There's nothing going on here, but even if there was, that would be none of your business. You don't get to decide who I date."

His face softens a bit when he looks at her. "No, but I have a responsibility to make sure you end up with someone capable of treating you right. Preferably someone whose body count isn't a thousand people deep."

The way the adrenaline pumps through my system at that statement—equal parts anger and shame—makes me want to tear Jameson in half. But he's not wrong.

Jules's hand lands on my forearm, gripping it tight enough that I take a breath. "Again," she practically growls at her brother. "None. Of. Your. Fucking. Business. You do *not* have a responsibility to make sure I end up with *anyone*. Who I end up with is my choice, and mine alone."

"I just want what's best for you," he tells her.

"Which isn't me." My comment comes through sounding just as tense as I feel. It's not a question, but I am looking for him to confirm if that's what he meant.

"Hey," he says, his gaze sliding from Jules to me where I stand next to her. "Nothing against you. I just want Jules to end up with someone—"

"Who you trust with her. And you've made it perfectly clear that isn't me."

I see the confusion in his eyes, and I don't know why I'm

so mad about this. He's watched me rack up one-night stands —fucking and forgetting women over and over—for a decade and a half. But he's the only person in Boston who knows about Cheri and Gabriel. So I guess I always assumed he understood why I never dated, why I wouldn't trust anyone enough to give them more than a night.

Jules moves her hand from my forearm to my abdomen, like she's holding me back, and then extends her other arm to Jameson's chest. It's only then that I realize how close we both are to throwing punches over this.

"Alright, you two clearly need a breather. Jameson, go home to Lauren, and let her explain to you why you're acting like an asshole."

"I'm not being an asshole." He sounds defensive.

"It's kind of your default. But not normally with either of us," she says, nodding her chin toward me while her hands remain firmly in place on each of us. "I get that you're not happy about this, but we're not asking for your opinion. *We'll* handle this."

Jameson's eyes flick back and forth between the two of us. "Fine." Then he looks back at me. "You better not hurt her."

"No one's going to get hurt," I say, with more certainty than I feel. Because if I've learned anything tonight, it's that I like Jules Flynn a whole lot more than I realized.

———

"I really might throw up," Jules says as we walk down the hallway of the office suite at the Rebels' practice facility early on Sunday morning.

"I tried to take you out to breakfast first," I remind her. "Coffee on an empty stomach is never a good idea."

"You don't even drink coffee," she reminds me. "And I'm not going to throw up because of the caffeine. It's nerves."

I take her hand, lacing our fingers together and giving her a little squeeze as we walk down the hallway. I'm so relieved when she doesn't pull her hand away that I stop walking and tug her back toward me. Her free hand flies up and lands on my chest as she spins around in surprise.

"Hey." I bend my head so I'm looking her in the eyes as she stares up at me. "Are you having second thoughts about this?"

"What? No." She shakes her head slightly, eyebrows scrunched up like she doesn't understand why I'm asking this.

"Jules, I know my reputation will come up again and again," I say, thinking about Jameson's reaction last night and imagining how fans will take this news. Will she be *the one who finally tamed Colt,* or will she be painted as *the poor soul who was last in a long line of women*? "I'm not sure how people will talk about you as a result, and if you don't want to do this, it's not too late to back out."

"As long as you're willing to stand up for me whenever necessary, and I do the same for you, we'll be fine." Her words are certain, her face is anything but.

"Us against the world?"

She lets out a small laugh, and it's so good to see a genuine smile from her that I can't hold mine in either. "Something like that," she says as her eyes search mine for a moment that ends too quickly. "Come on, we don't want to be late."

We approach the only open door, with the light streaming through into the somewhat dim hallway. I don't spend a lot of time up here in the offices, but the times I've been here, it's bustling. The whole space feels desolate right now, and that is a little intimidating, if I'm being honest.

AJ is sitting at her desk, her long dark hair obscuring her face as she looks at her phone. When I knock twice on the open door, her head snaps up, and she stands immediately, walking toward her couch area as she ushers us in. I introduce Jules, and AJ smiles as she extends her hand. "Alessandra Jones," she says, "but please, call me AJ."

As they shake hands, Jules tells her how much she likes her office. It's always amused me that AJ—who is literally the most powerful woman in hockey and whose entire reputation is based on being a complete ball-buster—has such a feminine office. There's a low cream-colored couch running along the glass wall that overlooks the practice rink. In front of it is a coffee table, and cushioned armchairs with frilly pillows are on either side.

Jules and I take a seat on the couch, and AJ sits in the chair on my other side. Next to me, Jules slides her hand back into mine, and I give her another supportive squeeze as I look over at AJ, waiting for her to say something.

"So the funny thing about being the only female GM in the league," she says, looking straight past me at Jules, "is that I tend to do things a little differently than some of my male counterparts. For example, I pride myself on knowing my players well—not just as players, but as people. I like to think one of the reasons I've been able to build the team I have here in Boston is because I inherited some great players, like Colt, who predated me. And I've been able to bring in the type of men I want, not for their skill on the ice, but because I know they'll have each other's backs."

Her eyes flick to me. "Which is why I find it absolutely *shocking* that I had to find out you're engaged from a goddamn fan website. You're a leader on this team, someone I've trusted from day one, despite how you're portrayed in the media. So being blindsided like this . . . either I'm fucking terrible at my job, or this"—she gestures between me and Jules—"is not what it seems."

Jules's fingers twitch, so I lean back against the couch cushions and pull our clasped hands into my lap, using my thumb to stroke circles on the back of her hand. I don't miss the way AJ's eyes track that movement before she glances up at me, eyebrows raised.

"You're not terrible at your job, and you know it." I'm so glad we decided not to lie to her, because that wouldn't have gone over well. As I explain what happened, and what we've decided to do, I watch her observe both of us closely and wonder what she sees.

When I'm done explaining the last eighteen hours, she gives a quick nod and says, "Okay, here are my initial thoughts." She looks at Jules. "First, at some point, I want to hear more details about this mentoring program because it sounds amazing and necessary. Second," she says, looking back at me, "there's obviously a reason you said you two were engaged, and I look forward to you figuring out what that was. Third, I agree with Jameson that the idea of continuing to fake this engagement is completely asinine, but also with both of you that there isn't a better alternative given the situation. And fourth, in order for this to work, you are going to have to convince *a lot* of people that you're in love.

There are probably already too many people who know the truth, and I appreciate being one of them. But I assume you're planning on telling the rest of the team, and Wilcott," she says, referring to our coach, "that you're really engaged?"

"Yeah," I say decisively, "I don't think anyone except you and Jules's family can know the truth. The more people who know, the more likely it is to get out."

"And the only thing that can make us look worse than we already do in this situation," Jules says with a sigh, "is if the *actual* truth was out there."

"I'm sorry you're in this position," AJ says, her voice uncharacteristically sympathetic. "But I agree with you on both accounts." Her eyes narrow in on us, sitting together, still holding hands. "Do you really think you can fake this, though?"

Jules and I glance at each other, and the memories of us in that alley come flooding back—the way she felt with her legs wrapped around my hips, pressed up against my body as she fucking devoured my mouth. Not a single thing about that moment felt like faking it. But unfortunately, I also can't shake the memory of Jameson making it clear that I'm not the kind of person he wants to be with his sister.

"Yeah, I think we can convince people," I say.

"Me too," Jules tells AJ.

"Well, good. Because that charity event for the pediatric hospital is this coming Saturday, and I expect you're now attending together," AJ says. "Which will give you the perfect opportunity to be seen out as a couple, at a team event. Plus, I assume Jules will be at the first playoff home game on Friday night?"

We leave tonight for our first two games in Florida, and

then we're back at the end of the week for a home game on Friday. I'd forgotten about that charity event on Saturday until right now. I'm about to tell AJ that Jules and I haven't discussed this yet, when she says, "Of course I'll be at both. Just like a good little fiancée would be."

I glance over at her. "You're going to have to tone down the sarcasm if you want people to believe you're marrying me."

"Well, luckily, I'm not," she says, her voice teasing. "But I can pretend in public."

"Be *very* careful," AJ warns, "because, given his reputation, people will be looking for any excuse to prove that Colt can't settle down. And if Colt looks like an idiot, this organization will too."

Jules nods as she pulls the side of her cheek into her mouth, creating a line beneath her strong cheekbones to stop herself from replying. As I try to imagine all the things she's *not* saying, it really sinks in what Jameson was trying to tell me last night . . . My reputation is incredibly tainted.

There's no way that's not going to come back to bite me in the ass the minute we officially announce this engagement —and Jules is the one who's going to be made to look stupid for falling for me.

But I can do things differently moving forward. I can be the man she deserves, even if it's only for appearance's sake.

Chapter Fifteen

JULES

I glance at my phone again as I wait for Graham to finish drying off after his shower. He managed to be in and out in ten minutes, which must be some sort of record. When he lived with me, it was a miracle if we could get him out in under half an hour. I guess the fact that I took him out to eat, and we got back later than planned, combined with him not wanting to miss any of his dad's first playoff game, lit a fire under his ass. I'll have to share this new strategy with Audrey when she gets home.

COLT

Tell me you don't have any plans tomorrow night.

He sent me the text an hour ago, but I didn't see it until we got home. In the living room, the TV's on and the players are already on the ice, so I haven't responded yet. He won't see my message until after the game anyway, so I have some time to figure out what I want to say.

I don't have any plans tomorrow night, but spending any more time with him than absolutely necessary feels like I'm inviting disaster. If I've learned anything in the last week, it's that I still make terrible decisions when he's around. Last weekend could have cost him his career, if AJ was mad enough, or cost me my professional reputation.

So no, I don't think it's a particularly good idea to do *anything* with him beyond what's required for our engagement to appear real.

I stand in the kitchen, close enough to hear Graham singing to himself in the bathroom, while I keep half an eye on the TV so I can give him a warning when it's about to start.

The camera zooms in on Colt as he does his warm up stretches. With his knees spread and ass out, Colt bounces lightly from side to side, stretching his inner thighs.

Why is that so hot?

"What are you looking at?" Graham's voice comes from right beside me, and it's so unexpected that I jump, sending my phone clattering to the countertop.

"Just checking how much longer until the game starts." Glancing down at the towel wrapped around his waist, I ask, "Are you going to get your pajamas on?"

"Yeah, I just wanted to make sure the game hadn't started."

"I promised to tell you if it did," I remind him. On the TV, the players start leaving the ice. "Oh, you better hurry up. They're going to do the pre-game stuff soon." I realize that I don't even know if there's a name for the players' entrance onto the ice, with lights and music, before the national anthem and the puck drop.

The buzzer rings, and I tell him, "And Morgan and Lauren are here."

"When's Mom going to be home?" he asks.

"In less than half an hour," I say as I reach over to buzz my friends into Audrey and Drew's place.

"I can't believe she's missing the beginning of the game."

"She's got her dance class, but she's leaving early so she can be home to watch some of the game with us before you go to bed. Better go get your pajamas on, or *you're* going to miss the beginning of the game."

Audrey's weekly Wednesday night dance class used to be a guaranteed time each week that I got to spend hanging out with my nephew. I didn't realize how much I'd miss that now that they live with Drew, and I only need to watch him when Drew is traveling. And once the playoffs are over, Drew will be home all the time, so I'm going to have to be even more intentional about scheduling time to see Graham.

Morgan and Lauren enter with a wide array of snacks and drinks and start setting them out on the kitchen island as we listen to the sportscasters talking about how Boston won the first game of the series two nights ago and speculate whether Florida can bring home a win on home ice tonight, before the series moves to Boston for Friday night's game.

"Where's Graham?" Morgan asks.

"Getting his PJs on."

"Okay, so once Audrey's home and he's in bed, we have *a lot* of questions about this whole fake engagement situation," she says. I'd explained everything to my family on Sunday night at our weekly family dinner, which I'd invited Morgan to so that everyone who had to know the truth was there. Except Colt and Drew, who'd already left for Florida. Colt said he'd talk to Drew on the flight down, given that they normally sit together.

"The types of questions we weren't going to ask in front of Jameson," Lauren adds. "Because we love you, and him, and don't want to embarrass you or send him to the grave early."

This is all fake—it's not like Colt would ever have feelings for me. So as long as I can keep my own feelings and thoughts under control, everything will be fine. This shouldn't be a big deal.

"Okay," I say, dragging the word out tentatively.

Graham comes running down the hall. "Auntie Lauren, why didn't you bring Iris and Ivy?" That kid loves his little cousins so much. He's going to be a great big brother someday.

Lauren bends down and kisses Graham on top of his head, reminding him, "Because they're already in bed. They don't get to stay up late to watch hockey games."

"But it's still light out," Graham says, clearly not remembering that the sun sets later in the spring. "And it would be more fun if they were here."

"Trust me, you don't want overtired three-year-olds around. They're not very fun."

The players take the ice and I try not to focus on the way Colt's moving around the crease, using the edges of his blades to rough up the ice so he doesn't go sliding across it when he tries to make a save. He's doing it in time with the music, like he's dancing, and even though it's an away game, a segment of the crowd is cheering and clapping along with his antics. He's hamming it up for the fans, like he always does, and it's a good reminder that everything with Colt is for show. Just like our "engagement."

During one of the commercial breaks, Morgan looks over and says, "Oh, I meant to tell you. I was able to schedule that interview with Rosie. This is going to be so amazing for getting some donors for the mentoring program. We can film it the week after next, but where would you like to do it? On a job site? In the Our House office? Your house?"

Morgan has done amazing things for our social media platforms and website since she took over our marketing six months ago. She seems to have a real knack for what will connect with potential clients.

"I'm fine with whatever makes Rosie feel most comfortable. Did she mention about her face?"

"No, what about it?"

"One side of her face is . . ." I don't know the right words to use here. Rosie refers to her face as "fucked up," but it's so much deeper than that. ". . . permanently damaged because of an abusive situation with her daughter's father."

"Oh my gosh," Lauren says, and I can tell she's doing that thing she does where she catalogs all the ways she could have had it worse with her late husband. His death uncovered a whole secret life he was leading, but thankfully, it also led her back to my brother.

"Yeah. He's in jail now, but she wears a permanent reminder of him. She's such a badass, but she's secretly really self-conscious about the scars. If we can film it so that we're focused on her at an angle that doesn't show that side of her face, that would be perfect."

"Of course," Morgan says. "I'll take some test recordings,

too, and show them to her to make sure she's happy with the setup before we start."

"Okay. Just let me know where and when, and no matter what else is going on, I'll make sure I'm there for the recording, too."

"I didn't realize you guys were already at the point of looking for donors until you told us what happened at that dinner," Lauren says.

"We weren't, really. But the opportunity to present at that nonprofit pitch fest felt like it would be a good chance to practice talking about the mentoring program and gauging interest. Turns out, I *really* wish we'd waited until we had the testimonial and had thought a bit more about how to strategically find donors who would be a good fit."

Morgan's laugh is more of a cute little snort. "Yeah, but if that hadn't happened, half the girls in Boston wouldn't hate you."

"Half the girls in Boston hate me? Why? Because I'm 'engaged' to Colt?"

"Pretty much," she says.

Graham comes back from the bathroom then, cutting our conversation short, and Audrey gets home shortly after. The rest of the first period is frustratingly uneventful, and by the time both teams head toward the locker room, the score is still 0-0. After their 5-2 loss earlier this week, Florida is apparently fighting back with a vengeance.

Graham is predictably whiny about having to go to bed with a 0-0 score, since he wants to know what's going to happen. It was easier to put him to bed mid-game at the beginning of the season when he just loved hockey, but now that he knows his dad plays for the team, he doesn't want to miss a minute. And if it was a weekend, Audrey would let him stay up even though he's a nightmare the next day when he's overtired. But it's a school night, so Audrey puts him to bed with the promise of waking him up at the end of the game to tell him the outcome.

"Are you really going to wake him up?" Lauren asks when Audrey comes back into the living room.

"Yeah. He's such a sound sleeper that I'll tell him, and he'll go right back to sleep. He won't remember in the morning, so I'll have to tell him again."

"Okay," Lauren says decisively as she pulls her long red hair over her shoulder and starts braiding it. "Graham's in bed, so let's talk about the HUGE elephant in the room."

I can't help it that my mind immediately jumps to wanting to make a dirty joke about how huge Colt is. That's got to be a perfectly normal reaction to having felt him pressed up against me in the alley, right? The heat runs along my skin as I remember the delicious feeling of being trapped between him and that wall, with my legs wrapped around him and nothing but the fabric of our pants between us. The way he was thrusting against me, running his hard length along my clit . . .

"Oh my god," Audrey says with a laugh. "What the hell are you thinking about right now?"

"What?" I shake myself out of that memory as quickly as I can, but the flush I can feel on my cheeks is evidence that I was just thinking about something that got me all hot and bothered.

"Holy shit," Morgan says. "Is this thing between you and Colt even fake? Because there was nothing fake about that look."

"I don't know what you're talking about," I say, and then realize that's about the most incriminating thing I could say in response.

"I think you do," Lauren chides. "This whole time, I thought it was Colt who had it bad for *you*, but—"

"Yeah, about that . . ." I've been meaning to ask her about that comment since we were on the phone Saturday night and haven't had a chance yet. "What the hell are you talking about? Because if there's one thing I'm absolutely certain about, it's that Colt doesn't have any feelings for me."

Audrey knows exactly what I mean, and why. But Morgan and Lauren both look at me skeptically, before Morgan says, "And you know that, how?"

I look toward Audrey for backup, because she knows I can't tell Lauren about what really happened in Vegas. I don't want Jameson to find out, and I don't want Lauren to have to lie about it. Audrey was in a similar situation this past fall, when Lauren figured out Drew was Graham's dad before Jameson did. I hate having secrets from my brother, but I also respect the fact that Colt is his best friend, not to mention his most lucrative client, and neither their friendship nor their business relationships should suffer because of my immaturity and inability to make good decisions when I was nineteen.

"Let's just say Jules had a little crush on Colt when she was younger, and it was clear that he didn't return the feelings," Audrey says. "And no, you *cannot* tell Jameson that, Lauren. Sorry. Hate to make you keep secrets, but teenage crushes are something only us girls should know about."

Okay, so I guess we are telling her at least *part* of the story.

"So you're telling me," Lauren says, with a tilt of her head as she narrows her gaze on me, "because he didn't return Jules's feelings when she was a teenager, that he couldn't possibly have feelings for her now?"

"Trust me," I say, thinking about the way Colt looked at me when Zach interrupted us in the alley, all that regret I saw before he opened his mouth to say it didn't mean anything. I would have known based on the look alone, but his words were the nail that sealed the coffin. His words only confirmed what I already knew. "He doesn't have feelings for me."

"Okay," Morgan says, but it sounds wholly unconvinced. "Maybe not the kind of feelings you had for him as a teenager. But the way he was looking at you at Audrey's engagement party?" She fans her face and collapses back against the couch cushion as she giggles. "Girl, he *wanted* you."

I'd been so focused on what happened between us in that alley that I'd forgotten the way he was staring at me from across the condo earlier that day. I hadn't recognized it as lust at the time, but given what happened that night, maybe it was?

"Regardless"—I shake my head—"whether he's attracted to me or not is irrelevant. If his 'recreational activities' are any indication, that man's attracted to every person with a pair of boobs. It doesn't mean there are actual feelings involved."

"And there's no way," Audrey adds, laying her hand on my thigh and giving it a squeeze, "that Jules would ever have feelings for Colt again."

Shit. I'm sure she meant to be supportive, assuring

Morgan and Lauren that this is all fake, but if their looks are any indication, she's sparked their curiosity further.

"And why not?" Lauren asks.

"Because I'm not interested in dating, much less marrying someone with his reputation," I say, hoping that sounds believable. It's a huge part of the truth.

"Oh shit!" Audrey says. "Florida just scored."

We all turn toward the TV in time to see the opposing players huddled together with their sticks in the air. Colt turns toward the goal and grabs his water bottle off the top of the net, and when the camera zooms in on him, he looks more pissed off than I'm used to seeing him, even during a game.

Fortunately, that goal and the subsequent fast-paced nature of the second and third periods have us so focused on the game, no one brings up the earlier conversation about Colt and me again. And I leave before the game is over, claiming that I have to get up early tomorrow, but really, I just want to make sure I'm not dragged into another interrogation about my past. Audrey is the only person who knows everything that happened in Vegas. And it needs to stay that way.

Chapter Sixteen

COLT

I face 200-pound men who are shooting rubber pucks at me at over 90 miles per hour on a regular basis. That fact alone means there's almost nothing that makes me nervous. So why, as I sit on Jules's couch waiting for her to get home from work, is my stomach twisted up in knots?

Pulling out my phone, I read through our text exchange from last night. It's embarrassing how frequently I've done this, trying to figure out what she's thinking and how she's feeling. She's so damn hard to read.

COLT

> Tell me you don't have any plans tomorrow night.

I sent that text a full hour before our game, and when I hadn't heard back from her before the game started, I was annoyed. I took a quick peek at my phone in between the first and second periods, which was a mistake. Her lack of response at that point pissed me off.

Why was she ignoring me? I was so busy getting myself worked up about it that I let a puck, which should have been an easy stop, fly right by me at the beginning of the second period.

That was the wake-up call I needed. This distractibility—me thinking about her when I shouldn't be—it's exactly why I don't date. No woman is worth fucking up my career over. Especially when I have so little of it left to enjoy.

I got my head on straight and didn't let a single shot past me after that, and we ended the game 2-1. Leading the series by two as we headed back to Boston was a great feeling, but I honestly couldn't enjoy the celebration with my teammates as we loaded onto the plane for our flight home—until her text came through.

JULES

I don't. Why, what did you have in mind?

COLT

A trip to the jeweler so you can pick out a ring, and then our first "official" date as a newly minted fake-engaged couple.

JULES

Do we have to?

When I'd chuckled at that, Drew's head snapped over to my phone screen so quickly I had to flip it over. Of course I'd pick the only woman in the world who's resistant to my charms. This couldn't have happened with someone who'd have made it easy.

You don't want easy.

I don't know where the thought comes from. But as I sit on the couch now, waiting for her, I have to admit that it's true. Every woman I've ever been with has been easy. Easy to get into my bed, and easy to leave. Even leaving Cheri, who I'd dated for two years and who was supposed to transfer to a college in Boston at the end of her freshman year so she could be with me, wasn't the painful part. It was getting over my brother's betrayal that gutted me.

Not only is Jules not easy, but she's a legitimate challenge . . . a puzzle I'm desperate to finish putting together while half-afraid I'll be missing the last piece. Somehow, that only makes me want to work harder at figuring her out.

COLT

Only if you want this to be believable.

JULES

What I want is for this not to be happening at all.

She's so much less snarky when she's within two feet of me. It's like her walls come down just enough for me to climb over them. It makes me wonder why those walls are there in the first place, and what I'd have to do to get them to crumble entirely?

COLT

Us against the world, remember? So start dreaming about what you want that ring to look like because you're going to be picking one out tomorrow night.

JULES

I work in construction, Colt. Can't we just get me one of those silicone rings so if it gets caught on something, I don't lose a finger?

COLT

There's no way in hell I'm buying you a $20 silicone ring as your engagement ring. Do you even know me? And you don't have to wear my ring at work. But you will wear it when we go out together.

JULES

Ooooh, just what I always wanted. A man to tell me what I will and won't be doing.

COLT

Trust me, you'd like it a whole lot if I was bossing you around.

It had taken almost a full half hour for her to respond to that one, and I was worried that I'd stepped over the line. It's one thing to flirt with a random woman you're trying to sleep with, and another thing entirely to flirt with your fake fiancée after promising your best friend you wouldn't touch her. We're not going to be sleeping together, so why do I enjoy teasing her like this?

JULES

Trust me, I'll be the one bossing you around.

I'd laughed out loud, jolting Drew awake in the dark plane. He looked up at me from where he was reclined, and quietly asked, "If this is all fake, why are you so goddamned happy?"

Am I happy? Is that what this feeling is? I sure as shit wasn't happy last night waiting for her to text me back. Or during the game, when I was so distracted by the fact that she hadn't texted me that I fucked up.

But in those moments where she did reply? Or right now, when I read through our text exchange, am I happy?

COLT

I look forward to that. A lot.

"**A**re you for fucking real right now?" Jules hisses in my ear as we stand in front of the glass display case at the world's most well-known jeweler. We'd arrive at the Newbury Street store via a private car and a back entrance, right at 6 p.m. when the store closed. No one but the clerk helping us, who already signed an NDA, needs to know that Jules didn't already have the ring.

"I'll give you two some time to consider these options, and if you don't like them, I'm happy to select some other choices. I'll be over there if you need anything." She nods her chin toward the corner of the room, far enough away that with the classical music playing quietly in the background, we can have a private conversation.

"Thank you," I tell her. Then I snake my arm around Jules's waist, pulling her against my hip so we're side to side, and turn my head to ask, "Is there a problem, Tink?"

"I can't wear one of these." She almost sounds scared by the thought.

"Do you remember how you said that no one who knows

you would believe we were engaged?" I ask, and she glances up at me, but doesn't respond—it's something that I notice she does a lot. It's like she lets her facial expressions speak for her and saves her words for when they're necessary. It's exactly the opposite of her family's refrain that she doesn't have a filter, and it has me even more curious about what she *doesn't* say. "Well, no one who knows *me* will believe I bought you any ring that wasn't like one of these."

She looks down at the selection of ostentatious rings. "Why, because you're showy and rich?"

"No, because I like to spoil the people I care about."

She stiffens. "Yes, but you *don't actually* care about me."

Is that what she thinks? I mean, I'm not in love with her, and never will be. I promised myself long ago that I was never going down that road again. But that doesn't mean I don't *care* about her. I wouldn't have gone to La Gallina last weekend, or stepped in like I did, if I didn't care. And I sure as hell wouldn't have kissed her to save her from having a panic attack.

"That's not true. And me getting you a cheap-ass ring would be a sure sign that I *didn't* care. We can't have people speculating."

"If your idea of a cheap-ass ring is anything smaller than four carats, you're even more pretentious than I thought."

I laugh at that. "Maybe I am. But that doesn't change the fact that I'm getting you one of *these* rings, since you didn't do what I asked and think about what you wanted ahead of time."

She grinds her teeth together as she looks down at the five rings set out on velvet pedestals on top of the glass case, then lets out a frustrated sigh. "Why don't you choose, then, since it obviously matters more to you than it does to me."

"You're being a brat just to prove a point, aren't you?" Reaching over, I take her chin between my fingers as I tilt her head so she's looking up at me. Why do I like it so much when she's difficult?

She just raises those light eyebrows and blinks, her long dark lashes descending over those blue eyes, as she bites the corner of her lip to hold in a smile. "Go ahead, choose one."

I let go of her chin and pull her in front of me, wrapping my arms around her like I think someone might do if they were actually picking out a ring for their fiancée. Then I lean my head down close to her ear and say, "You sure you don't want to choose? Because this is your last chance."

"I'm good." Her voice is full of amusement as she relaxes against my chest. It's then that I realize how right I was . . . when I'm close, or when I'm touching her, her walls start to come down.

"Okay," I tease out the word in a way that sounds just like *you're going to regret this,* as I lift my hand and motion the salesperson over. I turn my head toward her as she approaches, and right over Jules's head, I say, "My fiancée would like something . . . bigger."

―――――

Jules is still not speaking to me when we pull up to the outdoor driving range. The sun has almost set, and the bright lights illuminate the front of the building and the nets in the distance. Outdoor speakers pump music so loud I can hear it through the windows of the car as the driver pulls right to the front of the parking lot to let us out.

"Colt, *no*," Jules says with an enormous sigh.

"It's just golf. It'll be fun," I promise as I open the door and step out, holding the door for her. The driver rolls his window down and confirms that he'll be back for us in a few hours.

"Colt, I've never golfed. And I know that, like most hockey players, you spend a fair amount of your off-season on the golf course." It's true. It's one of the only sports I can participate in without violating my contract—they pay me way too much to risk me hurting myself in the summer.

"Right. So I'm going to kick your ass, and you're going to enjoy learning how to do something you're not already good at."

"You think that discovering I suck at golf is going to teach me how to loosen up and let off some steam?"

The disdain in her voice clues me into two things. First, she really hates to lose. And second, she honestly doesn't know what to do when she's not in control, except to back away, refusing to participate.

Resting my hand on her lower back, I guide her toward the front doors. "Why so tense? I'll make sure you can hit a golf ball by the end of the night. You might even enjoy yourself if you just relax and let things happen."

I get the sense that relaxing and letting things happen is exactly what she's trying to avoid, but I just don't know why. I'm determined to figure it out eventually.

We're greeted by name and shown to the bay I reserved on the top level—right in the middle of the action so that there will be plenty of evidence that we were out together. After choosing the right size clubs for each of us, and ordering some food and drinks, she looks out at the giant targets lit up along the grass, then at the nets surrounding the range.

"So how does this work?" Her voice is quiet, and not just because of the loud music surrounding us.

I step up behind her. "I'll show you how to hold the club and how to swing, then I'll walk you through it."

Is it wrong that the thought of wrapping my arms around her again, holding her hands in mine as I show her how to swing, has the blood rushing to my dick? Yeah, probably. Do I care? Not as much as I should.

She steps aside so I can demonstrate what to do, then she tosses me a ball. "Show me."

I bend to set up the ball on the tee, plant my feet in the slightly wide stance I prefer, wind up, and bring my club down to meet the ball. The satisfying ping of the golf ball leaving my club has me grinning at her with a cocky smile.

"Show off." She rolls her eyes, but she's smiling.

"You want to try?" I know she doesn't want to do this, but I need her to do it willingly, not because I'm forcing her to.

She shakes her head, but the way she's biting her lip as she looks at me has me thinking she's more willing than she's letting on. "C'mere."

Stepping across the turf, she says, "We have a little problem."

"And what's that?"

"I'm not left-handed."

I bark out a laugh. "Yeah, I should have thought of that. I'm sure I can figure out how to swing right-handed."

"This feels a little like the blind leading the blind," she

says as I step up behind her, lining us up at the right distance from the tee.

"We'll take a few practice swings before you try with the ball."

I line myself up, hyper-aware of how my quads are pressing against her hamstrings and ass, and I bring my arms around her to adjust her grip. Then I clasp my hands over hers and explain the mechanics of the swing. She glances to her left, where my head is dipped beside hers.

"Eyes on the tee, Jules."

She looks down, but presses her ass back into me in a way that has to be intentional. The way this woman doesn't back down does strange things to me—like making me want to spend more time with her.

I guide her through drawing her club back and bringing it down to the tee a few times so she'll get a sense of how to line it up to hit the ball. Then we practice swinging through, with me explaining how her body should be positioned at the end of the swing.

"You ready to try it on your own?" I ask.

"Not really."

"I think you are." What I really think is that I need to step away, because if my body is pressed up against hers like this for much longer, my reaction is going to be visible. And while I want people to see us out together, see me flirting with her, I don't need them to see me sporting a boner like a goddamned teenager.

Setting the ball on the tee, I look up at her. "Do it exactly like we just did, and you'll do fine."

Then I step back so I'm opposite her, and when she positions her hands on the club, the overhead lights shine off her ring, making me squint.

"Holy shit," I laugh. "The way the lights just caught your ring blinded me."

That's what I get for buying her a five-carat oval cut diamond with smaller diamonds lining the solitaire and the band. All-in-all, I think it's about six-and-a-half carats, and it's way more than what I was expecting to buy, but pissing her off is one of my favorite pastimes and you can't put a price on that kind of joy.

"Yeah," she deadpans, sending me a glare, "it's a bit much."

"Baby . . ." I make a show of stepping close enough to her that I can lean over and kiss the top of her head. "*I'm* a bit much."

"No doubt." With a sigh, she uses her index finger against my chest to move me back to the other side of the small patch of turf.

And then she winds up and smacks the ball like she's taking all her frustration out on it. It flies more than halfway down the range, and we're both so surprised that I scoop her up in my arms and spin her around.

"I can't believe you just did that. You're a natural." I'm beaming up at her as she laughs triumphantly.

She looks down at me with a smirk as I slow to a stop. "What can I say? I'm good with balls."

Chapter Seventeen

JULES

"Oh, no he didn't!" I say as I spin in my seat toward my sister, clutching my phone in my hand. On the ice several rows in front of us, the players are already warming up.

"What happened?" Audrey asks as she hands a big container of popcorn to Graham.

"He had me added to the WAG group chat."

Audrey bursts out laughing so loud that everyone near us turns to look at her. She fishes her phone out of her pocket, scrolls up a bit to find the right text thread, and then her shoulders shake with laughter again. "Ladies, let's welcome Colt's fiancée, Jules, to the chat. Most of you already know her, since she's Audrey's sister and Drew's future sister-in-law," she reads the latest text from Patrick Walsh's wife, Marissa.

From what I hear, Walsh—or Walshy as his teammates call him—is the most happily married guy in the NHL, and

Marissa serves as the "head WAG" since the team captain, Ronan McCabe, isn't married.

Not that I'd ever let someone get close enough to me that I'd get married, but if I ever found a guy who worshiped me the way Walsh worships Marissa . . . maybe I'd consider it. Someone with that level of open adoration and an anything-to-please-my-partner attitude might even convince me to trust again. But where do you even find a guy like that?

My eyes track over to Colt, where he's standing behind the goal, getting his water bottle set up. Behind him, girls holding signs with his name and clever sayings bang on the glass, trying to get his attention.

Not there, that's for sure.

But when he glances up at me and finds me staring at him, he skates over to the glass in front of us and motions for me. I roll my eyes at him, but don't dare refuse because I'm sure plenty of fans who are here early for warm-ups are watching this interaction.

Since photos and videos of us golfing together the other night started circulating all over social media, there's been even more interest in our relationship. Luckily, it's only the fans who seem to be paying much attention and they've been largely positive—they're surprised, but supportive. People's comments about the videos of us at the driving range together, especially when I hit my first ball and Colt picked me up and swung me around in celebration, focused on how "wholesome" we seemed.

And aside from a quick mention in our local Boston paper, there hasn't really been any other coverage of our relationship, thankfully.

I take the steps down to the glass, and when I get there,

Colt gives me a cocky grin as he circles his pointer finger in the air, indicating that he wants me to turn around. I sigh. I swore I'd never wear a player's jersey, and yet here I am with COLTIER written across my back.

I had just walked in the door from work this afternoon—sweaty and covered in a thick layer of construction dust—when he'd come downstairs, clearly on his way to the arena for the game.

The perfectly tailored navy-blue suit, with that sexy purple tie, had him oozing so much sex appeal that I'd momentarily lost my mind and agreed to wear the jersey he handed me. Once I realized what I'd done, I'd added, "One time only, to keep up appearances."

He'd just winked at me and said, "Sure, just this once." And then he'd headed out the door, leaving me to shower and get ready quickly so I could meet Audrey and Graham.

But now, as I sweep my hair over my shoulder and turn around so he can see his name on my back, I wish I'd left the jersey at home. He'd have survived, but I might not survive this.

Because in the stands above me, I can hear people cooing and murmuring, and I know they're talking about us even while I refuse to look up and check. They're taking pictures of this moment, which is exactly why he called me down here.

It's an important distinction that I need to remember: this isn't about him seeing me with his name on my back, this is about us performing for an audience so they'll believe that our engagement is real.

As I turn back toward him, I hope my face isn't bright red from embarrassment.

"You look good in my jersey, Tink," he says. It's loud enough for me to hear him through the thick plexiglass, but he's not yelling it for everyone to hear.

"So . . . WAG group chat?" I mouth the words as I hold up my phone against the glass, allowing him to see Marissa's text and all the "Welcome, Jules!" messages below.

He just gives me that devilish smile. "Good, you belong there."

If we were really engaged, sure, I'd belong in that chat. But knowing this is all going to be over at the end of the season, I don't understand why he asked to have me added. But I can't ask him right now because he's skating backward and calls out, "Meet me in the Family Room after the game."

When we close in on the end of the first period, the Rebels are up by one, thanks to a goal Drew scored on a power play. And that's when Jameson and Lauren finally slide into the seats next to us, Lauren asking, "What did we miss?"

"Where have you been?" Audrey asks.

"Babysitter issues," Jameson says, but Lauren's cheeks grow pink.

"I thought Morgan was watching the girls?" I say.

"She is, but the T broke down on the way out to our place, so then she had to get an Uber, along with everyone else who'd just gotten off the train."

"Why didn't you just go pick her up?" Audrey asks, and Lauren's cheeks get even pinker. *Ohhhhh.*

While Jameson says something about missing her call, I chuckle to myself, and Lauren elbows me and leans in, whispering, "Don't be a jerk or I'll start talking about Colt." That has the laughter dying in my throat.

When the period ends, AJ appears at the aisle and insists Jameson slide over so she can sit next to Lauren. I love the way she just comes up like a total boss and tells my brother what to do. Most people are intimidated by him, but I'm pretty sure nothing scares this woman.

She asks me for more details about the mentoring program, and as I explain how it works, she sighs and says, "God, I wish we had something like that in the league. Being a woman in this sport is tough, and I could have used a good mentor when I was starting out."

"Is that why you've been such a good mentor to me?" Lauren asks.

"I haven't mentored you," AJ says, looking over at Lauren like she's just said something patently wrong. Lauren works in marketing for the Rebels, and while AJ isn't technically her boss, she seems like she has her fingers on the pulse of all parts of the operation, whether related to the players or the business aspect of the organization.

"Of course you have. Starting the day you offered to bring a shovel if I needed to bury a body," Lauren says, and I haven't heard that story before, but I can guess it happened when Lauren found out the truth about her late husband. "And then you started inviting me to lunch, where you gave me all kinds of tips about how to survive in this male-domi-nated industry, and then Patrick got promoted, and I got his job as the head of marketing after only being here for, like, six months. You think I don't know you were behind that?"

"Good talent needs to be cultivated and rewarded," AJ says with a shrug.

"That's how it feels in construction, too," I say. "It's why I only hire women—"

"That's so badass." AJ meets my eyes with a bright smile. "I love that. In fact, I love it so much I might want to hire you."

I'm about to tell her that I don't work for friends, when I realize that she's not a friend. But she sure feels like a kindred spirit.

"You totally should," Lauren says. "Jules and Audrey did my whole house when I first moved back, and it couldn't have come out better."

I think back to the winter before last, when Jameson had us secretly remodel the entire upstairs of Lauren's house before she moved in, then refused to take any credit for it. His feelings for her were so obvious to everyone except Lauren—but then again, she didn't know the extent of the sacrifices he'd made for her until much later.

"I'll keep that in mind, because I just bought a new place and I think it's going to need some work. But I want to live in it for a bit first, and make sure that what I'm envisioning actually makes sense for the space."

"That's really smart," Audrey says. "I wish more people would do that. Most people think they know what they want, and they don't want to live through renovations, so they do them before moving in. But you wouldn't believe the number of people who want us to come back and change things once they've lived with them for a while."

The lights start flashing and AJ jumps up. "I have to run. Enjoy the rest of the game."

———

I'm standing with Audrey, who's got a sleepy Graham wrapped around her, in the Family Room. I've rarely been in here, since it's a space reserved only for players' families. Once or twice, I've come with Audrey post-game if it's not too late and she hasn't had to take Graham home to put him to bed. Tonight, he's half-asleep with his head on her shoulder, but I think she's hanging around just so I don't have to wait for Colt by myself.

Not that we've been standing here alone—there has been a parade of wives and girlfriends coming up to chat with us, some who I already know and some who are introducing themselves to me for the first time. But it would be a lot less comfortable if I didn't have my sister by my side. That's kind of how my life has been, Audrey always by my side, until recently.

I'm getting tired and wishing I'd just gone home, when Colt finally walks through the door. He's one of the first players into the room, which is highly unusual for a goalie, and he beelines straight toward me, wrapping me in his arms and giving me a full-body hug. I'm caught off-guard, as the only time he's ever hugged me before was the morning in Vegas after I almost wrecked my whole life.

I relax in his arms when I realize this is just for show. The Rebels had a tough game tonight, with Florida scoring in the last seconds of the game from a rebound off Colt's pads that their left winger was able to sneak into the goal from behind him. And, of course, a goalie who lost the game like that would want a hug from his fiancée, so he's giving his team-mates' families exactly what they expect to see.

When he releases me and steps back, he tells Audrey,

"Drew got off the bike a few minutes ago. He's showering and he wanted me to tell you that he'll be out in a minute."

"Okay, thanks," Audrey says, as Colt peeks around behind her and smooths his huge hand over Graham's head.

"He's completely out," he chuckles.

"Yeah, I can tell," she says. "He's dead weight."

"I'll take him for you," Colt offers.

"I don't want to keep you if you guys want to go. Drew will be along in a few minutes."

"We're going to meet up with some of my teammates for a while," Colt tells her, quickly glancing at me, "so we'll stay until they get out here."

"I'm sorry, what?" I agreed to go to tomorrow night's charity event with him, and I told him I'd meet him in the Family Room tonight. I never agreed to go hang out with his teammates. And what is he even thinking? The more time we spend together, especially around his teammates, the harder it will be to make this an amicable split at the end.

He turns away from Audrey and takes two steps over so that he's standing inches in front of me. Putting his hands on my hips, he pulls me even closer as he leans down and says, "Be nice. That was a tough loss, and I could really use a win tonight."

"A win?" My voice is all kinds of doubtful.

"Yeah, you know, like a night where you go along with this without acting like you hate me."

"What makes you think I'm acting?" I don't hate Colt, but I hate what being around him still does to me. I hate how it brings back memories of feelings I thought were long buried, and I hate how worried I am that it will bring back the feelings themselves. So I do what I always do when it comes to Colt—I push him away.

I feel his laughter as his chest shakes, and his voice is a low rumble when he says, "I think you *wish* you hated me, Tink."

Heat floods my body in a way that has me wanting to turn and run out the door, getting as far from him as possible. When did hearing him use my childhood nickname become a turn-on, instead of something that pissed me off?

I need to tamp my body's response to him as far down as possible. So I look up, stepping back as I say, "I think you *wish* I was better at hiding the way I hate you."

Drew comes up behind us right then, and with a low chuckle, says, "You two need to get better at the pretending part of this. You're lucky that it was me right behind you." He kisses Audrey's forehead and takes Graham out of her arms. "You kids have fun at the Neon Cactus tonight. We're going home."

"I'll bet you are," Colt says, wiggling his eyebrows like a lunatic. "I'm sure you have some adrenaline to burn off."

"At least I've got a way to burn it off." He wraps his arm around Audrey after she smacks his arm, then leads her out of the room like he can't wait to get her home.

Everyone I know is getting laid tonight . . . except me.

Chapter Eighteen

JULES

"I gotta be honest," Zach Reid says as Colt pulls me down onto his lap, nearly causing me to lose the contents of my margarita as I'm unexpectedly jostled, "I did not see this coming."

"See *what* coming?" Colt asks, amusement in his voice as he turns his head to look out at the bar that's become the unofficial watering hole of the Boston Rebels. A tequila bar is the last place I'd expect a hockey team to hang out, but even though you can order hundred dollar margaritas with top-shelf tequila, it looks and feels like a college bar. Shellacked wooden walls with neon signs hanging all around. There's a back area with pool tables, and the front of the space has booths lining the perimeter with a big bar in the center. And, being located in Beacon Hill, it's just far enough from the arena that fans probably don't flock here after the games.

"You two." Zach eyes me where I sit, probably looking as uncomfortable as I feel on Colt's lap. There's barely enough room for me to fit between him and the tabletop. It would have made a whole lot more sense for him to just push over and give me my own seat, like Zach just did for Ashleigh as we returned from the bar.

"What can I say," Colt says, running his nose up the side of my neck. "We're good at keeping secrets."

I can barely hold in the smile, because of all the things he's said in the hour we've been here, this is the one that stands out to me as incredibly true, but for an entirely different reason. Not only is the fake status of our relationship a secret, but we both have our own secrets, the entirety of which we haven't even shared with each other yet.

In all the years I crushed on him, I never imagined us faking being together. But the way he picked me up and turned in circles with me in his arms after I hit that golf ball the other night, the smile he gave me as he told me I was a natural, it felt way too real. And tonight, the way he keeps dropping his voice when he uses my nickname, the way he can't seem to let me be more than a few inches from him, it doesn't feel fake. Obviously, he's an incredibly good liar, which is something I would do well not to forget.

We fall into easy conversation as Ashleigh tells us about finishing up her first semester as an astrophysics PhD student in the Astro/Aero department at MIT. The girl is going to be a literal rocket scientist when she finishes her graduate work, and it amazes me how down to earth she seems even though she's obviously next-level smart. And then Zach is telling us about the vacation they have planned in July, and as Ashleigh's gushing about how excited she is to learn to scuba dive, she lets out a huge yawn.

"My girl's tired," Zach says. "Time to go home."

They could very well be going home to sleep, but just like with Drew and Audrey, I can't help but think that they're going home to fuck. Why is everyone around me happily paired off and getting laid regularly, and here I am, still a virgin at twenty-five?

As much as I don't want to date anyone—don't trust myself enough to be vulnerable like that—I really would like to know what it's like to share my body with someone else. If I could just get over the mental hurdle of it.

As we say goodbye and Zach and Ashleigh leave, Colt's thumb traces the column of my spine, just above my tailbone, and it sends a shiver up my back, causing me to squirm. His other arm wraps around my lower abdomen, anchoring me in place.

"You'd better stop that," he says, his words a dark caress that slides along my neck and curls behind my ear, making me shiver again. "Or we're going to have a big problem."

I can't help the laugh that shakes my body as I feel him growing hard between my ass cheeks. "I'm pretty sure we already have a *big* problem." I don't know what comes over me as I grind against him intentionally—a slow, circling press of my hips that I hope will quell the aching need building between my legs.

"Jules," he warns.

"Colt." My voice is teasing as I repeat the action. I'm only on my second drink, not nearly enough to blame my actions on the alcohol. No, it's my stupid inability to be in control of myself whenever he's around, but I'm not sure I really care at the moment.

"Here's how this is going to go." His growl reverberates

against me as his lips brush my earlobe again. "Either you stop that right now, or I'm going to slide my hand between your legs and make you come so hard this entire bar will hear you screaming my name."

The need that courses through me is like a hot flash, and I have the overwhelming desire to rip my clothes off. I slide my hips back and forth again and he hisses out a breath.

"Good choice," he says as his fingers trail from my abdomen along my leggings and down toward my clit, which is literally aching for his touch. Even though I shouldn't let him, I want his hands on me more than I've ever wanted anything. "Let's put on a convincing show."

His words are the slap that jolts me out of my lust-induced haze as my half-lidded eyes fly open and glance around the bar. I slide off his lap before he has a chance to stop me.

"Change your mind?" he teases, making me believe that was his intention all along—he was just seeing how far he could push me before I backed out.

"Shit, Colt. You can't say things like that to your *fake* fiancée."

"That was tame, Jules. You should hear the things I'd say if we weren't pretending."

I'm so tempted to throw out a taunting remark so that he'll elaborate, but now I'm hyper aware how many of his teammates at the surrounding tables are watching us, trying to gauge what's going on. And I'm not really in the mood for acting anymore.

"I'm tired," I say through a forced yawn. "I got up at five and now it's almost midnight. I'm going to head home."

Shifting in my seat, I move my legs out of the booth so I can stand, but Colt grabs the back of my jersey to hold me in place.

"*We're* going home." He leans over and kisses the top of my head, then lets me scoot out of the booth. As soon as I'm standing, he smacks my ass playfully, and when I spin in surprise, he's already right behind me, wrapping his arm around my shoulder and turning me toward the doors of the bar.

———

We don't say much as we walk back to the player's parking area at the arena, but Colt keeps his arm wrapped around my shoulders, his thumb tracing the line of my collarbone the whole time. He's quiet on the drive back to the South End, and I lean my head back, staring out the sunroof at the hazy night sky illuminated by the city lights, while we listen to the radio.

My mind is a mess, running through all the questions I have about what just happened. What I'm most wondering is: how is he so good at pretending?

The way he demanded I come show him his name on my back in front of the fans during warm-ups, how he hugged me in front of his teammates' families after the game like he couldn't possibly go another second without having me in his arms, how he forced me onto his lap and got me all wound up in the bar and how his body was responding to mine.

It's like he knows exactly what we need to do to convince

people this is real, and he's executing that plan perfectly. So perfectly, in fact, that it all feels a little too natural.

And then my mind does that thing I can't seem to convince it not to do. It flashes back to Vegas. Because that seemed natural too. The way Brock flirted with me all night, the way he held me like he adored me, the way he suggested I meant something to him. And then in the morning, when I woke up hungover and having made a terrible mistake, I discovered that not a single moment of it was real for him.

I'm swallowing down the lump in my throat when I realize that he's already turning into the alley that runs behind my house. Good. I'm suddenly desperate to get out of this car. I need to put distance between Colt and me. I need to remind myself that my judgment is fucked up, that I can't believe anything I'm feeling, and that this is all just an act for him.

My hand is already on the door handle when he pulls into his parking spot, and I have one leg out of the car before he even shifts into park.

"I need to ask you a question," he says before I can get out.

"How about another time?" I step out of the car and shut the door behind me, needing air, needing to clear my head. But he's out quickly too, following me up the back steps where he grabs ahold of the loose fabric on the jersey and stops me in my tracks. Then he steps up behind me, and because I'm on the stair above him, his head's level with mine.

"Why are you running away?" His words glide along my skin, raising goosebumps across my neck and down my shoulders.

"I'm not running. I just . . . have to pee."

"No, Jules. You're running. I stole glances at you that whole drive home, and you were so lost in thought, it was like you were in another world. Where'd you go back there?"

Squeezing my eyes closed tightly, I try not to feel or remember anything. I just want to go to my room, curl up in a ball, and forget that Vegas ever happened.

"I was just watching the sky, lost in the music, Colt. Don't make it into something it wasn't."

"We were listening to Britney Spears circa 2000. If you were lost in *that* music," he says, knowing that I despise pop, "you must be more drunk than I thought."

"I don't get drunk." I spit the words out. My father's an alcoholic and it only took being drunk once to know how easily I could fall down that rabbit hole of terrible decisions when alcohol is involved. I didn't drink for years after Vegas, and even now, I *never* have more than two drinks in one night.

"So are you saying that back at the bar, you weren't grinding yourself against my cock because you were drunk?"

The whoosh of air that leaves my lungs is an audible sigh. I'd love to use alcohol as an excuse, but now I can't.

"I'm saying that alcohol impaired my judgment, just like I'm sure it impaired yours." Being around him is what impaired my judgment, like it always does. But I can't tell him that, so I'll blame it on the margaritas.

"Jules, I outweigh you by a hundred pounds. Those two beers didn't even give me a buzz. Do you think I'd have driven you home if I was under the influence?"

"I guess not."

"You *guess* not? Seriously?" He must twist the fabric of the jersey in his fist, because it tightens around me even more as he pulls me closer to him. "I'd never put you, or anyone, in danger like that."

"I wasn't suggesting you would. I was just thinking . . . I don't know . . . that the beer made you . . ." *Horny?* Well, I sure as hell can't say that. So how do I explain what happened between us in the bar?

"Want you?" he suggests when I don't finish my sentence.

"Colt, I know this is all fake. Tonight was just one big show—for the fans and for your teammates—so they'd believe it's real. You don't have to worry about me getting confused and thinking that you *actually* want me."

He lets go of the back of the jersey and wraps that hand around my abdomen instead, pulling me against him so there's nothing, not even air, between us. His body is hard ripples of muscle pressed against me, but what catches me most off guard is the way the steel pipe he's packing in his pants presses between my ass cheeks.

His voice is almost deadly when he says, "Listen to me carefully, Tink. There's nothing fake about the way I want you. But I promised your brother I wouldn't touch you, and I don't go back on promises. Jameson's been like a brother to me for almost half my life, and I can't do that to him." He pauses for the briefest second before dropping his voice even lower. "But it doesn't mean I don't want to."

My breath hitches, a sharp intake that's overly loud in the quiet outdoor space.

Then he says, "Now go inside, disappear up to your room, and give me a minute to compose myself. Then, we're going to pretend like this didn't happen."

I don't know which hurts more: that he values his relationship with my brother more than what we could have together, or that he's so ashamed of wanting me that he never wants to bring it up again.

It doesn't matter, I tell myself as I reach for the back door. *You were holding him at a distance for exactly this reason. He's never wanted a relationship with you, and he never will.*

Chapter Nineteen

COLT

When we walk into the ballroom where the children's hospital is holding their charity gala, all eyes are on us. Even though I warned her what to expect, Jules still stiffens, drawing her shoulders back and holding her chin high—something I've noticed she does when she's uncomfortable. I squeeze her hand, then lean toward her, running my lips along her hair and whispering, "Relax."

"Everyone is staring at me," she says, turning her head and tucking her chin toward her shoulder to speak directly in my ear. "It's like they all know this is fake and I don't belong here."

I'm a bit afraid she's going to turn around and bolt, because that seems to be her default defense mechanism when she's scared.

"Jules," I say, dropping her hand and bringing mine to rest on her lower back while I guide her deeper into the room. My palm and thumb rest on the bare skin of her back, while my fingers splay across the gold fabric of this sexy-as-hell dress where it clings right above the curve of her ass. When she came downstairs in this dress tonight, I almost forgot all about what I told her last night—that nothing can happen between us. I don't want that to be our reality, but the truth is that I can't be what she's looking for, so I don't want to ruin the tenuous friendship we're building. "They're not staring because they think this is fake. They're staring because when you walk into a room, no one else is even worth looking at."

She raises her head to meet my eyes, and the look she gives me is nothing but a riot of confusion—like she can't trust my words and so she's searching my face to figure out my meaning.

"You seem to have lost the ability to speak," I tease as I brush my lips across the bridge of her nose. "I didn't think that was possible."

"Why would you say that when no one else is even around to hear? You don't have to sell this whole relationship when it's just you and me, you know?"

"You wanted to know why people are staring, and I gave you an honest answer."

Her jaw drops the tiniest bit as she runs her tongue along her top lip, and all I can think about is how she tastes. I want her to kiss me again. I want to experience that kind of possession I felt the last time our bodies came together, before we were so rudely interrupted.

In fact, sometimes it feels like that's all I can think about now . . . hockey and her. How she smells like her body wash and kissed me like she wanted to own me, the deep sound of her laughter and how I can tell there's so many things she's thinking but doesn't say, the way she can command an entire crew of construction workers and is seemingly completely unaware that what I feel for her is becoming more than just physical.

She's extraordinary: all the hard, driven parts of her brother, with the softer sentimental side of her sister. And as if I summoned her up in my mind, Audrey strides toward us. The smile she's wearing is so fake, I worry she's going to ruin this whole thing—that everyone will see through this. It's been hard convincing my teammates that this is real, and if they don't see a united front within the family, no one will buy this for a second longer.

Which is why it surprises me when she stops close to us, takes each of our hands in hers, and says, "I'm so sorry I got you both into this mess." Audrey seemed to accept this ruse just fine last night in the Family Room, which makes me think that Jules must have said something to her about the bar or our conversation when we got home. It has me wondering how she's really feeling about how close we came to something happening between us again.

"You didn't get us into this mess," Jules assures her sister.

"If I'd been at that dinner, none of this would have happened."

"Don't be ridiculous," Jules says. "You were where you needed to be. And it's fine. Colt and I will manage to get along through this ruse, and then everything can go back to how it was."

I don't know why I hate that idea so much, but I do. I really fucking hate it. I don't know when she grew up, or how I hadn't noticed. But the woman standing in front of me is so much more than just my best friend's little sister—even if I keep telling her that's all she is.

I don't want to go back to how it was, when I teased and tormented her like she was still a kid. No, I want to go back to that alley, where she squeezed her thighs into my waist while she kissed me so thoroughly that I still wake up hard after dreaming about it.

But we can't go there again.

Audrey's lips press into a line, and she looks like she's about to say something when Drew comes up beside her. He slips his arm around her waist, gripping her hip possessively. "What's wrong?"

The question is addressed to the whole group, but Audrey looks up at him. "Ugh, besides me fucking up my sister's life? Nothing."

"Hey," I say, "if you're implying that being engaged to me is fucking up her life, I'm insulted."

All three of them stare back at me.

"What? I'm kind of a catch . . . ask anyone."

"The only thing I'm likely to catch from you is a venereal disease," Jules mutters, barely loud enough for the four of us to hear.

Audrey's eyes widen, and Drew laughs into his beer before tilting it up and taking a sip. That beer looks like just what I need, and getting one gives me an excuse to get out of this foursome, where I feel like everyone is waiting to see how I'm going to fuck this up.

"I'm going to grab a drink," I say to Jules. "Do you want anything?"

"Just for this to be over as quickly as possible."

I bite the inside of my cheek because I don't think she

meant to be funny, but it's a relief that she's back to giving me shit after a whole day of avoiding me.

"Champagne it is," I say.

"I don't even like champagne."

"I thought it was your favorite?" Audrey calls her out.

When Jules gives her sister a death glare, I pull her back to me, enjoying the way I can feel her breasts pushed up against my chest as I duck my head and whisper, "I knew it was your favorite." I wait for her surprised inhale of breath, and when I hear it, I turn and head to the bar with a shit-eating grin spread across my face.

Not only am I here with the hottest woman in the room, but she's a whole lot more affected by me than she's letting on. I should stop taunting her, leading her down this path that leaves us both sexually frustrated. I should let us go back to what we were before this whole fake engagement situation. I should keep my distance, but I can't seem to stay away.

I'm waiting at the bar for my beer and Jules's champagne when McCabe wanders up to me. "Engaged, huh?" He could not possibly sound more skeptical if I'd told him I'd given up sex. "To Flynn's baby sister?"

"Ew, you don't need to make it sound sketchy, man."

He takes a swig of his beer while raising his eyebrows as if to say, *It is sketchy.* "How old is she?"

"Twenty-five."

His nearly black eyes focus in on me, and the sharp lines of his cheekbones narrow as his lips press together. "You've been sleeping with women all over the country, all season long. And you expect me to believe that you're getting married? To a twenty-five-year-old?"

"First of all," I say, "no, I haven't. I've *talked* to women all over the country all season. I haven't slept with anyone since well before Jules and I got together."

"And when was that, exactly?"

"October." I'll have to remember to tell Jules that's when we started our secret relationship so we can keep our story straight.

"So why were you out there pretending to be interested in other women?" He sounds more curious and less skeptical as he leans one elbow against the bar and turns toward me.

"Because we were trying to keep her family from finding out."

"Keep her brother from finding out, you mean?"

"Yeah." There's no way anyone would believe Audrey didn't know, and I'm glad Jules pointed that out before we tried to sell this whole show.

"How's he taking this?"

"He's . . ." I almost say he's fine with it, but there's no way that would be believable, especially since he's not even fine with it knowing that it's not real. ". . . coming around to the idea."

"You must really like her if you're willing to risk your friendship with him," McCabe says.

"Aren't you perceptive?"

"You're basically part of that family. You've always treated both those girls like they were *your* sisters." His eyes narrow again. "How are you now dating one of them?" He really isn't giving up on this.

Jameson isn't McCabe's agent, but McCabe joined the Rebels a year before Jameson retired, so they played together for a short time. And since Jameson represents nearly a quarter of the players on the team, and is good friends with

AJ, he's always around. McCabe knows him well enough to know how protective he is of Audrey and Jules, and he knows me well enough to know that I'd never jeopardize that friendship.

"Have you seen her?" I say, rolling my eyes as the bartender slides the two drinks I've been waiting for toward me.

"Yeah, total smokeshow. But you're not reckless. I still don't see you risking your relationship with that whole family just because she's hot."

"Obviously, I didn't go after her just because she's hot. She's also brilliant, she doesn't take any of my shit—"

He coughs out a laugh. "Yeah, she gives as good as she gets when it comes to you."

It's true, and anyone who's spent more than five minutes in our presence knows that. No one else aside from my teammates gives me shit like she does. "She balances me out," I say, because it's the type of thing I think you'd say about someone you were going to marry.

"I'm still trying to wrap my mind around you being in *love.*"

That word is like a cold rope of dread wrapping itself around my chest. In my lifetime, I've only told one woman I loved her, and she stabbed me in the back. The wounds may have healed, but the scars are still ugly.

"You'll get used to it," I tell him, even though I know that by the time he does, the whole thing will probably be over.

I hate the idea of this ending. I hate the reality that someday I'll go back to my condo in the Seaport, and Jules won't be there, or that I'll go on a date, and it won't be with her.

"Speaking of," he says, and nods toward the end of the bar where Jules is standing, her hands on the edge as she leans forward like she's trying to get the bartender's attention. I watch him notice her and head straight over there, like he can't get to her quickly enough. And watching her from here, I see exactly why—the gold V of her dress shimmers where it dips low between her breasts, and her blond hair hangs in soft waves over her shoulders. Even though I still call her Tink, like I always have, Barbie would be a more apt nickname these days. And tonight, she's Glamour Barbie. She's wearing makeup, which she never does, and it highlights the contours of her face, making her look even more spectacular than normal.

As the bartender talks to her, resting his entire forearm on the bar top so he can lean in as close as possible, I clear my throat.

"Better go get your girl," McCabe says with a laugh, then tips his beer at me while I grab our drinks and turn to walk toward her.

Despite the mirror that runs the full length of the bar, she doesn't see me coming. I'd like to imagine she's only giving the bartender her full attention because she's trying to be polite, but the way she throws her head back with a laugh has me about ready to punch this guy. Who does he think he is, making *my* fiancée laugh like that?

Fake fiancée, I hear Jameson's voice in my head, and I push it away. Tonight, we're supposed to be selling it like it's real, and my fiancée would never laugh at anyone else's jokes. Would she?

The bartender grabs a glass off the shelf behind him and walks a few steps away to fill it with ice, and I transfer her champagne flute to the hand holding my beer so I have a free hand. When I come up behind her, I smooth my thumb along the ridges of her spine, loving the way this dress leaves her back bared to me. Goosebumps erupt along the backs of her arms in response to my touch.

"Is that really necessary?" she asks, her voice husky as she turns to look at me over her shoulder.

I step up behind her, my right thigh pressed firmly against her ass, and set the drinks on the bar before planting my hand next to her so she's fully boxed in. Even though I told her I wanted her, but that nothing could happen between us, I can't stop myself from touching her when she's around.

I lean down and, keeping my voice low, I say, "There's no chance in hell that my fiancée looks like you do right now and I'm not all over her. So if we want this to appear real, you better be okay with me touching you."

I press my lips to her hair where it's tucked behind her ear and feel her sharp intake of breath.

"If you remember, *I* wasn't the one who had a problem with you touching me." The bitterness in her voice catches me off guard.

"Really? Because if I remember correctly, you were the one who slid off my lap when I offered to make you come." *Why am I tormenting myself—and her—like this?*

"And then you explained how you didn't want to want me like that, and said we were never going to talk about it again." Her saccharine tone couldn't be more fake, and it shows me just how much this actually bothered her.

"I *don't* want to want you, Jules," I admit. "I'm no good for you. You deserve someone who wants to fall in love, who wants to get married—and that's not me. I'll only hurt you."

"Like I told you last night," she says, straightening up and thereby forcing me to do the same. Then she turns in the space where she's sandwiched between the bar and me. "I'm under no illusion that you have feelings for me, or that you ever will. But since we have to sell this"—she trails her finger up my dress shirt and across my pec, then slides her hand into my suit jacket and over my shoulder—"how am I doing?"

I push forward, anchoring her between the bar and my hips. "You're doing so well." And then I dip my head and litter kisses along her jaw until my lips meet her earlobe, telling myself it's all for show. Taking her flesh between my lips, I let my teeth sink into her earlobe gently, then let go, whispering, "You're doing perfect."

Her fingers curl into my shoulder, and as she turns her head to look at me, her cheek slides along mine until her lips are only a breath away. Those eyes are a kaleidoscope of colors getting pushed to the edges of her iris by her quickly expanding pupils. Her look is desire and an invitation, but it's laced with resentment too.

"Now what?" The words fall from her full pink lips so softly she almost sounds lost.

I can feel myself growing hard where I'm pressed up against her stomach, and I clear my throat, reminding myself that we can't go down this path. It's too damn easy to forget when I'm around her.

"Now, you don't flirt with the bartender anymore."

She rears her head back as my words hit her like a splash of ice water. I didn't mean for them to come out all vindictive-sounding, but that's exactly how she took it—I can tell by the knowing look in her eyes, like I just proved her right. The notes of jealousy that I couldn't hide have clearly made her think that this was all because I didn't want her talking to the bartender, rather than me legitimately not being able to keep my hands off her.

And even though that's probably for the best, I don't like hurting her like that.

From beside us, a throat clears, and I look over to find Drew standing there, looking awkward as hell, like he just interrupted us having sex.

"Audrey sent me over here to remind you that 'selling this' doesn't mean mauling her sister in public."

"That's fine," I say, letting my gaze travel back to Jules where she's standing, breath ragged. I don't let myself look down where I know her chest will be heaving too, because if I caught sight of that cleavage from above, I'd have a *very* physical reaction. I'm already way too close to my erection being impossible to hide. "I'll save that for when we're alone."

"Colt, don't traumatize Drew," Jules says, the teasing lilt back in her voice and an insincere smile plastered across her face like she's certain I don't mean that. *If she only knew the things I'd imagined when we're alone.* She reaches over and grabs her champagne flute and a glass of water I hadn't even noticed the bartender leave next to us, then drops her voice and tells Drew, "I'll go reassure Audrey that I'm in entirely safe hands over here. Nothing but a little pissing contest getting the best of my *fake* fiancé."

Chapter Twenty

JULES

I'm more keyed up than I should be by the end of the night.

The number of times that Colt's hands have been on me has left me flustered and sexually frustrated. He knows just how to turn me on—a gentle touch that turns firm, his body pressed against mine, his tone bossy and seductive.

I don't know if I'm so transparent and my lust is so obvious that he figured this out easily, or we're just more sexually compatible than either of us probably would have guessed. What I do know is that I've been on dozens of first dates over the past couple of years, and not a single guy has gotten me revved up the way Colt can with a single touch.

"Here," he says, as he slides his suit coat off and drapes it over my shoulders while we walk across the lobby of the hotel where the gala was held. "It's cold out."

"Thanks," I mutter. While being wrapped up in his warm clothing that smells faintly of him, with his arm around me holding me to his side, is actually *exactly* what I want, the need to push him away and keep myself safe is greater now than it ever has been.

But I'm also aware that we're walking out with several of his teammates, and it would be beyond suspicious if I refused his jacket, especially while the lobby door is being held open and the chilly night air is sweeping into the space, so I go along with it.

He gives his ticket to the valet, and we say goodbye to his teammates, most of whom are half-wasted and piling into cabs to go home. I shiver as the breeze picks up again, tangling my long dress around my legs. Colt backs me into the corner of the stone walls, behind the valet stand.

"What are you doing?" My words are quiet because there are other couples huddled in this recessed area outside the doors waiting for their own cars.

He leans one hand on the wall behind me, his body close to mine. "Keeping you warm."

"Colt," I say, putting a hand on his chest to keep a little distance between us. "You can't keep saying you don't want me, then acting like you do."

"I didn't say I didn't want you, Jules. I said I couldn't have you. The difference between those two things is enormous."

"That's not fair to me." I'm determined not to be strung along like this. "You're saying one thing but doing another. It's confusing, and it's frustrating."

"You don't *seem* frustrated." His knuckles graze my jawline as he traces a path from my chin toward my ear, and at first, I lean into his touch. Then, remembering that this can only lead to even more frustration, I tilt my face away so his hand falls, but instead of lowering it completely, he rests his fingertips over my collarbone and his palm against my cleavage. I'm sure he can feel the way my heart is pounding, because his lips curve up at one corner into a smirk.

"My *body* is frustrated, Colt. You're toying with me like this is some sort of cat-and-mouse game. It's one thing to put on a show when we need to convince people." I glance around this waiting area and there's no one we even know left here. We could easily be standing side by side and no one would question whether we were together. "But what's this? Right now?"

"This is me, wanting to be close to you."

"That's not how *fake* works," I remind him quietly. I'm too frustrated to stop myself from saying something, even if it means I might reveal too much.

Leaning his face a fraction of an inch closer, his lips ghost over my forehead as he speaks. "How does it work, then?"

"You touch me only when absolutely necessary."

"Define absolutely necessary. Because this feels pretty damn necessary to me."

"No, absolutely necessary is only when other people are around. Only when we need to sell this engagement as real."

He shrugs. "Sorry, I am who I am."

"Yeah, well, I am who I am, too. And I don't let guys touch me and get me all . . ." I search for the right word, but Colt beats me to it.

"Turned on?"

"Sure. I don't let guys get me all turned on if they don't plan to do anything about it." I say this as though I've ever moved beyond kissing someone.

"Do you *want* me to do something about it?" His voice is a

seductive sound that curls around me. He sounds both hopeful and dubious at the same time.

I remind myself not to reveal too much. "Colt, I don't even know if you're asking that question seriously. All I know is, you're too good at faking it."

"I told you last night that I wasn't faking the way I want you."

"You also said you couldn't *do* anything about it," I say, my voice firm as I remind him that he was the one who said this was a bad idea. "But you never even asked me what I wanted, Colt. You're acting like this is all about you and your feelings. What about mine?"

His hand slides up from my chest to snake around my neck, pulling me closer as he dips his chin so that his lips meet my ear, and in that low, deep voice of his, he asks, "What is it you want, Jules?"

There's a moment when I consider being honest, telling him how much my body craves his. My pulse increases as I imagine us going home and not going our separate ways once we were there. We would be absolute fire in the bedroom, I'm certain of it with every fiber of my being. I want to know what it would be like to be with him in that way.

But that's all it would ever be with him . . . just physical. I'd be just another woman he'd fucked. Then at the end of the season, he'd cast me aside, like he has with every other woman who's shared his bed. It's what we'd agreed to earlier, and I'm not sure I could go back to being friends after sleeping with him.

Keeping my voice hushed, I tell him, "I want you to respect the agreement we had, and the promise you made to

Jameson. This is only for appearances, and you'll only touch me when absolutely necessary."

My hand still rests on his chest, and I use it to create a little more space between us. When he's pressed up against me, his hand over my heart or curled around my neck, I can't focus on anything but him. I need distance so I can think clearly. Based on his expression, he's not only surprised but also . . . disappointed?

"You're probably right," he says.

"Excuse me, sir," the valet says as he taps Colt on the shoulder, "your car."

Colt hands the guy a folded-up bill as he takes the key, then he guides me to the passenger side, where he opens the door for me, hands me my seatbelt once I'm seated, leans in, and says, "There's a photographer about half a block down, so try to look like you like me, yeah?"

I keep my head tilted up toward him as my eyes flick to the left, looking down the block. And sure enough, a guy stands there with a camera and a telephoto lens pointed right at us. What the hell? In general, hockey players are not famous enough that the paparazzi follow them around. But maybe there's more interest in our engagement than I thought?

My eyes flick back toward Colt just in time to notice that his face is only inches from mine and descending quite quickly. But he doesn't move in for the kiss I'm expecting. Instead, he cups my jaw in one hand while kissing my forehead gently, and then he's stepping back and shutting my door.

———

I spend the short ride back to my house debating the merits of having a frank conversation with Colt about why this is hard for me. He has to know I used to have a crush on him, but maybe he doesn't know the extent of it, and I'm sure he thinks I'm long over it.

The only way I can think to make him understand is to give him all the details about Vegas—to tell him why I went back downstairs after he brought me to my room, and to tell him what happened after I woke up in the morning. But I'd have to share things I've never told anyone but Audrey.

How would I tell him everything without him feeling absurdly guilty and without me looking like a complete moron? There is no way. Plus, I'm not sure I'm ready to be that vulnerable with Colt.

So we drive in silence while I rehash the past, all while still feeling the way he touched me over and over again tonight, and I arrive home even more confused and sexually frustrated than I was when I left that hotel ballroom with him twenty minutes ago.

"I'm going to bed," I say, the minute we walk through the door.

"Already?" he asks, glancing at the fancy watch on his wrist.

"It's after eleven."

"On a Saturday night," he says.

"Yeah, but I was up late last night because of the game, and I need to be up early tomorrow morning."

"What for?" he asks. Everyone knows I'm not a morning person, but it doesn't seem to matter. After years in construction, my body is wired to wake up before the sun, even on the weekends.

I press my lips together, realizing that I'm going to have to take my weekly video call in my closet, where he won't be able to overhear it, instead of at the dining room table where I normally chat with Jeannine. "I have my weekly therapy session on Sunday mornings."

The look he gives me is . . . I don't even know. Approving? Proud?

"Alright," he says, a small smile gracing his lips. "Goodnight, then."

As he turns and walks up the stairs, I watch him go, noting the way his dress shirt stretches across his back and his suit pants fit his ass. He lifts his arm, running his fingers under his collar across the back of his neck when he gets to the top of the stairs, then I hear his footsteps as he walks along the second-floor landing on the way to the stairs up to his apartment.

It's then that I realize I'm still wearing his jacket. I'm about to call out for him to wait so I can run the jacket up to him before he gets up to the third floor, but I stop myself. It's better if I don't, because meeting him in the hallway right outside my bedroom door has "bad decisions" written all over it. I'm going to have enough of those to unpack when I talk to Jeanine tomorrow morning. I don't need to add *losing my virginity to a man who told me he doesn't want to want me and said he isn't any good for me* to the list.

Instead, I hang his suit coat over the back of one of the kitchen chairs so he'll see it there tomorrow, turn out the lights on the first floor, and head up to my bedroom. And once I'm in my closet, I do what I do each night before bed: I take a moment to assess myself in the mirror.

You're strong.

You're sober.

You're safe.

It's the reassurance that I gave myself after I returned home from Vegas, and have given myself every night since. Tonight, I add another: *You're making good choices.*

Keeping my distance from Colt, except when necessary for keeping up appearances, is the right choice.

I reach behind me and tug at the small hidden zipper that starts at my lower back and unzips several inches down to my tailbone, then loop my thumbs under the thin shiny straps of the gold dress, letting them slide off my shoulders. The material brushes my hardened nipples as I let the dress drop to my hips, then I carefully step out of it, grab the hanger, and return the dress to my closet.

Then, in nothing but the thin lace thong I wore under the dress, I pad across the carpet to the top drawer of the island in the middle of my closet. And there, stored neatly in their boxes, is my entire collection of sex toys. I know exactly what I need tonight—I need a mind-blowing orgasm that will knock these thoughts of Colt right out of my head.

Taking my vibrator out of its box, I start to head back to my bed when I realize that the bedroom door is definitely not soundproof. *Colt's upstairs,* I assure myself, *it's fine.* This is one of the reasons I was so adamant that he stays in his space . . . I don't want him overhearing me getting myself off.

I pull my covers back and slip into bed, bringing a pillow down and adding it under my hips to tilt them back for what I know will be the best angle. Tonight, I need it deep. Rough even. I have another vibrator that's thicker and more power-ful, which I'd normally use when I'm looking for that type of experience. But my clit is aching and needs stimulation, and my nipples are pebbled and waiting for my touch, so this vibrator's combination of the thrusting, plus the clitoral stimulation, will allow me to use my free hand on my breasts.

I give it a few minutes, but even with how revved up I am, how badly I need this orgasm, my body won't relax enough to let me have it. My brain is too busy pushing the thoughts of Colt out of my head, because coming to images of us together defeats the whole purpose of getting myself off instead of asking him to do it for me.

Moving up onto my knees, I sink down so the vibrator is as deep as it can go, and my thoughts return to Colt, imagining what he'd look like if I was riding him like this. I'm so desperate to come that I stop fighting the pictures in my mind. Glancing into the mirror that runs across the dresser opposite my bed, I note how my full breasts bounce with the movement and imagine his mouth on them. I really want to be riding him instead of this damn vibrator.

I know how big he is because his damn erection has been pushed up against me numerous times this week. He'd fill me in ways this vibrator can't, and it's the images of us together, the imaginary feel of him inside me, of his tongue on me, our bodies slapping together, that finally tips me over the edge. The orgasm comes on so hard and so fast that I'm unprepared for it, and I'm crying out as I fall forward on one of my forearms and bury my face in the covers, groaning out my release while riding wave after wave of this orgasm.

When I finish, I turn off the vibrator, setting it aside as I roll onto my back and let out a deep sigh. And that's when I hear the creaking of the stairs outside my bedroom door.

No.

I try to assure myself that Colt was just coming down the stairs, and that he didn't hear anything. But as I lie there and listen, I hear him moving around upstairs. Which means he was coming up from the first floor and passing my room right as I orgasmed.

Fuck. Why the hell wasn't he upstairs in his apartment where he was supposed to be?

Chapter Twenty-One

COLT

I wake up exhausted, having tossed and turned half the night. I've never had to think twice about sleeping with someone so obviously willing, and having to exercise this kind of restraint is killing me. But she's Jameson's sister. She's off limits, and always has been. And I *promised* him I wouldn't touch her—something that's proving way harder than I expected.

As soon as I got upstairs last night and started undressing, I realized that I'd left my phone in my car. So I headed downstairs to get it, being as quiet as possible in case Jules was already in bed trying to fall asleep. On my way back in, I checked my messages to find *another* text from Gabriel, this time confirming the B&B reservation and telling me how much Mom and Dad are looking forward to meeting Jules.

With Game 7 on Friday night in Boston, there's really no excuse for why we can't drive up there on Saturday in time for the party, spend the night, and come back on Sunday. Especially since, if we win the series, the next one will start in Boston, so I don't even have travel plans as an excuse.

Plus, if I'm being honest with myself, I'm actually looking forward to a road trip with Jules. If I have to go back to my hometown and see my brother and sister-in-law for the first time in fifteen years, there is no one else I'd want by my side. Mostly because I'll be so focused on her that it'll be easy to ignore them, but also because she's fiercely protective, and I feel like she'll be the perfect buffer.

I feel safe with her. Not physically, because my body feels entirely out of my control every time she's around. But emotionally, she's one of the only people I can let my guard down around. I have a few close friends who I feel that way about, but she is the first woman who feels like she's giving more than she's taking. She'd go to bat for me, even while giving me sass about, if that's what it came down to. Just like I'd do for her.

I was so lost in thought about spending the whole weekend with her that I almost didn't notice the low moan coming from her bedroom door as I passed by, but the second time, the sound finally registered in my brain, and I fucking froze in that hallway. That low, slow groan of satisfaction turned hurried, coming out faster with a higher pitch, and I knew *exactly* what was happening on the other side of that door. I could picture it so clearly—the way her back would arch, her tits bouncing with each thrust, her lips parted and panting as she chased that orgasm.

It was enough to send all the blood in my body rushing toward my cock, and as if someone had injected it with concrete, it expanded and hardened so fast it ached—for her touch, for those sounds she was making to be for me, for the feel of her skin against mine and the taste of her on my tongue. I ached for her with an intensity I'd never felt before, and the sound of her hissing out a low *Yessss* had me turning and heading up the stairs before I blew my load in my pants right there outside her door.

I had barely shut the door to my apartment before I turned, one hand already in my pants as I rested the other against the front door, hearing her sounds in my head as I quickly jerked myself off to the visions I'd had in the hallways.

And now, even after finally getting some sleep, I still can't get those images out of my head. I want to know what every inch of her body looks like. I want to know what her skin feels like sliding along mine. I want to taste her, to know what she sounds like when she comes on my tongue. I want to push inside her and see what her face looks like when I'm filling her completely—so full that there's not a centimeter of her that's not taken up by me.

But I can't. I can't do *any* of those things, because despite my reputation and my past, one thing I will not do is go back on my word. Not when it was given to my best friend, who has stood beside me through some shit, who has made sure my career and my future weren't affected every time I made a dumb, impulsive decision. He trusts me to take care of her, and I couldn't do that to him just because I'm fantasizing about her.

I am not my brother.

It takes me longer than it should to pack up my shit for

our pre-game skate, so I'm running late as I take the stairs two at a time on my way out. Jules said she had her therapy appointment this morning, so I'm hoping she's tied up with that and I won't run into her on my way out. I need to get her out of my thoughts, and getting on the ice is the only sure-fire way I know of to clear my head like that.

But when I come down the second flight of stairs, I catch sight of her on the far side of the kitchen. She's bent over at the waist, taking something out of the under-counter microwave, and her short workout shorts are doing nothing to cover the bottom half of her ass cheeks, which has me wondering what type of underwear she's wearing—which has my mind going to the exact place I don't want it going.

She must hear me, because she straightens up and spins around, two hands clutching a steaming coffee mug. "Oh, hey," she says, like she's surprised it's me. There's a split second where I wonder if the sounds I heard last night were actually her in there with someone else, and that thought makes me even more ashamed of getting myself off to visions of her.

"Who else would be coming down the stairs in your house?" I ask.

She lets out a small laugh. "No one. I just . . . sometimes I forget you live here too."

I grab my baseball hat off the counter and slip it on my head backward. "I love being so forgettable."

Her eyes crinkle in the corners as she looks at me, trying to assess my meaning. "Trust me . . . you're not forgettable." She mutters something under her breath as she brings the coffee cup to her lips and takes a sip. Then she's clenching her teeth and lips together in pain, before swallowing and saying, "Shit, that was too hot."

"Why were you heating your coffee in the microwave?" I ask. Everyone knows that things heat unevenly in a microwave. She's lucky she didn't burn her lips or tongue.

"I always reheat it. I never seem to be able to drink a cup before it gets cold."

I set my bag on the floor next to me. "You should get one of those mugs that just keeps it at a constant temperature for you."

"I didn't know there were mugs that did that. I'll have to look into it." She nods at my bag. "Are you headed to the rink?"

"Yeah, pre-game skate. I'll be back in the early afternoon, and I, uh . . . I always take a nap before the game. I don't know if you have any plans that would be loud—"

"No." She shakes her head. "I know that's part of any hockey player's routine on a game day. I'm actually going shopping with Morgan this afternoon—I need something to wear to the anniversary party this weekend—so I'll stay out of your way."

I want to tell her she's never in my way, but in this case, it really is better if she's out of the house. Maybe then I'll be able to sleep without thinking about her? "You mean to tell me that within that expansive closet of yours, you don't have anything you can wear to that party?"

"I don't have anything I *want* to wear to the party, which is pretty much the same thing. What are you wearing?" she asks. "Just so I know how dressed up to get."

"I'll probably wear a tie. That's about as much as I've thought about it. Everyone will get dressed up, but it's like 'small-town dressed up,' not 'big-city dressed up,' you know?"

She smiles, laughter shaking her shoulders. "Yeah, I think I know what you mean. So how small is this small town? I thought you grew up in Montreal?"

"No, a small town about forty-five minutes outside of the city called Pinevale."

"I thought all the town and city names in Quebec were French?"

"They are. But you don't speak French, so I'm just going to use the English names, for your sake."

"Damn Latin never comes in handy," she says, as she raises her cup and blows on the surface of the coffee before taking a small, tentative sip. "Not that I ever travel . . ."

"Wait, you've been out of the country before, right?"

Lifting her eyebrows, she shakes her head.

"But you do have a passport, right?" Holy crap, how did I not think to ask this before?

"Yeah, I've just never used it."

I exhale a sigh of relief, because if she wasn't able to come, there's no way I'd be going. That thought has me realizing how dependent I've become on having her in my life, and I have to remind myself that we can be friends, but nothing more.

"Alright, I've got to go. I'm already cutting it close." It takes so long to get all my goalie gear on, I arrive earlier than most of the other players. "Will I see you after the game?"

"I don't think I can stay for the whole game. I have to be up at five tomorrow because we're getting a big shipment of lumber at six." She lets out a small groan as she sags back against the countertop. "The neighbors at this new house we're starting on this week are going to freaking love me tomorrow morning."

"You should get some gift cards for a local coffee shop and drop them in everyone's mailboxes with a *Sorry for the early morning* note," I suggest.

"That's actually kind of genius."

"So, will I not see you before I get on our plane after the game tonight?" I ask.

"Ahhhh . . . " She gives me a fake sad face. "Are you going to miss me?"

You have no idea.

"No," I huff out a laugh. "But I have a little going away present for you before I leave."

Her eyes widen. "I know we're supposed to be engaged and all, but this better not be like the gifts Drew sends Audrey when he's traveling."

"Why? What does Drew send Audrey?"

Those blue eyes widen even more and then she slow blinks. "Oh my god, pretend I didn't just say that. Please."

"Why, what's he send her?"

"Nothing. And don't you dare ask him, either. That would be a total violation of my sister's privacy."

"Ahhh, so something sexy, then?" I'm teasing her just to see if I can get her to blush. As the pink creeps into her cheeks, I step around the kitchen table so I'm directly in front of her. "Why, is that the kind of goodbye gift you'd like?" She's full-on blushing now, which only makes me want to push this a bit further. "Because that could easily be arranged."

"Don't make promises you don't plan to deliver on, Colt. Per your choice, we're keeping this platonic, remember?"

Wait a minute. "That's not what I said. I said I *couldn't* do anything about it, and you said you wanted me to respect our agreement and the promise I made to your brother." My voice drops lower. "Are you telling me that now you *don't* want to keep this platonic?"

"Let's not have this conversation again," she says breezily, but I can tell she's more affected than she's pretending to be, and not just because of the way she's holding that coffee mug between us, her forearms pressed right over her nipples like she doesn't want me to see what my being this close does to her.

"As you wish," I say, stepping back. "So, this is goodbye? For the next few days, at least?"

"What time are you leaving here tonight for your game? I can make sure I'm home in time to say goodbye."

———

She didn't make it home in time to say goodbye, but she sent me an apology text detailing how crappy her afternoon had been, and as we stand in the hallway waiting to take the ice for our second home game of this series, I'm trying not to let it bother me.

It's not that I expect her to drop her own plans—I wouldn't have even expected that if this was a real engagement. But standing there in the kitchen this morning, I'd known the perfect gift to get her, and I didn't want to wait for some special occasion to give it to her. I'd gone to three stores after our pre-game skate before I found exactly what I was looking for, and I stopped by one of those fancy card stores to get a pretty gift bag that was big enough for it. I'd just wanted to see her face when she opened it. Instead, I left it sitting on the kitchen table with a sticky note that said, "Open me tonight."

"Why are you in such a fuck-off mood?" Zach asks. But he looks like he knows the answer. "Not trouble in paradise, I hope?"

How do I even answer questions like that? Am I supposed to pretend to be a lovesick fool over her? Or should I be acting like everything is perfect?

"Just gearing up mentally," I say.

"Dude, don't take this the wrong way, but you play like shit when you're pissed. I know Hartmann's starting the game tonight, but you better get your head on right before you take the ice."

"I'm sorry, Zen Master." I taunt him in a way that has a few of the players closest to us looking over. Zach is our resident Aikido black belt, so-calm-you-can't-shake-him guru, but at this moment, his advice is not wanted. "Am I not chill enough for you tonight?"

Zach just looks at me like I'm pathetic and snorts out a laugh. "Your funeral, man. I'm just trying to keep you alive."

And then the music is blasting and the fans are cheering, and we take turns slapping our hands against the giant Rebels symbol on the wall as we head down the hallway and onto the ice. And when I skate past our bench, I glance up six rows where I know Jules will be sitting.

Holding up her phone, I can barely make out a picture of her rechargeable mug—the travel kind so she can take it to work with her, too—as she mouths, "Thank you!"

But that's not the thing that has the smile splitting my face in half. No, that's because, despite saying "only this once" before Friday night's game, she's wearing my jersey again.

———

Hartmann goaltends for the first two periods, and when I go in for the third, it's because he gave up two goals in the last five minutes. Our 4-1 lead going into the second period is now a narrow 4-3 lead.

"Nothing gets by you." Those are the instructions Wilcott gave me in the locker room between periods, and they hang heavy on me. Winning the game will be up to our other five players on the ice. Losing it will be up to me.

Florida's getting sloppy and if we can just keep it together and play smart, we can prevent them from tying it up before the period ends.

With three minutes left in the period, Drew narrowly misses a goal. That's when it gets ugly.

We're exhausted. They're exhausted. Tempers are high and so it shouldn't be a surprise when the next face-off turns into a brawl that sends Drew to the sin bin for two minutes. With the power play advantage, Florida pulls their goalie so they have six players on the ice ready to score. They're taking a risk to get the tie because they want that additional over-time period to give them a chance at winning.

I block four shots before the fifth goes wide, and I leave the crease to stop it with my stick. But there's no one to pass it up to because Florida's covering all our players, so I send it to the boards near the center line, hoping that if the puck advances into their neutral zone maybe one of our players can get to it on some sort of a breakaway. With an empty net on the other side of the rink and about twenty seconds left on the penalty clock, it's our best shot at scoring.

But the puck ricochets off the boards at the perfect angle, and heads straight toward the wide-open goal. I hold my breath, even as I know how unlikely it is for a goalie to score. Somehow, though, even as two of Florida's defensemen skate back toward it as fast as they can, the puck goes into the net. The sound of the buzzer fills the arena, and can barely be heard over the deafening roar of the home crowd.

It's the first goal of my entire professional career. Our fans scream the Rebel Chant at the top of their lungs while they swing the white towels with the dark and light blue Rebels logo above their heads.

I take the moment to skate to the bench, high-fiving my teammates who are also losing their fucking minds. And then I continue on, stopping at the glass right past our bench. Jules is already in the aisle, running down the stairs toward me when I stop and point at her. She comes to a stop before me, blowing me a kiss before I yell, "That one was for you!"

Her eyes widen and she shakes her head at me like I'm crazy, so I wink at her before turning and skating back to our goal so we can finish the last few seconds of this game. And long after the game and the never-ending interviews with the press, I find her waiting for me in the Family Room even though she said she wasn't staying until the end.

It's close to midnight, and she's clearly tired, but I'm thankful she's waited. The team is headed to the airport in a few minutes, and we'll be gone until Thursday unless we win our first game and close out the series. I'm having strangely mixed emotions about not seeing her for that long.

I stop short, leaving a few feet between us as I hold my

arms out for her, because I need her to come to me. And she does, wrapping herself in my arms, saying, "I couldn't let you leave for Florida without congratulating you."

When her lips meet mine, it occurs to me that this is the first time she's kissed me, and not the other way around. And I'm starting to wonder if the line between what's fake and what's real is getting as blurry for her as it already is for me.

Chapter Twenty-Two

JULES

The sun's only been up for an hour and already my bag is packed and sitting by the back door. I rarely travel, so I don't really know what I'm supposed to bring for a weekend with my fiancé's family. It's only one night away, but we have the party tonight, and then breakfast at his parents' place tomorrow. And the weather looks unpredictable, with a forty-degree range in the daily temps.

I'm strangely nervous about the whole thing—about meeting his parents, lying about our relationship, staying in the same room as him at the inn. He'd called to ask if we could get a room with two beds because he's "a big guy and sharing a small bed would be a problem," and was politely told that they didn't have any rooms with two beds, but that there was a couch in our room, too. I've offered to take that, but he only laughed and said he'd take it. I don't know how he thinks he's fitting his six-foot-four frame on a couch comfortably enough to sleep, but okay.

I think I'd be less nervous if he hadn't been gone all week. Luckily, they'd won the series during Game 6 in Florida, so they didn't have to play last night's home game. I thought that might mean we'd have more time to talk about this weekend at some point yesterday, but he was booked up all day with practice, and the media, and an appointment with his massage therapist, then he went out with his teammates last night. He invited me to come along, but I'm a nervous traveler and was afraid I'd be a mess today if I didn't get enough sleep. But I tossed and turned until I heard him come up the stairs anyway, so maybe I should have just gone out?

I'm headed out to get my sunglasses from the center console of my truck, busy thinking that I'm glad Colt's driving today, when I hear a too-familiar voice. My shoulders stiffen and I press my eyes closed for a moment. Even though I'd been expecting this a couple of weeks ago, I guess I must have let my guard down because my father's voice catches me by surprise.

"You're headed out early for a Saturday morning."

I turn slowly and find him leaning back against the exterior brick of our row house, one foot resting on the wall next to his opposite knee. His tattered jeans and T-shirt with small holes along the seams are practically stiff from the filth, and even from six feet away, he smells like the inside of a trash can on a hot day. The hollows under his eyes are a purplish gray, and his sallow skin sags along his gaunt cheeks, where there's not an ounce of fat to fill it out. His body's so thin it looks like the wall might be holding him up.

"What are you doing here?" It's the same question I ask him every time he shows up. Usually, it's even earlier on a weekday, and he catches me heading out to work. He's never come by on a weekend, which might be why he's caught me so off guard.

"I need some cash."

"I told you last time, I'm not giving you money anymore. Not unless you go to rehab."

"Rehab's a waste for a guy like me. I don't want you spending your money on that."

"No," my voice is harsh as I look him up and down, "you just want me wasting it on alcohol and drugs instead?"

His head rears back in surprise. I never talk back to him. I'm always the obedient daughter, the only person in his life who's still willing to help him out. I don't know why I've held on to the hope that he's going to change, but I'm finally realizing he never will.

"Listen, girl," he says, his nostrils flaring as he takes a step toward me. "You are where you are because of me. You think you'd be running your own construction company if I hadn't taught you everything you know? The least you can do is help me out now."

Behind me, the back door slams and I jump in surprise. Colt's next to me so fast he must have jumped down the back steps because there's no way he could make it down the six stairs that quick.

"With all due respect," he says, his voice level and firm as he places a reassuring hand on my lower back, "if you're going to speak to my fiancée that way, you're going to answer to me instead."

Dad looks at Colt, and his eyes widen in recognition. They've met a handful of times, back before Dad left, when we used to go to all the Rebels games to watch Jameson play.

Clearly, Dad hadn't heard our engagement news, which makes me wonder if he still follows hockey at all.

His dull blue eyes, once so bright and similar to mine, slide over to me. "Ahhh, getting yourself hitched to a hockey player, eh? And you can't spare a Benjamin Franklin for your old man?"

Colt's hand flies out, pulling me behind him as he steps forward in front of me. I don't feel threatened by my father, who is so emaciated from his addiction that he can't possibly weigh more than I do, but once again, Colt is putting himself between what he perceives as a potential threat and me.

"She's my daughter, and I'm not talking to her through you," Dad snarls. Everything about him—from the way his knees are a little bent to the way his lip curls up to bare his teeth, or what's left of them anyway—reminds me of a mangy dog about to attack.

"You're done talking to her, period," Colt says. "You clearly don't deserve whatever sympathy she has left for you. Now get out of here, or I'll call the cops and tell them you're trespassing."

The way Colt is keeping his calm, the way he doesn't let my dad's veiled threats affect his outward demeanor, surprises me. He's level-headed, yes. But I saw him just about lose his shit a few weeks ago when I was being threatened, and it makes me wonder why he hasn't gone into attack mode this time too. Whatever the reason, his calming presence is calming me, too.

"We'll talk about this later," Dad says to me, then he makes a hideous noise in the back of his throat that sounds like he's coughing and choking at the same time, before he spits a wad of phlegm at Colt's feet.

To his credit, Colt doesn't react. We just stand there together, watching him hobble down the alley. It's not until Dad turns the corner onto the sidewalk that I realize I'm holding Colt's hand. I don't even know when that happened.

"Hey," I say, squeezing. "You didn't have to jump in like that. I don't need protecting."

He obviously didn't absorb that message after what happened at the restaurant, but at least there was no catastrophic fallout this time.

"I know you don't. You could have handled him by yourself . . . but I wanted you to know you didn't have to." Then he turns, giving me a quick kiss on the forehead that has me softening toward him even more. "Don't forget your sunglasses."

We're an hour into our drive north when Colt says, "So, you want to talk about what happened back there with your dad?"

I shift in my seat, bringing my travel mug with my always-warm coffee up to my lips and noting, as I do each time I use it, what a thoughtful gift it was. "Not particularly."

"How often does he come around asking for money?"

"You asked if I wanted to talk about it, and I said no."

"Well, I'm going to need some basic information, Jules, so I know whether I need to be worried about him coming back."

"Colt, you saw him. It's not like he's a threat." At least, this confrontation didn't result in a panic attack like I had after the interaction with Jerome.

"Do Jameson and Audrey know he still comes around?"

I glance out the windows at the evergreens lining this part of the highway. Now that we're farther north, the trees are just starting to get their leaves, whereas they are completely filled in back down in Boston. "No."

"And why do you think that is?"

"Because I haven't told them," I say, swallowing roughly.

"Has he contacted either of them?"

"I don't think so."

"Would you know if he did?"

"Yeah."

"And why's that?" He's led me straight to the point I don't want to let him make. I know exactly why my dad only ever approaches me.

"Because if he had, either of them would have told him to fuck off, and then told the rest of us about it."

"So why haven't you done that?" He's got one arm loosely gripping the top of the steering wheel, and the ends of his sandy hair curl up from under his backward ball cap. Outwardly, he's relaxed, but I can tell just by the line of questioning that he's not.

"What do you want me to say, Colt? That I feel bad for him, and that despite the fact that he left us, I feel some obligation to help him?"

"That's a start. Does your therapist know you've helped him out in the past?"

"You're jumping to a lot of conclusions for someone who heard, like, five seconds of our conversation."

"The kitchen window was open, Jules. That's how I knew he was out there in the first place. It's not like I'd have recognized him if I hadn't heard your conversation and known it was your dad."

It's true that my dad is barely recognizable. I remember when I was still very young, back when Jameson was in high school and my parents were happily married—Dad used to look so much like my brother looks now, but without the dark eyes. Jameson got those from his own mom, but otherwise, they're practically twins. Their personalities couldn't be more different, though. Where Jameson is fiercely loyal, staunchly determined, and completely disciplined in all aspects of his life, Dad's a loose cannon of bad decisions. It's why I try so hard to be more like my brother—I don't want to end up like my dad.

"No," I say finally. "My therapist doesn't know about my dad."

"And why not?"

"I don't know, Colt," I say, sarcasm heavy in my tone. "Because I have so many other issues to talk to her about that this one hasn't come up yet?"

Besides, I'm well aware that just about every issue in my life stems from my father in the first place. There's a reason they call them "daddy issues."

"So how about this," he says. "When you talk to her tomorrow morning, let's tell her about what's happening with your dad, and see what she says. Or, I can tell your brother."

My incredulous laugh comes out sounding an awful lot like a snort. "Are you fucking giving me an ultimatum? We haven't been together long enough for that. And also, what do you mean *let's* talk to her about it. Are you planning to join my therapy session?"

"I'd like to," he says. His eyes flick from the road to me quickly before he refocuses them straight ahead. "If you're open to it."

Is he even for real right now? "Why in the world would I be open to that?"

"I just want to be there when you tell her what happened. Then I'll leave."

I genuinely laugh at that. "No, you won't. Because she's going to have a lot of questions for you, Colt."

"For me?"

"Yeah. Like she's going to ask why you keep jumping in to save me in situations I can clearly handle by myself. And why your first instinct was to say we're engaged. And why you have probably hundreds of former hookups in your contact list and haven't slept with anyone in half a year, but you can't keep your hands off me."

His lips curve up into what I can only imagine is a classic Colt smirk, but I can't tell for sure since I can only see his profile. "You sure those aren't the questions *you* want to ask?"

"I think those are the questions that *anyone* who knew about our situation would have," I say, hoping he doesn't glance over here and see how my face is heating up. He hit the nail right on the head, because those are exactly the questions I want answers to. "Besides, I canceled tomorrow's appointment already."

"Why would you do that? You could have still had a video call with her."

"I didn't know what our plans would be, or if I'd have a private place to take the call."

"Jules, those appointments are important. We could have

moved plans around and made sure you had space so that you could have been on that call."

I feel oddly defensive that he's questioning my judgment here. It's not like I don't think they're important, it's just that I couldn't imagine how I'd take that call when we're sharing a room at the inn and have some sort of breakfast plans with his parents. At the same time, I'm touched that he's willing to reschedule things like that.

My feelings for him, and about him, are getting so damn complicated.

He reaches for his phone where it rests on the charging pad and hands it to me. "2-6-3-8."

"What?"

"That's my passcode. Enter it."

"Okay . . ." I drag the word out as I unlock his phone. "Now what."

"Open my contacts."

"Why? I don't want to see what's there." Is this some form of torture, making me look at the long list of women he's slept with, with details about the location and experience noted prominently in their name?

"I'm pretty sure you do, actually."

"I kind of hate you right now." I hate him the way you hate something you know you want, but can never have. I hate the way he always thinks he knows what I'm feeling. And I hate it even more that he's always right.

"You don't hate me, Tink. You just wish you did." *See? Bullseye, every freaking time.* "Now, open my contacts."

I do as he says, wrinkling my nose in advance of what I imagine I'll find there. But I'm not really sure how to process the screen I land on.

I use my finger to scroll through the contacts, all thirty of them. And I recognize, or can at least place, every single name. His parents and brother, his teammates, my brother and sister . . . I'm about to object that I'm not in there, but find myself listed near the end as *Tinker Bell.*

I know why he's showing me this, but I still feel the need to hear him say it. "Yeah, so?"

"I deleted them all. And blocked them. And turned off my DMs on social media."

"Why would you do that?" I try to keep my tone nonchalant, making it sound like this makes no difference to me. But it does matter, and we both know it.

"For exactly the reasons you think."

I'm about to tell him that he doesn't know what I'm thinking, but we'd both know that's a lie. So instead, I just say, "Hmmmm." I'm so intent on looking out the window at the passing trees like they are the most interesting thing in the world that I startle when he places his hand just above my knee and gives my leg a little squeeze.

When he doesn't pull his hand back, I relax into the seat. I'm starting to feel safe any time Colt's hands are on me, no matter how dangerous that might be.

Chapter Twenty-Three

COLT

"Why did you buy so many of those?" I ask when she comes back to my car with about ten boxes of Hot Tamales.

"They're your favorite, so I grabbed them all."

It's no secret that I'm addicted to cinnamon—it's my favorite flavor of candy, gum, and tea. I don't know what I like about it so much, except that it reminds me of my childhood. Mom was known for her apple pies, which were heavy on the cinnamon and sugar, and she baked one every single holiday no matter what time of year. I find it oddly touching that Jules apparently bought out all the cinnamon candies in the gas station.

We drive in silence, with me holding my hand out every few minutes and Jules dropping a few Hot Tamales at a time into my palm, but she looks lost in thought, so I haven't tried to engage her in conversation. We're only a couple of miles from the Canadian border when Jules says, "I'll sleep on the couch tonight, Colt."

It seems tonight's sleeping arrangements are weighing on her mind. "I really don't mind," I tell her. I do mind, because I know I'll get a crap night of sleep, but I'd rather it be me that sleeps poorly than her.

"Colt, you're used to sleeping in that ginormous king-size bed you insisted on moving into my house because Jameson's existing bed wasn't big enough. There's no way you're going to be able to get comfortable on a couch."

"I brought my bed with me when I moved in because I sleep there *every* night that I'm not on the road. I'll be fine on the couch for *one* night."

"You sure you didn't bring that big bed for all your hookups?"

I've made it abundantly clear that I haven't hooked up with anyone in months. I even showed her my updated contacts in my phone. But she's not willing to let go of my reputation— kind of seems like she's clinging to it so she doesn't have to see that maybe she's a part of the reason I'm changing.

"I don't do sleepovers."

"Because you need that big bed all to yourself?" I can tell by the way she curls her legs up onto the leather seat and turns toward me that she's teasing.

"Because I don't want to set any expectations."

"Don't worry. Not only are we *not* going to be sharing that bed tonight, but even if we did, I wouldn't have any expectations that it meant something."

"Maybe that's your problem, Jules. Maybe you don't expect enough." I chance a quick glance at her so I can watch the flush of embarrassment creep across her cheeks. It's too damn easy to make her blush, and I enjoy it too damn much.

"Like I said"—her voice is defensive—"I wouldn't expect anything from *you*."

"What if I was your real fiancé?"

Shut up, you idiot, my brain screams. Why am I letting her know that I've even considered that, when I've already told her that I can't act on anything I'm feeling toward her? I'm a fucking mess.

She coughs out a laugh. "Colt, the world would have to be ending before I'd actually agree to marry you." Despite her words, there's no heat behind them. It's clearly an attempt to rebuild those walls she occasionally lets down around me.

"You're going to at least have to pretend that you like me if we're going to sell this engagement this weekend."

"Nah, you'd never marry someone who was always fawning over you. That would be the surest sign ever that this wasn't real. You need someone to put you in your place, Colt. And I plan to do just that, even in front of your family."

———

Driving through my hometown is surreal. Everything's the same, yet everything's different. Same buildings on Main Street, different stores. Same high school, with a huge new addition off the side. Same grocery store, new name.

It's been so long since I've let myself think about this place, and about what I'm missing by not coming home, that I actually have a lump in my throat as we drive through the center of town. As if she knows how I'm feeling, Jules reaches her arm over and rests her hand on my thigh. It doesn't have the calming effect I'm sure she intends. Instead, it has my heart beating faster. Or is my heart rate increasing because now that we're here, I'm going to have to tell her what happened between Gabriel, Cheri, and me so long ago?

My GPS directs me to take a left, but I'd have been able to find the inn without it. Pinevale is small enough that you don't come here unless you're visiting someone. There's only one inn in town. But when we pull up to the white Victorian with its contrasting pale sage green gingerbread trim and wide front porch with floorboards painted in the same shade, I realize my mistake. I've waited too long to tell Jules the truth about my past.

Because sitting in three of the rocking chairs on the front porch are my brother, my mom, and my dad—and they wave enthusiastically when we pull in.

I drive to the farthest parking spot I can find, down at the end of the wide circular driveway, and then turn toward Jules in my seat. "I haven't seen my brother in fifteen years, and I wasn't expecting him to be waiting for us."

"It's going to be fine," she says, squeezing my thigh, but I feel like she's saying it as much for her own benefit as for mine.

"No, it's not. Because I haven't told you everything that happened between us, and there's no way it's not coming up right now, and no matter what's said, I need you to pretend like you already know all of it."

"Uhh . . ." She glances behind me, and when I look over my shoulder, my family is standing on the grass waiting for us to get out of the car.

"Please, Jules," I whisper, then take her hand and bring it

to my lips. "There's no way they'll believe that this is real if you don't already know the whole story."

"When were you going to tell me?" she asks, her brow furrowing.

"When we got inside." I brush my lips over her knuckles. "Please play along."

Dropping her voice, she says, "I like it when you beg." Then she turns and is opening her door, leaving me speechless for maybe the first time in my life.

Mom must go around to the passenger's side the minute Jules's door opens, because as I open my door, I'm face to face with my dad and my brother. On the other side of the car, I can hear Mom gushing over "finally" meeting my fiancée.

Dad holds his arms out and wraps me in a hug, and when I pull back, Gabriel extends his arm, offering me his hand to shake. I just look at it, then up to his face, nodding in acknowledgment before I head to the back of my SUV, popping open the lift gate and pulling out our bags.

Mom and Jules come around from the other side of the car, and my mom takes one look at my carry-on suitcase and Jules's over-the-shoulder bag and says, "Where's the rest of your stuff?"

I point at the suitcase and say, "That's mine," and then at the bag sitting on top. "That's hers."

"Wow, you pack light," she says to Jules.

"I'm pretty low maintenance."

Mom laughs and says, "Good. Someone in the relationship should be, and I know it's not my son." Then she introduces Jules to my dad and brother, and I don't miss the way

Gabriel eyes me after Jules shakes his hand, as if to say: *See, at least she's mature.*

"So," I say as we walk up the path to the wide steps leading to the porch. "What are you guys doing here? I didn't expect to see you until the party tonight."

Mom looks away as we climb the steps, and Dad says, "We thought maybe it was best if the first time you and Gabriel saw each other again was . . . more private."

"See, now I completely disagree," I say, setting the suitcase down with Jules's bag on top of it once we reach the porch. "I came here to see you guys. I have nothing to say to him, and the party would have been the perfect place for us to avoid each other."

"You can't avoid me forever," Gabriel says, frustration ringing out in his tone.

"Want to bet?" I push the front door to the inn open, ushering Jules through. I'm about to shut the door behind me when Dad's hand shoots out and holds it open and I hear my family shuffle in behind us.

"Hey, Patrice," Dad says to the woman standing behind the counter. Her auburn hair has a few streaks of gray in it, and she looks familiar. But she's too young to have been friends with my parents when I was growing up, and too old to have been in school with me. I can't place her, and I wonder how many times that's going to happen tonight.

"Thanks for setting aside the sitting room for us," Mom says. "We'll head back there while you get Mathieu and Jules checked in."

"Sure thing. It's all yours until teatime at four," the woman says, before turning her attention back to us. "My, my," she says, looking at me. "Haven't you grown up?" Then she turns to Jules. "This little devil child was in my third-grade class my first year of teaching. He gave me *such* a run for my money."

"Oh my god," I say with a laugh. "Ms. Wilder?"

"I've been Mrs. Benson for quite some time," she says. "When Roger's parents decided to retire about ten years ago, we took over the inn so it would stay in the family. I'd had enough of dealing with eight-year-olds by then."

"I'm surprised you made it that long after having to deal with this one," Jules says with a smile as she pokes me in the side. "I've known him since he was a teenager and he's barely matured since then."

Mrs. Benson lets out a laugh, the kind that comes from deep in your gut, and then says to me, "I'm glad you found someone to keep you in line."

"Oh, she does more than just keep me in line," I say, unable to resist.

Jules rolls her eyes, and I do my best to ignore the way that makes my dick twitch, as always. "See what I mean," she tells my former teacher. "He's pretty much still a child."

"But the most successful one to have ever left Pinevale." Pride is evident in her voice. "It's been a lot of fun watching you play over the years."

"Oh? Are you a Rebels fan now?" I tease. We're *deep* in Montreal territory, and if there's one thing people around here take seriously, it's their loyalty to their local team.

"As if," she says with a laugh, then turns and grabs a key with a pale green retro tag off a hook behind her. "You're in luck with the room. I know you were concerned about the size of the bed, and we had a cancellation for this weekend. The couple that was supposed to take the honeymoon suite had to change their plans, so that room is all yours. It's going to be the last door at the end of the hallway." She points to the wooden stairs next to the registration desk. Then she turns back, winks at Jules, and adds, "Biggest bed in the Pinevale Inn."

I'm already afraid of what we're going to find when we get up there. "I'm sure the original room will be just fine," I say, because at least we know that one had both a bed and a couch.

"Nonsense," she insists. "Besides, we already rented out that room to your cousin, Lane. He and his wife were on the waitlist, and now they won't have to stay with your aunt and uncle." She purses her lips, and we both understand exactly why this is better for Lane and his wife—my aunt is a raging bitch, or at least she was when I was younger. It doesn't even surprise me one bit that Lane went to Ottawa for university and has lived there ever since. "They checked in about an hour ago and were so grateful for the room."

Jules looks at me and, with laughter in her voice, says, "Guess we get the honeymoon suite a bit early." Holding out her palm to get the key from Mrs. Benson, her eyes meet mine again. "Why don't I go get our stuff settled in the room so you can have a few minutes to catch up with your family?"

It's the perfect solution, really, as it allows me to explain the situation to her privately, later, instead of her hearing the drama unfold when I sit down with my brother for the first time since he got my girlfriend pregnant.

"Oh no, honey," Mrs. Benson says, gently pushing Jules's

hand away. "I promised the Coltiers that I'd take your stuff up so you all can catch up before tonight's party. You guys go ahead."

She steps around the desk and grabs the handle of the suitcase from me. *Well, fuck.*

Chapter Twenty-Four

JULES

"Let's just start by clearing the air," Gabriel says the minute we sit on the couch across from him and his parents, and Colt's grip tightens around my fingers to the point that it's nearly painful. I have the feeling that this is the only thing preventing him from losing his shit, even though I don't know why, so I just squeeze back, hoping he knows I'll back him up however he needs me to. "I apologize. What Cheri and I did was wrong . . ."

In the pregnant pause that follows, Colt grits out, "There better not be a *but* following that statement."

"There is, and you know why," Gabriel says. "You two hadn't been happy since before you got drafted."

I'm trying to put the pieces of this puzzle together, and my best guess is something happened between Gabriel and the girl Colt was dating before he went pro.

"She was planning to move to Boston to be with me once

her freshman year was over. You were supposed to keep an eye out for her at college, not sleep with her."

Ohhh. So his brother slept with his high school girlfriend when, it sounds like, they went to the same college and Colt came to Boston for hockey? But Gabriel is four years older, so the math doesn't quite add up. Why would he have been at college when Colt's girlfriend was a freshman?

"We didn't mean for it to happen, and you know it."

"Do I?" He drops my hand, leaning forward so both his elbows rest on his knees. "Because it sure seems like the minute I was out of the country, you were falling into her bed when you were supposed to be focusing on medical school."

"Guys." Mr. Coltier says this the way I imagine he must have a hundred times a week while they were growing up, like they're fighting over the last cupcake or something equally trivial. Mrs. Coltier glances at the glass door to the hallway like she wants to make sure no one is standing beyond it and potentially hearing this conversation.

I rest my free hand on Colt's back, gently pressing against his spine so he knows I'm here for him.

"Dad, he went after her while she was still dating me." Colt's voice rises a little with anger, but he's not yelling. He's just clearly pissed off. "While she was still coming down to Boston every weekend that I wasn't traveling. He was sleeping with her *at the same time* I was. We had to have a fucking paternity test to figure out who the father was, and you just want me to forgive him for that?"

I focus on breathing in and out through my nose in an attempt not to react to this piece of information. Cheri was pregnant and, at least for a little while, Colt wasn't sure if that child was his. The fact that he's never had a serious relationship in all the time I've known him makes so much more sense now. How do you ever trust after a betrayal of that magnitude?

"You don't have to forgive him," Mrs. Coltier says. "We just need you to accept that it happened, and move on."

"Maybe it's good that we had this conversation," Colt says, as his hand slides over to my knee, cupping my leg in his huge hand. His voice is calm, but from where I sit, it's impossible not to notice how he's practically vibrating with rage. "It allowed us to establish that Gabriel and Cheri are both cheaters who are obviously suited to each other. And besides"—he glances at me—"I think everything turned out exactly like it was supposed to."

He stands, holding his hand out to me, and I take it, letting him pull me up from the couch. And as we walk from the room, I don't turn to say goodbye. We'll be seeing them again soon enough, and right now, Colt needs me more than they need my good manners.

We don't say anything as he swipes the key from the tray it's sitting on at the front desk, or as we climb the stairs to the second floor, or as we walk down the hallway hand in hand. And when I follow him through the door into the bedroom, he turns quickly, reaching out and closing it behind me. I'm stuck between him and the door, watching his ragged breathing as he looks down at me like he's at war with himself.

Reaching out, I rest both my hands on his chest and then slide them up to his shoulders. "I'm sorry that happened to you," I tell him, and he sucks in a breath before slowly exhaling, the scent of cinnamon gliding over my skin.

"I'm not."

That's the last thing I expected him to say. "Really? Why not?"

He leans down, resting his forehead against mine. "Because if it hadn't been him, it would have been someone else."

"Are you sure?" I ask. Because it sounded like Gabriel and Cheri might still be together, which leads me to think she's not cheating on him.

"We weren't in love. We were holding on to a relationship from our childhood even though we should have said goodbye when I left for Boston. Besides," he says, as his hand smooths along the side of my neck and into my hair, his thumb caressing the space behind my ear, "I don't want to think about what my life could have been like. I wasn't lying when I said that everything turned out exactly as it should have."

His breathing is still ragged, like he's losing his grip on his control, and his lips are closer to mine than they were a moment ago. I want him to kiss me with every fiber of my being, but I don't want it to be because of Gabriel and Cheri.

"Yeah," I say, with a teasing little laugh, "because having a fake fiancée is really how you pictured things ending up."

"Tink." He says my nickname like he's chiding me. "You're not a consolation prize."

"I didn't say I was." I glance around the honeymoon suite, with its white shiplap walls and frilly white bedding, so I don't have to look at him. But he takes my chin and guides my head back so I have no choice but to lock eyes with him.

"You're acting like you wouldn't be my first choice, in any situation, every single time."

Now it's *me* who's struggling to breathe. What is he talking about? My eyes search his, trying to determine his meaning.

"If you weren't Jameson's little sister . . ."

It's the sucker punch I wasn't expecting, but should have been. His relationship with my brother will always be more important to him than whatever is growing between us.

"I'm going to take a shower," I say, slipping under his arm and grabbing my bag where it sits on the bed. I don't stop to get my toiletries out; I just take the entire bag into the bathroom with me. And then I stand under the spray of the shower, turning the water as hot as I can possibly tolerate it, and wonder why I keep letting him lead me on like this when I already know how it's going to end.

Even though there's clearly something between us, he's never going to choose me.

Chapter Twenty-Five

COLT

I'm leaning back against the bar, watching Jules as she chats with my mom. There's ease in the way they get along, my mom welcoming her into our family with open arms because she's thrilled to see her son happy. This is exactly why I asked Jules to go along with this—I wanted to show my family that I'm fine.

The difference between when I asked her to fake this whole engagement and now, is that I actually *am* happy. I'm not pretending, and it's almost entirely because Jules is here with me. Even the earlier argument with my brother where I finally admitted how much he hurt me, it felt like letting go in a way that freed me to finally be happy again.

Tonight, Jules is wearing a black jumpsuit with an open back covered in black lace. It dips low enough in the front that her cleavage is on display, but not so low that it's not still classy. For someone who spends their days on a construction site, she sure cleans up well.

I watch as she tosses those blond waves over her shoulder, laughing at something my mom said, and I realize that even as gorgeous and glamorous as she looks now, I'd rather have her in a tank top and shorts padding around the house barefoot with her hair in a bun and no makeup. I've lost count of the number of times I've come downstairs for some made-up reason because the thought of us both being in the same house but not being together gives me hives.

Watching my parents renew their vows earlier, all I could think about was how I never thought I wanted what they had —or at least, since Cheri and Gabriel betrayed me, I *told* myself I didn't want that. But today, with Jules by my side and her smile so genuine as she watched my parents together . . . I don't know. I keep wondering what life would be like with her.

I don't know what to do about these feelings I have, and how at odds they are with the promise I easily made to my best friend a couple of weeks ago. I'm starting to wonder if he might be okay with us being together if he knew how real my feelings are—that this isn't just because I'm desperate to get her in bed, this is me wanting and needing to be with her every minute possible.

I've been viewing this situation as analogous to Gabriel and me fifteen years earlier. Jameson is asking me to look after his little sister, just like I asked Gabriel to look after Cheri for me. But is it really the same? Gabriel and Cheri getting together was a betrayal of my trust because she and I were dating. It's not the same with Jameson and Jules . . . she's his little sister whom he raised. Making things real between us, as long as we didn't go behind his back, wouldn't be betraying his trust or our friendship. I don't think?

"I never thought I'd see *you* looking lovestruck." My dad's voice comes from directly beside me, but I was so focused on Jules that I didn't even notice he was there. His hair is grayer in a way I hadn't noticed earlier.

"I mean, look at her," I say, as if it's her looks that have me feeling all these conflicting emotions.

"Yeah," my dad says, "but it's not the way she looks. It's the way *you* look at *her*—and the way she practically glows when you do."

I press my lips between my teeth, wishing I could ask his advice about this, about how to handle it with Jameson so I don't break his trust, but still get what I want. But I don't just want her—I *need* her in my life.

However, I don't have any reason to believe she wants me in the same way—for anything more than a physical relationship. I also don't have any reason to believe she doesn't want more. Aside from the sexual frustration, she's kept her feelings well-hidden as we've tried to navigate this engagement situation together. Clearly, we need to talk.

"She's pretty incredible," I say, because my dad's looking at me like he's wondering why I'm lost in my own head. "She makes me feel . . ." I'm not sure where I'm going with this, so I say the first thing that comes to my mind. ". . . complete."

"I think that's how you know you found the one," Dad says.

I'm about to respond—to ask him how you can ever be sure that someone is *the one*—but then Jules is walking toward us, a big smile on her face. When she comes to a stop in front of us, she says, "Mind if I steal my fiancé away for a dance? This is my favorite song."

As she drags me onto the dance floor, I laugh and say, "Of course 'Landslide' is your favorite song."

She wraps her arms around my shoulders, pulling me close. "Why is that so predictable?"

"Because Stevie Nicks wrote that song when her life was in upheaval. It's all about self-reflection and going after what you want and the fear of making big changes, of letting go."

I feel the "Hmmm" she lets out in response as it reverberates between our chests. "It always makes me think of my dad."

"Is that a good thing?" I ask. I can't imagine how it would be, given what I saw between them this morning, but I know she has good memories of him.

"In a way. He used to play a lot of Fleetwood Mac on job sites. I definitely get my musical taste from him. Anyway, this song always reminds me of how choices have consequences —how they can be a turning point, or the avalanche that does you in."

It occurs to me then that in the two weeks we've been "engaged," she hasn't had a single panic attack . . . that I know of. "Is that how you feel when you're not in control? Like an avalanche is coming?"

"I don't know, Colt," she says as she looks up at me and winks. "I never lose control long enough to find out."

I glance up from my phone, where I was taking a second look at the photos of my condo that my contractor sent minutes ago, and Jules and I just flipped through. The electrical has all been redone, and the plumbers finished their work earlier today. Pretty soon, we'll be ready for insulation and drywall, and I suspect that once that's done, the rest of the renovation will go pretty quickly.

The thought of moving back to my condo has a thin layer of sweat breaking out across my skin. The only thing I miss about that space is the view, and even as spectacular as it is, it doesn't have me wanting to move out of Jules's place.

Next to me, she toys with the lime in her drink as she stares across the restaurant, where Cheri stands next to Gabriel at the bar. Her hair is the same shade of blond as Jules's, ashy with some light brown undertones, though hers ends just below her shoulders while Jules wears hers longer. Cheri's got blue eyes too, but they're lighter and washed out compared to Jules's.

Cheri's aged well—she has the natural look of a woman who's spent a lot of time outdoors, doesn't use much makeup, and has chosen to wear her age instead of trying to cover it up in an attempt to look younger. She also looks happy. Gabriel was right about the fact that they are better together than she and I ever were.

"Is that why you were never attracted to me?" Jules asks quietly.

My head snaps toward her, and she looks like she's in pain, so I reach out, looping my hand around her hip and turning her toward me. Then dipping my head close to hers, I ask, "What are you talking about, Tink?"

"Back when I used to have a crush on you. Is that why you weren't attracted to me?" She nods her chin toward Cheri. "It's pretty easy to do the math. I was nineteen in

Vegas, the same age that you guys were when she slept with your brother. Did I remind you of her?"

My other hand moves to her chin, my thumb on one side of her jaw and my fingers on the other as I tilt her face up so she's forced to look me in the eye. "I was never *not* attracted to you. I just never let myself look at you that way. Partially because you have blond hair and, yeah, since Cheri, I've never been with a blonde. But also, because I always thought of you like a sister."

"Zero difference between Audrey and me, huh?" she asks, but her voice is taunting me like she wants to crack me open and figure out all my secrets.

"Not back then."

"What about a couple weeks ago? If it had been Audrey at that dinner, and Jerome grabbed her instead of me, would you have ended up in that alley with her instead?"

Jerome. That's the asshole's name. Noted.

I press my lips together and swallow before saying, "No."

"Why not?"

"Jules, why are you pushing me like this? Trust me when I say you don't want to know the answers to these questions."

"Why? Because you *can't do anything* about your attraction to me?" She mimics my words back to me.

"You are such a brat sometimes," I practically growl. Why does it turn me on when she acts like this? "But yes, that's exactly why."

"Tell me, if it had been Audrey . . .?"

"It wouldn't have been her."

"What does that even mean, Colt?" She rolls her eyes, and I step in close enough that I have to drop my hand from her chin because there isn't room for my arm between us. God, she drives me crazy—the way she pushes and taunts me has me wanting to back her up against the wall and have my way with her.

"It means that I wouldn't have gone to that restaurant in the first place for Audrey. And I sure as hell wouldn't have let her practically fuck me through her clothes like you were doing in that alley."

Her gulp is so loud I'm glad no one is around to hear it except for me.

"Why not?" she asks, a challenge flashing in her gorgeous blue eyes as they lock onto mine.

"I don't have the same protective instincts toward her that I feel for you, and I've *never* looked at her the way I look at you."

"And how do you look at me, Colt?"

"I'm starting to think you're not just taunting me." I shake my head as I stare down at her. "Now I'm pretty sure you're trying to *torment* me."

"Torment you how?" She rolls her eyes again like she knows it'll get a reaction out of me, and I clench my jaw so I don't surge forward and invade her mouth like I want to do. The tension between us is ever-present, like a spark ready to turn into a blaze.

When I don't respond, she says, "Because I'm reminding you that you're attracted to me after you've told me you don't want to feel that way? Sorry, I forgot I'm supposed to focus on your feelings and not my own."

My fingers curl around her lower back to rest on the curve of her ass as I pull her flush against me. "Are you saying you have feelings for me?"

"Relax, Colt." She lets out a sigh. "I got over my crush on you after Vegas."

"What?" I bark out the word so sharply she flinches.

"What part of that requires explaining?"

My hand instinctively tightens on her hip, anchoring her to me. "All of it, Jules. Because it sounds like you're saying that what happened in Vegas had something to do with me."

I'm expecting her to laugh and say that no, that wasn't what she meant. But I'd know she was lying. Why else would she have gotten over her crush on me after Vegas if what happened there had nothing to do with me?

Instead of giving me an explanation, she digs her heels in, asking, "Why do *you* sound mad about this? You're not the one who almost ruined their life with their inability to control their own emotions."

"Because if you had feelings for me before Vegas and you went and married someone else while we were there, I have to wonder if it was because of something I did. Or didn't do. I don't know. But I have *never* wanted to hurt you—not now, and certainly not back then. So if I did, I deserve to know what happened. And to have the chance to make it right."

She looks away. "It was a long time ago, Colt. It can't be made right."

"The fuck it can't." The words are low and feral, and I watch her shiver as they coast over her skin. "We need to talk about this, and we're not doing it here. Let's go."

Chapter Twenty-Six

JULES

6 Years Ago
Las Vegas, NV

Is this what being drunk feels like? Exhilarating and terrifying and freeing, all at the same time?

Brock reaches across his body and intertwines the fingers of his left hand with mine, while his right arm circles my waist, anchoring me to his hip as we navigate through the small tables at the outdoor French bistro. I don't think I'm swaying, exactly, but everything feels fuzzy and lovely, and it's certainly easier to walk in a straight line when he's helping me.

"Oh my God," I gasp as I glance up at the lights of the Eiffel Tower sparkling above us. "We're in Paris!" I've never left the country before, and I'm shocked and delighted that I'm in France and don't even remember the trip here.

The smacking sound he makes when his lips land on my

cheek is adorable. He can't seem to keep his mouth off me, which is fine by me, because his kisses are a million times better than the drunk frat boys who are always trying to steal kisses at the MIT parties I've been to this year.

"We're outside the Paris Hotel, not actually *in* Paris." He says it with the same voice you'd use to tell a child they're silly, and that has me in a fit of giggles.

I don't know why everything is so funny, but I'm happy and I'm enjoying this feeling. It's sort of a new one for me. Brock makes me happy. Well, Brock and whiskey sours and delicious French meals at an outdoor cafe under the Eiffel Tower, and some after-dinner drink with a name that had something to do with Paris and burning. Whatever it was, it was strong but delicious and went down easy—so easy that Brock had two.

"I'm pretty sure this actually *is* Paris," I say, glancing from the outdoor bistro tables of the French cafe we're walking through and back up to the Eiffel Tower.

"Sure thing," he says and presses his lips to my temple as his fingers snake a figure-eight pattern over my hip bone.

His touch has my skin on fire, but, like, if fire was pleasant. It makes me glow. I've never felt like this before. Is this what I've been missing out on? Why was I holding out for Colt when there are so many other attractive guys out there?

Once we're out of the cafe, he points out the Bellagio's fountains across the street. They're in the middle of their spectacular show, so we head over to watch them. Standing there with my back pressed up against his chest and his arms wrapped around me, holding me tight, with the lights and the fountains and the music all coordinated, he leans his head down and says, "How about we go back to my room after this?"

My laugh is light and flirtatious, the alcohol pumping through my veins has me feeling warm and tingly. "Brock," I say, nervousness creeping up on me. "I'm not sleeping with you tonight."

I've never even done anything more than kiss a guy, and the thought that he expects more than that from me has me so nervous I could throw up.

"I wasn't planning on getting much sleep." His thumb runs back and forth over my wrist, and it's sending sparks of desire through me. He might not be the man I'd envisioned losing my virginity to, but that man is currently fucking some random woman he'll never see again in a Vegas hotel room. *This man*, however, has been nothing but sweet and attentive and wonderful to me all night.

I giggle as his lips trace a path up my neck and consider what it would be like to actually give myself over to him. Everything he's doing—the way he touches me, the way his lips feel on my body—is amazing. Now, though, I'm suddenly feeling the effects of that after-dinner drink. The fountains in front of us look like a big moving blob of water, and the notes of the music blend together in a way that feels over-whelming.

I want to talk to Audrey. I want to ask her what I should do here. But knowing that she had a one-night stand last summer that resulted in pregnancy and her facing single motherhood when the baby is born, I already know what she'd say. I'm on the pill, though, and I can make sure he wears a condom too. Double protection. Still, accidents happen, and I don't want to be a single mom. The only way to avoid that, though, is to wait until you're married to have sex.

Yes! That's it, my brain screams. *Tell him you can't have sex until you're married.*

When I say that, his chest shakes with a low chuckle. "Okay, let's get married, then. We *are* in Vegas, after all."

"I didn't come to Vegas to get married." I'm proud of myself for remembering this fact right now when everything is starting to feel fuzzy.

"Neither did I," he says, then pulls my earlobe between his teeth. "But we'd be good together, don't you think?" He takes one of his arms that was around my waist and moves it up, sliding his hand between his suit jacket that I'm wearing and my dress so that he can cup my breast in his hand. His thumb toys with my nipple in a way that has me instantly crossing my legs to relieve some of the pressure building there.

Right now I want to have sex with him. But I don't want to be a single mom, either. *Marriage is a good solution*, my brain tells me, and in my drunken state, I don't even think to question it.

"Okay," I sigh, leaning the back of my head against his shoulder. "Let's get married, then."

He spins me around to face him and smacks a big, wet kiss on my lips. "Pretty sure I'm the luckiest guy in Vegas."

"Because you're going to hit the jackpot tonight?" In my mind, this is the funniest thing I've ever said, and I almost collapse into another fit of giggles.

He's laughing right along with me, pulling me into his arms. "Exactly." Then he flags down a taxi, and as we pile in, he asks, "Where's the closest place to get married?"

"You have a marriage license already?" the guy asks.

Brock and I both let out big, drunk sighs. "Nope."

"You're in luck," he says, "the Marriage License Bureau is open until midnight, so I can get you down there with just enough time to get your license, then bring you back to a chapel."

Brock flashes his shiny, white grin at me, then says, "So we're definitely doing this, right?"

When I nod in agreement, my head keeps bobbing up and down until I feel like I'm going to be sick. So I lean back against the headrest and crack the window open, breathing in the fresh air as we go speeding down The Strip.

"They're not going to approve the license if you two are wasted," the driver says.

"We're not wasted, just tipsy. Right, babe?"

My eyes are closed, and it doesn't really register that he's talking to me, until he squeezes my thigh. "Right?"

"Yep, just tipsy," I lie. "I'm tired, too." The long day and night, combined with all the alcohol we've consumed, have me feeling like I want to lay my head in his lap and sleep.

"Alright, we'll be at the bureau in five minutes," the driver says. "You'll need identification."

"You've done this before, I take it?" Brock asks.

"Several times a night," the guy responds.

My eyes stay closed as they chat, and it feels like only seconds later Brock is shaking me awake. "You sure about this?" he asks, pressing a kiss to my forehead in the sweetest, gentlest way.

"Positive." In fact, this is probably the best idea I've ever had. Or ever agreed to? At this point, I've lost track of who suggested this in the first place.

My head pounds, the pain so intense I wake up wanting to cry. Everything aches. Do I have the flu? I had it once when I was twelve and it felt a lot like this—a lot like wanting to die. My stomach flips over in a way that has me thinking I'm going to vomit, but then it must flip back the right way because the feeling passes.

Where the hell am I? Everything feels like it's moving. Maybe I'm on a boat?

I breathe through my nose because I think that's what you're supposed to do when you're in pain? Why does everything hurt? I try to remember the last thing I was doing before I went to sleep, and that's when it hits me: I'm in Paris! No, that doesn't make sense; I can't be in Paris. I was in Las Vegas yesterday. Yes . . . *Vegas. The game. Dinner afterward. The casino. Brock flirting with me. Whiskey sours. Colt demanding I leave. The woman in the pink dress. My broken heart. The hotel room floor. Brock's text.*

I haven't opened my eyes, but I can feel the tears leaking down my face. And the memories just keep coming.

The elevator ride down to the casino. Brock flirting with me, taking me to dinner. Candles and an outdoor bistro. The Eiffel Tower. And then it gets fuzzy . . . A car ride somewhere? Paperwork? Elvis?

No, the last things don't make sense. We were at dinner, we left, the Eiffel Tower was above us, then we walked across the street where there were lights and music and water.

I hear movement next to me, so I open my eyes. The stark morning light through the hotel room windows blinds me at first, and I squeeze my eyes shut again. Did I not pull the curtains shut last night? No, that can't be right. Audrey was already back in the room asleep when I went out, and it was pitch black in there. She had to have pulled the curtains shut.

I crack my eyes open ever so slowly, trying to let myself adjust to the light. My head pounds harder, begging me to just go back to sleep. Anything to escape this pain.

My eyes are open probably halfway when the body in bed across from me comes into focus. *Brock.*

Fuck, what am I doing in bed with Brock Lester? We flirted, yes. We went out to dinner. But why am I in his hotel room, and not my own? I'm lying on my right side, so I reach out my left hand to nudge him awake. And just when my fingers poke his shoulder, that's when I see it. Sitting prominently on my left ring finger, the stone catches the light, shooting rainbow daggers back into my eyes. I pull my arm back quickly, suddenly not wanting to wake him, but it's too late.

He opens his eyes, takes one look at me, and says, "Why are you still here?"

Ouch. This is not the Brock I remember from last night— the one who flirted with me shamelessly, told me I was beautiful, kissed me like he meant it, and apparently . . . married me?

My jaw drops open in shock as I consider his question and this reality. He doesn't remember that we're married. Maybe we're not? Maybe this ring is some sort of sick joke.

When I fail to respond, he says, "You were much more talkative, and prettier, when we were both drunk."

I need to say something, but I'm at such a loss for words. I've never been spoken to like this before, so I have no idea how I'm supposed to respond. Is this what it's always like "the morning after?"

Instead of saying anything, I hold up my left hand in front of his face.

"What the fuck?" he says, and as he goes to grab my hand for a closer inspection, we both notice the ring on his finger. His hand pauses midair, and he looks from it to me, then rolls on his back and groans out "Fuck!" at the top of his lungs. His fists are clenched and so are his teeth, and every muscle in his upper body flexes in rage. It's enough to actually scare me out of my stupor.

I jump off the bed and hold my palm to my forehead, pressing to relieve some of the pressure, as I stare down at him. "What the hell was that, Brock?"

My eyes flick from him where he's lying on the bed, to the hotel phone on the nightstand. Room 712. I still don't know where I am, exactly, but at least I have a room number. And at least I'm fully clothed, unlike him. He's in nothing but boxers, eyes transfixed on the ceiling.

"That was the sound of someone whose girlfriend is going to kill them."

"You have a girlfriend? Seriously?" Of all the things I should be upset about right now, I choose to focus on this?

"Yeah."

"Then what the fuck was last night?" I can feel the bile sloshing around in my stomach, threatening to come up at any minute as I continue to press on my forehead because it feels like if I don't, my brain might explode.

He glances over at me like I'm trash that got stuck to the bottom of his shoe and ended up on his hotel room floor. "I was just trying to piss your brother off. *It didn't mean anything.*"

"Piss Jameson off? Why?"

"None of your goddamn business, Jules."

Who is this asshole, and how is he so entirely different from the man I was with last night? "So everything last night . . . it was all just an act? A lie?"

The bile sloshes around more, burning as it creeps up into my esophagus in waves that mimic the shame and anger flowing through me.

He looks toward the floor-to-ceiling windows of what I'm now noticing is a pretty nice suite—not the kind with a separate bedroom, but there's a couch, chairs, and a table over in one corner of the spacious room, and a kitchen with an island and several chairs in the other corner.

Then he looks back at me, his eyes sweeping up and down my body. Given how hungover I am, I can imagine what I look like standing there in my sparkly dress from last night, my hair a mess, my makeup smeared from the tears.

"Honey," he says, like I'm the most pitiful creature in the world, "guys like me don't go for girls like you."

I grab my phone off the nightstand, then sprint for what I hope is the bathroom door. Luckily, I guess right, and I shut and lock it behind me, then collapse, my knees crashing onto the tile floor as I lunge for the toilet and empty the contents of my stomach. It's probably at least a half an hour before I stop retching, even though it's been nothing but dry heaving for most of that time.

Brock hasn't come to check on me, but I also appreciate that he's not kicking me out of the room in my state. How sad is it that my standards are so low, I'm thankful my husband isn't throwing me out into the hallway?

Finally, I open the map app on my phone and check to see where I am. Not in my own hotel, as it turns out. I try to stand, but my legs are shaking like crazy, and I collapse back onto the floor. I can't ask Brock for help. I don't even want to go out there and see him again, and I don't really feel safe in his presence after the way he reacted to finding out we're married.

Pulling out my phone, I text Jameson the hotel name and room number I noted on the phone earlier.

JULES

I need you to come get me.

I think about what Brock said about wanting to piss him off, and it makes me wonder what bad blood exists between them. Suddenly, I'm terrified that Jameson will kill him, and it'll be my fault.

JULES

You should bring Colt with you.

Second only to Brock, Colt is the last person I want to see right now. But he's generally level-headed and never gets truly upset about anything. More than once I've seen him calm my brother down.

JAMESON

What the hell are you doing there? You're supposed to be in your hotel room.

JULES

Well obviously I'm not. Just come get me and I'll explain when you get here.

And then I set my phone on the floor and dry heave into the toilet a few more times. If this is what being hungover is like, why would anyone drink? It makes me think of all the mornings my dad was bleary-eyed but cracked a beer for breakfast anyway because he claimed it chased the hangover away.

That's the model Dad set for us: alcohol and bad decisions.

I watched him go down a dark path. His heartbreak while my mom was dying led to heavier drinking, the drinking led to bad decisions that nearly bankrupted his company and broke our family apart, and the inability to control that drinking led to him walking away.

In retrospect, his leaving probably saved us. I don't want to think about what Audrey's and my life would have been like if he'd stayed. Jameson was a better father figure to us than our dad ever was.

And I don't want to go down "Flynn Road," as Dad calls it. It's the same road his father walked before him, succumbing to alcoholism and a premature death from it. And it only took one night in Vegas, with too many drinks and a broken heart, to have me following in my father's footsteps.

I will never be him. I won't allow it.

I owe it to my family, and to myself, to be better than he was. It's why I've been so damn careful. Until now.

The banging on the hotel room door starts a few minutes later. Or maybe I've dozed off with my head on my arms where they're folded across the toilet seat? There are angry voices in the hallways outside the bathroom door, then Jameson knocks and says, "Jules, open the door."

I push up to standing, holding on to the countertop for support as I walk to the door. And when it's open, Colt's standing there. Jameson's behind him with one hand around Brock's neck, while Brock holds his hands in the air, saying, "I swear I didn't touch her, man."

"Shit, Tink." Colt's words are a whisper as he reaches his hand out to me. And without thinking, I extend my left hand into his grip. He freezes when he sees the ring, then holds up my hand for Jameson and Brock to see. "What the fuck happened last night?"

And that's when all hell breaks loose. Jameson's got Brock on the floor before I can even blink, and Colt scoops me up, cradling me protectively in his arms as he stands in the doorway of the bathroom looking at the skirmish below. I wince when Jameson's fist connects with Brock's jaw, but Colt turns us toward the door. "Do you have everything?"

"My phone." I nod my chin toward the bathroom where it sits on the countertop, and he reaches over to grab it with one hand while holding me to him with his other arm like I weigh nothing. "We'll be outside."

He flips the lock to the hotel room door, propping it open as we exit—I assume, in case he needs to get back in there to help my brother—but he doesn't set me down in the hallway. "Do you want to talk about it?"

"I *never* want to talk about this. In fact, promise me now that you'll never bring it up again."

I watch his throat bob and his lips twist together before he says, "This wasn't your fault."

"Promise me, Colt. We're not talking about this now, nor ever again."

He sighs, and it's a deep movement that, from my vantage point in his arms, feels like it deflates him. "Okay, Tink. I promise."

Chapter Twenty-Seven

COLT

Present Day

"You're not saying anything," she whispers, the sound escaping from where she's pressed up against my chest, with my arms wrapped around her and my shirt wet from her tears. It's so similar to the way I cradled her in my arms that morning in Vegas that it has my heart seizing. At least this time, we're in the quiet of our own room at the inn, and hopefully by now she knows I'd do just about anything to make sure she feels safe.

I'm so consumed by my own guilt that I don't know what to say. She got drunk and married him because I hurt her. Not intentionally, but it was me being oblivious to her feelings that drove her straight into his arms. All for what? Some random chick I never saw or thought of again. I was supposed to be taking care of her, and knowing that not only did I fail her in that, but I actually caused the whole situation, has a knife twisting inside my gut.

It didn't mean anything. I think his words—the same ones I said to her in that alley a couple of weeks back—will haunt me forever. She deserves so much more than that. She deserves to mean *everything* to someone.

"I had no idea."

"About what?"

"About why it happened. I mean, I got the sense that you had a crush on me when you were younger, but I thought you outgrew that when you were old enough to figure out . . ."

"That you were the biggest fuckboy in the league?" she suggests when I don't provide an end to that sentence. Then she lets out a small laugh and relaxes against me. "Yeah, I always hoped there was more to you than your reputation. And I think I was right."

"I think maybe you're the only one who ever tried to see beneath the mask."

"What Gabriel and Cheri did to you . . . Colt, if I'd have known, I don't think I would have suggested forgiving them."

The fact that she is even considering what happened between me and my brother, right now, after telling me what happened to her . . . I don't know if she's just extremely empathetic, or if she's trying to turn the conversation away from the huge bomb she just dropped.

"You didn't," I remind her. "You said I didn't have to forgive them, that I could just choose to move on. And that advice, I think, begs the question: why haven't *you* moved on from what Brock did to you?"

"Besides the fact that this was only six years ago, not fifteen?"

I can tell she's joking, trying to buy time to decide how to answer the question. "Touché."

"It's not that I can't move on because I haven't forgiven Brock. It's because what happened back in Vegas proved to me that I can't trust *myself*."

"I think what you learned, Jules, is a lesson we all learn the hard way . . . you make really bad decisions when you're drunk."

"No. I learned that when I let go of control, I fuck up my life. Alcohol is one way of losing control, but there are others."

"Like what?" I ask, wondering how deep her control issues go.

"I don't know." I can feel her shrug her shoulder where it rests against my bicep. "I never test my limits. Being vulnerable in any way . . . it's a no from me."

"Jules, that's . . ." I stop myself before I say *ridiculous*. How can she possibly grow, or be a fully functioning human being, if she keeps herself so closed off? ". . . limiting your life experiences, don't you think?"

She shrugs again.

"What are the things you'd want to do if you weren't afraid of losing control?"

"You're not my shrink, Colt."

I can already feel her walls coming back up. "No, I'm not. But unlike your therapist, I'm here right now. And you need to talk this out."

The hum of her disapproval rattles around in her throat, but her fingers trace the tattoos on my right biceps.

"Let's play a little game," I suggest. "Here's the sentence frame: *if I wasn't afraid of . . . blank, I would or wouldn't . . . blank*. I'll go first."

"Okay." Her agreement is tentative, like she might change her mind if I don't offer something worthy.

"If I wasn't afraid of getting hurt again, I would drop my one night only rule. Your turn."

She pauses, sighing as if she's not sure where to start. "If I wasn't afraid of making terrible decisions, I would try more than two drinks in a night just to see what it's like."

"If you ever want to get drunk, Jules, I'll happily stay sober and make sure you're safe. You can try drinking again, and I won't let you do anything you'll regret."

She shifts on the bed, curling into me like she's burrowing into blankets. She's trying to get cozy with me, and I don't have the typical urge to get up, move away, invite her to leave. No, I want Jules curled up with me for as long as she wants to be here.

"Maybe someday," she says finally. "Your turn."

"If I wasn't afraid of becoming irrelevant, I wouldn't try so hard to live up to my reputation."

"Hmmmm." That sound rattles against me again, and I'm about to remind her that it's her turn now when she says, "If I wasn't afraid of losing control, I would date."

"You're afraid of losing control on a date?"

"No questions, Colt," she says. "Just finish the sentence frame. Your turn."

My chest shakes with laughter because I'm finally figuring her out. Knowing she lashes out when she's scared—especially of being vulnerable—makes it so much easier to understand her.

"If I wasn't afraid of hurting someone else the way I was hurt," I say, releasing a heavy breath, "I would be open to a relationship."

"You think you'd hurt someone else the same way you were hurt?"

Of course not. After what Gabriel did to me, there's no way I'd ever cheat. But there are a lot of other ways to hurt someone just as much.

"No questions, Jules. Just finish the damn sentence," I say, mimicking her.

"Fine," she huffs like she's irritated that I used her strategy on her. "If I wasn't afraid of losing control, I wouldn't still be a virgin."

I freeze. I think I stop breathing and my blood stops flowing, because everything inside of me comes to a standstill. I couldn't have heard her correctly. And then my body jolts itself back alive in a flash of heat that flows across my skin painfully.

"What now?" I croak out the words,

"No questions . . ." she says, but I tighten my grip on her with my left arm and use my right hand to tilt her chin up so she's looking at me.

"Jules, you can't lead with a sentence like that and not offer an explanation."

"I don't owe you an explanation, Colt."

"You're right. But . . ." But what? I don't deserve to know this about her, or know anything else that she doesn't want to tell me. ". . . maybe talking about it would help?"

"I've talked about it ad nauseam with my therapist and my sister."

"And has that helped?"

"I'm still a virgin, aren't I?" The question is sassy and sardonic, but it seems to hide real pain—or real fears, at the very least.

"Can I ask you a question that's probably going to piss you off?" In response, she rolls her eyes as if to say, *Everything you do pisses me off*. But I think I'm learning that this is just part of her defensive strategy. "How do you know for sure? I mean, you were so drunk you don't remember getting married. Are you *positive* that douchebag didn't take advantage of you?"

She burrows her cheek into my chest. "Look at you getting all possessive," she teases, trying to redirect the conversation so she doesn't have to answer the question. I wait her out and finally, she says, "I was having my period. I still had my tampon in that morning."

"God, Jules," I say as I stroke her cheek. "I'm so fucking sorry."

"It's not your fault."

"Yeah, it really is. I always felt guilty because, even though I made sure you got back to your room safely, it didn't stop everything that happened afterward. Now I know that it *truly* is my fault."

"I was in charge of my own emotions and my own decision-making that night, Colt. I'm the one who's responsible. Just like I'm the one who has to decide when I can trust someone enough to move past what happened."

"What's preventing you from taking that last step?"

Why am I asking her these questions? Why am I prying into something that isn't my business? Is it because she's quickly become one of the few people I trust enough to share my secrets? Or is it because I can't stop thinking about her? Can't stop imagining us together? Have pictured myself having sex with her almost as often as I've taken a breath lately? Jerked off to images of us together? Want her so bad that I'm having a fucking crisis of conscience over her?

"You mean, besides the lack of quality men in this world?" she says.

"Yeah."

She sighs, and I think she's done with the conversation. But then she says, "I think sex is one of those things where I would have to trust another person implicitly in order to be able to . . . do it. And I've never met a guy I can trust like that."

I have so many thoughts about that—about the fact that sex doesn't have to be an emotional experience, how it can just be about blowing off steam and feeling good. But I guess I don't have the control issues or the fear that Jules does, so it's easy for me to disassociate sex from emotions.

"You've never met a single guy you trust enough to have sex with?"

She lets out a little snort of laughter. "The circle of guys I trust, and the circle of guys who want to sleep with me . . . they just never seem to overlap."

Do you trust me? The question is on the tip of my tongue, but I don't dare ask it.

Her family is my family, and they don't want me with her. Jameson is my best friend, so he told me what everybody else was thinking: I'm not good enough for Jules. And they're right. I'll hurt her in the end, or she'll hurt me. Either way, I can't risk damaging my relationship with the Flynns. Even if, for a brief moment, every once in a while, in quiet times like this when it's just the two of us, I go stupid and think there's a chance Jules and I could actually work out.

Chapter Twenty-Eight

COLT

"Colt," she whispers while poking me in the stomach. It's still dark out, but the light is starting to creep in.

I rub one eye with the back of my hand but can't rub the other because she's got her head on my pillow, our faces pressed together, so that I don't have access to it. "What time is it?"

She snuggles in closer. Our legs are already intertwined, as we apparently wrapped ourselves around each other in our sleep. As she shifts, her thigh presses into my cock and she laughs, a low, throaty sound that has me growing even harder against her. She hums her approval. "Time for you to listen to the brilliant idea I just had."

"Okay." The word is full of trepidation because she sounds wide awake and excited. After her sadness before falling asleep last night, this has me on high alert.

She keeps her eyes locked on me when she says, "I think you should be the one to take my virginity."

"No." I don't even think about my denial before it's out of my mouth. I don't have to. There's no way I'm sleeping with my best friend's little sister. *Especially* now that I know she's never had sex with anyone else. Her face doesn't fall, and she doesn't look crushed—which I take as a good sign. She just continues to stare at me like she's waiting for me to say more. "Jules, you deserve your first time to be with someone special."

"And you don't think you're special?" she challenges, but there's something in her eyes that softens.

"I think our situation is already complicated enough. It's hard enough to keep my hands off you when I'm supposed to. You *asked* me to keep my hands off you unless it was absolutely necessary, and now you're asking me to have sex with you?"

"Oh, I'm sorry," she says. "Am I sending you mixed signals? How's that feel? Confusing, isn't it?"

"That's even more of a reason we shouldn't have sex. Adding sex to our already confusing situation would just make things that much harder."

She snorts out a little laugh, which is quickly becoming one of the things I adore about her. "I don't think you could get much harder." She presses herself against my length as she runs her hand up my chest and rests it along the side of my neck.

"Jules, no. This is a terrible idea."

"I told you last night that there was no overlap between the guys I trust, and the guys who would want to sleep with me. But when I woke up this morning, with your hugely hard dick pressed into my stomach, I realized that *you* are the overlap."

I could tell her that I wake up this hard every morning, that it has nothing to do with the way my body is wrapped around hers, but that would be a lie. And more importantly, it would hurt her.

"It's the perfect solution," she says, seeming so sure of herself. "Because I know you're never going to have feelings for me, so I don't have to worry about getting hurt. And because the relationship is fake, the sex would be too."

She only wants me for sex. The realization guts me—it's exactly what I was afraid of. She's becoming my favorite person more and more each day, but to her, I'm just someone who can fulfill a physical need. But my body doesn't seem to care. My dick is raring to go.

"You can't fake sex, Jules. It doesn't work like that."

"Really? Because based on what I've heard from other women, they're faking it a lot of the time."

"Trust me, Tink," I say, unable to help the way my voice drops low as I bring my hand up and tuck her hair behind her ear. "You wouldn't need to fake it."

She presses herself forward, into me. "I'm going to need you to prove that theory."

"This is the worst idea," I groan, even as my dick grows harder. "We can't go there."

"What about everything *except* sex?"

The temptation to make her beg for me to fuck her, and then deliver, is so overwhelming that my hips thrust forward into her of their own accord. *Fuck.* I shouldn't have done that, because now she's wrapping her leg over my hip, and using her calf to pull me forward so I'm lined up with her center.

"Fuck, Jules." I rest my forehead on hers. "We can't."

"Why not? What's going to happen if we do?"

I'm going to fall for you. "One of us will get hurt." And that "one" is bound to be me.

"Colt, I already told you, I'm not under any illusions that you'll develop feelings for me. And I won't let myself have feelings for you. So it's perfect."

The thought of her having sex with me to get over that hurdle but it meaning nothing to her, bothers me so much, even though in the past that's always been what I'm looking for in a hookup—something casual, where no actual feelings are involved.

But this time, my feelings are involved. Can I do this with her, even knowing it means nothing to her?

Her hips tilt forward, sliding along the length of me again, and before I can talk myself out of it, I thrust forward to meet her. The low groan of pleasure she admits rattles through me.

"We've already kissed," she says, her tone way too seductive to ignore. Sliding her hand up to my jaw, she traces her thumb along my lower lip. "So that doesn't feel like it should be off limits."

"You are playing such a dangerous game right now," I growl before sinking my teeth into her thumb. I'm barely holding on by a thread, and she's lying here trying to gnaw through that last frayed string of my control.

"It's not dangerous, Colt." She pushes me onto my back and straddles me, hovering just above me. She's wearing my T-shirt and some skimpy underwear, and even though I'm in the sweats I put on last night when we got back from the party, I can feel the heat radiating off her through the thick fabric. "It's perfect."

Crossing her arms in front of her, she grips the fabric at the bottom of the shirt in each hand and raises her eyebrow at me. "Tell me not to take this shirt off and we can stop right here." She glances down at my crotch, where my dick is standing at attention as much as the fabric of my sweats will allow, and then she rolls her hips forward, pressing along my length. "But I don't think you want to stop."

I want to be the kind of person who's strong enough to resist her, to put a stop to this before we go any further. Instead, I say, "We're not having sex."

"I'm fine with that, as long as you give me an orgasm. I'd at least like to know that I'm capable of orgasming with someone other than myself."

"You've never . . .?"

With a shake of her head, she starts to lift her shirt slowly, like she's giving me time to stop her if I want to. Even though I should put a halt to this before we cross over into territory that we can't come back from, even though I'm going to enjoy this now, but it'll hurt later, I watch in fascination as the shirt rises to show me her creamy skin. There are three freckles on her abdomen, and I reach my thumb out, tracing them while I try to memorize their exact locations. Then the undersides of her breasts come into view, and *fuuuuuck*. She's stacked like the Playboy models in the magazines my friends and I used to steal from my neighbor's recycling bin.

"Fuck it."

I sit up quickly, my hands sliding under the shirt and ripping it up and over her head so fast she lets out a surprised gasp. Then my hands are on her breasts, cupping them so I can run my thumbs over her nipples, and she's holding my face in her hands and kissing me while she grinds herself against my cock.

I feel like a horny teenager with not enough control over my body any time she's around. Lying wrapped up in her limbs and trying to resist her while she offered herself up to me for the past few minutes has me already on the verge of exploding. If she keeps rubbing herself along me like that, with just the perfect amount of pressure, I'm going to come in my pants like a fucking amateur.

I kiss my way down her neck, and then take a moment to admire a sight I never thought I'd see. Her breasts spill out of my hands, her nipples pebbled under the rough pads of my thumbs, and below that her abdomen flexes and contracts as she controls the movement of her hips, and every time she pulls back, I can see the neatly trimmed V of curls through the sheer underwear, right where her body runs itself along my sweats.

As soft as they are, I'm wearing these pants like armor, knowing that if I remove them, I'll fuck her senseless. But I already told her that we're not having sex, and I need to stick to that, at least, since we're already hurdling over so many other lines.

There will be a lot to think about later, probably a lot to talk about too, but I don't care at this moment. All I care about is proving to her that she can let go of her iron grip on control long enough to come by someone else's hand . . . or mouth. I haven't decided yet.

My face descends to her breast, capturing her nipple and pulling it between my lips, smoothing around and over it with my tongue while Jules moans, "Yes, Colt!" and my cock surges up, seeking the friction of her body as it presses into mine. I suck her into my mouth until I hear that small grunt of pain, then pause and smooth my tongue over her again, before switching to the other breast. She hums approvingly as I give her other nipple the same attention, and her hips move faster as she grinds into me harder.

The familiar sensation at the base of my spine tells me I need to slow the fuck down before I'm coming in my pants, but the way she's rubbing herself up against me, so carefree and unguarded and willing to let me touch her in any way I want—it makes me hesitant to pull back. I don't want her mind to go into overdrive trying to figure out what it means if I slow us down, or worse yet, drawing the wrong conclusions.

"This is too good," I say, trying to explain myself, "and I'm too close. So I'm going to need you to stop pressing yourself up against my cock like that."

"Oh yeah," she says, her voice husky and teasing at the same time. "Or what?"

"Or I'm going to embarrass myself," I say. Trailing my mouth up the side of her neck, I nip at the cord of muscle there. "And I'd much rather focus on giving you that orgasm you requested."

"I need you to give me the kind of orgasm that has me seeing stars," she says as she reaches up and tugs on the gold necklace with the star engraved on it that she always wears.

"Jules," I say as I flip her onto her back, using my extended arm to prop myself up over her. "I'm going to give you the whole fucking supernova experience. And then every time you touch that necklace of yours, you're going to remember exactly how it feels to explode."

She relaxes into the bed and lets her knees fall to the

sides. Her thong is tiny, a soft black lace that's now drenched. Hooking my thumbs around the fabric, I press her legs together so I can slide them off her, then I press them to my face, breathing in her scent, before I tuck them into the pockets of my sweats, telling her, "I'm keeping these."

"Hey, I made those!"

"You *made* them?"

I have so many questions, but she just mumbles, "I'll tell you later," as her knees fall open again, baring that perfect pussy to me. Aside from the little V of curls at the top, she's completely bare—pink and shimmering with her arousal.

"So fucking pretty," I say, reaching a hand out to circle my fingers lightly over her clit. "The way you're so wet for me . . ." I bend down and press a kiss along the inside of her knee. "So needy."

Trailing kisses down her inner thigh as I continue circling her clit with light pressure, I make sure to keep my eyes on her face. I want this experience to be perfect for her. I'm confident she knows what she likes when she does this to herself, but since no one else has done this to her, she may not know how to tell me what she needs.

Her eyes flutter shut, and her hips raise to meet my hand, adding additional pressure where my fingers graze against her sensitive nerve endings. Okay, maybe she does know how to show me what she needs.

Increasing the speed as well as the pressure, I kiss my way up to the apex of her thighs and I breathe in deeply, inhaling her scent. And then, I slide my tongue from the back of her pussy all the way up to the front, pulling my fingers away as my tongue laps against her clit to match the tempo of her hips as they move against my mouth. Her soft pants turn into low moans of pleasure that have me teasing my fingers along her entrance.

As I lift my head, she whispers, "Please don't stop."

"Grab those pillows behind you and prop yourself up so you can watch. I want you to see what it looks like when someone takes care of you like this, and I want to watch you fall apart on my tongue."

She arches her back as she reaches for the pillows above her head, and the movement has the tips of my two fingers pressing into her entrance enough that her mouth falls open as she lets out a low, throaty groan. When I slide both fingers into her at once, she hisses out a "yes."

"Come on," I say when she freezes, focusing on me inside of her instead of on getting herself set up on those pillows. "Prop yourself up so you can see the way your greedy little pussy is devouring my fingers."

"Jesus, Colt." Eyes wide, she sits up enough to prop one elbow behind her and get the pillows situated under her upper back. Then she lies back against them, her eyes locked on me, and I curl my fingers up, stroking her from the inside.

She closes her eyes as her hips meet my fingers thrust for thrust. "Eyes on me," I say, and her eyes snap open. "I want you to watch every second of this, so that you remember the first person who ever made you scream their name."

"I won't be screaming your name," she says with a laugh.

I bend my head back down to her clit, circling it with my tongue before sucking it between my lips. The moan she lets out borders on a scream, so I lift my head again and say, "Want to bet?"

I'm determined to give her an orgasm that beats anything she's ever experienced and is more than she ever hoped for.

Using my tongue on her clit while my fingers sink deep inside her, I have her moaning and thrashing, chasing that orgasm in mere minutes. Trailing my free hand up her side, I skim my palm along her breast and over her nipple before I spread my thumb and fingers to grasp the base of her throat. I only apply light pressure, not enough to prevent her from breathing, but it sends her body into overdrive. Her hips slam into my fingers as she sets the tempo, and by the way she's gasping my name in between moans when she finally comes, I'd say I was successful in helping her let go of control long enough to show her who owns this pussy. Because as I pull my fingers out of her and use my tongue to lap up every bit of her cum, there's only one path forward . . . us, together.

"I love the way you taste," I tell her.

"Oh yeah? How do I taste?"

I lean forward, planting my elbow on the bed next to her shoulder as I bring my lips to her forehead. "Like you're mine."

"I didn't know 'mine' was a flavor," she says, her sass fully back intact like she didn't just fall apart on my tongue. "What does it taste like?"

"You."

Chapter Twenty-Nine

JULES

Colt's parents' house is chaotic and loud, but still warm and inviting. His aunt and uncle sit at the kitchen table, sipping tea and eating croissants while his cousin, Lane, plays video games with Colt's nephew, Simon. Simon is the spitting image of Gabriel—he has a dark complexion with dark brown hair like his dad, but he has his mom's pale eyes.

I know he said that sometimes his nephew comes down to Boston with his parents, and it makes me wonder how Colt feels every time he sees Simon, who is the literal embodiment of his brother's betrayal. He's also an incredibly good-natured teenage boy, and from what I can tell, he seems like he really looks up to his uncle.

Colt said yesterday that everything worked out exactly as it should have, which makes me think of the saying my mom used a lot: *Everything happens for a reason.* After she died, I hated that saying with the burning passion of a thousand suns. It felt like a lazy way to dismiss real pain and suffering with a casual promise of a better future.

But now, when I look at Colt's family and think about how different his life would have been if that baby had been his, or I think about how different my life would have been if my parents had both survived my mom's illness and my brother hadn't retired from hockey to raise us . . . I don't know that I disagree with the saying as much as I used to.

Both of those things led to good. Not that our lives wouldn't have each been good without those catastrophic events, but they'd be different. We definitely wouldn't be in this complicated as hell situation we're in . . . but it's feeling less complicated, and more real, by the minute.

Colt tightens his arm around my shoulder where we stand, leaning against the kitchen counter near the stove where his mom is heating the kettle to brew more tea.

"I got you that cinnamon kind you like," she tells Colt, and then asks me if I drink tea.

"Sometimes? I drink it like my dad used to, with some milk and sugar."

"How very Irish of you," Colt says and kisses the top of my head. "You want to try my favorite kind? I'm sure it's good with milk and sugar."

"Sure." I relax into his side, feeling more at peace than I've felt in a long time, despite the fact that Gabriel and Cheri are standing on the other side of the island. Based on their history, it should be awkward, but Colt seems more okay with it than he was yesterday. I'm trying not to read too much into it, though it does seem that me being here with him is what's making the difference.

"How are you feeling about round two of the playoffs?"

Gabriel asks him. Next to me, Colt stiffens the tiniest amount—it would be imperceptible to anyone not touching him.

"Good. Carolina's got a really strong defense this year, but so do we."

They talk for a few minutes about the game, and based on some of the details he mentions, I realize that Gabriel must follow his brother's career closely. As his mom hands us our mugs of tea, I wonder if Colt is picking up on this too.

"Jules and I are going to take our tea down to the pond. I want to show her where I learned to skate. But also," he says specifically to Gabriel, "I got tickets for Mom and Dad to come see the game on Thursday. I realize you guys probably have work and Simon probably has school, but I could get three more tickets if you guys want to join them."

Gabriel looks at Cheri, and her mouth pops open, but she seems lost for words.

"You don't have to decide now," Colt says quickly. "Just let me know."

And with that, he moves his hand to the small of my back and guides me through the sliding glass door that leads to a raised deck. We follow the stairs down to the ground, and then take the steps built into the steep hillside to the pond below. When we get to the dock, Colt unfurls a heavy wool blanket that he must have grabbed on our way out.

The crisp spring morning air smells damp, the way soil does after it rains. He wraps the blanket around his shoulders and then sides so that his butt is on the blanket and there's just enough space between his legs for me to sit on it too. I settle in, leaning back against him and sipping my tea as he pulls the blanket around us to ward off the chill.

"I'm proud of you for what you did back there," I say.

"Inviting them to the game?"

"Yeah. I know it took a lot for you to extend that olive branch."

He exhales and his breath skims the top of my head and then condenses with the mist surrounding us. "It was a lot easier than I'd worked it up to be in my mind."

"I think that, maybe, that's what moving on feels like."

"Yeah . . . maybe."

Sitting on the dock watching the mist come off the water and the sun try to peek through the grey clouds, I marvel at the fact that I'm in Colt's arms . . . and have been for the last few hours. I was still ravenous for him after that single mind-blowing orgasm early this morning, but he wouldn't let me take it any further than we had.

Instead, he wrapped me in his arms and fucking cuddled me, and I fell back asleep while pressed up against his chest with his arms around me. I woke up at some point when he got up and went into the bathroom, and I'm pretty sure he took care of that erection that had been pushed up against me when I fell asleep because it was absent, and he was more relaxed when he came back to bed to pull me right back into his arms.

When the alarm went off a few hours ago, I was afraid things would be awkward, especially since the only other time I'd ever woken up in a guy's bed had been a nightmare. But everything has felt so natural, so easy, that part of me is waiting for the other shoe to drop.

"So you learned to skate on this pond in the winters, I assume?" I ask after a few moments of silence.

"Yeah. I probably spent more hours of my life on this

pond, skating in the winter and swimming in the summer, than anywhere else, ever."

I look out across the "pond," which is actually larger than a lot of lakes in New England. "When I was a kid, my mom used to take us up to her aunt's house on Lake Sunapee in the summers. Sometimes we'd just go for the weekend, and other times we'd stay for a week or two. It was this amazing old hunting lodge overlooking the water, and I'd go down to the dock and just sit there in the shade and read in the mornings. It was my absolute favorite place in the world, but I haven't been back in years."

"What happened to it?"

"Nothing. It's still in the family, but my dad never took us up there once Mom died—he never got along well with her family. I inquired about buying the house last year. I'd love to remodel it and make it something that could be enjoyed year-round. I had all these visions of going up there with my whole family for holidays and such. But my great-aunt's kids are not interested in selling. Apparently, it's their favorite place, too."

"I love that you have a favorite place," he says. "But I'm sorry you don't get to go there anymore."

I shrug against him, and he hugs me tighter. "Is this your favorite place?"

"I don't think I have a favorite place. I loved it here when I was a kid, but this is my first time sitting on this dock in fifteen years. It's not even the same dock. The old one was long, narrow, and wooden. This new one is quite a bit nicer."

I glance along the floating platform that we're sitting on, which is connected to the shore by a short, permanent dock.

It's coated in droplets of water and, despite the blanket beneath me, I realize that my jeans are damp.

"Did it rain overnight?" I ask. I didn't hear the rain, but there's a layer of moisture clinging to everything, and I can't tell if it's just from the mist.

"Not sure," he says, his whispered words brushing up against my ear. "I was too busy listening to you scream my name to notice whether it was raining."

"First of all, that was this morning, not last night. And second, I did *not* scream your name."

"Want me to demonstrate what you sounded like?" His voice is husky as he smooths his hand against my stomach, anchoring me back against his chest. "Or maybe"—he toys with the button at the top of my jeans—"I should just slide my hand in here and do it again? You'll have to be quieter this time, because sound carries over water, and if we go back to talking at a normal volume, they'll be able to hear everything up at the house, and across the pond, too."

"Don't you dare," I whisper, even as my hips tilt forward, seeking out his hand. I know they can't see us from the house because of the trees, but I didn't realize they could hear us. "I do not need the mortification of everyone listening to me having an orgasm on your parents' dock."

"Jules, now that I've given you *one*, I kind of want to see how many times I can make you come. I bet I could get at least two out of you right in a row, maybe more."

An uneasy feeling washes over me. I can't explain where it comes from, but the uncertainty and mistrust are there, rearing their ugly heads. "Why? Do you compare notes with your teammates to see who can dole out the most orgasms in one go, or something?" I'm joking—it's not like I really believe he does this. But guys *do* talk, and I don't want to be the subject of their conversations.

The sudden clink of his mug on the dock sends a few birds scattering out of the tree above us, their black wings taking shape against the mist coming off the water as they swoop low over the pond. Colt uses both hands to grip my waist, lifting and turning me so I'm sitting on his knees. I reach down and set my mug on the dock as well, thankful I'd almost finished my tea so I didn't spill it everywhere.

"Do you *really* think I'd do something like that, Jules?" Annoyed notes of frustration ring out in his quiet, but tense, voice.

"What can I say? I know hockey players." I give a little shrug to hide how uncomfortable I am. It was so much easier to talk about my past last night, shrouded in the darkness. Sitting a foot from him and looking him dead in the eye in broad daylight is different.

"Really?" The word is skepticism come alive. "So your brother, then?"

"No, obviously not him. I'm sure he slept around a fair bit before Lauren, but I'm confident he doesn't talk about their sex life with other people."

"Jameson's always been incredibly discreet," he confirms. "So what about Drew, then?"

"God no, he was so gone for Audrey the minute he saw her again. He's like a goddamn golden retriever with the way he needs all her love and attention."

"Okay, so what other hockey players do you know?"

I lift an eyebrow but don't say anything.

"If this is about Brock fucking Lester, and you're lumping me in with him, I've got some thoughts about that." His jaw clenches so tightly I'm afraid he's going to shatter some teeth, so I cup his face in my hands and smooth my thumbs over his cheeks, hoping he'll relax a bit.

"I hate that what he did has colored my perception of all men, but it is what it is. He wrecked my confidence and my ability to trust myself."

"Jules, let's get one thing straight. Brock is an asshole and what he did was wrong. He was too fucking blind to see what he had right in front of him—"

"Story of my life." I don't mean for that to slip out, to reference that Colt, also, apparently couldn't see me right there in front of him, despite how desperate I was for him to notice me. But it comes out anyway.

"Don't you dare compare me to him," Colt practically growls in an attempt to keep his voice low. "I *saw* you. But you were my best friend's little sister, and I was never planning to let myself see you *like that*. I also wasn't at a place in my life where I could trust any woman enough to let her get close to me, and there was no way in hell I'd have slept with you and then just never talked to you again, which was what ninety percent of my hookups were."

"And the other ten percent?" I ask, letting my curiosity get the best of me.

"I definitely had some repeat hookups, but that's all they ever were to me."

"And now? What about us?"

I'm so fucking proud of myself for asking this question. It would be so easy to give in to the fear of discussing the future of this relationship, to ride out this high and wait to see where it goes. But I deserve to know where we stand right now, even if that might evolve and change over time.

He brushes his lips against the bridge of my nose. "We're not ready for this conversation, Tink. I know you think we are. Hell, maybe you are, but I'm not. You've got work to do to be able to trust me enough for this to be real, and I've got work to do to prove to you that I'm worth trusting."

What does that even mean? Just as I'm about to ask, a throat clears from behind me and the floating dock rocks as someone steps onto it.

"Ummmm," Gabriel's uncertain voice sounds from behind us, "I'm supposed to tell you that apparently there's cake? And Mom and Dad would like you to join us for it."

I turn my head, and he's got his arm bent over his head as she scratches the back of his neck, clearly uncomfortable to have interrupted our conversation. It seems impossible that we didn't hear him coming, so either he's some sort of stealthy ninja, or we must have been intently focused on each other. I pray that we were quiet enough that he didn't hear what we were saying, since the whole point of this ruse was that he and Cheri would think Colt was happily engaged and had moved on.

"Okay," Colt says as I stand, "we're coming." He gets up, but I don't miss the wince as he stands, and when my eyes flick over to Gabriel, I see that he didn't miss it either.

"Thanks," Gabriel says, "for the ticket offer. I have to see if I can get someone to cover my shift at the hospital and make sure Simon can miss school on Thursday and Friday. But as long as that works out, we'd love to be there for the game."

Colt's gaze is locked on his brother, and I watch his throat bob as he swallows down whatever emotions he's working through. I'm not sure what he's feeling, but it certainly seems like these two are long overdue for a private conversation.

"You know what," I say quickly. "I'm going to run up to the house so I can use the bathroom before we have cake. You guys take your time." Turning, I practically sprint up the dock, across the outcropping of rocks, and up the staircase built into the hillside, all the while hoping that giving them a few minutes alone is the right choice.

Chapter Thirty

JULES

Colt's body stills over mine as he says, "Are you sure you're ready for this?"

My entire core clenches, feeling the emptiness that I need him to fill. I run my hands up along his sides marveling at the way his cut muscles create ridges and valleys.

"Oh, believe me, I am more than ready." When he still doesn't move, I say, "Colt, now."

He hesitates a moment longer, and then he pushes into me, filling me so completely that there's no room for anything else. I'm not even sure there's space for air to fill my lungs. Nothing in my entire collection of vibrators could have possibly prepared me for this fullness, this feeling of being joined together with him, or the way it feels as he brushes his fingers over my nipple while he says, "I'm going to make you come so hard, they'll hear you screaming in the suburbs."

I close my eyes as I adjust to his size and the delicious

sensation of him dragging his cock along my inner walls, and then pushing back into me, filling me as far as I can take him. "Yes. Please, Colt . . ." I groan out the pleading words.

I'm about to tell him how amazing it feels now that he's finally inside me, but something is poking me in my side, a persistent nudging that won't go away. I go to swat at it when I open my eyes back up and realize that I'm in Colt's fancy SUV.

Fuck. It felt so real, just like it always does in my dreams.

My underwear is so damp I'm worried he'll be able to smell my arousal. I'm so turned on that I just want to close my eyes and jump right back into the dream. But that poking at my side happens again, and I glance over to find Colt looking at me. "Hey . . . we're home."

"Okay," I croak out because my throat is so thick with longing I can hardly speak.

"You alright?"

"Yeah, I was just in the middle of a dream, is all."

"Yeah, there was quite a bit of moaning in that dream," he teases.

Shit, what is wrong with me—why did I have to say that? Why couldn't I have just said my throat hurt or something? And as much as I try not to let it happen, I can feel the flush creep up my neck and into my cheeks. He smirks at me like he knows exactly what I was dreaming about. It probably isn't hard to figure out.

"So," he says, "Walsh just texted, and he and Marissa have a babysitter for tonight so they're going out to dinner, and they want to know if we want to meet up for drinks afterward? Can you make that work?"

He sounds so hopeful, and the fact that he *wants* me to go

has me wanting to say yes. But the responsible part of me knows I shouldn't. It's been a long weekend of travel, and I should unpack. Plus, I have to work tomorrow morning, and 5:30 a.m. comes at the same time every day, no matter how late you stay up the night before.

You'd probably stay up reading anyway, my brain reminds me, because it knows all about my romance book addiction and is using it against me.

"I have to work tomorrow . . ." I don't finish my sentence because I can't make myself say no, even though I know I should.

"Come on, Jules. We won't stay out too late. We need them to believe that we're engaged, and I'm sure my fiancée would be too smart to let me go out on my own."

Oh. So that hopeful note in his voice wasn't because he wanted to spend more time with me, it's so we can keep up appearances. I shake my head at my own hopeful stupidity.

What did you expect?

"So you're saying that you're not trustworthy enough to be out on your own without your 'fiancée'"—I actually use air quotes around the word to emphasize our fake status, mostly because I need the reminder myself. He doesn't seem to have much trouble remembering that this isn't real—"and you need me there to babysit you?"

"No, I need you there to protect me from the women who will be all over me if you're not around." The blasé way he says this, as if he knows women will flock to him even though they know he's engaged . . . it pisses me off. I don't know why. I'm not sure if I'm angry that other women would move in on "my man," or if I'm pissed on his behalf that having to fight off women constantly is his norm. Or am I just jealous?

That's when it hits me: this is the dynamic that he created and has played into since he was a nineteen-year-old rookie with a broken heart. He's chosen to remain single; he's flaunted the many women and his party persona very publicly. And he's done it all to show Cheri and Gabriel that—whether it was true or not—he didn't want what they had.

Now that I understand his past, everything about his fuck-boy status makes a lot more sense. But what I still don't know is whether he actually didn't want to be tied down, or if it was a defense mechanism to protect his heart and make it seem like he was much happier this way.

"I don't really feel like going out," I say, wanting to retreat to my bedroom, take care of this ache between my legs that's left over from my dream, and then sleep until tomorrow morning. I look out the window at the back door, wanting to get inside and away from him so I can figure out what I'm feeling . . . because suddenly, I'm sad. Sad for him, and sad that I had to go and fall for someone who doesn't even want to have a real conversation about what's happening between us, because he doesn't think we're "ready" for a real conver-sation, whatever that means. "It's been a long weekend."

"Tink." He reaches across, sliding his hand around the back of my neck and gripping me possessively. I like it, and the way his thumb strokes my jaw, more than I should. "What's wrong?"

"Nothing."

"I know it's not nothing. I just don't know what I did."

"I'm just tired." I don't want to talk about my feelings when I'm so unsure of them myself.

"You just slept for two hours," he says, using his fingers around the base of my skull to turn my head so I'm facing him. He eyes me like he's trying very hard to understand me, and still can't. Which is fine. Half the time, I don't understand myself.

I shrug and say, "And yet I'm still tired."

"Are you getting sick?" The concern in his voice about does me in. I need to get out of here.

I reach over for the door handle. "No, I just . . . I need to go inside."

Hopping out of the car, I rush up the stairs to the back door, leaving him to bring our stuff inside.

Two hours later, I'm standing in my closet, putting the finishing touches on the new bra I just created. Now that I've had some time to let my emotions decompress, and to process this weekend while also working on something creative, I'm feeling centered again.

What's happening between us still feels nebulous and uncertain, but at least I've figured out what he meant on that dock. He said that we both had work to do—me to learn to trust him, and him to show me he was trustworthy. That's not something you say to someone you're just fake dating. That's something you say to someone you *want* to build something with. But the problem isn't really that I don't trust *him*. It's that I don't trust *me*. And that's the part I don't know how to get over.

As I tuck the sewing machine back down into its cabinet, there's knocking on my bedroom door. I half expected it, and it still takes me by surprise.

When I open the door, he's standing there in jeans and a collared shirt with the sleeves rolled up to his elbows so that some of his tattoos peek out. He looks so delicious I have to gulp down my sigh.

"I'm not going out without you."

I cross my arms over my chest. "Why not?"

He reaches up and grips the doorframe as he leans in closer. "Because I don't want to. I want to be wherever you are, and I'm sorry if I made it sound like I only wanted you to come out to make this relationship look real. I was feeling a little desperate to say whatever would get you to hang out with me, and obviously that was not it."

I hug myself a little tighter, fighting off the flutters awakening in my stomach. "How do I know *this* isn't the thing you're saying now because you're desperate for me to come out with you tonight?"

"I don't really care if we go out, Jules. But after spending the weekend with you, I don't want to be without you."

I try to keep my walls up, to keep myself safe, but when he says things like that, it's harder and harder to remember why I need those walls to begin with.

"What if I want to stay home?"

"Then I'll stay with you."

I glance over at the clock on my nightstand and am surprised to find that it's not quite eight o'clock. "Fine, I'll go. But I need to change."

He bends down and swoops me over his shoulder so quick I barely have time to shriek before he's walking through the door to my bathroom and heading toward my closet.

"Colt, stop."

He freezes.

"I can change by myself."

"What is it about this closet that makes it so secretive, huh?" he asks. "Does it turn into a sex dungeon or something?"

I laugh. "What in the world would a virgin need a sex dungeon for?"

He pulls me down, letting my body slide along his until my feet meet the floor. His voice is even deeper and more gravelly than normal when he says, "Why do you keep emphasizing the fact that you're a virgin?"

I reach up and hook my finger into the space above the top button on his shirt. "Because I still need someone to help me out with that situation."

Leaning forward, he kisses my forehead. "We can revisit this when you have a better answer."

Then he's turning me toward my closet, and he smacks my ass to push me through the door, telling me I have fifteen minutes to get ready.

"I can't believe you're here!" Audrey squeals when Colt and I slide into the booth at the Neon Cactus.

"Why's that?" I ask, feigning an air of nonchalance that I certainly don't feel. Obviously, I know everyone sitting at this table: my sister and Drew, Zach and Ashleigh, and Walsh and Marissa. But there's something about being here with other well-established couples, when this thing with Colt and me has only started to feel real recently. Zach and Ashleigh have only been together since right before Christmas, but she moved in with him weeks after they met because she was relocating from Seattle to Boston, and he insisted it didn't make sense for her to get her own place.

"Because you have to work tomorrow morning," Audrey says.

"So do you." I shrug.

"Yeah, but I'll stroll into the office whenever I feel like it, which will probably be about three or four hours after you leave for work."

"Must be nice," I say with a little roll of my eyes. Then again, I'm often home long before Audrey finishes up for the day. "I'll be fine. It's just one night. Plus, we're starting a little late tomorrow because we're waiting on a delivery."

"How was Montreal?" Walsh asks.

I look at Colt, waiting for him to respond. He just shrugs, still looking at me, and says, "It was interesting."

They pepper us with questions about what it was like for me to meet Colt's family for the first time, and it's a relief when the waitress comes over to take our drink orders. Colt and I are both being purposefully evasive, and I'm half-afraid someone's going to call us on it.

By the time we're on our second round of drinks, the conversation has shifted to the upcoming series against Carolina. Colt's lazily tracing figure eights on my bare thigh when Walsh starts going through the list of players, and what their strengths and weaknesses are.

Colt slides out of the booth and holds his hand out to me. "Let's go play pool."

"I don't really play pool," I tell him, but I take his hand and let him pull me up to standing.

He dips his head and says, "I'll teach you." When he sees my doubtful look, he adds, "I think we established that it's good for you to try new things. Look how much fun you had golfing."

"That wasn't exactly golfing." I laugh as we walk over to the pool tables in the back. Predictably, most of them are empty on this Sunday night. "It was more like hitting balls at an outdoor party."

"Well, this won't exactly be pool either, because I'm going to be playing on both teams."

"So, speaking of trying new things," I say, my lips pursing. "Maybe tonight should be the night I try having more than two drinks."

"You think you should be making that decision when you're already drinking?"

"Colt, I've only had two. And I don't have to get up as early tomorrow as normal. Plus, there's virtually no one here except our friends. And there are no twenty-four-hour wedding chapels nearby."

"So those are your reasons to try drinking again?"

"No, those are my counterarguments. I've spent too many years letting one night of bad decisions affect my life. I just want to see what it's like to be buzzed when I know I'm safe."

"I'm a little nervous about you making this decision less than twenty-four hours after I made the offer, and with two drinks already in you."

I stop in front of the rack of cue sticks lined up on the wall. Turning to look at him, I say, "I'm going to have a couple more drinks. Are you going to make sure I'm safe and don't make any bad decisions, or not?"

"I'm always going to make sure you only make *good* decisions, Tink."

I grab a pool cue off the wall, but Colt's hand covers

mine. "That one's way too short for you. You need something longer."

Lifting my margarita, I say, "That's what she said," before taking a sip.

His hand is on my hip as he steps in so close I have to look up to see his face, and now my old-fashioned glass with the salt rim rests along his pecs. "Trust me, no one's *ever* said that to me."

I feel my throat bob as I swallow down the longing with the sweet, tangy margarita. "Those women just had more of a filter than I do."

"Bullshit, Tink." Taking my drink, he sets it on the edge of the pool table before bringing his hand to the back of my head and threading his fingers into my hair. "You might have everyone else fooled, but no one has a stronger filter than you do. And it's the things you *don't* say that have me most curious."

Goddamnit, why does he always have to *see* me?

Trying to change the subject, I bat my eyelashes at him. "So, how long of a stick do I need, then?"

He presses his lips together to hold in his smile and raises an eyebrow. "I guess we'll find out." Turning me so I'm facing the wall where the pool cues are hung, he lifts one out of the stand and holds it up to me. "This will do."

Then he takes one for himself, and I barely have a chance to grab my margarita before he pulls me over to the table in the back corner. The only light is the long one hanging over the table, and the angled shades ensure it only illuminates the green felt and barely anything beyond. We're shrouded in darkness back here, and I'm certain that was his intention.

He sets our cue sticks on the table and then goes about

racking the balls, the same way I used to see my dad do it at the bar down the street from our house. Audrey and I spent a lot of time there with him when Mom was sick, because of course that's where an alcoholic takes two pre-teen girls on a Saturday afternoon. I never really enjoyed playing pool, but I'm a boss at darts.

Once the balls are racked, Colt steps up behind me, his feet spread on either side of mine. His hand lands on my hip, gripping it possessively—it feels like he's always looking for a way to hold on to me.

That's just wishful thinking, I remind myself. Because every time he's not holding on to me, he's pushing me away. It's like he can't make up his mind. We're drawn to each other, no doubt, but he's clearly unwilling to do anything about it because of some stupid promise he made to my brother. I have half a mind to just ask Jameson if he'd actually care if anything was happening between us, but I don't want to potentially damage their friendship. That's a conversation they need to have, when and if Colt's ready to have it.

"I'm going to grab myself another drink before we start." Colt's words flow into my hair, sending a shiver down my neck and spine. "Do you want one?"

"Yeah. Let's try the coconut margarita this time."

"Sounds good. And I'll make sure you don't do anything crazy after drinking it."

The only crazy things I want to do are with you.

"We're stopping at four, no matter what." I can remember how four drinks felt. I was happily buzzed at that point. But the bad decisions started right after that, because once I hit four, I felt like I should keep going, and going hard.

"No matter what." He nods his agreement. "Let me go get

us another round, and you can practice taking some shots with this white ball." Reaching out, he picks it up off the table, tossing it in the air and catching it again. "I'll leave the rack on the balls, so you don't mess them up."

When he heads to the bar, I glance over at the table where our friends are sitting, and Audrey is staring at me. Then she takes her phone out of her bag, taps it a few times, and mine buzzes in my pocket.

AUDREY

You good?

JULES

I'm great, why?

AUDREY

This is seeming less and less fake each time I see you together.

JULES

You want my honest response?

AUDREY

Always.

JULES

It's feeling less and less fake the more time we spend together.

AUDREY

Are you sleeping with him?

I can feel the alcohol coursing through my blood. Not enough that I'm drunk, but enough that my filter is fading fast. It's the only reason I'm honest with her.

JULES

Not yet.

AUDREY

Are you sure this is the path you want to go down with him?

I barely stop myself from making a joke about going down on him.

JULES

We'll see.

Audrey's gaze flicks over to the bar, then back to her phone.

AUDREY

Are you having a third drink?

She knows about my two-drink limit, and it's the same one she has. Not because she's had a bad drinking experience like I have, but because with our family history, she doesn't want to tempt fate.

JULES

Yeah. Colt said he'd make sure I'm safe and don't make any bad decisions if I wanted to have more than two, and I'm taking him up on the offer.

AUDREY

Who's going to keep you safe from HIM???

JULES

Trust me, I'm plenty safe from him. He's got an iron will and finds it way too easy to resist me.

AUDREY

I trust you, but this feels like playing with fire.

I glance up to give her a reassuring look, but Colt's between us as he walks toward me with a margarita for each of us in his hands.

JULES

I promise you, everything is going to be fine.

Chapter Thirty-One

JULES

I don't know what's wrong with me, but I am absolutely *living* to drive Colt crazy. He doesn't want to want me? Fuck that. I'm going to make sure he can't resist me by the end of the night.

Actually, never mind, I know exactly what's wrong with me—this is the liquid courage of four margaritas. Will I regret this in the morning? Possibly. Do I care? Not in the least.

Leaning back against him while he bends over me to help line up the pool cue, I revel in the feel of his hard length where he's cradled in the crevice between the pockets of my jeans. He shifts his weight forward, pressing his rock-hard dick into me. He wasn't lying. I'm absolutely convinced that no woman has ever thought she needed something longer when she was with Colt. I should probably be scared of the size of his dick. Instead, I'm trying to encourage him to use it to deflower me.

"What are you laughing about?" he asks, his voice extra-husky and quiet, even though his face is next to mine.

It's then that I realize my chest is shaking as I try to hold in the giggles. "The word 'deflower.' It's such a bizarre word. Like, who thought of using that word to describe taking someone's virginity?"

Colt's sigh is so forceful it engulfs me in his margarita-scented breath, then he stands. I miss his body heat immediately, so I stand too. Turning toward him, it's hard to miss the tortured look on his face—the way his eyes focus in on me with longing, but his jaw ticks with the effort of restraint. *Good.*

"What's wrong, Colt?" My voice is the kind of teasing that borders on mocking. "Does it bother you that I'm a virgin?"

"It only bothers me that you keep bringing it up."

I take my fingertips and trail them down the front placket of his shirt, over the ridges of the small buttons, and stop when I reach the buckle of his belt.

"Why shouldn't I bring it up? It's not something I'm ashamed of." Tilting my chin up defiantly, I meet his heated gaze. In the low light, his eyes are practically black, and they're so focused on me that I almost shrink back and admit that it's a lie. That I am ashamed—not of my status as a virgin, but of my inability to be trusting and open enough with another person to give myself over in that way. But I could, with him.

He grips my jaw, tilting my head up so I'm forced to look at him. "Why do you *really* keep telling me you're a virgin?" His hand slips down my throat until he's got his fingers resting along the side of my neck. I'm certain he can feel the way my heart is racing, pumping blood through me so fast that I can feel my pulse pounding beneath his fingertips.

"Because you can solve this problem for me."

"Wrong. Answer," he grits out, his voice low and growly.

"What do you want me to say, Colt?" I ask, already knowing the answer. He wants the truth. He wants to know why I'm asking *him*.

"Why me, Jules?"

"I already told you this morning." I feel myself sway as I look up at him. He's not gripping my neck hard enough for me to lack oxygen, so this dizziness must be the alcohol. I think the fact that I can deduce this means I'm not *that* drunk? "You're the one person who, I think, wants to sleep with me, *and* who I also trust."

"That might be the start of it," he says, his eyes searching mine, "but that's not the whole reason."

"Oh yeah? What's the whole reason, then?" My tone is back to mocking him.

"When you figure it out, you let me know."

"Colt," I say, letting my body slump back against the pool table. "You are the ultimate tease. You know I'm willing, and I know you want me. Why are you making this so hard?"

"Trust me, Jules. One day, you'll be glad I did."

"And why's that?" I ask, crossing one foot over the other as I lean back farther.

"Because when we finally have sex, it's going to *mean* something." He steps up close, spreading his legs so one of his feet is on either side of mine. "And no amount of begging me for my cock is going to convince me to sleep with you before then."

My laugh is a bark. "I'm not *begging* you for your cock!" I reach one hand behind me to steady myself on the pool table, but my palm lands on one of the balls, it moves under my weight, and I fall backward onto the table.

Lying there across the hard felt table, with a ball under one of my shoulders and Colt looming above me, I can't stop laughing. Of course that would happen, and of course he looks mad about it. To everyone else, he's the happy-go-lucky goalie, but apparently I bring out this always-glowering side of him. Lucky me.

Actually, it is kind of lucky, I think to myself, *because annoyed Colt is HOT*. He always has been, which is probably why I've always taunted him.

"Alright, then," my sister says, stepping up next to him. With the darkness behind her and her fair skin lit up by the light above the table, she looks like an angel. A mad angel, who God would send down to punish the wicked.

I must say as much, because she rolls her eyes and says, "I'm not an angel, Jules, and I'm not mad." Then she looks at Colt. "How much did you let her drink?"

"Like three and a half drinks."

"Well, she's clearly had enough." Audrey reaches her hand out to me, and I grab hold, letting her pull me up to a sitting position. When we're face to face, I realize that she looks like she could use a hug. So I wrap my arms around her and give her the biggest bear hug possible.

"You're very huggable," I tell her.

"You're very drunk." She's using her *I am not amused* voice that she uses on Graham when he's done something she finds funny but shouldn't, like when he sticks French fries up his nose and claims they're extra-long boogers.

"I'm only a little drunk. *Trust me*, I know the difference." I let go of her then, and almost lose my balance again because my butt is perched on that narrow wooden ledge around the table, but she and Colt both reach out for me, each grabbing a different arm. "And I'm not going to do anything stupid this time. Colt promised he wouldn't let me," I tell her, then look at him. "Right?"

"Right. But I am taking you home because that third drink hit you harder than I thought."

"It was probably the fourth."

"What? I took the fourth away from you after you had like two sips."

"Yeah, but you set it on the counter there," I say, pointing to the empty glass where it sits on a ledge along the wall. "And I drank it when you weren't looking." I sound so damn pleased with myself.

"Oh my god, are you a fucking child?" Audrey asks with a laugh. Of course she's laughing—alcohol makes me funny.

"Don't know." I shrug and look down at my body, which appears fully grown to me. "I don't think so. I think I'm too big to be a child."

"Jesus," Audrey laughs. Then she turns to Colt. "I hope you're planning to walk home. She needs the fresh air and some movement to help sober her up."

"Yep, walking all the way," he confirms with a nod.

"But we're a long way from our house," I whine.

"No, we're not. We can be there in twenty minutes. Provided you can walk in a straight line."

"I totally can." My head bobs in agreement like I'm reassuring both of us, even though I have no idea if that's true. Everything is pleasantly fuzzy. But the thought of walking home with Colt's arm around me opens up the possibility, in my mind at least, that I'll be able to convince him to sleep with me. Surely, he needs to do something about that massive erection he was grinding against me a few minutes ago, just as much as I need him to do something about the painful ache between my thighs.

I hop off the ledge of the table, but the ground's closer than I expect, and so when my feet hit it, I topple toward him. Wrapping my arms around him, I'm hoping to pass it off as intentional, and say, "Let's go!"

He tucks me under his arm, and turns me toward the table of our friends, but then I realize if we're walking home, I need to use the bathroom first. Audrey offers to go with me because she seems to think I'm not capable of peeing alone while tipsy, and when we come out of the bathroom, Colt's over at the table.

There are two additional women there now, and I'm not sure when they arrived, but I don't like the familiar way one of them is resting her hand on Colt's arm while she leans into him and whispers something in his ear.

"Who's that?" I ask Audrey, nodding my chin toward Colt.

"Oh, do you remember my roommate from college? Jasmine?"

"From senior year? The one who basically ghosted you after you got pregnant and couldn't go out partying with her?"

"Yeah, the very one. I haven't seen her in years, but when she showed up here tonight and I invited her to sit with us, I regretted it almost immediately. Apparently, she's . . . famil-iar . . . with a lot of the guys on the team."

"Looks like she knows Colt pretty well." I hate the acidity of my tone. He's been with other people; it's not like I don't know that about him. At least he hasn't been with anyone else in a long time.

Audrey grasps my forearm and gives me what I think is meant to be a reassuring squeeze. "It's okay if he has a past. It's only the present and future that matter. Don't let that get to you."

I wonder for a second if my brother would feel the same way. He knows Colt in a way neither of us do. He's seen him living his wild ways. And it makes even more sense to me now why he'd make Colt promise not to touch me. It doesn't change how I feel, or what I want, but it helps me understand Jameson's insistence.

We walk up behind Colt and Jasmine as he slides her hand off his arm and says, "I've told you I'm not interested." There's a hard edge in his voice that even drunk me doesn't miss. I wonder if he's slept with her in the past. I wonder if I'll have to ask that question about every woman he knows?

You're not actually engaged, I remind myself. *Who he's slept with in the past is none of your business.* Still, I hate that he's been with so many women, whether it meant anything to him or not.

He glances over his shoulder like he senses me standing there, and his face is nothing but happy and grateful to find me standing there. Pushing back his chair, he steps toward me, asking, "You ready?"

"You're not going to introduce me to your friend?" I ask, giving him a little wink so he'll know I'm giving him shit. To be honest, I just want this chick to meet his fiancée, because either she doesn't know he's engaged, or more likely, she knows and doesn't even care.

"Jasmine," he says, glancing down at her, "this is my fiancée, Jules. Jules, this is Jasmine."

"Nice to meet you," I say, but I don't even bother extending my hand. Instead, I wrap my arm around Colt's waist and say, "Let's go home, babe."

We head straight toward the door of the bar, and on the way there, he says, "Babe, huh?" with a laugh.

"Felt appropriate in the moment. I've never seen you needing to be rescued before."

"I didn't need to be rescued, but I'm glad you were there, anyway."

The steep hills and uneven sidewalks of Beacon Hill are more of a challenge than I expect, but finally we arrive at the Boston Common, where the streets give way to wide, more modern sidewalks. They don't have the charm of Beacon Hill, but they're a hell of a lot more practical.

"Are you really going to make me walk the whole way home?" I ask.

"Yes, I am," he says, sounding very proud of himself.

"Why's that?"

"Because you need to sober up a bit, and I'm taking good care of you."

I laugh and give his chest a light smack. "You're barely putting up with me."

He comes to a stop, his arm around my shoulders making me stop as well. "What are you talking about? I *enjoy* taking care of you. You're one of my favorite people."

"Yeah, well, you like everyone, so that isn't saying much."

"No, I tolerate everyone. You, I actually like."

———

I wake up feeling like I'm both suffocating and incredibly turned on—neither is a normal morning occurrence for me. Opening my eyes, I find my face pressed into Colt's bare chest. One of my legs is wrapped over his hip, and my center is right up against the hot, hard cock he's pressing into me. The slow drag of him along my clit has my eyes rolling back in my head, but when I tilt my head back to ask him what he's doing in my bed, not to mention why he's dry humping me in my sleep, I realize that he's still asleep.

Shit, did I wrap myself around him and start this? *Ewww, I am such a creep.* One who clearly needs to take care of some business that obviously wasn't taken care of last night.

Despite my many attempts to convince him we should have sex, Colt was resolute that we were "only making good decisions." Which makes me wonder if that means that sex with me is a bad decision? Or if it's just drunk sex that would be a bad decision?

I try to lift my leg off him and roll onto my back as discreetly as possible, so maybe I can hop in the shower without waking him. My mouth is dry, my head has a dull ache, and I might be sweating out tequila at this point. Still, I don't feel *that* bad—nothing like last time. And I didn't do anything crazy like go and marry some asshole hockey player. Wait . . . I hold out my left hand and look at my ring finger just to make sure, and sure enough, there's a five-carat ring sitting there. At least I know why this time.

Next to me, I hear Colt chuckle. "Did you forget you were wearing that?"

I glance over at him. "Yeah. I had had this moment where I was like 'at least I didn't get married,' and then I saw the ring and . . . you know . . ."

"I promised I'd take good take care of you." His voice has a small undercurrent of hurt, like he thinks I didn't trust him.

"I know, and you did. It's just . . ." I pause, and he waits patiently for me to tell him what it is. ". . . I'm used to being the one who's in control of my decision-making. I like feeling strong and safe, and knowing that it's because of me and not because I'm relying on someone else."

"Sometimes, strength is knowing when to let other people help you. You don't have to do everything yourself, Jules."

My laugh is muffled because I'm pressing my lips together to stop the scoff from escaping. Taking care of others has been my entire life. It's my love language, but sometimes I do wonder: who's taking care of me?

"You don't," he insists. "You're always so busy helping everyone else, doing things for other people, sharing your strength so they can be strong too. It's okay to let people help you, too. Not because you can't do things yourself, but so that you don't always have to."

His words remind me of what he said after my confrontation with my dad a few mornings ago. It brings tears to my eyes, making me feel uncomfortably vulnerable. I'm way too keyed up sexually to be having an emotional or meaningful conversation like this. So I do what I always do, I deflect. "Right now, the only thing I need help with is an orgasm to take the edge off."

"Wow," he says, barking out a laugh. "Way to slow roll right into the whole using me for sex thing this morning."

"Listen, I have to leave for work in"—I raise my head to look at my alarm clock, which is on the other side of him. Shit, I still have well over an hour, which is way more time than I actually need—"not too long. So if you're not going to help me take care of this problem right now, I guess I'll have to do it myself."

"By all means," he says with a smirk.

"Awesome." It's spoken with all hard edges and bitterness. Of all the things he wants to help me with, why can't this be one of them? "I'm hopping in the shower. I'll leave the door unlocked, in case you change your mind." I roll out of bed and pad toward the bathroom.

"I'm not going to change my mind," he calls out. And just for that, I leave the door open a crack. He can listen to the fucking orgasm that I have to give myself because he's being obstinate about us having sex, or he can leave. Either way, I'm going to prioritize taking care of myself.

Chapter Thirty-Two

COLT

She literally has no idea how hard this is for me.

Which is probably for the best, honestly. She's wrapped herself around my heart so tightly it actually hurts. It might be because it's the first time in the last fifteen years that I care about someone, but I'm determined to take it slow with her.

Achingly, painfully slow, apparently.

For me, this isn't about sex. And I can't move forward with her until I know it's not just about sex for her, too. I don't want her to use me so she can check *lose my virginity* off her list. But I absolutely will be the first—and hopefully last—man she ever sleeps with. As soon as she finally figures out why she wants *me* to be her first and is willing to be honest about it.

As I listen to Jules turn on the shower, I grab my phone and re-read the text messages Jameson and I exchanged last night after she fell asleep.

COLT

Got the name of that investment guy Jules had dinner with.

JAMESON

How'd you manage that?

COLT

She was drunk. . . .

JAMESON

You let her get drunk? Do you not remember what happened last time?

COLT

Don't worry, I took good care of her.

Last night, I watched the dots appear, then disappear, as he typed. I imagined he was typing something about how I was supposed to be taking care of her last time, too. I know we're past that, but we wouldn't be if he knew the real reason it all happened. Just as I was giving up hope that he'd reply, his message came.

JAMESON

Name, please. I will have Derek get us more info.

Jameson's personal assistant, Derek, is a man of many talents—and getting Jameson exactly the intel he needs is one of his specialties.

COLT

Jerome Waters. Tell me when you have more info and we'll pay him a visit.

JAMESON

Don't make plans for tomorrow evening.
Derek will have what we need by then.

I've just finished re-reading when the first moan comes from the bathroom. It's distinctly sexual. The kind of sound that makes my dick strain against my boxer briefs. I want to know exactly what she's doing that's resulting in that sound. Is she touching herself? Is she thinking of me while she does it?

The second moan is significantly louder. The kind that I'm certain she wants me to hear. I glance over at the door and notice that it's cracked open. Light is streaming through, but from where I'm lying on her bed, I can't see anything.

She moans again, so loud I'd probably hear her if I was upstairs in my own apartment, and I have no doubt whatsoever that it's for my benefit. She wasn't even this vocal yesterday morning when my face was between her legs and she was coming on my tongue.

I should get up and leave. She knows my willpower is only going to last so long, so she's testing me. And even though I know exactly what she's doing, I still can't make myself go. My dick is so hard it's painful, and all it wants—all I want—is to be with her.

You don't have to have sex with her, I tell myself. *There are plenty of other things that will satisfy both of you until she figures her shit out.*

My feet hit the floor before I've even decided I should get up, and I take the few steps to the bathroom tentatively. Through the crack in the door, I can see the top half of her on the other side of the glass. One of her arms is resting against the wall under the showerhead, her back arched and her face tilted up so the shower spray hits her tits and rolls down her flat stomach, as her body rocks backward and then forward. She's letting out small grunts of pleasure, and I can't contain my curiosity—what is she doing to pleasure herself?

I tap the door slightly, pushing it into the room just enough that I can see the rest of her body. I regret it instantly, because the image in front of me is straight out of a porno and will live rent free in my head forever.

Her fingers circle her clit slowly as she leans back onto some sort of a dildo suction cupped to the wall of the shower, and watching her pussy take it over and over has a grunt escaping straight from the back of my throat. As she turns her head and looks at me, there's not even a hint of surprise on her face—it's like she knew I'd be standing there eventually.

"Fucking hell, Jules."

Raising her eyebrow as if to challenge me, she asks, "You joining me?"

I couldn't say no right now if my life depended on it. Even the awareness that this could jeopardize my friendship with her brother and make me an outsider in this family I've found for myself in Boston, even knowing that this is taking what we started yesterday morning to a whole new level, one we can never come back from . . . none of that feels like a reason to stop myself from accepting her invitation. In fact, it all feels like a reason I *should*—a first step in making this permanent.

I don't know what permanent means for a guy like me, or if it's even what she wants, but it's suddenly the only thing I can think about: I want her in my life forever. I want to come home to her after a road trip, I want her at my games with my last name on her back, I want to wake up with her in my arms, I want to make her grilled cheese sandwiches when she doesn't feel like cooking, and make sure her dad doesn't come around harassing her for money. I want to take care of her, and mostly, I want her to want me for more than sex.

I bend, sliding my boxer briefs to my ankles before I step out of them. Her eyes are huge and her smile is feline as she eyes my cock where it stands at attention, straining to be near her.

She sinks back onto that dildo as she stands, and with her ass pressed against the tile wall, she leaves room for me to step past her and into the shower.

"Get in here." Her words are practically a purr even while she's being demanding.

I take a step closer, noting the way her back is arched so she can tilt her hips to accommodate the toy, while still standing up enough to leave me room to fit through the opening left where the glass wall ends. Her shoulders are back, and the water runs down her chest in rivulets—I want to trace their path with my tongue, I want her nipples between my lips, I want to feel the way her whole body shakes when she orgasms.

"I love that you think you're giving the orders here," I say.

One more step and I'm at the edge of the shower, I'm teetering on the edge of my sanity as well. Stepping over that marble ledge and *not* having sex with her is going to take every ounce of self-control I have. But she deserves better for her first time than being fucked in a shower. Hopefully, there'll be plenty of opportunities for that later.

"I'm glad you're already in the shower."

"Why's that?" she asks coyly.

"Because I fully plan on getting you dirty, and this will make it easier to clean you up afterward."

Reaching out, I wrap my hand around the back of her neck as I step into the spray. The water hits my back, and her slick breasts slide along my chest, resting my other hand on the wall behind her as my mouth crashes onto hers.

It's a greedy kiss, full of the need and longing we've both been reluctantly holding on to. Our lips and teeth and tongues clash like we're devouring each other, both of us fighting for dominance in this situation. I'll give it to her, because I know she wants to feel like she's in control . . . but I'm going to make her fight for it first.

Her hands skim up my sides lightly, then she hooks her arms up my back, pulling me closer to her so she can slide her body against mine as she starts rocking her hips. I feel her groan of frustration a moment later.

"What's wrong, princess? Am I too tall for you to rub your clit along my cock like you're desperate to do?"

"Yes," she pants.

"Allow me, then."

I drop to my knees, and when my tongue meets her clit, she hisses out a deep, guttural, "Yes!" I know she's close because she's been in here for a while already, but this first time, I want her coming only because of me.

I scoot back on my knees and with the shower raining down on the back of my head, I pull her forward so her toy slips out of her. She cries out at the loss, but I fill her with my fingers, and then she's moaning my name interspersed with expletives and grunts of satisfaction. As I increase the speed and pressure with my tongue, I'm rewarded with the sweet sounds of her pleasure. Not the fake moans she was letting out before to tempt me, but the real ones that are quieter, deeper, and more desperate.

Sucking her clit between my lips, I run my tongue over it as I hold it in place, and her moans turn to raspy cries of pleasure as her muscles contract around my fingers, gripping me so solidly my dick is painfully jealous.

Her eyes shut tightly, her face scrunches up, and her lips part. As the orgasm rolls through her, heavy breaths replace her cries and finally she opens her eyes and stares down at me.

"Holy shit, Colt. You keep delivering orgasms like that and you're going to ruin me for all other men."

"It's almost like that's the point, Tink." If the last twenty-four hours have proven anything to me, it's that she's *mine*. Even if she doesn't know it yet.

I stand, cupping her face in my hands and kissing her like I want to brand her with my tongue the same way she's somehow branded herself onto my heart.

But instead of telling her how I'm feeling, I say, "Hearing you come like that, and knowing I'm the only man who's ever made you make those sounds, that fucking does something to me."

Her response is lifting one leg and wrapping it around my lower back, anchoring our hips together so I can't help but thrust my cock along her warm center, still slick with her cum. She hums out an appreciative sound. "You could be the first man to be *inside* of me, too, you know."

I try to hold in the smirk, but the way her eyes flare makes me realize I haven't been successful at that.

"Oh, don't worry. I *will* be."

"Now, Colt," she says, her voice pleading as she slides herself along my cock. I call on every ounce of restraint I possess, telling myself that this will be worth the wait—for both of us.

"No, not now, Jules. When you're ready."

"I. Am. Ready."

"Not when you're ready to fuck me—when you're ready to admit *why*."

She leans her head back against the tile and lets out an exasperated growl. "The *why* is because I want to have sex with you. And you very clearly want to have sex with me, too. Why isn't that enough of a reason?"

"Because when we finally have sex, it's going to change things. I want more than just sex with you. And right now, I don't think either of us know what 'more' means, or what that would look like, and we deserve the chance to figure it out before we fuck it up by having sex."

"Colt . . ." She slides herself along me, her breath coming out in desperate little puffs of air. Fuck, she's sexy when she's panting for me like this. "I need you."

"No, what you need is to come again, and I'll make sure that happens."

She releases a frustrated sigh. "I can't come a second time."

"Like hell you can't."

"I've tried."

"Well, we haven't tried together," I say, stepping back and lining her up with the dildo that's still attached to the tile wall. The relieved hum that she lets out as it slips inside her has her lips parting, and she licks them as she looks down at my cock. She reaches out tentatively, glancing up at me before gripping the base and bending forward, bringing her tongue to circle the head.

The sheer effort it takes not to push into her mouth has me gritting my teeth so hard I can feel every cord of muscle in my neck straining with the effort. She dips her head, taking my cock between her lips and swirling her tongue around the head again, before pulling back and looking up at me.

"I guess if we aren't going to have sex, this isn't a terrible alternative. I've always wondered what it would be like to suck a guy off while another fucked me—"

"And this is as close as you're ever going to get to that fantasy," I say, "because I don't share."

"That's good," she says breathily, leaning forward and using her flat tongue to lick her way from my base to my tip before circling over the sensitive flesh at the top. "Because neither do I."

And then she slides me into her mouth until I hit the back of her throat, but somehow, she doesn't gag. She just tightens her lips and tongue along my cock as she welcomes me in farther than should be possible, and then she's using her hand and her mouth to give me what might be the best blow job I've ever had.

I'm not sure what's sexier right now—the way she's deep throating me, or the way she's doing it while slamming her hips back onto that dildo? Or is it the small hums of satisfaction and the way they reverberate along my cock? Is it the way I've wrapped her hair around my fist as I rest my hand at the base of her skull to help set the right pace, or the way she moans when I lean forward, sliding my hand under her ribcage until I've got her nipple between my fingers?

She likes that so much that I release her hair so I can use both my hands to play with her nipples until she's moaning louder, and her movements turn nearly frantic. Seeing her about to come unhinged like this, with her mouth around my cock, has me close as well. Leaning forward a bit, I stretch one of my arms beneath her so I can reach her clit. That hot bundle of nerves is already swollen from her last orgasm, and it pulses beneath my fingers, coated in the evidence of her arousal.

The moan she lets out at the contact has an electrical current racing through me. It starts at the base of my spine and travels straight to my balls, and I can feel them tightening up, so I move my hand from her breast to her ribcage and guide her off my dick.

"Grab hold of my shoulders," I say.

"What?" She looks down at my dick longingly. "Why?"

"Because I want to see you painted in my cum," I say as I grip my cock, jerking my hand up it quickly, and circling my fist over the head before sliding back down my shaft. "And then when I'm done, I'll clean you off, but we'll both know that you're my dirty girl."

My fingers press harder on her clit as I pick up the pace, and she's breathing heavily as she continues sliding her hips back and forth along the dildo.

"Say it." I grind out the words while trying to hold in my orgasm until she's there with me.

A groove forms between her eyebrows. "Say what?"

"Tell me you're my dirty girl," I say, lifting my fingers off her clit so I'm barely touching her. She whimpers in response. "And then I'll let you come again."

"Yes," she says with an eager nod, shocking me when she

doesn't argue. She's so desperate for this release, and it's a goddamn pleasure to watch her let go of her control like this. "I'm your dirty girl. Now fucking *make me come*, Colt."

Pinching her clit between my fingers, I gently stroke her from all sides. As she cries out over and over with the orgasm that rips through her, I finally stop holding back. Ropes of my cum shoot across her stomach and up onto her breasts, as I press my forehead to hers and I let out an anguished groan myself.

I'm not used to these feelings accompanying sex, and it's almost too much . . . too overwhelming, too thrilling and scary at the same time. I'm falling so fast and hard for her and there's absolutely no question in my mind . . . she's it for me.

When we're both spent, I pull her to me, letting our bodies press together as I run my hands up her back and into her hair. Tilting her head backward, I let all my affection for her pour out through a tender kiss. The way Jules slides her arms over my shoulders, one hand moving into my hair and the other down my spine as she holds me to her, I'm praying she feels the same way.

"I know I didn't give you *exactly* what you wanted, but hopefully it'll hold you over?" I ask the question like I'm teasing her, but there's a small, vulnerable part of me that's worried that being with me like this won't be enough for her. That she won't be willing to wait, to let this grow into something that's more than just physical for her. And that thought terrifies me because Jules has already burned a hole straight into my heart, and if she doesn't feel the same way about me, I'll probably bleed out.

Chapter Thirty-Three

JULES

"What do you think of this?" Morgan asks as she brings the camera over to Rosie, to make sure that she doesn't move from her seated position, so that if she's happy with the angle, we can re-record from the same place.

Rosie takes a look at the camera as Morgan plays the clip back and says, "It's fine. I don't know why I even care about showing the other side of my face." She sounds like she's disappointed in herself.

"Because you've been through hell," I say, "and you don't need to be reminded of it. We can show the world what a badass you are, without having to dredge up your past."

I want her to know that part of what makes her strong is how much she's endured and overcome, but that's not the only reason she's amazing.

Rosie takes a deep breath and says, "Yeah, but would this testimonial be more powerful if I talked about my past? That way, people would know what you helped me overcome to achieve what I did."

I hear the side door open in the kitchen, and glance over to see Colt walking through it before I say, "*You* overcame that. *You* did the work. I just gave you a little guidance."

Rosie shakes her head. "You really don't see it, do you?"

"See what?" I ask.

"Your worth."

Tears spring to my eyes and my nose waters, and I have to sniff and look away before I start crying. When Morgan first suggested developing some sort of school-to-career pipeline to help more women enter the trades, I never could have imagined the women I'd meet. Rosie was the first woman to accept the offer of mentorship, and while we've been able to help a dozen more women too, Rosie will always hold a special place in my heart. As apparently, I do in hers.

Colt steps up behind me, wrapping his arm around my waist and pulling me to him so my back is against his chest as he presses a kiss to the top of my head. "She really doesn't," he says. "But if we keep working on her, maybe we can convince her."

A smile spreads across Rosie's face. "And who are you?"

"I'm Colt, Jules's fiancé." He lets me go as he leans forward and holds his arm out to shake her hand, and even as I glance over at them, I'm still in shock. He's introduced me to his family and friends back home as his fiancée, and to his teammates and their wives and girlfriends too . . . but it's the first time I've ever heard him introduce *himself* as my fiancé. And I'm trying really hard not to read too much into it, but the pride I heard in his voice keeps me teary-eyed.

Rosie's eyebrows are practically at her hairline as she

shakes his hand, then looks at me. "You got engaged and didn't even say anything? Where's the ring?"

"I don't usually wear it during the week because I don't want anything to happen to it at work." And, you know, because we're not really engaged.

"The woman wanted a silicone ring," Colt tells Rosie. "And I insisted on something a bit more . . . traditional." He reaches into his pocket. "It's funny, though, because I just picked this up for you today."

He holds out his hand and in his palm rests a silicone ring made up of small gold dots linked together. I had no idea they made silicone rings in anything other than plain bands. "It's actually . . . beautiful."

He looks down at me with his lips quirked up slightly in a knowing smile. "It reminded me of the gold disk on the necklace you always wear." Instinctively, I reach up and run the disk with the stars between my thumb and forefinger, and then Colt takes my hand and slides the ring onto my finger. "That's better."

"Alright," Rosie says, her voice overly loud. We both turn to look at her, where she's sitting with Morgan still standing next to her, fanning her face. "Now I'm about to cry because you two are too cute. So before I go and ruin my mascara, can we film this video?"

We all laugh, and then Colt says, "Okay if I stay?"

I'm about to tell him that it's better if we have some privacy for this, when Rosie says, "Of course you can."

When Morgan begins recording, Rosie shocks the hell out of me by starting out talking about her abusive ex-boyfriend and how she escaped that situation, all so she could give her daughter a better life.

She explains how isolating electrical school felt because there were only three women in the entire program, and how hard it had been to build connections with her classmates or see herself being successful in that field.

"And then, one day, they announced a guest speaker. It was an optional thing, after classes were already over, and I almost didn't go because it meant I'd have to pay for an extra hour of babysitting, and Lord knows I didn't have the money for that. But something told me I needed to be there."

My throat tightens, and Colt wraps his arm around my abdomen, pulling me back against him again.

"And there was this woman, all blonde and looking like Construction Barbie, talking about how we *needed* more women in the trades, and how she was organizing a mentoring program to connect women in trade school with women already working in the field. At that point, I was almost ready to give up on this path. I could have just dismissed her, thinking that her experience and mine were too different. What could this woman, who looked and talked like she was some rich girl from the city, possibly know about helping a woman like me? As it turns out"— Rosie turns to face the camera, moving her long hair back over her shoulder so the jagged, raised scar along her cheek is clearly visible—"everything. See, one of the things Jules taught me is that some of us wear our scars on the outside . . ." She points at her own face. "But some people wear their scars on the inside and use their pain to help others."

Her eyes flick to mine, and she notes the tears streaming down my face before she looks directly at the camera. "I'm so glad I didn't let my initial assumptions, based on nothing more than outward appearance, dissuade me. Because this mentoring program . . . it saved me. Not only did it provide the guidance and support I needed to figure out how to make it through electrical school, but it's also helped me line up the work experience I need before I can sit for my exam and get my journeyman license. Now that I'm working and have a steady income, it's the first time in my life I feel like I can breathe. I have absolutely no doubt that the day I earn that license is the day I fully break the cycle of poverty and abuse I was born into. And I'm equally certain that without this mentoring program, I wouldn't have been able to do it."

I'm pressing my fist into my lips so hard I can taste blood, but it's the only thing preventing my sob from escaping. I knew we'd helped Rosie, and a dozen other women like her, but I honestly didn't know how much. And it kills me that we have a waiting list and can't help more people until we get the funding to expand the program.

At this point, Rosie breaks down crying, and I don't even think about it before I step out of Colt's arms so that I can cross the room and wrap her in my embrace. "You healed me too . . . I hope you know that. You showed me what true strength looks like."

A million thoughts are running through my mind at this point—thoughts of gratitude for the privilege that's allowed me to do this work, and sadness for the women who have walked this path before me all alone. But none of the thoughts are screaming louder for my attention than the one that says, *"You need donors NOW."* At a minimum, we need to hire someone to run the nonprofit—to recruit and coordinate the mentors and mentees, to handle all the administrative stuff that I simply don't have time for.

I think back to how both Jameson and Colt have offered donations. I said no, initially, because of my pride. Because I didn't want the mentoring program to succeed based on relatives donating, I wanted it to succeed because other people in the industry saw the need and recognized how we met it.

But does it really matter where the money comes from, if it helps us do the work we need to do? And once the foundation is in place, maybe that will free me and Audrey up to look for other donors.

Rosie pulls back, saying she needs a minute to collect herself, and she's going to step outside. I point her toward the sliding glass door off the living room that leads to the tiny backyard, and she steps through.

"Wow," Morgan says. "That was . . . powerful."

I wipe my face and turn toward her and Colt, who stands slightly behind her where I left him. "Yeah. I wasn't expecting to get so emotional."

"I think that's how you know the work is worth it," Morgan says. She glances at me and then over her shoulder at Colt. "You know, I think I need a minute too. I'm going to take a quick walk." She turns and heads out the front door, leaving us alone in the living room.

Tenderness lines his features as he gazes at me with what I can only describe as some combination of love and pride. "I hope you know how amazing you are."

I wipe under my eyes again, hoping I've gotten most of the streaked mascara off my cheeks. "Remember when you offered to donate? I hope you have your checkbook ready," I say.

He steps up close and wraps his arms around me. "There's no one I'd rather invest in than you."

———

"So," Morgan says as she takes a sip of her drink and eyes our friends where they sit around the table now littered with drinks and appetizers. "Since Jules isn't telling you what happened this afternoon, I guess I will."

"It wasn't a big deal," I say, shooting her a look.

"Like hell it wasn't," she says, then shares the story of filming Rosie's testimonial, beginning with Colt giving me a new ring and ending with Rosie and me sobbing in each other's arms.

"Holy crap," Audrey says. "I can't believe I missed that. The *one* day I have an offsite meeting?" She'd been at the house of our next clients, reviewing their renovation plans so we can order the necessary materials once they're approved.

"You missed the best part," I tell Morgan as I reach into my purse for the check, then hold it up in front of me with two hands.

"How many zeros is that?" Audrey asks, snatching the check from my fingers. She looks at it, then up at me. "Are you for real?"

"Are you going to tell us what it says, or just tease us?" Lauren asks.

"It's a donation, from Colt, for a hundred thousand dollars." Audrey's voice is full of awe.

Lauren turns toward me. "Have you talked to your

brother about that?" It sounds an awful lot like, *You're going to be in so much trouble when your dad gets home.*

"No, why?"

Lauren sighs. "Because I was telling Jackson and Nate about your nonprofit when we were visiting them at Blackstone last week . . . and Jameson mentioned that he'd wanted to invest, and you wouldn't let him because you didn't want handouts from family. Is Colt not family?"

I'm sure my face reddens, because suddenly my mind is reeling with images from our shower this morning. He very clearly doesn't see me like a little sister anymore.

"I came to a really important realization when Rosie was talking today," I say quickly, trying to get those thoughts of Colt out of my head. I tell them about my epiphany that maybe all we need is a bit of starter money from whoever wants to donate it, regardless of why they're donating, to let us start growing the program.

"I wish you'd talked to me about that." My sister sounds hurt. "I mean, I know this program is really your baby, but so far, we've made all the big decisions together."

"Audrey," I say, looking over at her. "I'm so sorry, I was just so excited at the prospect of helping more women, and you've said all along that it shouldn't matter who donates, so I thought I was doing what you would have wanted me to."

She shrugs. "It's fine. You're right. I'm just being . . ." she trails off and looks away before glancing back. "I don't even know. It's just weird, like you have this other person now that you go to before me, and I'm used to being that person who helps you make decisions. Now you have Colt."

I give her a small smile. "I know *exactly* how you feel."

She tugs at her necklace, and I see now how we both do

the same thing when we're worried or uncomfortable. It's like the small reminder of our mother, who gave us our necklaces, soothes us. "Is this how it felt when Drew and I got together?"

"Yeah, especially once you moved out."

Reaching across the table, she squeezes my hand. "I'm sorry."

"It's natural that things will change . . ."

"Yeah, I guess I just didn't see this coming with Colt."

Morgan sighs. "You should have seen them together today. He is *so far gone* over her."

"So, is this not fake anymore?" Audrey asks.

"I don't know," I say. It sure as hell doesn't feel fake. "Things are definitely . . . shifting."

"What's that even mean?" Lauren asks, her brow furrowing with what looks like concern.

"It means we're figuring it out."

"Please tell me you're at least getting laid," Morgan says. She clearly has no idea about my status as a virgin because I've never told anyone but Audrey, and now Colt.

"Not exactly," I say, biting the inside of my lip. "But . . . things are definitely heating up."

"I really don't want to know this." Lauren makes a sing-song voice as she playfully covers her ears. Then she drops her hands and says, more seriously, "Because when Jameson asks me if I think anything is actually going on between you two, I want to be able to say that I don't know."

"Well, since I haven't *actually* given you any details, you can say that you don't know anything." I laugh to myself, because this reminds me so much of when Drew first came back into Audrey's life, and Audrey refused to give Lauren any details because she wanted her to have "plausible deniability" if Jameson asked her any questions.

The waiter comes over then to see if we want another round of drinks or more food, and after we order, the conversation turns toward Lauren's upcoming bridal shower. She'd insisted she didn't want one, as there was absolutely nothing she and Jameson needed.

Honestly, I think she's still just traumatized by memories of the bridal shower her ex-mother-in-law threw for her in Park City, before she married her first husband, Josh. Lauren knew almost no one there, except her mother and sister who had flown out, and her mother-in-law had made her feel like the whole event, which she'd insisted on throwing, was an enormous imposition.

So it felt like a small victory when Lauren finally agreed to let us have a small brunch as long as there were no "silly wedding games." As we chat about the upcoming event, I'm relieved that the conversation doesn't come back around to Colt and me.

But as if he knew I was thinking about him, my phone buzzes with a text.

COLT

What time will you be home tonight?

JULES

Not sure, why? Miss me already?

I don't know where Colt went once we were done filming Rosie's testimonial. He'd said he "had something to take care of," kissed my forehead, told me he'd see me when I got home from dinner with my friends tonight, before heading out the door.

COLT

You know it.

JULES

We just ordered another round of drinks.

COLT

Let me know if you need me to come walk you home.

JULES

LOL, you really DO miss me, don't you?

Why does that realization tug at my heart so much? I told myself that I didn't have to worry about falling for Colt, because there was no way he'd ever fall for me. But if he has, what's stopping me from falling, too?

COLT

Like I'd miss breathing if there was no air.

Chapter Thirty-Four

COLT

"If this goes wrong and I get arrested—or worse, benched—I'm blaming you."

"Me?" Jameson says as he pushes the button for the thirty-third floor. "You're the one who gave me his name and suggested we pay him a visit."

"Yeah, well, I'm still blaming you if I don't get to play tomorrow because of this."

"We're not going to jump him, you idiot." Jameson rolls his eyes. "We're just here to let him know that his company is officially no longer a sponsor of the Boston Rebels."

This is news to me. "How the fuck did you make *that* happen?"

"I showed AJ the footage from the restaurant's security cameras, which clearly show him grabbing Jules and getting up in her face, and she took it to Frank," he says. Frank Hartmann is the billionaire owner of the Rebels, and our second-string goalie's dad. He has a largely hands-off approach and generally lets AJ manage all aspects of the team, and only occasionally gets involved in the business operations. The fact that he put his foot down on this is surprising, to say the least.

"And they rescinded his sponsorship based off of what they saw?" Given how much money a sponsorship involves, and how little actually happened in the restaurant, this seems unlikely.

"It didn't take much to convince them that if that video got out and people found out Jerome was a sponsor, it would reflect poorly on the organization."

"And who has access to that video besides you?"

"No one. But they don't need to know that." Jameson eyes the lights above the elevator doors and sighs when he sees that we're only at the twenty-fifth floor.

"How the hell did you even get that? And how long have you had it?"

"I got it the night it happened, and that's all you need to know."

"Jesus. So who's taking over the sponsorship?"

"I was so tempted to write a check and have Our House be the new sponsor," he says, and I laugh out loud.

"Jules would have been so pissed, but it would have been total poetic justice."

"Yeah, but in addition to pissing my sister off, it would have been a fuck you that made no sense financially for me. So it'll go to the next corporation on the waiting list for a sponsorship opportunity."

The elevator dings as we arrive on the thirty-third floor, and Jameson mutters, "Let me do the talking," right before the doors open.

I follow him as he approaches reception, and the young guy sitting there looks from Jameson to me, his eyes lighting up with recognition. "Oh my god," he says, clearly a little starstruck. "You're Colt."

"This is my client, *Mathieu Coltier*." Jameson emphasizes my full name as if to point out that this guy and I aren't on a nickname basis, even though no one but my family, and occasionally the hockey sportscasters, has called me Mathieu in fifteen years. "We're here to see Jerome Waters."

The guy pulls at the knot of his tie as he glances toward his computer screen. "Is he expecting you?"

"Yes," Jameson says, "and we know the way."

He starts walking past the reception desk quickly, and I assume I'm supposed to follow.

"You can't just barge into his office," the guy calls out from behind us.

"Watch me." Jameson doesn't turn his head back toward the guy, but his words carry across the mostly empty office. Apparently, things wrap up right at five here.

"Does he know we're coming?" I ask Jameson quietly as I follow him. He somehow seems to know exactly where he's going.

"Derek got a meeting on his schedule, but no, he doesn't know it's us."

I don't bother asking how Derek managed this, because the guy's clearly a magician.

When we get to the large double wooden doors with Jerome Waters engraved across them, Jameson doesn't bother knocking, he just pulls them both open and we stroll through. Jerome is at his desk and glances up with a distinctly annoyed look across his face. Then his eyes narrow in on me.

"You." He spits out the word like I disgust him, which is fine, because the feeling is very mutual. Then he looks back and forth between Jameson and me, and I can't tell if he recognizes my best friend or not. Jules mentioned that Jerome was a huge Rebels fan and season ticket holder, but it's been over a decade at this point since Jameson played, so maybe he doesn't remember him.

"I'm Jameson Flynn," he says, holding out his hand to Jerome, who dubiously extends his own hand before Jameson crushes it in his grip. "I'm a former Rebels player, Colt's agent, Jules Flynn's big brother, and close friend of just about everyone on the Rebels' management team. So on behalf of my family and the entire Rebels organization, I'd like to give you this."

Jameson reaches into a pocket on the inside of his suit coat and hands over a folded piece of paper. The groove between Jerome's eyebrows deepens as he unfolds the check. "Why are you giving me a check from the Boston Rebels?"

"I'm glad you asked." Jameson's voice drips with sarcasm and reminds me what a shrewd businessman he is. I never saw this side of him when we played together, but he has just the right disposition for negotiation and he doesn't mind doing something underhanded every once in a while, if it's really necessary. "This is a pro-rated refund on your sponsorship for the team. Your signage has already been removed from the rink, your logo is no longer on the website, and you'll never be listed as a team sponsor again."

"What? You can't do that," Jerome says, sounding an awful

lot like a man who's never been challenged . . . or at least, never defeated.

"Funny, I already did. You fucked with the wrong family, Waters. Next time you decide to lay your hand on a woman, I hope she cuts off your fingers like my sister should have done."

"Nothing even happened." His gaze flies to me. "You made a big deal out of nothing."

"Nothing?" The word rips from my throat like a roar. "You put your hands on the woman I love, and you think that's *nothing*? You're lucky that all we did was rescind your sponsorship. Piss me off again, and we'll come after your business next."

He scoffs. "Like there's anything you could do to my business."

"Would you like to try me?" I ask. "Because that's exactly what will happen if you don't stop running your mouth."

I have no idea what I'm even saying. I wouldn't know the first thing about going after his business, but the man who's been my best friend for most of my life and is standing right next to me looking at me like I'm amusing him, will know exactly what to do.

"You can leave now," Jerome says. He's backing down but trying to do it without losing any authority—as if he has any in this situation.

"Gladly," I say. "And by the way, we didn't touch your season tickets. I wanted to make sure that you're still able to enjoy watching me win."

With that, we turn and leave. We don't speak until we're in the elevator and the doors have closed.

"So you love her?" Jameson asks the question without

looking at me. He's eerily calm, which has me a little worried.

"Yeah, I'm pretty sure I do."

"Does she know yet?"

"I'm trying to show her every day."

"I'm having a really hard time being okay with this," Jameson says, turning to me. His jaw ticks, and I realize there's a lot he's not saying.

I steel myself against his disapproval. I wish it wasn't this way, but I understand why it is. "I'm telling you what my intentions are. I'm not asking for your permission."

"That's good, because you don't have it. She's my baby sister. She's way too young for you. And you've got a reputation and a past that she shouldn't have to deal with. I hope that you truly have changed your ways like you seem to think you have, and that you deserve her. But just know: if it goes badly and I have to choose, I'm always choosing her."

The elevator dings to let us know we're at the ground level, right as I say, "As you should."

My best friend walks out of the elevator and across the lobby, and I stand there, hoping that I'm doing the right thing. Hoping that Jules will one day trust me enough to feel the same way, because if she doesn't, I've just ruined my relationship with the only family I have in Boston.

When she gets home from dinner with her friends, I'm sitting propped up against the pillows on her bed, watching some game footage from Carolina's last series in preparation for our first game against them tomorrow.

She didn't take me up on my offer to walk her home from the restaurant, but there was no way I wasn't seeing her tonight.

After two nights in a row of sharing a bed with her, I'm in no hurry to get back up to my own bedroom. *Is it too soon to move my bed down here into her bedroom?*

She takes one look at me, lying there in nothing but a pair of black athletic shorts, and says, "Change your mind about fucking me?"

"Nope. Change your mind about just using me for sex?"

"Nope." The way that word comes out of her mouth—hard and certain—is at odds with the way her eyes soften while she looks at me.

"Come here."

She walks around the bed to the far side, where I slept last night. And as she comes up to what I'm already thinking of as "my side of the bed," I turn so my legs hang off the edge and I pull her between my knees, holding on to her hips as I look up at her.

"I missed you."

Staring down at me, her face heats under my gaze, then she closes her eyes and shakes her head with a little laugh. "I missed you, too."

"I need to tell you something, and I need you to stay calm and not panic when I do."

Her exhale is shaky, but she manages to squeak out, "Okay?"

I should probably tell her where I was tonight while she was at dinner. I should tell her about Jerome, and about my conversation with Jameson. But that doesn't seem as pressing as the reality she doesn't know she's going to face when she walks into Liberty Arena tomorrow night.

"You know how we're playing Carolina in this next round of the playoffs?" I ask, and she nods in response. "Do you know who plays for Carolina now?"

She shakes her head, but I can see on her face that she realizes there's only one reason I would ask her this question. Closing her eyes, her head drops forward.

"I didn't realize you didn't know. When Gabriel started talking about Carolina yesterday, I expected some sort of a reaction, but I thought maybe you were just holding it in because we were with my family. But when Walsh started listing the players off at the bar last night, and you didn't tense up or seem uncomfortable, that's when it finally occurred to me that you didn't know."

"Is that why you wanted to play pool? So I wouldn't accidentally hear his name?"

I use the tips of my fingers to massage her lower back, hoping she'll relax from the rigid pose she adopted the minute she realized Brock Lester now plays for Carolina. "Yeah. That, and I wanted to get you alone. I have a hard time sharing your attention with others."

A single, silent laugh shakes her body. "Well, I appreciate you making sure I didn't find out from someone else. After Vegas, I made it a point not to follow hockey because I never wanted to think about, or hear about, him again."

"You don't have to come to the home games this week if you don't want to. As much as I would love to have you there, I will completely understand if you stay home. I don't want you to do anything you're not totally comfortable with."

She slides one knee up onto the bed, resting it against my hip, and then does the same with the other so that she's fully straddling me. Wrapping her arms around me, she clings to me like a koala, and I've never been so happy to be smothered in my life.

Holding her tight against me, I realize that the only thing I want in the world is for her to feel safe, and for me to be the one who makes her feel that way.

"I'm not sure if I can go to the game," she murmurs into my neck, her hot breath caressing the muscles there. "But also, the thought of staying home when everyone else is there . . . Why should I have to miss out, because of him?"

"Don't come if it's going to be too hard. Or do if it helps you feel like you're over what happened. Whatever you feel is going to be best for you is what we'll do."

She sits up and cups my jaw in her hands. "Part of me wants to show up in your jersey and prove that I've moved on."

"Jules." Her name is rough coming off my tongue. I don't know how to be vulnerable and ask the question that needs to be asked, but I want her to be honest with me about how she's feeling, and I won't know unless I ask. "*Is* that what it would mean? Because last time you wore my jersey to a game, you did it to keep up appearances. If you wear it now, is it because you've truly moved on?"

Her thumbs stroke my face, running along the line of my cheekbones above my beard. "I think so?"

I wish she knew for sure, but this is progress, at least. She's still got work to do to learn to trust, and I need to keep being there so she knows she can trust *me*.

"I'm not here to break down your walls," I tell her. "You

put them up, you have to choose to dismantle them. But don't fucking think for one second that I'm not going to climb over them whenever I can, hoping that eventually you won't feel like you need them anymore."

She presses her lips to mine gently, raining tentative kisses across them before moving to my nose and my forehead. "I know. And I'm working on it. I promise."

"As long as you're doing it for *you*, Jules. I don't want to move faster than you're ready for," I say as I rest my palm in the space between her breasts. "I'm going to be here for as long as it takes, because you're worth waiting for."

Chapter Thirty-Five

COLT

"I know I'm starting," I tell Hartmann as we take the ice for warm-ups, "but you'd better be ready to play tonight."

"Are your knees bothering you?" He asks the question with complete empathy, unlike my teammates who give me shit for being the oldest player on the team, because he knows what it's like even though he's only a couple years into his career.

"No. Because there's at least a fifty percent chance I'm getting into a fight tonight, and if I do, I plan on winning."

"Whose ass are we kicking?"

"You're not kicking anyone's ass, because we need you to goaltend if I get kicked out."

"Okay, whose ass are *you* kicking?"

"Brock Lester."

Hartmann snorts. "That guy's such a douche. What did he do this time?"

I consider what I can say that won't betray Jules's confidence or invade her privacy. "It's an old grudge about something that happened a long time ago."

"And it's just rearing its ugly head now?" His eyes squint as he looks at me, then he looks past me at the stands and nods his chin in that direction. "You sure it has nothing to do with her?"

I turn and find Jules descending the steps toward her family's seats right behind our bench. I didn't think she'd be here—when I left for the arena this afternoon, she still wasn't sure. But now, she's strutting down the stairs like she owns the whole damn arena. Her hair is in loose, bouncy curls and she's wearing a touch of makeup. Her bootcut jeans with heeled boots make her legs look a mile long, and over her tucked in scoop-neck T-shirt that shows quite a lot of cleavage, she's wearing a Rebels playoff jacket.

I'm pretty sure the WAGs start working on those way in advance. I think they wore them for the first round and Jules wasn't wearing one, so I'm not sure where this came from. But the navy-blue satin material of the oversized starter jacket shimmers, while the Rebels logo on the front breast sparkles.

When she sees me looking at her, she gives me a little fist bump in the air with her left hand, and her ring almost blinds me. Good. I want everyone to know she's mine.

I skate toward her, and she walks straight past her family, sitting in their seats, and meets me down at the glass. And just like the first time I saw her in my jersey, I loop my finger through the air so she'll turn around. Like last time, she rolls her eyes at me but turns, sweeping her long blonde hair over her shoulder so I can see COLTIER where it arches across her shoulder blades.

When she's fully turned around and facing me again, I say, "You trying to kill me, Tink?"

She just smirks at me and presses both her hands against the glass. And that's when I notice that not only is she wearing her engagement ring on her left hand, but she's got the gold silicone ring on her right.

Someday, I'm going to propose to her for real—I'm certain of it. And I hope she'll still want these same rings, so we can remember where we started, and see how far we've come.

"Where'd the jacket come from?"

"Marissa unexpectedly dropped it off at my house a couple hours ago."

"That the only reason you're here tonight?"

She gives me a small smile. "*You're* the only reason I'm here tonight."

My fucking heart is in my throat as I drop my gloves and press my hands against hers. "Wish me luck."

"You don't need luck," she says. "You got this." Then she blows me a kiss and turns to head up to her seat. I stand there, watching the way her jeans cling to the curve of her ass as her hips sway with each step, until McCabe skates up, spraying me with ice.

"Dick."

"Get your head in the right place, Colt. This is too important of a game to be distracted."

"I'm not distracted," I say, now even more focused on the game, and on giving Brock Lester the beating he fully deserves. "Speaking of this game. You should know that I'm probably going to get a game misconduct, so just be prepared."

"What the fuck are you on about?" Half the things that come out of McCabe's mouth sound like he's growling. Good luck to the woman who ends up having to put up with his surly ass.

He's a single dad, and his dating life was severely curtailed this past summer when his ex showed up at his place to drop off their newborn—whom he didn't know about until that moment. Since then, he's a dad first. He rarely goes out anymore, but he was dating this chick named Annabelle at the beginning of the season, which is how I met her friend, Jasmine. Seeing her at the bar the other night reminded me of exactly why I stopped sleeping around.

A shiver runs through me when I think about how meaningless all the sex I've had in my life has been . . . It only makes me want Jules more. I want to know what it would be like to sleep with someone I actually care about.

"Dude," McCabe growls when I don't respond. "What the hell are you thinking about?"

"Nothing."

"About that penalty, then?"

I tell him the same thing I told Hartmann about Lester. "I'm surprised Lover Boy doesn't want in on that fight," McCabe says, referring to Hartmann's nickname, which Walshy gave him because he said the heart in his last name equates to lover and his baby face makes him look like a boy, not a man.

"Why would he?"

"They played together in high school, I think. Or juniors or something. I know there's bad blood there, somewhere."

"Well, tonight, he's mine. I'm just waiting for him to say something, and then it's gloves off."

"You sure? In all your gear?"

"Don't worry about me, I'll be fine."

———

It's near the end of the first period before Lester makes it anywhere near my crease. But from that point forward, he makes it a point of being there as often as possible. Not because he's looking to score, but because he's trying to be an agitator.

The first few comments he throws my way could be mistaken for friendly banter. Things like "Nice save, keep" and "Way to not be a sieve."

When he gets a little too close, skating back onto the crease, I reach out and shove him forward so he's out of my way, telling him to "move along."

At the beginning of the second period, he shoots and I knock the puck away with my glove when I really should have caught it. "Sloppy," Lester mutters as he skates up, "just like your fiancée."

"The fuck you say?" I spit out.

"You heard me. You enjoying my sloppy seconds?" he asks as he skates just out of reach like the fucking coward that he is. The puck is still in play, and I can't take my eyes off it for a second, but the minute he's close enough again, he's going down.

I get my chance half-way through the third period, when he skates backward just as the whistle blows to stop the play, and says, "Just remember, I had her first."

"Like hell you did." Dropping my stick, I reach out and grab him by the neck of his jersey, pulling him back and slamming him to the ice where he slides into the net. He tries to get up, but I'm throwing my mask off and pinning him to the ice with my knees as I rip my glove and blocker off before pummeling his face.

"You were too drunk to get it up, you fucking lightweight. So don't ever speak about Jules as if you've known her in that way. She might have worn your ring for a night, but she's going to wear mine for the rest of her life."

I don't actually know if that's why they didn't have sex, but I have to imagine that being too drunk at least had something to do with it. And I'm relishing the thought of him thinking that this is what Jules remembers about him, that this is the story she tells about their wedding. It's so much better than the reality of how he shook her confidence and made her question herself.

In a matter of seconds, I've pounded his face until it's bloody and his nose is twisted and ugly—all before the refs are able to pull me off him. It's only then that I notice the fighting going on all around me.

And when I'm given a game misconduct penalty, I happily skate off the ice and head to the locker room. Whatever fines I get from the league, or whatever lecture my coaches give me, it'll be worth it. Because for the rest of his life, Brock Lester is going to look at his now-crooked nose and remember the beating I gave him for disrespecting Jules. And she'll remember that she's worth fighting for.

Chapter Thirty-Six

JULES

I don't know what it is about watching my fake fiancé fight my ex-husband, but it does something to me—elicits some sort of primal need to claim him and be claimed by him. I don't even want to know what Brock said that made Colt fling him to the ice and pound the shit out of him; I just want to kiss his face and tell him how much I love him for it.

Wait . . . what?

"What's wrong?" Audrey asks, glancing over at me after we watch Colt skate off the ice. Below us, Drew is lining up for a faceoff, but Audrey's eyes are flitting between her fiancé and me, her face contorted into a worried grimace.

"For a second there, I just had this thought that terrified me."

"Yeah," Audrey says, throwing an arm around me and squeezing me to her side as she looks back at the ice. "Love can be like that."

How does she know what I'm thinking? "But I don't . . . I can't . . ."

"Yeah," Audrey says, "you can. It's okay, Jules. Don't you think, after everything, after the way he keeps showing you he cares, that it's okay to trust him? Okay to care about him in return?"

"I'm so scared," I whisper, reaching across my body and taking her hand where it rests on my shoulder, squeezing her fingers. "I can't fall for him. Not when we already agreed it was all fake."

"How long do you think it's been since it was fake for him?" she asks quietly while her gaze darts back and forth, following the puck along the ice. Now that Colt's not in the game, I'm just staring at her, trying to figure out what she's talking about.

"What do you mean?"

"When's the last time this felt fake? Like the last time that you thought he was just putting on a show for people?"

I think back, before this weekend when we went away, trying to figure out when things changed. It didn't feel fake at the party, even though I was worried he was only touching me, only paying attention to me, for show. But that was the last time I needed to worry about it, because from that moment on, whether it was just the two of us or we were with other people, there was never a moment that it felt like we were pretending. No, as soon as I stopped reminding him it was all pretend, it stopped feeling fake.

And the way he takes every opportunity to touch me, to hold me, to tell me he cares and that he'll wait and that I'm worth it . . . it can't be fake for him either.

He's slowly, brick by brick, dismantling the walls I've

built around my heart. He said I had to be the one to take those walls down, but he's doing it for me every single day in the way he shows me how he feels.

"Oh my god," I gasp, and instead of looking at me in shock, Audrey just smiles. Lauren looks over at me from the other side of Audrey. Jameson headed to the locker room the second that Colt got a game misconduct, so at least he's not here to witness his sister realizing she's in love with his best friend.

"I knew you'd find the right person someday," Audrey says. "I just never thought it would be Colt."

My laugh is almost a bark. "Yeah, me neither."

Teenage me couldn't even have dreamed up how great he actually is. And the fact that I thought this whole thing was "safe" because there'd be no way he'd ever have feelings for me? The irony is too much.

"I always kind of thought it would be him," Lauren says, one eyebrow raised.

"Did you now?" I ask. I'm so tempted to say that the only reason she could believe that would be because she didn't know what happened in Vegas. But none of that seems to matter anymore, so I hold my tongue. "I need to go see him."

Audrey tells me how to get to the door closest to the locker rooms. "You're going to have to text him to come meet you, though. They won't let you in there."

And then I'm running up the stairs to the exit and following her directions. I don't text him, though, I call. When I get his voicemail, I tell him where I'm waiting for him. I'm only standing there, chatting up the security guard, for a few minutes before a loud cheer goes up in the arena, which I assume either means the Rebels scored again, or we won the game. Maybe both.

And then the heavy metal door flings open, and Colt is striding through the door in his suit, heading straight toward me. He wraps me in his arms, burrowing his face into my neck and breathing in deeply.

"You good?" I ask.

"Yeah," he says, but doesn't let go. Instead, he clings to me like I'm the only thing holding him up.

I pull back, cupping his face in my hands and looking every square inch of him over. "You sure?"

"I'm completely fucking positive, Tink. I feel fantastic." Then he kisses my nose and says, "Let's go."

We're at the Neon Cactus having a drink with his teammates when the text comes through.

LAUREN

> You know Jackson's husband, Nate? His dad is interested in your nonprofit and wants to meet with you.

JULES

> He's interested in donating?

LAUREN

> Yeah, apparently Nate told him about it after I explained it to him and Jackson. He owns a ton of commercial property in Boston and is interested in donating. But I think he also genuinely wants to know more about the program and may want to be involved somehow.

My stomach drops when I think of the last guy who wanted to be "involved" in our nonprofit.

I turn my phone toward Audrey and her eyes scan the screen before she raises her eyebrows and says, "Do you want to meet with him?"

"I keep thinking about how I felt when we finished recording that video of Rosie. That realization that we need the money *now* so we don't have a waiting list a mile long. So yeah, I think we need to move on this."

LAUREN

I'm going to send you his contact info. Nate told him you'd reach out if you were interested.

"Do you want me to be involved in this?" Audrey asks. "Or do you want to handle it yourself?"

I realize that my sister is putting the ball in my court, letting me decide if I want this to be an "us" thing, or if I need to go by myself like I did last time, just to prove to myself that I can do it.

"This nonprofit, like Our House, is *ours*. I can't, and don't want to, do it without you."

"From a business perspective," Audrey says, leaning over and resting her head on my shoulder, "yes, it's ours. But you are the face and the lifeblood of this nonprofit, Jules. You're the one with the passion and the knowledge that helps these women. I couldn't do it without you, but you certainly could do it without me."

I hear her acknowledgement of what I bring to this process, but it doesn't change the fact that Audrey and I are in this together.

Tilting my head to the side, I rest my cheek on the top of her head. "Even if I *could* do it without you, I don't want to."

Nate's dad's contact comes through via text a moment later, and I don't let myself think too much about it before I tap on the number to send a message.

JULES

Hi, this is Jules Flynn. Nate suggested reaching out to you about the mentoring program for women in the trades that my sister and I recently started in Boston. He mentioned that you might be interested in donating or being involved. I'd love to talk more about that opportunity whenever you have time.

JAY DAVENPORT

How is tomorrow, late afternoon? I have some time around 5pm.

Audrey sits up and we just look at each other. I wasn't expecting a reply this late at night, or for a meeting so quickly.

"Let's do it," she says.

JULES

We can make that work. I'll send you some info tomorrow in case you have a minute to look through it ahead of time. Where would you like to meet?

He texts me the address to his office in the Davenport building downtown, right near the old State House, and it's only then that I have the "ah ha" moment of realizing exactly what a big deal he is. Jackson's husband, Nate, while obviously wealthy, is so down to earth I would never have guessed that he's part of the historic Davenport family that the landmark building is named after.

"What's going on?" Colt's voice is low, the words spoken directly in my ear from the opposite side of me.

"Just setting up a business meeting with a potential donor tomorrow."

"At . . ." Colt glances at his watch. ". . . eleven at night?"

"Yep."

"Why do you need more donors? Should I have made a bigger donation?"

"You can't be our only donor, Colt."

His hand slides along my lower back and loops around my waist, pulling me toward him. "And why not?"

"Because I don't want to milk you for all you're worth," I say, squeezing his strong thigh playfully where it rests beneath my hand.

His laugh is deep, and his breath ruffles my hair when he says, "I think I'd be okay with you milking me for all I'm worth, Jules." I know he's not talking about money right now, and immediately my thoughts go to yesterday and the way he left his release all over my body. I cross my legs to quell the ache between them as the memories rip through me. I need this man. I need him in my bed, but I also need him in my life and in my house.

I need him taking care of me the way that only he can— the perfect balance of showing me how strong I can be and holding me in my moments of weakness.

Looking over my shoulder at him, I shake my head through a laugh. "I think you should take me home."

His hand presses into my belly as his thumb strokes the underside of my breast. "I was thinking the same thing."

We scoot out of the booth, saying our goodbyes, and I tell Audrey we'll chat tomorrow morning about the meeting. McCabe looks at his phone, grumbling about his nanny being flighty and unreliable, and slides out of the booth with us. We walk out together, and even though they're both heading back to the arena to get their cars, Colt tells McCabe he'll see him later.

As McCabe speeds on ahead, Colt backs me into the glass wall of a storefront half a block down the street from the Neon Cactus.

He steps in close—not enough that he's touching me, but enough that I can feel the current of sexual tension humming between us. His stance is wide, so I barely have to look up at him as he reaches out to stroke his thumb along the tender flesh of my lower lip.

"I don't want to leave after the game on Thursday," he says, his words a whispered admission.

"And I don't want you to go." But he has to. We both know it. I don't know how many more years he plans to play, but the thought of feeling like this every time he travels, and knowing that he's gone about half of every season . . . I don't know how I'd do it. I don't know if that's even what he wants?

Leaning forward, he rests his forehead on mine. "Is this what falling in love feels like?"

My stomach flips over almost painfully in my belly, and I have to clear my throat because it feels too thick to speak. "I don't know. But I think . . . maybe it is?"

"Are you telling me I'm not in this alone?" The vulnerability in his question hits me hard.

I guess this is what Audrey meant when she asked me when the last time was that it felt fake. And I can't remember anymore, because in all honesty, it stopped feeling fake almost immediately.

"I don't even know what *this* is, Colt. But whatever it is, I'm in it with you."

Colt leans down, kissing me tenderly, before he pulls back and says, "You've gradually become the single most important person in my life. None of this is fake for me. I'm not sure it ever was."

His tender kisses turn needy and insistent, and I want to be alone with him. I want his clothes off and our bodies pressed together, and I'm not willing to wait a second longer. When I tell him as much, he links our fingers together, pulls me to the edge of the sidewalk, and hails a cab.

"What about your car?" I ask, even though I don't want to waste time going to get it.

"Fuck the car. I'll get it tomorrow."

He opens the cab door for me, and I slide in behind the driver, and when Colt gets in, he tells the driver the address and promises him a good tip if he can get us there in five minutes or less. We speed through the streets of Boston, as Colt's hand moves up my inner thigh and his fingers trail between my legs. As he runs his fingers along my seam, pressing the thick fabric of my jeans into my clit, I have to swallow down the moan that wants to erupt from the pleasure he's already bringing me. He teases me over and over until I'm craving him in a way that feels nearly uncontrollable. I want his fingers inside me so I can fuck them right in the back of this cab.

And then the cabbie takes the turn a little too fast, and I'm thrown toward him. He easily captures me in his hands and sets me on his lap. I'm sitting on his huge erection while he quickly undoes the button of my jeans and pulls the zipper down, and I'm hoping the cabbie can't hear the drag of metal against metal over the music he's playing.

Colt slides his hand down the front of my jeans, dipping his fingers into the front of the lace thong I sewed myself and sliding his fingers along my slick seam before bringing the moisture up to circle my clit. My back arches as I react to his touch and he brings his other hand under my shirt, running his thumb over my nipple as he slides one long finger of his other hand into me. The contact—him entering me while also stroking my breast—has me bucking my hips to meet the shallow thrusts of his finger. His movement is hampered by my jeans, and in this moment, I have no shame. I'd pull them down right now if we weren't already turning onto my street.

"Alright," the cabbie says after clearing his throat like he knows exactly what we're up to back here. "Under five minutes, as promised."

When Colt pulls his finger out of me, I want to cry. I need him so badly I'm not sure I can wait until we get into the house. But I don't have a choice, because he's pulling my shirt down over my open jeans, then opening the door for me. He reaches into his wallet and takes out several bills, which he hands through the opening in the divider between the front and back seats before he steps out of the cab himself.

The way his pants are tented at the zipper as he stands on the sidewalk, looking at me through a lust-filled haze, has me reaching out to stroke him. He lets out a groan, then grabs my hand and pulls me up the front steps, clearly in as much of a hurry to get naked with me as I am with him.

As soon as the door closes behind me, he's pressed me up against it, pulling my legs up so they're wrapped around his waist, and then he's thrusting his enormous and ridiculously hard cock against my clit. The sensation has me moaning into his mouth as his tongue tangles with mine. I slide my hands along his shoulders and push his jacket down until he lets it fall off each arm before bringing his hands back to my ass. I thread mine into his hair, dragging my fingertips along his scalp gently. It's a caress at first, and then I'm digging my fingers into his head, pulling him closer, changing the angle as I pour all my feelings into that kiss.

A minute later, he pulls back, looking at me in awe and saying, "Holy shit, Tink. You kiss like you're ravenous."

"I am," I say with a small shrug, "for you." And then I'm holding on tightly with my legs and pulling my shirt over my head.

He looks down at the sheer lace bra and hisses out his appreciation. "Look at you," he says, gazing down at me as my chest heaves with heavy breaths. A small, private smile graces his lips. It's nothing like the one he flashes for everyone else, and it makes me wonder if anyone but me has gotten to see it.

Before I can ask, he's turning and striding across the entryway to the kitchen. He glances at the table, then turns toward the countertop instead and sets me right on the edge. It's the perfect height, because I'm still wrapped around his waist exactly where he wants me, but now his hands are free to explore.

"This bra is . . ." He looks down at me and shakes his head slightly, like he's forgotten how to speak.

"Thanks. I made it myself."

"Really?" His eyebrows raise as he trails his fingers lightly across the lace, like he forgot that I told him this about the thong he kept.

"Yep. The underwear too."

"This I have to see." He hooks his thumbs into the open waistband of my jeans. "Lift," he commands, and I press up on the countertop to lift my ass off it so he can slide my jeans down over my hips. He pulls them gently down my legs, kneels to remove my shoes and pull the jeans over my feet, then tosses them to the side before standing back up.

My legs are spread on either side of his hips, my heels resting on the drawer pulls below. He stands there staring at me, his eyes raking up and down my body before he finally looks up and meets my gaze. "You are so fucking beautiful."

"Is that why you like me so much, now?" My tone is teasing, but I need to hear from him how he feels. He said he was falling in love, but why?

Stepping forward so that he's between my open legs, he grips my hip bones and leans in to say, "Fuck no. You've always been beautiful, but I never really knew you until recently. It's who you are—your generosity, your honesty, the way you always take care of others, the way you turn prickly when you're hurt, and the way you'll open up to me even when you won't with others—that has me truly falling for you. Now I can't imagine my life without you in it."

His admission seems to suck all the oxygen from the

room. It's so cliché, and yet it must be true, because I'm having a hard time breathing.

"I feel like you're freaking out internally right now. It's okay if you don't feel the same way yet," he says.

"I do." The words barely make it past the lump in my throat, and I can feel my nose heating up the way it does when I cry.

I should be happy—this is what I always dreamed of having with him. But instead, I feel raw. I'm on the verge of tears because he's peeled back all the layers, seen who I really am, and . . . it's made him like me *more*? It's made him love me, even? I didn't know this type of vulnerability with another person was something I could ever let myself experience.

"I don't know what the future looks like for us, Jules," he says as he leans down and rests his forehead on mine. "I just know that my only path forward is with you."

"Yes." It's a whispered plea coming off my lips, both because that's what I want with him, and because he's reached out and is running his thumb along the damp lace of my thong, then stroking upward to my clit. And as he teases me, I undo his tie and unbutton his shirt, until I'm sliding it off and pulling his undershirt up and over his head.

I want him naked, but for now, this view—the hard ridges and planes of his abdomen and chest, his strong arms, his muscular shoulders and neck—will do. This man is *mine*, and I will enjoy him.

When he brings both his hands to my shoulders and hooks his thumbs under the straps of my bra, dragging them down my biceps, I hook my legs around his waist and pull him flush against me. I already miss the feel of him, and as I tilt my hips up, grinding myself along his hard length, he frees my breasts from the lace. His thumbs toy with my nipples as he watches me writhe against him.

"Goddamn, Jules. You keep grinding yourself against me like that and we're not going to make it to the bedroom."

In response, I tighten my hold on his hips and press myself against him even harder. "I *need* you, and only you. Whether you knew it or not, it's always been you. And right now, I need to know what you feel like inside me."

Chapter Thirty-Seven

COLT

I scoop her up and set her on the ground in front of me, and she practically shrieks when her feet meet the cold tile of the floor. Dragging the stretchy lace of her sexy-as-hell bra down her waist and over her hips, I let it drop to the ground. And then I turn her toward the entryway and give her ass a light smack, saying, "Let's go."

"Where are we going, exactly?" she asks, her feet remaining planted in place.

"Upstairs." Stepping up behind her, I drop my voice when I say, "because the first time we have sex, it's not going to be on the kitchen counter."

"But another time?" she asks, her voice hopeful.

"There's pretty much no surface in this house where I haven't already imagined you spread out before me. I'll take you wherever you want, whenever you want. But not this first time."

"Such a gentleman," she teases as she reaches behind her and grasps my belt buckle, pulling me along as she walks across her entryway in nothing but her thong.

I step behind her as we approach the front door. We didn't turn any lights on, and it's unlikely someone's on the sidewalk outside her brownstone but, just in case, I make sure to block her from view with my body. And then when we reach the stairs, I pull her hand off my buckle.

"I want to watch you walk up those stairs, just like I did earlier tonight at the arena. But instead of imagining what you look like naked, I'm going to enjoy every moment of seeing all of you."

She glances over her shoulder at me as she takes the first step. "You were picturing me naked during your warm-ups?"

"I'm always picturing you naked, Jules. Get used to it."

She takes each step, just like she did at the arena tonight, and the gentle sway of her hips above her muscular thighs and ass has me wanting to grip her hips and watch myself slide into her from behind.

When she looks back at me and says, "Are you coming?" I take the steps two at a time, and she does as well, as we hurry to get to the bedroom. But the minute she crosses the threshold to her room, she stops, and I have to put my hand up on the top of the door frame so I don't run right into the back of her.

I snake my other hand along her bare waist and pull her back to me, relishing the way her hair feels pressed up against my bare skin.

"What's wrong, Tink?"

She turns, running her palms along my chest on their way

to my shoulders before she wraps her arms around my neck. The feel of her breasts against my chest has the blood rushing to my dick so fast I almost feel lightheaded.

"What makes tonight different than all the other nights you turned me down?"

"You really don't know?" When she shakes her head, I say, "I needed you to feel the same way about me that I feel about you. I didn't want you to sleep with me because I was convenient and willing, I wanted you to want *me*."

Her voice is practically a whisper when she says, "I've always wanted *you*, Colt. I just never thought you'd feel the same way. I'm sorry if . . ." She takes a deep breath and lets out a sigh. "I'm sorry if I made you feel like I was using you to cross something off my bucket list."

I kiss the bridge of her nose. "I'm one hundred percent fine with you using me for sex, now that I know how you feel." Bringing my hands to her inner thighs, I scoop her up so she's wrapping her legs around me again, and walk over to the bed, where I set her on the edge and step between her parted legs. "In fact, I see *a lot* of sex in our future."

Without breaking eye contact, she undoes my belt, then unbuttons my pants and pulls the zipper down. As she slides them down my thighs and lets them pool at my ankles, my cock strains against the fabric of my boxer briefs now that my zipper is no longer holding it back. Jules reaches out and touches me, cupping her hand and smoothing her palm along my shaft as she brings her fingers to my head, circling it before she hooks her thumbs into my briefs and lifts them over my dick to push them down my legs.

As she leans forward to do so, her lips part and she sucks

me into her mouth. It's impossible to resist pushing into her as her tongue laves against my length, and her hum of approval makes me do it again. She doesn't seem to mind me hitting the back of her throat, which makes me wonder if she has a gag reflex at all. *Something to explore another time*, I think to myself.

She grasps the base of my cock with one hand as the other slides down between her legs, and then she's moaning around me, and I watch in fascination as her fingers dip into her underwear and work her clit with the same tempo she's taking me into her mouth. I reach out, brushing my palms along her nipples, and she moans again, sending shock waves through my body and spurring me on. Her hand begins moving frantically between her legs as she lets me fuck her mouth, and when she starts moaning through the orgasm she's giving herself, it's all I can do to hold myself off from coming right down the back of her throat. But I cling to that last, thin thread of self-control because there's no way we're not having sex immediately after she's done.

As her orgasm recedes, she releases me from her mouth and looks up into my eyes as she licks a circle around the head of my cock like some sort of vixen. Then she's standing and sliding her thong down her legs before she steps forward and presses her fully naked body against mine. I sweep her legs up in one arm while I hold her back, cradling her as I take a step toward the bed and lay her down.

"You're a fucking masterpiece and I want to see every inch of you," I say, standing over her and taking in the sight of her long limbs and muscular body. The bed dips under my weight as I plant my knees between her legs.

She lets her knees fall open, baring herself to me, and I suck in a breath at the sight of her—even in the moonlight streaming through the window, I can see her smooth skin glistening with evidence of her orgasm.

Planting one hand above her shoulder, I lean down and kiss her forehead. I'm about to promise her that I'll take it slow, be gentle with her, when she says, "I can't even tell you how many times I've dreamed about this."

"I don't know what you dreamed up, Tink, but I can promise you, this is going to be so much better."

She reaches out and strokes the entire length of me, and I almost lose my mind and push into her bare. *Shit.* "I, uh, I have to go upstairs and get a condom. I don't have one on me."

"I have a whole drawer full," she says, nodding her chin toward her nightstand.

"Why do *you* have a whole drawer full?"

She cocks an eyebrow at me. "Because I planned on having a lot of sex with you when you finally gave in." With slow, gentle strokes, she continues sliding her hand along my shaft, making me impossibly hard. "What are we waiting for?"

I take a deep breath, exhaling slowly. "This is going to change everything."

"Good." She gestures toward the nightstand again, and so I reach over and slide the drawer open, grabbing a condom out of a bowl they're sitting in. As I tear the foil packet open, she says, "Show me how to put it on you."

The sight of her lying beneath me, using her long fingers to roll the condom over my tip and down my shaft with so much care and reverence, is doing funny things to my heart.

This couldn't be more different from all the one-night stands I've had in the past—mostly because I want to see this sight every night for the rest of my life.

When her hand reaches the end of my cock, I lean in to kiss her, and she sucks my lower lip into her mouth, sinking her teeth into it lightly like I've noticed she likes to do. As she wraps one leg around my ass, pulling me closer to her, I know what she wants, but I want to make sure she's ready. Reaching between us, I slide my fingers over her clit and down to her entrance. She's so wet that two fingers slip into her tight pussy easily.

"Colt, when I said I wanted you inside of me, that wasn't what I meant," she growls against my cheek after pulling away from the kiss, making me chuckle.

"You're adorable when you're frustrated."

"Please, don't make me wait any longer."

"Well, if you're going to beg—"

"I'm not begging," she says, using her lower leg to push down on my body until my cock hits my hand. "But I will if you want me to."

I slip my fingers out of her and make sure I'm lined up with her entrance, and as I push into her, I tell her, "There's no reason to beg for something I can't wait to give you, Jules."

She sucks in a breath when she takes the first couple of inches of me, and then she relaxes as I drive my hips forward slowly. She's hot, and tight, and wet, and lying there with all her hair fanned out beneath her, and those big blue eyes staring up at me, she's basically a goddess. The dream girl I didn't know I was looking for and was lucky enough to find anyway.

She winces when I'm not even all the way in yet, and I freeze. "Are you okay?"

"Just . . . so full. I've never been this full."

"Not even with your extensive toy collection?" I tease.

Her eyes widen. "How do you know about that?"

"Besides the one I got a first-hand view of in the shower, you mean? You told me all about your collection on our walk home when you were drunk."

"No, I didn't," she says, tilting her hips up to take more of me. "There's no way I was that drunk."

I lean my face down and nuzzle into her hair next to her ear. "So you're saying you told me about all your different vibrators while sober. Got it." I draw my hips forward, pushing into her farther.

And then she tightens her leg over my ass and slams her hips up so I enter her completely. She hisses as her muscles contract around me, and I swear to God I see stars.

"That's better," she says on a breath. "Stop treating me like I'm going to break. I need you to fuck me like you mean it."

"Like I mean what, exactly?" I ask as I start to move inside her with long, slow strokes.

"Like you mean all the things you said to me earlier tonight."

Moving one of my knees up under hers, I smooth my hand up her ribcage on the opposite side of her body, letting my thumb graze under her breast and across her nipple. And then I'm sliding my palm around her collarbone and up her neck until I'm cupping her chin in my hand.

Kissing her lips lightly, I whisper, "The problem is, I don't want to fuck you like I'm falling in love with you. I want to fuck you like I'm trying to ruin you for every other man in existence."

I feel her chest shake with laughter and I still because I can't figure out why that would make her laugh. She responds by tightening the walls of her core and squeezing my cock, then she reaches out and cups my cheek in her hand.

"You already *have*, Colt. You've shown me how I should be treated by a man. You've shown me that I can trust you, and that I don't have to control everything. Now, I just want to lose control with you. So fuck me however you want to because I'm going to love it no matter what."

Her words unleash whatever part of me I've been holding back. I am absolutely feral for this woman, and determined that she know it, feel it, and understand it before this is done. And as I move inside her with abandon, she meets me thrust for thrust. Our lips, tongues, and teeth tangle together as we devour each other wholly—it's like the first time I kissed her in the alley, but a hundred times better, too. While I kiss her, my free hand explores her body, caressing and gripping the smooth expanse of her skin, learning every nook and cranny of her. I want to memorize every single thing about her, so that I can still feel her with me when I leave for a road trip later this week.

I don't want to go.

Later on, when I'm not in the middle of having sex with the girl of my dreams, I'll have to figure out what it means that I've had that thought twice tonight. I've never dreaded going on a road trip. I've never wished I was home with a woman instead.

Then again, I never had anyone like Jules in my life before.

"Yes," she hisses as I drive into her deeply. As I bottom out, I tilt my hips so the end of my cock hits the ridges deep inside her that I know will help her orgasm again. With my body grinding against her clit, and her legs wrapped so tightly around my waist that I can barely pull out of her, I know I'm hitting all the right places.

"Holy shit," she says, her breath catching, "please don't stop."

"There's no chance we're stopping, Tink. Not until you're screaming my name so loud someone alerts the media."

She wraps her hand around the back of my head and pulls my face to hers, sinking her teeth into my lower lip before she says mumbles into my mouth, "How about you make me?"

"Don't worry, I plan to."

I bring my other knee up under her other thigh and wrap my arm around her lower back as I continue with the deep thrusts that have her chanting, "Yes, fuck yes," over and over. And then her chants are practically screams, as her muscles pulse around me while her orgasm overtakes her. And when she yells, "Oh my god, oh shit, Colt!" I trail gentle kisses up the side of her neck and behind her ear as I let her ride the waves of her release on my cock.

The feeling of her coming on me, the way her body rhythmically squeezes mine, has electricity flowing through my veins until the pulsing in my balls has me emptying myself into her in several long, hard thrusts.

"Holy shit," she says as I collapse on my elbow, hovering just above her. Her lower body is still wrapped around mine, but she exhales until the rest of her is almost lifeless beneath me. "I don't know what that was, but it was magic. Is it always like that?"

I look down at her flushed cheeks, the way she's still panting and not letting me go. I want to be joined to her like this forever.

"No," I tell her honestly. "It's *never* like this. Except with you."

Chapter Thirty-Eight

JULES

"Alright, we'll be in touch then," Jay Davenport says, shaking my hand and then Audrey's as the elevator dings to alert us to its arrival on his floor of the building.

Meeting with him has been the polar opposite of my meeting with Jerome weeks ago. Jay has been nothing but professional, explaining that his interest in the program is because—with the number of commercial properties he owns in downtown—he has his own crews for repairs and renovations but has trouble finding qualified, reliable people to keep on staff. When he told me what the starting salary was at his company, I was floored. That kind of income could make a huge difference in people's lives, and I'm thrilled that he's specifically looking to hire women too.

"Thank you so much for your time," I say as we turn and step into the elevator.

"Looking forward to working with you," Audrey adds, and then the doors close.

We turn toward each other, and I hold my index finger to my mouth as I look up and watch the floors count down while the elevator descends. When we've gone down fifteen floors, I figure that's far enough, and I reach over, bracing my hands on Audrey's shoulders as I say, "Holy shit!"

Both of us are squealing with excitement, because the donation he just promised us is a game changer. We'll be able to help so many people, and I'm confident that his guidance will be extremely valuable as we grow the mentoring program.

"Okay, we need to meet with Morgan and figure out our next steps," Audrey says. Morgan's only official role in Our House is to run our social media accounts, but this mentoring program was her brainchild. We'll need her help messaging out more information about expanding the program, and she may even be able to help us recruit a director for the non-profit. Her recently acquired MBA, combined with her social media experience and her willing-ness to share her wealth of business knowledge, have been invaluable.

"Can you set up some time with her?" I ask as the elevator arrives at the lobby . "I have to run over to the Seaport and see the progress on Colt's condo, but I can make time tomorrow or Friday."

"Wait, is Colt's place done already?"

"God no," I tell her as we cross the lobby. The fact that she thinks damage that extensive could be cleaned up and rebuilt in the past several weeks is proof that she knows very little about the construction side of our business. "But drywall is going up tomorrow, so he wants me to look at everything before it's all closed up."

"Alright. I'll text you and let you know when Morgan's free so we can meet and figure out next steps."

We go our separate ways, me to where I parked my truck down the street, and her toward the Boston Common because she says it's too nice of an evening not to walk home. Getting over to Colt's building in the Seaport is easier than I'd expect at this time of day, mostly because Boston traffic seems to start well before rush hour and is generally better by the time I'd expect it to be bad.

I leave my truck with the valet, who tells me it'll be parked next to Colt's in the garage, keys inside, when I'm ready for it. And then I'm headed up to the thirtieth floor. Colt greets me at the door, but I hardly notice him as he stands there taking up most of the doorframe, because in the space beside him, I have a clear view directly out the floor-to-ceiling glass walls. And with the sun already on the horizon, Boston Harbor looks like it's on fire with ribbons of gold and orange dancing across the surface of the water.

"Holy shit," I sigh, one hand pressed to my chest. "This view . . ."

Colt looks down at me. "I'd say thanks, but I don't think you're talking about me."

"You're so full of yourself." I laugh as he pulls me to him, circling his arms around my back and pressing a kiss to the top of my head.

"If I had my way right now, you'd be full of me too."

"I don't know why I like you so much," I say, rising onto my tiptoes so I can trail kisses across his jaw.

"Because I'm a likable guy."

I snort out a laugh. "You're tolerable, I suppose." I don't

know why I keep pretending to resist him—but it's like a defense mechanism I can't let go of after so many years.

"You seemed to tolerate me just fine when I was buried inside you last night." The words are a low caress against my ear and send a shiver down my spine.

I can't help the way my body tries to curl into him, how my hips want to rise and meet his, how my skin wants his rough hands skating gently across it, how my core aches to have him inside me again.

"Meh," I say, and go to move past him.

But he captures my hand in his, pulling me back to him as he drops his voice so deep it's practically a growl. "Every time you try to push me away, I'm going to pull you right back. If I'm going to fall, you're coming down with me."

A chill runs up my spine as his words sink in, and then my hands are sliding up his chest and my arms are snaking around his neck as I pull him close. "I'm right there with you. I'm sorry I keep pushing you away. I know it's a defense mechanism, I just don't know how to stop it."

"You'll know."

"What does that mean?"

"It means that you'll know when you can fully trust me because you won't feel the need to do it anymore."

I gaze up at that perfectly sculpted face. "I do trust you, Colt."

"You're getting there." He dips his head and kisses my forehead.

I'm about to tell him that he doesn't get to decide when I trust him enough. But then he spins us around and shuts the door behind us, pushing me farther down the hallway toward his living room. The view is fucking spectacular.

As I come down the few steps to the sunken living room, which has to be bigger than the entire first floor of my brownstone, I can see the islands of the harbor dotting the water. Beyond them, the horizon is streaked with the same orange and gold as the water, but with pinks and lavenders as well. Because we're on the Eastern Seaboard, we don't get true sunsets over the water in Boston. But every once in a while, before it dips below the buildings on the other side of the city, the sun reflects off the water and the sky like this, giving us a textbook-perfect sunset.

"What do you think?" Colt asks, coming up behind me where I've stopped in the middle of his living room.

"I still can't believe this view."

"I meant about the condo?"

I glance around, and between the steel studs, the foam insulation is neatly cured. The electrical wires and plumbing tubes run exactly where they should. "How can you expect me to talk about work with a view like this?"

His eyes flick toward the windows, then back at me. "The view's okay."

"Okay?" I drag out the word. "What the hell are you talking about? How could you be desensitized to a view like this?"

"Trust me, you just get used to it." He reaches out, pulling me to him like he always does. I love that he can't seem to keep his hands off me, and always wants me as close as possible. I always thought that I'd hate it if a man were clingy, but with Colt, I love it. Knowing that he could have anyone, and only wants me—it's the reassurance I didn't realize I needed. "This view, though," he says, focusing in on my face, "I can't get enough of this view."

I smooth my palm along his jaw, cupping his face. "Good. You'll need to get your fill tonight, though, because after the game tomorrow, I won't see you for almost four days. Not that I'm counting," I add hastily.

"Clearly."

"I don't like feeling this way."

"What way's that?" he asks, amusement tinging his words.

"I hate the ups and downs—being thrilled to see you when you're here, and then missing you like crazy when you're gone. It's too much."

"There's no such thing as too much, Tink. You can never be too excited to see me, or miss me too much when I'm not here."

"But I don't want to feel all those emotions," I tell him. Life was simpler when I got up every day, worked my job, mentored a few women, spoiled my immediate family, and occasionally made some beautiful lingerie, and then went to sleep to do it all again in the morning.

"More things to talk about in therapy, it sounds like."

"Yeah, I promise I won't cancel this weekend's meeting," I assure him.

"Good. Okay, so can you take a quick look around, let me know what you think of everything so I can give them the go ahead to put the walls up tomorrow?"

"Sure." As I walk the perimeter of the large space, looking at things the way I know an inspector would, it occurs to me that if they're putting walls up tomorrow, the inspector must already have signed off on everything.

When I ask him why he's having me look at it in that case, he just shrugs and says, "I want to make sure it's done right, and I know you'd never accept anything less than the best work."

"Everything looks good," I say, crossing the room to where he stands, waiting for me near the sliding glass doors.

He takes my hand, leading me out to the large and incredibly private balcony. Full walls on both sides prevent you from seeing onto any neighbor's balcony. It's a full-on outdoor room out here, and the only view is directly out beyond the glass half-wall, toward the ocean.

It was beautiful the last time I was here, but we were distracted by the wreckage that was his apartment—and I was so busy trying not to eavesdrop on his conversation with Gabriel—that I didn't fully appreciate this view.

He gestures to the large sectional couch off to the side. There's a coffee table with two place settings and heaps of takeout containers stacked there. "I got us Italian."

We're sitting on pillows we've put on the floor and are almost done with dinner, when I finally work up the nerve to ask the question that's been bothering me since I first walked in here. "So, are you looking forward to this renovation finally being done?"

Leaning back against the couch, he lifts his arm and rests it along the cushions as he turns toward me. "I'm dreading it, actually."

"Why?" It springs from my mouth, because his place is beyond amazing and it's going to be even better than before when it's done. I know that for a fact because Audrey and I helped him pick all the finishes.

He just stares at me. "Why do you think, Tink?"

My lips part, but the words don't come. So he reaches up,

tracing my lower lip with his thumb as he waits for me to speak.

"Why don't you tell me, so we can avoid this whole guessing game," I say, hating the way I can't make myself admit that I *hope* it's because the thought of not living with me is tearing him up.

His hand slides from my face to my neck, holding the side possessively, like he's reminding me I'm his.

"Because I don't want to be two feet away from you, much less halfway across the city. I don't want to spend a second away from you that I don't have to. So no, I'm not looking forward to my place being done, because I don't plan on moving back in here unless you kick me out."

My breath is trapped in my lungs, which refuse to expand. Then I take a heaving gasp, and nod out toward the ocean view. "You'd give all this up to live in your fake fiancée's childhood home?"

"I'd give *everything* up to be with you. It's not even a question." He sighs, his fingers tightening around the back of my neck. "The only way I'm moving out is if we break up. And if you remember, the only way this is ending is if *you* break it off."

"And if I don't?"

"Then I guess you're stuck with me . . . and that ring."

I stiffen involuntarily, and he gives me a questioning look.

"It's not that I don't want to be with you. But I don't want my inaction to be the reason we stay together."

"What do you mean?"

"Being together should be a conscious choice, not the default thing that happens because I don't end it."

"Isn't *not* ending it a conscious choice? We agreed that we'd stay together until the end of playoffs. If we decide to stay together beyond that, isn't it a choice?"

Shrugging, I pause for a moment as I try to put my feelings, and worries, into words. "Colt . . . I . . ." I take a deep breath. "I've never done any of this before. I've never fallen for someone. I've never had sex with anyone. I've never been in love. It's . . ."

"We're going to take this slow, because I know that's what you need. But I want to remind you . . . you *have* done all of that before. *You've done it with me.* And as scary as you're finding all of it, just know that I am too."

"Is this what love feels like? I don't even know, and I'm not sure you do, either," I admit. I don't want us to fall into this because it's convenient—because we like spending time together, we cohabitate well, and the sex is great. It has to be based on more than that . . . doesn't it?

"I was nineteen—a damn child, and a fool one at that— the last time I told someone I loved them," Colt says. "I thought I knew then what love was, but that wasn't it. My heart didn't literally ache when I was away from her. I didn't spend every spare moment planning ways to spend more time with her. She wasn't the first thing I thought of when I woke up, or the last person I wanted to see before I fell asleep. I didn't know what every single sound she made meant . . . never even thought to catalog that information away like I do with you. So don't tell me I don't know what love is. I've experienced what it *isn't* well enough to know what it *is.*"

My heart is pounding, in response to his admission, so I lean toward him, resting my head in the hollow where his raised arm meets his shoulder. "I'm sorry. It's not that I don't have these feelings. It's that I don't know how to deal with them. Emotions scare me."

"At least you can admit it." Stroking the back of my head, he leans down and plants a kiss on top of it. "And they scare me, too. We're learning, together. I think maybe you just need to remember what you told me last night."

"What was that?" I ask.

"You said I'd already ruined you for any other man. That I'd shown you how you should be treated, that you can trust me, and that you're not afraid of letting go of your need to control things when I'm around. And then you said you were going to love me no matter what."

"Did I really?" My heart feels like my chest is constricting around it. Every word of that is true, but I must have been feeling especially safe and secure to say it out loud. Either that, or sex made me lose my mind.

"I think that maybe," Colt says as the beginning of a smirk quirks his lips, "you are more honest when you're naked."

"Are you trying to get me naked right now?" I ask, eyes narrowing playfully.

His hand slides down to the buttons of my sleeveless blouse. "I'm always trying to get you naked."

The way the heel of his hand grazes my nipple as he toys with the first button has a wave of longing rippling through me. I push up on my knees and swing my leg over his so I'm straddling him. I already knew I had a high sex drive, but now having had sex has made me feel like an addict. All I've thought about every waking moment today is having him inside me again, as soon as possible.

"Someone's eager." He chuckles, and the vibrations run

along my abdomen, like the shock waves of a bomb detonating. Between my legs, I can feel him growing hard where my center is pressed up against him, so I slide my hips forward and back right along his length, pulling a deep sigh from the back of his throat.

"Now that you've shown me what sex can be like, you're going to have to provide a repeat performance so I know it wasn't a fluke."

He glances up at me, taking his eyes off the narrow buttons he was undoing. "A fluke, huh?"

I raise an eyebrow in response, taking over and unbuttoning the last two buttons without even looking at them. Sliding the blouse down my arms, I toss it onto the couch.

Colt sucks in a sharp breath when my bra comes into view. It's made of a stretchy sheer nude-colored mesh, with the palest pink flowers embroidered right over my nipples. The drag of the embroidery over my hardening peaks has me feeling extra turned on, but the heat in his eyes almost drives me over the edge. "Did you make this one, too?"

"Yep."

"Are you going to show me how you do this?"

"How I make them?" I clarify, and when he nods, I say, "Sure, someday. But right now, all I want to do is show you how to take it off without ruining it." My fingers meet between my breasts, and I fold the two pieces of the plastic clip forward so that the clasp opens, and then I pull the bra open in the front.

"You are so goddamn stunning," he says, his eyes focused on my breasts and then moving up to my face. "Not just the way you look . . . but everything about you. I didn't expect you." His hands skim my breasts on their way to my chest, where he presses his palm against my sternum. "You take up all the space in my heart."

Goddamn. "You seem to have fixed all the cracks in my heart, too."

"I feel like I put most of them there," he says, his voice low and raw. "The least I can do is help repair them."

I reach between us for his buckle, wanting to get these pants off as quickly as possible. "Stand for a sec," he says as he works to push his pants down, but is hampered by the way I'm sitting on his lap.

I do as he asks, and with my legs spread on either side of him, he's looking right at my thighs, where he sits on the ground with his back against the frame of the outdoor couch. And as he pushes his pants and underwear down his legs, kicking off his shoes and following them with his remaining clothing, he leans forward. Then his hands are pulling my skirt down over my hips, and he brings his nose to my center, inhaling deeply through the thin scrap of fabric.

"Jesus, Jules. I can tell how much you want me." He presses his tongue against my already damp underwear, licking me through the sheer material, and making me gasp. "You're so wet for me."

He glides his tongue over me, adding additional friction as he circles around my clit, while reaching up and cupping my breasts together, dragging his rough thumbs over my sensitive nipples in a way that brings me along quickly. "Fuck that feels good," I breathe out. "But it's not enough. I need you, Colt."

Pulling back, he smacks my ass lightly, and I look down at him in surprise.

"Hands on the railing. I want to see myself enter you."

"Aren't you . . . worried someone is going to see us?"

His chuckle is deep. "On the thirtieth floor? Look around, Jules," he says, and I turn, my eyes scanning the horizon.

There are no other buildings, and only a few small boats dot the water of the harbor. In the distance, Boston Light is sending its beam of light out into the ocean as a warning to ships that land is near. But for me, it's a beacon, calling me home, showing me that I'm exactly where I'm meant to be.

"Who's going to see us?" he asks.

I lean toward the glass wall with its steel-framed railing along the top, planting my hands there and spreading my legs slightly as I tilt my ass up toward Colt. The hum of anticipation that flows through my body has me practically shaking, and it's a relief that it's from excitement and not fear. I've never felt so comfortable around anyone before.

"My god, you're a fucking vision," he says, kneeling behind me. Strong hands grip my thighs as he moves my thong to the side and licks me from my clit all the way along my slit. "I can't wait to be inside you." His tongue returns to my clit, flicking back and forth over it in quick, sure strokes that have me tingling all over.

In front of me is nothing but the inky blue sky dotted with a few stars, and the ray of the lighthouse sweeping the horizon. Thirty stories below me, cars and pedestrians move along the street, completely unaware that up on this balcony, Colt's got his face buried in me, his tongue working overtime to bring me my first orgasm of the night.

My core tightens, my muscles pulling together rhythmically, wanting to grip him but instead finding an empty chasm. "More," I say between the quick, shallow pants that seem to be all my lungs are capable of. "Please, Colt, I need more."

When I see movement on the floor near me, I glance down, realizing that he's groping around in the dark for his pants. He's probably looking for a condom.

"I love you on your knees like this for me, but I want you inside me *now*," I insist, as my legs quake and my muscles contract. "I want to come all over you before you fuck me into oblivion."

"Jesus, Jules," he groans. But instead of the reprimand it usually feels like when my family says it, with Colt, it sounds like he's praying. Worshiping me. "I need a second to find a condom."

The waves are moving through my core, threatening to tip me over the edge. "No, you don't. We're fine. I have an IUD. As long as you're clean?"

"I am," he says, pulling my thong down in one quick movement. Then he leans over against my back, his huge, hot cock resting right along my ass, as he asks softly, "Are you sure? Because this—having sex like this—is huge. It's a first for me, too."

I glance over at him, where his chin rests on my shoulder. "I'm glad I can be your first for something, too."

"You're my first for just about every single thing besides sex, Jules." He reaches down, dragging the tip of his cock along my wet seam, teasing me as he presses it over my clit. I can't hold in my moan as I rock my body against him, needing the friction and pressure against that bundle of nerves. What I *really* need is him filling me. "And you're never doing this with anyone else. This is forever."

My thoughts are a jumbled mess as I try to absorb what

he's saying, what he's promising. But I can't seem to find my words, all I can do is groan out a "Yesss," as he presses into me, entering me slowly. The sensation of his skin on mine, inside me and all around me, has me pressing back into him, taking all of him at once.

He lets out a whispered, "Holy shit," as he starts to move. His fingers make their way around my hip and down to my clit, giving me the friction I needed there as he thrusts inside me, and I feel like I'm about to explode all around him. I was already so close, and the tingling sensation spreads through me quickly, until I'm grunting each time I sink back onto him.

"Look at you," he says, and I look up over my shoulder at him. He's standing behind me, watching me take him as he pushes into me. "Look at that beautiful pussy, taking me so well. You were fucking made for me." Increasing the pace, his jaw clamps together, the words barely escaping through gritted teeth as he says, "You're mine."

"I'm yours," I agree, as I use the railing at the top of the glass wall for leverage to help me push back into him and set the pace I need. And when my muscles contract within my core, it's a completely new sensation—it's not the manual stimulation on my clit that's bringing me to orgasm, it's the way that ridged head of his cock slides along the deepest recesses of me. I swear I see stars that aren't there as white-hot heat pours through me, every drag of his dick threatening to tip me over the edge and into euphoria. And when it happens, I cry out, followed by a promise. "I'll always be yours."

Chapter Thirty-Nine

COLT

"You are on fire tonight," McCabe yells at me when I snag another puck. For a second, I thought the slap shot might get by me. But at this point in my career, knowing exactly where the puck is at is almost second nature. I didn't even have time to look for it as I snagged it out of the air, but the whistle signals the stop of play.

"Don't fucking say it," I tell McCabe as I toss the puck at the ref for a face-off.

"Not saying shit," he says. He knows what I mean. I don't want him to even mutter the S-word, even though right now, as we're up 3-0 with less than a minute left in the third period, it's on everyone's mind. I haven't had a shutout in a while, and I'd love to have one on home ice with my whole family and Jules in attendance, but I'm also superstitious as hell and don't want to jinx it.

As the players line up around the circle to my left, one of Carolina's forwards, Martin Levesque, shoots a look over his shoulder at me. He's been coming at me all game, with comments like, "You broke Lester's fucking face."

That's right, I did. Not only did I fracture his nose, but he has a hairline fracture in his cheekbone. I saw the pictures that were posted online and despite how bruised and swollen he was, I didn't feel an ounce of fucking regret. I sure as shit hope he felt some, though.

The fine the league levied and the way my goalie coach ripped me a new asshole . . . those were incredibly small prices to pay. Jules will never get the apology she deserves from him, but hopefully his broken face at least helps avenge her.

As soon as the puck drops, Lester's asshole friend skates backward toward me. He's not lining up to receive a shot. The puck is down near center ice, but the ref won't call him offsides unless someone passes to him. He keeps his back to me and plants himself right in front of me. And then the top of his stick flies right at my face, catching in my mask as he pulls me forward and throws me to the ground.

I hear the whistle, and when I get up, I don't move to fight him. I just laugh at him and say, "Tell Lester I said I hope his face looks like that forever. And enjoy the rest of the game in the penalty box. We could use a fourth goal on a power play, anyway."

The refs get to him before my teammates do, which is lucky for him, because if there's anything that'll get you an ass kicking in hockey, it's touching the other team's goalie. And when Walsh sinks the puck into the other net, I take a moment to skate over to the sin bin and personally thank Levesque for his terrible judgment.

I feel like I've aged ten years in the time it takes me to get all my gear off, shower, listen to the post-game pep talk Wilcott gives us, pack up my gear for our trip down south, and talk to the media. Everyone wants to discuss the shutout, and all I want is to spend as much time as possible with Jules before I have to get on that plane tonight.

I'm finally heading over to say hello to my family and goodbye to Jules when a text comes through from a number I don't recognize.

UNKNOWN NUMBER

> Hey Colt, it's Jasmine. I need to talk to you after the game. Can you tell me where to meet you?

I don't know what it is about this woman that makes her incapable of taking a hint. When she was hitting on me the other night at the Neon Cactus, asking why I never call her back, I explained that I'm engaged and very much not interested. Is she one of those women who only wants you more when they think you're playing hard to get?

Instead of responding, I block this number too. I told my fiancée that I'd blocked all the women in my contacts, and I mean to keep that promise.

Jules is the first person I see when I walk through the doors, but she's deep in conversation with my nephew and doesn't notice me. Her blond hair is in a ponytail, and she's talking with her hands, which she only does when she gets really excited about something. As I come up behind her, Simon says, "That's so cool. I'd love to be able to learn from you. Maybe I can visit over the summer and shadow you on a job site for a couple days? I mean, if you don't mind."

Simon is currently a sophomore at a technical high school, training to be a carpenter. He has always loved building things, and he's particularly talented when it comes to woodworking. The fact that he wants to learn from Jules, and the way Cheri and Gabriel are looking at her like she's amazing and accomplished, has me kind of choked up.

It's ironic that this whole thing started because I couldn't get over what they'd done to me, but as soon as Jules was in my life, their betrayal ceased to have the impact it once had.

"Mathieu," my mom's voice rings out when she sees me standing there. I notice Jules lean in and say something to Simon, but I can't hear what it is because Mom's already thrown her arms around me and is chatting away about the game.

"What a game for us to come see!" Dad says, as he claps me on the shoulder. "You did well."

"Yeah," Simon says. "The shutout was great, but I can't believe we missed the coolest fight ever the other night."

"Yeah, what the hell happened out there?" Gabriel asks. "It's not like you to fight."

He's right, and it only reinforces my suspicion that he's followed my career closely despite me refusing to talk to him. His voice carries the notes of *proud big brother* any time he mentions hockey.

I glance at Jules before I say, "It was a long time coming."

"Why?" my dad asks. "What did he do to you?"

I've seen the replays. It's obvious that Lester was taunting me before I gave him a beating. But I'm not going to repeat what he said—they don't need to know about Jules's past, unless she decides she wants to tell them.

"He was defending me." She speaks up, and everyone—me included—is so surprised that we all fall silent. "I had . . . a thing with him a long time ago. And Colt was standing up for me."

"Good," my dad says, with a decisive nod, at the same time my mom says, "No one messes with our family."

There's a tightness in my chest that's almost painful. It's pride and longing and happiness, all mixed together, but instead of it making me feel lighter, I feel heavy. This trip to North Carolina is weighing on me. I don't know why I'm so opposed to leaving her, why the thought of being away from her for four days has me wanting to claw my way out of my own skin.

Is this how the other guys feel when they leave their wives and girlfriends behind? I'll have to ask Drew or Walshy.

We stand around chatting for a bit and the topic of the shutout comes up more than once. At one point, while my family is discussing the game, Cheri turns toward me and quietly says, "I'm really happy for you."

"Thanks," I say. "I mean, shutouts don't happen often, so I'm pretty happy too."

"I meant about Jules," she says, and there's nothing she could have said that would have shocked me more. "You found someone who makes you happy in a way I never did. I'm so sorry how everything went down back then." *How everything went down* feels like a vast understatement, but it's not worth making a fuss over since she's actually apologizing. "Mistakes were made, and I didn't own up to my part in them. I let Gabriel handle everything, and I've always felt like I should have told you how sorry I was. I know it probably doesn't matter to you now, but I'm apologizing anyway."

"It matters," I say, determined to take the high road here. It's easier now that I truly have moved past what they did. "Thank you for apologizing."

"Hey." Jules's voice is smooth as she steps toward me, coming up to my side and snaking her arm behind my back as she pulls me to her. "Nice job out there tonight."

Cheri steps away, giving us a little privacy in the otherwise crowded room. I turn toward Jules, pulling her into a hug and pressing my face to the top of her head. "I'm going to miss you so fucking much," I tell her.

"You're just going to miss being in my bed."

My chest shakes with a silent laugh. "I'll miss that part too."

"It's only four and a half days," she says, looking up at me, but it sounds like she's reassuring herself as much as me. "You'll be home by the time I wake up on Tuesday morning. We can do this."

"*You* can do this. I'm not so sure about me." I press my lips together between my teeth because I'm afraid my damn lower lip is trembling with how much the thought of being away from her has me about to tear up.

"You're going to be fine. You spent the last fifteen years traveling for hockey."

"Yeah, well, I was never falling in love before." I bend to give her a gentle kiss, trying to savor this moment—the way she feels wrapped in my arms, and the way her whole face softens when I admit my feelings.

"Time to go," someone shouts from behind me, and it

only makes me cling to her more tightly. I'm not sure how I've fallen so fast, and so hard, for someone I've known for so long, but I can no longer imagine my life without her. Someday, I'm going to say the three words that have been running through my mind nonstop the past few days. But I'm forcing myself to wait until she's ready to hear them.

And when I finally pull away and turn to walk out the door, Walsh walks up beside me.

"Does it get easier?" I push the words out through the lump in my throat, and even out of context, I'm pretty sure he knows what I mean.

"In some ways. And then it gets harder again with kids."

I don't tell him that Jules doesn't want kids—a decision I'm completely fine with. I'd have kids with her if that's what she wanted, but at this point in my life, I'm already an honorary uncle to her nieces and nephew, and that works just fine for me. We can spoil them relentlessly but still have our nights and weekends to ourselves, have actual adult conversations without being constantly peppered with questions, and take vacations alone. The best of both worlds, if you ask me.

Chapter Forty

JULES

"I deeply regret my life choices right now," I tell Morgan as I set the bolt of tulle on my farmhouse table and look around at the mess of fabric, vases, and candles scattered around my kitchen.

Morgan sighs, then takes a deep gulp from the bottle of hard cider she just opened. "She's going to love it, and that's all that matters. Right?"

"Of course. But we are not crafty people. Why didn't we just do this at a restaurant?"

"Because we wanted it to be personal, and we wanted to be able to hang out all day."

"Well, we should have just hired someone to plan this all."

"All we're doing are the table arrangements and the photo booth," she reminds me. At least we decided to have it catered, because as much as I enjoy cooking, I find I'm doing a lot less of it now. Partially because stress was always a motivating factor with my cooking, and with Colt around all the time, I'm either less stressed or just better able to handle it.

I glance over at the ten-by-ten whitewashed wooden backdrop that stands against one wall of my entryway. Building it was the only part of this party that I've felt equipped to help with. We have strands of leaves and flowers that need to be intertwined and hung along the wooden frame, and a custom-cut banner with adorable gold letters that will hang beneath the floral swag. But the vases and candles and the fresh flowers that will be delivered tomorrow, all of those decorations feel very much outside of my wheelhouse, even though I know we're creating something spectacular that Lauren will love.

"I should have taken Graham home for bed and let Audrey stay and help. She'd probably be a lot better at all this than me."

Morgan laughs. "Jules, you work with your hands. You're great at this stuff."

"Being good at something and enjoying it are two totally different things."

The only thing keeping me going is knowing how much Lauren will love it, and I'd do just about anything to make her happy. Even her gift, which I really hesitated to make, since it will mean divulging my secret hobby to my friends, was custom designed because I knew she'd love it.

Morgan's phone buzzes on the table, and she flips it over to look at the notification. As I pull over another hurricane vase to wipe out before placing the candle inside, I watch her eyebrows scrunch together. She taps the screen, and her eyes narrow as she reads whatever it is.

"Everything okay?" I ask when she sets her phone down on the table, but doesn't look back up.

"Uhhhh . . ."

"Okay, now you're kind of scaring me. What's wrong?"

She raises her eyes to meet my gaze, and her face has gone full-on pale. Her eyes are huge, like a deer caught in the headlights, and she reaches up, smoothing her hand over her strawberry blonde hair where it's pulled back into a bun. Her lips part, but no words come out.

"What the hell, Morgan? What's going on?"

"I . . ." Picking up her phone, she taps the screen and hands it to me. And as my eyes scan the direct message that was sent to the Our House account, which Morgan manages for us, my stomach drops so fast I'm afraid I'm going to throw up.

JASMINE WATERS

Hi, this message is for Jules. I've been seeing your "fiancé" since October. I'm sure you didn't know about me, just like I didn't know about you until I met you last week. Just thought you'd want to know that he's a liar and a cheater. Message me back if you want more details. I've got receipts, and I'm happy to go to the media with them if you don't respond.

Taking a screenshot, I send it to myself from her phone, then hand it back to her and pick mine up off the table. I quickly send a message off to Colt before I can think twice about it.

JULES

What the fuck is this all about?

"I know who that woman is," I tell Morgan, my voice barely more than a whisper.

"Seriously?"

"Yeah, she was at the Neon Cactus . . . I don't know . . . like a week ago? Colt and I were about to walk home," I say, remembering how pleasantly buzzed I was feeling at the time, "but I went to the bathroom first, and when I came out, she was next to him, leaning into him and running her hand along his arm."

Bile rises into my esophagus, burning as it comes up, and I swallow hard to prevent myself from throwing up. *Deep breaths. In, two-three-four, out, two-three-four.* I repeat the breathing technique that sometimes can prevent me from spiraling into a full-on panic attack.

"But she wasn't there *with* him, right?"

"No, we went together to meet up with some of his teammates right after we got back from Montreal." I shake my head, because my brain feels cloudy—like it's having trouble completing its most essential functions: thinking, as well as reminding my heart to beat and my lungs to breathe.

In, two-three-four. Out, two-three-four.

"He was very clearly pushing her away when I came out, but I don't know . . . she seemed surprised. At first, I thought she was surprised he was turning her down, but maybe she was actually surprised he was engaged?"

My stomach turns over again, and that takeout sushi that we got earlier tonight feels like it's gone rancid and is trying to make an escape.

"What did he say about you two meeting at the time?"

"Nothing. He introduced me as his fiancée, and we left together."

"Did you ask him about her?"

"I'm sure I meant to, but I was a little drunk—"

"Wait, what?" Morgan cuts me off. Everyone knows I never have more than two drinks. Ever.

"Yeah, story for another time," I say, unsure how to explain that I'd trusted Colt enough to lose my inhibitions. I'd trusted him enough to do a lot more than that—like hand my heart right over to him after, how long? A few weeks? A month? "Anyway, we walked home, and I forgot to ask."

"Jules, I know that message looks damning, but I've seen you two together. He does *not* look at you like he's holding anything back. He lives with you. You two have been insepa-rable. How could he possibly have been dating someone else?"

I close my eyes, trying to remember every last detail about Colt—all the ways he's been here for me and made me feel safe. And the idea that he could have been with someone else the whole time not only feels logistically impossible, it doesn't check out at all with what I know of his character.

Morgan's right, and I knew it without her having to say it: he's held nothing back with me. He's shared his feelings all along. He's done everything he could to let me know that I'm safe with him. He isn't the kind of person to cheat.

But then *why* is she sending this message?

My phone rings in my hand, and I glance down to see a picture of Colt lighting up my screen. "It's a video call," I tell Morgan.

"I'll give you some privacy. I'm going to head downstairs to your office and call Audrey. Is it okay if I let her know what's going on?"

I nod, and as soon as she opens the door to the basement,

I answer my phone. I don't say anything, just prop it up on the bottle of cider Morgan left behind and raise my eyebrows in question.

"You know that's not true, right?" he asks, his gaze littered with concern. He's walking down a street, the midnight blue sky peppered with streetlamps behind him as he walks quickly.

"It doesn't *feel* true," I say, but the hesitation is there in my voice. "But if there's no truth at all in it, why would she send it?"

"I slept with her one time," Colt insists. "Last fall. I'd only seen her in passing until she showed up at the Neon Cactus the other night and I introduced you two."

"So why is she claiming it's more than that?" I ask.

The thoughts spiraling through my head are taking up so much of my focus that I forget to breathe. I know this feeling. I haven't had a single panic attack since Colt and I have been together, but I can feel it coming on. More gradually than normal, but it's there just the same.

"Did you catch her last name?" he asks as he steps through a doorway. I think he's in the lobby of his hotel now.

"I was more focused on the message."

"Waters."

"Shit." The world carries on a long exhale. Is Jasmine related to Jerome?

"Yeah. And so, I think this is my fault. Well, mine and your brother's."

"What's Jameson have to do with this?"

"He and I may have paid a visit to Jerome's office earlier this week."

"You *what?*" I practically spit out the words. "You *knew*

that I didn't want you getting involved like that. It was over, and I wanted it to stay that way. What the hell did you two do?"

He steps into an elevator, and while the video breaks up a bit, the sound carries through just fine. "His company was a sponsor of the Rebels. When AJ saw the video from the restaurant—"

"There's video footage from the restaurant?" My voice is shrill, and my heart picks up pace.

"Jameson had it."

"What the fuck?" I whisper.

"I guess he got a copy of it just in case it was necessary to . . . I don't know. Anyway, AJ talked to Frank Hartmann, you know, the owner of the team, and they agreed to rescind Jerome's sponsorship of the team."

"What does that have to do with Jasmine?"

"I'm guessing that Daddy losing access to the team—his luxury box, the special events for sponsors, that type of thing —really pissed her off. And given that I've turned her down repeatedly, I'm guessing that when she found out, this is the little revenge plan she hatched."

Colt's walking down a long hallway with beige wallpaper and fancy lights, then he's heading through the door to his dark hotel room. And still, I'm silent, because I'm busy processing all of this.

And the question I asked myself that night at the Neon Cactus rattles around in my brain, trying to cast as much doubt as possible: *Am I going to have to worry about this with every woman he knows? Has he slept with them all? Are others going to come out of the woodwork, for whatever reason, trying to cause drama?*

I'm not cut out for this. I like peace. I like stability. And in the wake of this situation, I worry about whether Colt can give me either of those things.

His eyes flick to the top of his screen, then back at me. I rest my elbows on the table and lean forward, holding my head in my hands, forcing myself to breathe in slowly through my nose, and exhale through my mouth, like I'm training myself to do when these feelings come on.

"Your brother will be there in about five minutes."

That has me looking back up at him, as a new wave of anxiety spikes, crashing over me until I feel like it's holding me under water. "What? Why?" I can barely speak.

"Because I was worried about how you'd react to this, and I didn't want you to be alone."

"I don't need a fucking babysitter." I barely get the words out because my lungs feel like they can't expand, and I fold forward, resting my head on the table.

"Jules!" Colt's voice is a bark, and in my surprise, I sit up and look at him. "Eyes on me. You're going to be okay. *We're* going to be okay. Just breathe."

I want to breathe, I really do, but I'm finding it hard to make my lungs function.

And then I take a moment to take stock of my body, realizing that perhaps I can't breathe because every single part of me is tense. I need to release some of this. I start by focusing on my shoulders, letting them fall so they no longer feel like they're by my ears.

"Good girl," Colt encourages me from the phone. I close my eyes and focus on letting my abdomen relax. And then I take a breath. It's shallow, but knowing I can get oxygen helps calm me just a little more, and I'm able to repeat the action. "You're doing so well."

Once I'm breathing normally, I look up at him, my eyes full of tears. "Thank you."

"You did that," he says, right as Morgan walks through the basement door. "You're the one doing the work to get things under control. I'm not even there."

"Yeah, and yet you are *still* here for me, even from several states away."

I'm about to tell him how much that means to me when Jameson bursts through the side door. He takes one look at my tear-stained face, and then he's yelling at Colt through my phone.

"You don't get to burst in here and start yelling at people," I say, interrupting his mini-tirade. "You caused this. You and Colt, deciding you were going to handle something that I already asked you guys not to get involved in—that's why we're in this situation. I'm not the scared nineteen year old who got drunk-married in Vegas and needs you to discreetly handle my divorce so no one finds out. I'm a grown-ass woman and I can take care of myself, *especially* where my business is concerned. You two getting involved in this only fucked things up. And right now, I'm done talking to both of you about this. I'm going to bed."

And then I head for the stairs, leaving my phone sitting on the table so they can finish their conversation.

Chapter Forty-One

COLT

Please explain to me why Wilcott just told me you won't be at practice tomorrow?

Jules needs me.

Your team needs you. What the hell is wrong with your priorities?

For the first time in my life, my priorities are just right. I'd retire early before I'd risk losing her.

Your choice.

Just make sure you're back in time for tomorrow night's game.

Jameson's asleep on the couch when I come in the front door, but the sound of me shutting and locking it wakes him. His voice is groggy when he says, "I have half a mind to kill you."

I cross my arms over my chest. "Yeah, you mentioned that earlier."

"I warned you not to hurt her."

"This isn't something *I* did to Jules. This is a self-absorbed, pick-me girl stirring up drama because *you* went to AJ and Frank and got her dad's sponsorship of the team revoked."

"None of this would have happened if you hadn't slept with her in the past."

"Yeah." There's truth in that statement, but this didn't happen *because* I'd slept with her. This is a pissy woman with a half-baked revenge plan, fucking with the wrong people. Just like her dad did. "It also wouldn't have happened if you hadn't gotten involved."

"Yeah."

We stare at each other across the dimly lit space. I assume he's considering his role in these events, just like I am. It felt damn good to deliver that refund check to Jerome and tell him his sponsorship had been revoked, but if I had realized what would happen as a result, I wouldn't have gone through with it.

"When I went up and tried to talk to her last night," he says, "she told me she was going to sleep and I should go home."

"Dude, you can't come in hot like that with Jules or she's just going to shut down."

He looks at me like he's assessing the fact that I know this about her and he somehow doesn't. There's a whole lot I know about her that he doesn't, but I'm not going to rub that in. He's basically been the father figure in her life for over a decade, and I don't want him to feel like I'm stepping between them in any way. Unless he tries to stop us from being together . . . then the gloves will come off.

When he glances at his watch, his face tells me he's just realizing it's three in the morning. "How the hell did you get a flight here this late?"

"I chartered a jet."

"What the hell? How much did that cost?"

"It doesn't matter. There's nothing I wouldn't spend to be here for her. I'm going upstairs now. Can you lock the door on the way out?"

"Hey," he says as I head toward the stairs. I stop and turn back to face him. "Thanks."

"For what?"

"For becoming the person she deserves."

There's so much to unpack in that statement. He's right that I haven't always been worthy of her, but at least he sees that I'm working to be that person now.

I give him a nod. "Let's talk once we've all had some sleep. There's a lot we'll need to figure out before I fly back to North Carolina this afternoon."

"Alright," he says. "How about I come back around ten?"

"Sure."

Jules's door is shut, and when I crack it open and peek in, I realize that she's curled up on her side, still fully clothed and on top of the sheets. The curtains are wide open, and the moonlight casts a cool glow in the room. I take my clothes off, and the minute I climb onto the bed, she rolls over. Then she sits straight up like she's just awoken from a nightmare.

"Oh my god! What are you doing here?" She reaches for me like she's not sure if I'm real or not, and I meet her hand, lacing our fingers together and squeezing lightly. Just being in her presence again heals something in me—it's like there was this gaping wound, and her touch has stopped the bleeding. I fucking hate being apart from her, and I'm not sure what to do about it.

"There was no way I wasn't going to be here for you after the shitshow that happened tonight." I pull her close to me, wrapping her in my arms. "Especially because it seemed like you had a moment when you weren't sure if you could trust me, and that gutted me."

Her face falls. "There *was* a moment when I wondered if there was any truth to her accusations. But when I thought about it, it was obvious that her claims were impossible. Since you've lived here, you've done nothing but show me that I can trust you. You've been here for me, and with me, non-stop. I know you'd never cheat—that's just not in your character."

"I'm so sorry this happened. I'm sorry that Jameson and I got involved. I know we wouldn't be in this situation if we hadn't stepped in."

The relief I feel as she rests her head on my shoulder is indescribable. She slides her hand along my abdomen like she's going to wrap her arm around me in a hug, but her fingers hit gauze and tape and she pulls back. "What's this?"

I lift my arm. "Take it off and see."

As she reaches out to peel back the tape holding the six-inch square piece of gauze, her nose scrunches up like it always does when she's intensely focusing on something. It's cute as hell and I just want to lean in and kiss her, but I don't want to interrupt her from seeing what's under that bandage.

When she gently pulls the gauze away from my skin, she sucks in a sharp breath. Right there, directly under my heart, is an intricately inked pair of Tinker Bell wings. Her eyes fill with tears.

"When did you get this?"

"Tonight. I'd just left the tattoo studio and was headed back to the hotel when you messaged me."

"Why this, though?"

"C'mon, Tink," I say, my words and tone clearly indicating that she already knows the answer to the question. But she obviously needs to hear me say it. "You've worked yourself so deep into my soul, there's no reason you shouldn't be inked on my skin as well."

She burrows her face into my chest, and I feel her tears as they slide down her cheeks and meet my skin. And as I wrap her in my arms and hold her tight, she whispers, "I love you so much."

I press my lips to her head, grateful that she's finally trusting her own feelings.

"I love you too, Jules. I always will."

She squeezes me tight. "I know. And that's the only reason I'm not afraid of falling . . . because I know you'll always catch me."

―――

I'm in the kitchen making a pot of coffee when Jameson arrives the next morning. He's got Lauren and the kids with him, which I wasn't expecting, but right behind him, I see Audrey and Graham, followed by Morgan, and it all makes sense. Their family is coming to stand shoulder to shoulder, to be with Jules and to figure out how to fix this mess Jameson and I created.

"Where's Jules?" Lauren asks as she looks around the kitchen. There are fake flowers and strands of leaves, along with candles and glass vases, everywhere. I know they're hosting a bridal brunch for Lauren here tomorrow, and I'm guessing she wasn't supposed to see all of this now.

"Upstairs getting dressed. She just got out of the shower a few minutes ago."

It was a long night, full of tears and admissions of our feelings, and promises about our future. We were both too tired for anything physical, but I'd more than made it up to her this morning—which means we are now running quite late.

"I'm going to get a movie started for the kids," Audrey says, heading toward the family room as Graham, Iris, and Ivy all follow her.

"I'll get this mess cleaned up," Morgan says as she starts scooping up supplies and heading toward empty cardboard boxes that sit in the entryway.

Lauren moves toward the stairs, and in the now-empty kitchen, my eyes meet Jameson's. There's a lot that passes through that look—two former teammates who remained best friends and business associates, recognizing that we are now going to be linked together as family.

We help Morgan put away some of the decorations, and

then Lauren and Jules are heading down the stairs. Even in leggings and a tank top, with her face free of any makeup and her wet hair pulled back into a low bun, she takes my breath away.

I guess this is what love feels like—not the desperate need to cling to someone, but the deep peace they bring you just by being there.

With the kids in the living room watching a movie, we all gather in the kitchen. Surrounding the coffee and the box of pastries that Lauren and Jameson brought, we spend some time figuring out the next steps.

"AJ thinks you should have a statement prepared in case Jasmine tries to go public with this story," Jameson says.

"You told AJ what happened?" I ask. Out of respect for Jules's privacy, I'd been careful not to give her any details when we texted last night.

"Like there was another option," he says, releasing a sigh. "You're my client, and this woman is trying to fuck with your career."

"No, she's trying to fuck with my personal life."

"And you think that, had she been successful, it wouldn't have impacted your performance?" He looks at me like I'm an idiot, but he's right—if Jules was hurt, it would have fucked with my game.

"Point taken."

"Do we think there's a chance that she actually might go public with this?" Jules asks as she tears off a piece of a croissant, seeming more calm than I'd have expected.

"I think we need to be prepared for anything," Lauren says. "The Rebels can write up a statement corroborating your story, so that's ready to go too."

"You're doing PR now too, not just marketing?" I ask.

"No, communications handles public relations. But part of my new role as the director of marketing is to facilitate a more coordinated approach between marketing and communications, and I can easily reach out about this."

I had forgotten she got promoted when the former director of marketing was given the vice president position recently.

"I really hope Jasmine doesn't go that route," Audrey says. "But it does seem smart to be prepared, in case."

"Her making this claim publicly would be bad for everyone involved, her included," Morgan adds. "And her father will come out looking the worst in all this."

"I think that's the key to stopping this," Jameson says. "If we write up a statement from Colt and Jules, and the team writes one up too, I can share both statements with him. We'll offer not to publish them if he calls his daughter off."

Jules laughs, and we all look at her. "So we're basically going to go tattle on her to her dad. Got it."

"Do you have another suggestion?" Jameson asks her.

"Nope. She's acting like a fucking child. Tattling on her feels like the appropriate response, actually."

Two hours later, everything is finalized. We have the approval we need from the Rebels' management, and Jameson heads out to meet with Jerome. Everyone else trickles out, and Jules and I are left in the kitchen alone.

"When do you have to head back?" she asks.

"A car is picking me up in about fifteen minutes. My flight leaves in an hour and a half."

She steps forward, resting her forehead against my chest and wrapping her arms around my waist. I wish I didn't have to leave her, especially since I'm not even playing tonight—unless something goes wrong with Hartmann. Or I wish I could bring her with me, but I know she can't miss Lauren's shower tomorrow, or work on Monday.

"Thank you for everything last night. For helping stop that panic attack, and then flying back last night. I didn't expect that at all, but I'm so glad you were here today."

"I'm always going to be here for you, Tink. My job makes me travel a lot, but it won't be forever."

She looks up at me. "You're not thinking about retiring, are you?"

"I only have one more year left on my contract."

"But you're still playing amazingly well. They'll want to re-sign, don't you think?"

"We'll see how I feel about things next season. Right now, I'm just excited for this season to end—after we win the Cup, of course—so I can be around all summer."

"Maybe we can go away for a bit," she suggests, and there's a lightness in her blue eyes I want to keep there. "Like this summer, after Jameson and Lauren's wedding? I never take time off, but I'm sure I can manage to sneak away for a week or two."

"I'd like that. Why don't you think about where you'd like to go, and I'll take care of making the plans?"

"That sounds perfect."

I'm just about to leave, when there's a knock on the back door. Jules glances over and whispers, "Fuck." And when I follow her gaze, her father stands with his back to the door. His hair is greasy and thinning, his shoulders slumped, and his shirt is dirty.

"Do you want to talk to him right now?" I ask. Because as

much as I want to head out there, guns blazing, to take care of this for her, it should be her choice.

"No, not really."

"Can I take care of this?"

She sighs, but it sounds like it's full of relief. "By all means."

He doesn't turn around until I open the door, and by then it's too late for him to leave because I've stepped out, cornering him against the metal railing of the brick stairs.

"I thought I made it clear that you weren't welcome around here anymore," I say.

"I want to talk to my daughter."

"You don't deserve to talk to her. You don't deserve whatever help you plan to ask for. You don't deserve her time, or her attention, or her money. So until you can clean yourself up, you need to disappear into whatever sewer you came from."

"Who do you think you are?"

I'm pretty sure he asked me that last time he was here. So this time, I will make myself crystal clear.

"I'm the man who's going to marry your daughter. And I'm going to take care of her, and protect her heart, and show her what it's like to be loved—since she clearly didn't see that from the way you treated her mom and then left her and Audrey."

"You don't know anything about me," he spits out.

"Oh, but I do. Sadly, though, you don't know anything about your kids. All three of them are successful. All three of them are engaged. All three of them are happy. And you don't know the first thing about any of it, because all you care about is scrounging money off your youngest whenever you can catch her feeling sorry for you. But that ends now. Don't come around again unless you've cleaned up your life, or genuinely want help doing so."

I step back so there's room for him to pass me and walk down the stairs.

He stands there for a moment, unmoving. Then quietly, still looking down at the steps, he asks, "And if I do want help?"

"Then you know where to find me. But you don't try to contact Jules again, unless you want me to get Jameson and the police involved in this."

He purses his thin lips and gives me a curt nod as he heads down the stairs. As I watch him go, I hope that he will take me up on the offer, but I know his history well enough to know how unlikely that is. In the meantime, I'll have a security system installed so I feel better about her being here when I'm gone.

Chapter Forty-Two

JULES

"Today has been perfect, and you are all amazing, beautiful, strong women," Lauren gushes as she toasts us with her glass of champagne.

She's standing at the head of the table, which now has plates of food scattered all along it, amid the decorations that everyone helped pull together yesterday afternoon. There's no way Morgan and I could have done all of this without everyone pitching in, especially with how exhausted I am after what happened Friday night.

As Lauren sways to one side, she puts her free hand down on the kitchen table to steady herself. I haven't been counting her drinks, but I'm pretty sure she's past just being tipsy.

I reach for the champagne and top off everyone else's glasses to finish the bottle, because I don't want Lauren to have any more and get sick or be hungover. Then Petra stands and comes to the head of the table, wrapping her arm around Lauren's waist and anchoring her to her hip.

"*You* are an amazing, beautiful, strong woman," Petra tells Lauren as she takes the champagne flute from her hand and hands it to Morgan. "Look at everything you've accomplished in the last year and a half—moving across the country with your two little girls, creating your dream life here, getting back into sports marketing and kicking so much ass at your new job that you already got a huge promotion, and giving Jameson a chance to prove how much he loved you, even after you'd been hurt and were scared to trust again. And you've surrounded yourself with women who bring that same energy—who are bold, smart, compassionate, and willing to take big risks."

She glances around the table where Lauren's two other best friends, Jackson and Sierra, sit along with Morgan and Paige, Audrey and me, and AJ, who literally flew in this morning for this shower and is headed right back to North Carolina when we're done.

Lauren rests her head on Petra's shoulder. "I couldn't have done any of that without every single one of you."

"That's literally what friends and family are for," Morgan says.

And as we sit around chatting about Lauren and Jameson's upcoming wedding, now less than two months away, Lauren looks at me and says, "I think Audrey's next, but are we planning a bridal shower for you after that?"

All eyes turn toward me. Half the people sitting at this table know that Colt's and my engagement was fake, but the other half don't. The natural answer to keep up the charade should be, "Of course!" But I know what she's really asking me—are Colt and I going to stay engaged?

"I think so?" I say.

"Why is that a question?" Petra asks.

"How much time do you have?" I joke as a laugh escapes me. "Because it's a *really* long story."

"We're here until tomorrow," Jackson says, her bright green eyes gleaming conspiratorially as she leans in, and Sierra and Petra nod along.

So I swear them all to secrecy, then I start at the beginning—six years ago in Las Vegas—and tell them everything, even things that no one but Audrey knew until now. I stop the story when Colt left to head back for his game yesterday. And I don't mention how he called me as soon as he got back to his hotel post-win last night, and talked dirty to me as he watched me make myself come over and over again.

"It was obvious from the minute you entered my office that this wasn't fake for him," AJ says. "You took a little more time to warm up to the idea. But after everything that went down this weekend, I've never been more sure that it's real for both of you."

"The whole fake engagement thing aside," Petra says, her face lighting up in a way that makes it seem like she's just had a great idea, "can we just talk about this mentoring program for a minute? Because that is one of the most badass things I've ever heard."

"It was Morgan's idea, actually," I say, and Petra looks at her assistant with something akin to pride. "I just ended up being the face of it because I'm the one who's got the contracting experience."

"I want you to let me donate to your nonprofit," AJ says,

looking between Audrey and me. "I know I'm not in the field, and I can't contribute as a mentor, but I'm an enormous fan of women going into spaces that were traditionally dominated by men, and showing that we can kick ass there too."

Lauren laughs, then says, "Yes, you sure are."

"And I want to interview you about it," Petra says, but I shake my head adamantly.

"No. It's just in its infancy. Your show focuses on women who have done groundbreaking things in their field, like AJ has. All I've done is help a few women feel comfortable working in a male-dominated industry."

Audrey's scoff is sudden and loud. "*All you've done?* Jules, do you not understand how life changing that's been for people?"

"I want to see that video you said you guys filmed about Rosie's experience," Petra says. "Even if you're not ready for me to interview you, I can share that video broadly, get more people interested in donating."

I shake my head. "You all are moving so fast. How about if Audrey, Morgan, and I spend some time finding a director for this nonprofit, and then once things are more in place, we can circle back? I'm afraid that the only thing worse than not growing our program would be growing it too quickly. There are so many things we still need to work through to make sure we can grow this program successfully, and I don't want to get ahead of ourselves. But then, yes. We can talk about sharing that video out more widely, if Rosie is okay with it," I say to Petra, "and we can talk about potential donations," I tell AJ.

I carefully steer the conversation back to Lauren, because I feel guilty that Colt's and my story has dominated the last half hour of her bridal shower. By mid-afternoon, everyone is tired from all the food, drinks, and conversation, so when AJ says she needs to head to the airport, everyone else starts saying goodbye too.

"Walk me out?" AJ says to me as she stands.

"Sure." After she hugs Lauren goodbye, I follow her to the front door.

"You know, I could get you a ticket if you wanted to come to the game tomorrow night."

My lips part but the words don't come, because my brain is busy trying to figure out whether that's possible. Finally, I say, "I would love to be there. But I'm not sure if I can miss the next two days of work."

"Think about it and let me know. The offer is open."

"Thanks. I'll let you know either way."

"I hope you can come. Because not only am I convinced that he plays better when you're there, but I think that what you and Colt have is really solid. I've known him for years, and I've never seen him care about anyone like this before. He's a different person around you . . . a better version of himself, for sure."

"Thanks, AJ. That means a lot." I don't need outside validation to know that what Colt and I have is real, and worth holding on to. But the fact that it's so obvious to others, too, makes it even more special.

———

"I have to go get Graham from Jameson's," Audrey says. "I'm sorry. I feel bad leaving you when there's still some cleanup to be done."

I glance around the first floor. The food is put away, the dishes are done, and we've gotten almost all the decorations taken down. The only thing that remains is taking apart the big wooden backdrop, still laden with flowers, leaves, and the banner—and there's no rush on that.

"It's fine. Thank you so much for staying so long. I know it's exhausting when Drew is traveling and you're doing the single parent thing."

Even though Audrey was a single parent for five years before Drew came back in her life, raising Graham was always a team effort, with Jameson and me helping out a lot.

"It's getting easier as Graham gets older, actually. He's becoming so independent. I kind of miss him being little," she says wistfully.

"You thinking about having another?" I know Drew regrets missing out on so much of Graham's childhood, and he's told Audrey multiple times that he wants more kids with her.

"I mean . . . I'm not *not* thinking about it." She gives me a little wink.

"Are you . . .?"

"No," she says with a laugh as she grabs her keys off the counter and steps toward me, "I'm not pregnant. But I'm starting to think I don't want to wait too much longer before we grow our family. I don't want Graham to be much older than his siblings. He's already about to turn six."

"Just think how much older than us Jameson is, and we're still all close."

"That was different."

We've talked a lot over the years about how we were still little kids when Jameson left for college, and even though he came back to Boston four years later to play for the Rebels, he was busy living his life. When Mom died, and Dad left, the three of us were all each other had. Our relationships with each other would undoubtedly be different if it weren't for our shared tragedy.

"I know. And I'm sure you and Drew will know when it's the right time," I assure her. "But please, aside from Drew, promise me I'll be the first person you tell."

She gives me a kiss on the cheek. "You're my person, Jules. Of course you'll be the first one to know."

It hits me then that, until Colt was in my life, I'd kind of felt like I'd lost Audrey to Drew. I couldn't be happier that my sister had found the love of her life, but I missed having *my person* around all the time. But now that I have Colt, I get it. I get how she feels about Drew. I get why there's someone she goes to now before she comes to me. Because that's exactly how I feel about Colt.

There are things Colt knows about me—like my panic attacks, and the fact that Dad still comes around sometimes—that even Audrey doesn't know.

So after Audrey leaves, I pull out my laptop and look at the project management software I use to keep track of all the work Our House is doing. Right now, we only have one project going on, and everything is set up for the next one already. I could put someone else in charge and take two days to be there for Game 4. With Boston up 3-0 in the series, it's entirely possible that tomorrow night's game could be the one that clinches the series for them . . . and I don't want to miss that if I don't have to.

I pull out my phone and shoot off a message to AJ.

JULES

> Can I take you up on the ticket offer?

AJ

> Of course.

JULES

> Let's not tell Colt. I'd like it to be a surprise.

AJ

> I love surprises!

JULES

> That's shocking, actually. You don't seem like the type that would want to be caught off guard.

AJ

> I love surprises for OTHER people. Most importantly, Colt's going to love this surprise.

She sends me the details for where to meet her tomorrow night, and I set about booking a flight down there, making sure I get in early enough that if there are any delays, it won't cause me to miss the game.

Chapter Forty-Three

COLT

"Looking good, Lester!" I call out to him where he's stretching just on the other side of center ice. "The cage is a nice addition. Helps block out the sight of your ugly face."

Unlike Games 2 and 3, he's suited up tonight, but he has two black eyes and his nose is taped under the metal face cage he's sporting. Hopefully, the cameras have zoomed in on him at some point, and Jules is watching at home so she can see firsthand the condition he's in now.

I'm hoping he gets some ice time tonight, because we don't plan on there being a Game 5 and half my team now wants their shot at him. When they asked why I'd pulled him down and beat the shit out of him, I only gave them a three-word answer: "He hurt Jules."

Doesn't matter how or when, because if there's one thing I'm more certain of now than ever, it's that karma does come back to you in the end—and he deserved this. I'm not a violent guy by nature, but if you hurt someone I love, there's no way I'm not getting involved.

I skate over to the visitor's goal to rough up the crease, then sink to the ice to get some stretches in before my teammates start taking shots at me. I can hear the fans behind me, banging on the glass to get my attention. It's not like when we play at home, but there are definitely fans that have traveled here for the game. I focus on my stretches, tuning them out as I lean from one side to the other to make sure my abductor and adductor muscles are well stretched.

A few minutes later, my teammates are waiting to practice some shots, so I grab my stick and get into position in front of the net. But despite the pucks all around and the fact that I'm ready, no one skates forward to take a shot. They're too focused on something behind me.

That's when McCabe rolls his eyes and circles his finger in the air, just like I did to Jules when I wanted her to turn around so I could see her wearing my name on her back. I move out of the crease, turning to skate behind the net, and that's when I come face to face with her.

My heart pounds powerfully at the sight of her—it can't be. How is she here? Then I notice what I think has everyone staring—her WAG jacket is wide open, and instead of a plain white shirt like she wore at our last home game, this one has a big red fabric heart sewn into the front. And in thick block letters that match the Rebels font, my name is spelled out over the heart.

She made that. For me.

She finally let me see her closet Saturday morning, showing me where she sews all the sexy lingerie she designs. And sometime between then and now, she made the decision to surprise me at this game, and crafted this shirt, so I'd know she's mine.

I've been hers since the moment I kissed her in that alley. I tried to fight it at first, but it was no use. Sometimes it felt like I'd be waiting forever for her to admit that she was mine too. But somehow, Jasmine trying to pull us apart actually brought us closer together—made us realize what we stood to lose, and made us both want to fight to keep what we have.

When I told her I loved her the other night, her first response was, "I know." Which means I did what I set out to do. I showed her how I felt, proved she could trust me, and made her feel safe and secure in her feelings for me.

My jaw must be hanging open from the shock of seeing her, because her laugh is airy as she smiles down at me. She seems more certain about us, and more carefree, than I've ever seen her.

I skate right up to the glass, pull my glove off, and put my hand up. She meets it with hers.

"I love you," I tell her. "I love you so fucking much."

She laughs again. "I love you too."

As I skate back to the net, ready to warm up, I'm more driven to win than I've ever been. Because if we win the series in Game 4, we'll have a whole week off before the next series starts. And that's a lot more time to spend with her.

———

Jules is standing next to AJ, waiting for me right outside the locker room post-game, as I walk out in my suit, dreading the flight home. The second she sees me, she comes barreling toward me. I drop my bag so I can catch her as she jumps into my arms, wrapping her legs around my waist like she's a koala.

She nuzzles her face into my neck, breathing in deeply as she squeezes her arms around me. "You did it."

"We all did it."

"Yeah, but that save you made on the penalty shot right at the end secured the win."

"I was just determined to be able to spend next week with you."

We'll still have practice, but without games I'll be home every night with her.

"I can't wait," she says. And then she lowers her voice, her lips ghosting across my ear. "I also made lingerie that matches the shirt, and I'm really looking forward to modeling it for you the minute we get home."

"Jesus, Tink." I squeeze her tighter to me, wishing we were alone and naked.

"Speaking of going home," she says, sitting up in my arms, "AJ said I could come on the team plane with you guys."

"Good." I press a kiss to her lips. "You're sitting with me, then."

Drew must have come out of the locker room right behind me. "Hey, where am I going to sit?"

"I don't fucking care," I say as Jules puts her feet back on the ground and I turn toward him. "You can sit with AJ."

His eyes flick over to where she stands, chatting with Coach Wilcott, and he drops his voice low. "No way."

Next to him, McCabe says, "You can have my seat."

Drew and I turn to look at him in surprise, because not only is he giving up one of the best seats on the plane, but he and AJ barely tolerate each other. It's not a hostile relationship, exactly. They've always maintained a level of professionalism, but it's easy to tell that he doesn't like her, and she seems like she puts up with him because she has to. I'm pretty sure that years ago, she was the Assistant GM in St. Louis when he played there, right before he was traded to Boston. He's never mentioned it, though, so I've never asked.

"It's no big deal," McCabe shrugs. "I'm going to be sleeping. Why do I care where I sit?"

Given that I haven't been able to sleep on a flight home this entire season, I'm fully expecting that I'll be wide awake all night, gazing at Jules as she rests in my arms. But that's not what happens. She cuddles into my side before the plane takes off, and about half an hour into the trip, she falls asleep. And somehow, with her curled up next to me and our seats reclined, I sleep on a flight home for the first time all season.

When we get back to Boston, I bring her back to *our house* —the one she grew up in, the one she started her business in, the one I moved into as her temporary roommate, the one I am planning on living in for as long as she wants to stay here.

It's almost four in the morning when we arrive home, but I'm more well rested than normal. So when we get upstairs, I follow her into her closet, no longer a secret room I'm not allowed into now that I know about her sewing projects and exactly which drawer she stashes her vibrator collection in. And as I slide her jacket off her shoulders, and undo her belt, pulling her jeans down those long, muscular legs, she's left standing in front of me in nothing but an almost transparent thong with a big red heart sewn across the front. It exactly matches the one on her shirt, but without my name.

She turns slowly so I can see the back, and along the thin strap that runs above her ass cheeks, she's sewn gold letters that read: COLT. If it was anyone but her—anyone else at all —I don't think I'd like seeing my name written across someone's ass. But because it's Jules, because it's yet another way she's marking herself as mine, the caveman deep inside me puffs up his chest.

With my hands on her hips, I lean in and kiss the side of her neck. "This is a whole new way of seeing my name across your back. I kind of love it."

"I thought you might," she says, her voice husky as she moves her hands to the hem of her T-shirt and pulls it over her head. Looking down over her shoulder, I can tell that the bra is made up of the sheer fabric from the front of her thong, no hearts or my name anywhere, just nearly transparent fabric shimmering across her breasts and doing nothing to hide the stiff peaks of her nipples.

My thumbs trace the letters across the back of her thong as I kiss my way down the side of her neck and across the ridge of muscles above her collarbone. Then I take the strap of the bra between my teeth and slide it over her shoulder. I'm about to do the same with the other side, but she's impatient, as she so often is when it comes to sex, and doesn't want to take it slow.

Reaching up, she pulls both straps down, then says, "You're wearing entirely too many clothes," as she hooks her thumbs into the stretchy fabric around her rib cage and slides the bra down over her hips, letting it fall to the floor.

Standing there in nothing but her thong, I wonder if there will ever come a day that all the blood in my body doesn't rush to my dick when I see her naked. Hopefully not.

She steps forward, pushing my suit coat off my shoulders and tossing it onto the bench beneath the window. Then she's undressing me with her eyes closed because I can't stop kissing her, can't take my hands off her, can't stop touching every part of her until she's sighing into the kiss, pressing her body forward until we're skin to skin.

"That's better," she says.

"No. *Better* will be when I can taste you," I tell her as I lift her hips and set her on the countertop of the island in the middle of her closet. "It's been too long."

I kneel before her, lifting her knees until they're over my shoulders, and then I reach out, tracing the red heart to where the pointy end sits right over her clit. My fingers continue down to find her underwear soaked.

"Clearly, I missed you too," she says. I know she's perfectly capable of taking care of herself, but the thought of her, here without me for the last two nights, has me determined to provide her with multiple orgasms that will put her vibrator to shame.

Sweeping her thong to the side, I reach out with my tongue, savoring her taste as I lick up every last drop of her arousal. And then I feast, bringing her to orgasm in what has to be record time before I'm flipping her over so she's bent forward over that island and sliding into her from behind, watching her take me inch by inch.

The pace is fast and hard, how she likes it best, and I enjoy every one of her cries as she chants my name while she comes. And when I carry her back to the bedroom, the sun is already rising. I smile to myself as I settle us in our bed, thinking how lucky I am to hold this woman in my arms every night.

When I envision my future, all I see is Jules. We can live here if that's what she wants, or in my condo, or somewhere entirely new. I don't care, as long as it's with her.

And one day, when she's ready, she's going to be my wife. I'll spend every day reminding her that she's worthy of a forever kind of love . . . because that's exactly what I intend to give her.

Epilogue

COLT & JULES

COLT

Two Months Later

"Are you nervous?" I ask Jameson as we walk toward the side door that will lead us from this small room out to the altar of the church. I can't stop my hand from twitching so I shove it in my pocket.

He looks me up and down. "Not as nervous as you, apparently." His voice is dry but amused. "What has you so fidgety?"

I haven't told Jameson about my plan yet. Everyone knows we're headed to Bora Bora for two weeks after the wedding. No one, except Drew, knows we're headed somewhere else first. And because I want to make sure Jules is surprised, I'm going to keep it that way until we get back from our vacation.

"Dude, if I'm feeling like this about seeing Jules walk down that aisle, why aren't you more nervous to see Lauren?"

"I already saw her."

"Isn't it bad luck to see the bride before the wedding?" I ask. I don't know a ton about weddings, but that seems like one of those superstitions that's stood the test of time.

"Like I'd go a whole day without seeing her."

"I knew you were whipped from the minute you asked about that marketing job with the Rebels two seasons ago." I roll my eyes, remembering when Jameson first started talking about his former colleague who was relocating back to Boston—the way he was always going out of his way to help her, whether it was to set her up with an interview for a new job, or to go watch her kids when she couldn't get home in time during a snowstorm. He'd claimed that she was just a friend, but even before I met her, I could tell something was different in the way he talked about her.

"You're one to talk. When's the last time you were away from Jules for more than eight hours?"

"Not since the finals." I'm not too proud to admit that I've been following her around like a lost puppy since then, even while recovering from a knee injury I sustained in our last game.

She keeps joking that she's going to get tired of me if I'm always around, but there's no truth in her words, which she proves over and over as she rushes back to me any time she has to be away, too.

"Exactly. So don't give me shit for seeing Lauren on our

wedding day. Besides, we wanted to take some first look pictures before the chaos begins."

"So that's where you went." An hour ago, Jameson told me he had to take care of something, and he'd meet me in this room before the ceremony. I watch the way his eyes get misty as he stares off into space. "Shit, you cried, didn't you?"

In typical Jameson fashion, his jaw ticks as he holds his emotions in.

"Don't worry, man," I say and clasp him on the shoulder. "There's, like, a ninety percent chance I'm going to cry when I see Jules, and we're not even the ones getting married."

"Yet."

"Yeah, we'll see. She's not ready for that yet."

"You guys just going to stay engaged forever?" Jameson asks.

"Not sure. First, I have to really propose, and she has to really say yes."

"Bora Bora?"

"It's been three months," I say dryly. I'd have married her yesterday, but even I know that three months is quick. She's still wearing my ring, over a month after we were knocked out of the playoffs, which was our end date. We've had endless talks about the future, but she's never said the word "marriage." I did think about proposing to her on our vacation this week, but I'm waiting for her to let me know, without a doubt, that she's ready for a lifetime commitment.

"Dude, you wouldn't be okay without her. You know that, right? It's like being with her has altered some part of your brain chemistry, and you're no longer Colt, you're Jules and Colt."

"I'm fine with that."

"Me too," he says with a nod. "You're a better version of yourself this way."

"So I was a dick before?"

He sighs. "You were just you. And right now, you're acting awfully cagey. It reminds me of all the times you did something I was going to have to fix, but you didn't want to tell me."

I chuckle. I used to do such stupid shit and try to hide it before expecting him to fix it, instead of owning up to my mistakes.

"Don't worry," I say as I reach for the door and pull it open. "I'm not planning anything sketchy." If we don't get out of this small room, just him and me, I'm probably going to break down and tell him my plan.

We enter near the altar of the church right as Drew is ushering Graham, in his little six-year-old-sized tux, out of the church through the doors into the entryway. Which must mean the bridal party has arrived.

The other groomsmen—Lauren's friends' husbands, Nate, Beau, and Alex—meet us at the front of the church, joined shortly after by Drew, whose amused expression makes me wonder what kind of pandemonium is going on out there. With Lauren's three-year-old twins as flower girls and Graham as the ring bearer, not to mention Lauren's seven bridesmaids, I imagine it's quite the scene.

When the music plays, and the bridesmaids start walking in, I can't take my eyes off Jules. As always, she's the most stunning woman in the room—she's wearing minimal makeup, but her blue eyes sparkle under those long dark lashes, and her lips are glossy and so fucking delicious looking that I want to meet her halfway down the aisle and kiss the shit out of her. But I refrain, because it's my best friend's wedding.

When she gets to the end of the aisle, she gives me a wink and then takes her place on the steps leading to the altar. Morgan is the last bridesmaid down the aisle and she's flanked by Lauren's twins, who are doing a great job throwing petals onto the runner, and only occasionally stopping to say hi to people. Graham comes down the aisle with the rings, followed by Lauren's Maid of Honor, her sister, Paige, and then everyone is standing.

When the doors open and Lauren steps through—her white lace dress clinging to her small frame all the way down to her knees before fanning out toward the ground, and her face covered in a short veil—my best friend clears his throat several times.

And I don't even want to give him shit about it because I'm choked up too, thinking about what it will be like to one day see Jules walking toward me like Lauren is walking toward Jameson.

We've already started our life together, much like they have, but there's something about the idea of a ceremony where we commit to each other in front of our friends and family that has me suddenly feeling very impatient.

———

JULES

"Hey, Tink." Colt's voice wakes me up. Or maybe it's the way his hand is stroking my face gently, and the familiar feeling of his thumb tugging at my lower lip like it so often does before he kisses me. "We're here."

I open my eyes and see nothing but darkness out the tinted windows of the big, black SUV. I didn't mean to fall asleep, and I hate the way I feel—confused and incoherent—when I'm woken up with anything less than a full night's rest.

"Where are we?" I ask. I guess when we left the reception and he said we were staying somewhere else before tomorrow's flight to Bora Bora, I anticipated a short drive to a hotel. Instead, we're somewhere pitch black. It feels like we're in the middle of nowhere. If I weren't with Colt, I'd be terrified to wake up not knowing where I am or how I got here.

"You'll see." He opens the car door, and there's nothing but the sound of crickets and the gentle rustling of leaves. The air is markedly cooler than when we left the wedding, and I don't know if that means we're far away or if it's the middle of the night, or both?

Two months ago, this not knowing would have been enough to send me spiraling into a panic attack. Today, I just inhale a deep breath of the crisp evening air—taking note of the earthy, damp smell as a hint that we're not near the city—and give Colt's hand a squeeze.

Stepping out of the car, he holds his hand back toward me, and I take it again, sliding across the back seat. "Where are you taking me, exactly?"

"You'll see."

He uses the flashlight on his phone to light the way, and I hold on to his arm tightly as we follow a paved path down the gentle slope of a hill. We're surrounded by trees so thick I can't see how wide the path is, or even see the sky through their branches above us. But after only a minute of walking, there's light ahead. We reach the end of the path and the full moon above glows brightly, a marked contrast to how dark it was under the thick trees. In front of us is a large, level clearing and beyond that, the gently lapping waves of a lake.

But the part that takes my breath away isn't the spectacular view in front of me, where the earth and water meet with trees and mountains all around us and the bright smattering of stars in the dark sky. No, the thing that takes my breath away are the hundred or so glass hurricane vases with candles set up in the middle of the clearing. They're in the shape of a large rectangle, with lines of candles inside forming smaller rectangles.

I glance up at Colt, and his look as he gazes down at me is full of love, but also . . . nerves?

"Oh my god, is this what I think it is?"

His low rumble of a laugh fills the space. "I highly doubt it."

"Okay," I say, wondering if that means he isn't proposing to me tonight? "So, what is this, then?"

"Let me walk you through it," he says, walking toward a straight line of candles that run parallel to the shore, and closest to the road we just walked down.

I follow beside him, his arm wrapped around my lower back protectively, like he's trying to make sure I don't trip. Which is good, since the first thing that happens as we step into the clearing is that the toe of one of the flip-flops I put on at the reception catches on a tree root sticking out of the uneven ground, and I start to fall forward. Colt's arm keeps me upright.

He stops between two candles, dead center on the line. "I

want you to imagine a big front porch here, with a doorway." Moving forward, he brings me along. "This is the entryway. To the left"—he points—"is a den. To the right is the dining room." He walks a few steps farther between two rows of candles.

"Beyond that is the kitchen"—he points right—"and on the other side of this wide hallway is the bathroom." He leads us a few more steps closer to the lake. "And this is the great room. Imagine a wall with several sets of French doors surrounded by windows overlooking the water, and outside, a large screened-in porch where we can set up rocking chairs to watch the sunset."

It's the rocking chair reference that does it for me, and I gasp. "Colt . . . is this . . ."

"The floor plan of your great aunt's house on Lake Sunapee? Yes."

"Is that where we are? In Sunapee?"

"No. And I think you'll like this better, actually. Follow me through our glass doors to our porch and down to the lake," he says, and walks forward, through a row of candles. We're only about thirty feet from the water now, and I can see a brand-new dock jutting out into the lake. The dock is at least twenty-five feet long with a huge platform at the end that would be a perfect place to set up chairs and read a book, or dive into the lake on a hot summer day.

He steps up onto the dock first, then holds out a hand to me as I step up onto it.

"You going to tell me where we are now?" I ask, wishing my phone wasn't sitting back in the car so I could just take a look and see exactly where I am.

When we get to the end of the dock, he wraps his arms

around me, pulling me to him so my back is resting up against his chest. He kisses the top of my head, then extends his arm, pointing out at the lake. "I thought you would like it here, because this little cove is quiet and private, but we still have views of the mountains across this part of the lake. And the big lake is right down there." Lifting his arm to the left, he points to an opening beyond which all I see is water sparkling in the moonlight.

"Where are we?"

"Lake Winnipesaukee."

My heart skips a beat. Audrey and Drew have been looking for a place up here over the last few months, because he grew up coming to his family's cabin on this lake every summer and wants to continue the tradition with Audrey and Graham.

"So that I can be close to Audrey?" I ask.

He turns us toward the shoreline and that's when my eyes land on a house, its windows lit up in the moonlight, sitting just to the side of our future house. There is a fairly narrow line of trees between our properties, and I'm actually surprised it's so close to where our house will be. Coming out from that house is another dock, running parallel to this one. There are no other properties in this small cove that I can see.

"I hope we like our neighbors," I say, hugging his arms where they wrap around my abdomen.

His chest shakes against my back as his low laugh rumbles against my hair. "We do."

"Are you . . ." I can't even fathom what he's telling me. There's no way my sister bought a lake house and didn't tell me. Is there? "Did Drew and Audrey buy that house?"

"Drew bought it, and we subdivided the property. I had this area cleared so that I could build you your dream house right next to your sister. I have the original plans to your great aunt's house, so we can rebuild it exactly if you want," he says, and now it makes sense why he was able to describe a house he'd never been to. But how did he even get those drawings? And how long has he been planning this? "Or you can have Audrey design you something completely different. But I knew that, either way, you'd want to be involved."

I look up at him, almost unable to breathe because the realization of what he's done for me has my heart expanding in my chest so that there's no room for anything but my love for him. "You know me so well."

"And yet not as well as I want to," he says. "I feel like I'll never stop wanting to learn new things about you."

"What happens when you run out of new things to learn? Or get bored of me?" I ask. It's not a real fear, but every once in a while, the doubt creeps in.

"Impossible." He squeezes me tighter. "Do you remember when we were sitting on the dock at my parents' house, and I said I didn't have a favorite place?"

"Yeah, of course I remember." I just didn't realize he was taking such careful notes about the place I loved so much.

"I finally figured it out. My favorite place is wherever you are."

My god, this man! It's like knowing how to love me is just second nature to him. I have no idea what I did to deserve him, only that I will do whatever it takes to always show him I feel the same way.

My heart races when I tell him, "My favorite place is with

you too. I want to spend forever with you, making all kinds of new memories in new favorite places."

In the quiet night air, with no one but the crickets keeping us company, I can hear the way his breath hitches at my admission.

He puts his hands on my shoulders and steps back as he turns me toward him, and then he says, "I'd have married you already if I thought you were ready. I want to spend every day of the rest of my life making you happy."

"That's perfect, then." I smile. "Because I also want to spend every day of the rest of my life making you happy."

His hands slide down my arms, and he takes my fingers in his big palms, sliding his thumbs over the two rings I wear—the engagement ring that never really felt fake, and the silicone band on my opposite hand—as he sinks to one knee.

My eyes fill with tears so quickly that I almost can't see him when he says, "Jules, I know we've been engaged for months already. Nothing about us together has ever felt anything except perfect. From the first moment I kissed you in the alley, I was yours, completely. I've never had to pretend with you, except when it comes to letting you know how much I want to spend the rest of my life with you. I've been waiting until you were ready to talk about forever, so that I could finally ask you for real: will you marry me?"

I sink to my knees on that dock, my hands flying up to cup his face as my lips crash onto his. And between kisses, I tell him, "Yes. Absolutely and without a doubt, yes." And then I kiss him again, before I say, "I've wanted you since the moment I first laid eyes on you, Mathieu Coltier, and even though my feelings for you have changed and grown in a hundred different ways in that time, I never could have imagined us here, now. I never could have imagined how unimaginably wonderful you are. How perfect you are for me. How much I want to be perfect for you, too—"

"You already are, Jules. Just as you are," he says as he kisses my nose. "There is absolutely nothing about you, about us together, that isn't already enough. And I can't wait to spend every single day, forever, with you."

———

We're lying tangled up together, sweaty and naked, on the enormous bed that takes up a good quarter of the adorable tiny house trailer on our new property. I don't know how I hadn't noticed it when we first came down what I now know is the driveway, but it sits off to the side under the trees. The big window above the headboard faces the lake, so I'm already looking forward to that view first thing in the morning.

I still can't believe everything Colt has done over the last month—how he bought this property with Drew and cleared land for us to build my dream vacation house; how he had this cute little trailer set up so we'd have a place to stay up here this summer as we make all the plans to start the build in the fall; how he and Drew planned this surprise so he'd show me our future house tonight, and Drew will bring Audrey and Graham up here to see their new house tomorrow.

Or today, actually, as it's now somewhere in the early hours of the morning as Colt kisses his way up the inside of my thigh. I groan and tell him, "I can't come again. Twice is enough."

"I bet you can give me a third," he says with a cocky grin, and when his hot breath meets the opening of my pussy, my entire core clenches and I'm pretty sure he's right. "Besides, you haven't let me taste you yet."

"Since this morning, you mean?" I ask with a laugh. This man loves to eat, and I know I'm incredibly blessed. If I'm only ever going to have sex with one person in my entire life, I appreciate that he's committed to pleasing me in every way possible.

His tongue slides over my clit, warm and rough, with enough pressure that I moan out his name. And as he slides two fingers inside me, I wish it had been more than two minutes since we'd had sex so I could have him inside me again. His fingers are great, but there's nothing better than the way he fills me perfectly with his cock.

"I will never get enough of you, Tink," he says, and the wet, sloppy sound of his fingers sliding into me while I'm still filled with his cum is its own kind of filthy pleasure. He strokes his tongue over my clit again and again, until I'm practically panting, and then says, "I need you to promise me something."

"Anything," I gasp, eager for him to stop talking and get his mouth back on me as soon as possible.

"Whatever you decide on for this house, please don't make it one of those crazy huge mansions like you see on this lake."

He knows me well enough to know that's not at all the kind of house I'd build. "Why not?"

"I never want us to live in a place that big," he says decisively. "I never want to be that far away from you. In fact"—

he wraps one arm under my leg and anchors my hip to the bed—"I think maybe this is the perfect house for us."

"You can practically reach both sides of this trailer when you stick your arms out. How could this be the perfect place for us?" I laugh, until his tongue strokes over my clit again, making my hips buck while he holds me firmly to the bed.

"Because," he says, lifting his head to look up at me between my thighs, "I love the idea of always having you within reach."

"Oh yeah," I tease as I reach down to stroke his face. "Why do you always want me within reach?"

"So I can do this, any time I want." Returning his face to my center, he swirls his tongue over my clit as his fingers stroke me from the inside.

"Yes," I hiss, my fingers gripping his hair, "I can see the appeal." The vibrations of his laughter send ripples of longing throughout my body as he works me closer to the edge, until I'm almost ready to tip over into the abyss. "But I promise to let you do this any time you want, anywhere you want, in our new house."

"In that case," he says, just as he meets my eyes with a demand, "come for me."

"Make me," I taunt.

The way he holds my clit between his lips, sucking on it rhythmically as his tongue slides over it, sends lightning through my veins. And then I'm screaming his name as the waves of pleasure crash over me, again and again and again, until I think I might not be able to breathe.

My body feels like a pool of liquid as he climbs over me and lays himself beside me, pulling me to him. "God, I love to hear you come," he says, kissing my shoulder, "but I think we need to invest in the best sound-proof insulation and sound-proof windows on the planet. Because I don't want to share those sounds with anyone, and you know how sound carries across water."

"Fuck," I sigh, "now the whole lake knows you're here and what you're doing."

His laugh shakes the whole bed. "Luckily, there are no other houses in this cove. I doubt the sound carries that far. But unless we want to traumatize your sister's family when they arrive tomorrow, we'll have to practice being quiet."

I never want to be quiet where Colt is concerned. I want to love this man out loud, and I want the whole world to know how much I love him. But he's probably right that the whole world doesn't need to know about our sex life.

"Yeah," I tell him, running my hands over his skin, "we'll need lots and lots of practice."

His teeth sink into my shoulder with a playful nip. "Don't tempt me. We do need to get some sleep."

"Are we actually headed to Bora Bora tomorrow, or was that just an elaborate ruse to get me up here? I'm okay either way," I tell him.

"Our flight is tomorrow night. Let's get some sleep so we can spend some time with your sister tomorrow, then we'll head to the airport. That overwater bungalow I got us will actually be the perfect place for us to practice being quiet," he says. "We'll be pros by the time we get back here."

"Are we spending a lot of time up here this summer?"

"As much as you can manage with work."

I'm more thankful than ever that I've been able to build such a competent, wonderful team of women at Our House. Because despite already taking the next two weeks off to go to Bora Bora, I'm now thinking that I should take Fridays off this summer so we can spend long weekends up here, dreaming about and planning out our future vacation house.

"I already can't wait," I tell him, kissing his neck as I snuggle into him and close my eyes. "We're going to build something amazing here—not just the house, but the whole life we're creating together."

"Our life is already pretty damn amazing, and it's only going to get better," he promises, and it's with visions of our future together—with the person who makes me feel loved, and safe, and cherished, in a way that I didn't even know was possible—that I settle into a deep, happy sleep.

Want more Colt and Jules? Get their steamy bonus epilogue here.

Curious about Zach and Ashleigh? They have a novella, THE TRADE UP, which you can download here.

THE END

Join My Reader Group

Not ready to leave the world of the Boston Rebels? Join me in my Facebook reader group, where we're always talking about the Rebels!

CROSS-CHECKED
Boston Rebels, Book 3

McCabe & AJ

Some people might call it a grudge, but in reality, hating Alessandra Jones is more like an obsession.

AJ is the league's first female general manager, and my boss. As the team captain, I have to play nice with her—in public, at least.

But in private, the gloves come off. And then one time, our clothes do too.

We vow it won't happen again.

Not only can we not stand each other, but we're in tense negotiations over my contract right now, and AJ is up for the league's GM of the Year award. Getting involved wouldn't just be a PR nightmare—it would be unethical.

It doesn't help that we have a history, or that she and my daughter adore each other. When AJ is injured protecting my baby, there's no choice but to move her into my place.

Taking care of someone I hate shouldn't feel so right. Getting to know her better shouldn't break down my defenses. She's hurt me once before, and I'd be a fool to trust her again.

But the more time we spend together, the more I realize that maybe I'm not obsessed with hating her . . . maybe *I'm just obsessed with her.*

Books by Julia Connors

FROZEN HEARTS SERIES

On the Edge: Jackson & Nate

Out of Bounds: Sierra & Beau

One Last Shot: Petra & Aleksandr

One Little Favor: Avery & Tom

On the Line: Lauren & Jameson

BOSTON REBELS SERIES

Center Ice: Drew & Audrey

Fake Shot: Colt & Jules

Cross-Checked: McCabe & AJ

Goal Line: Luke & Eva

Penalty Play: Aidan & Morgan

HARTMANN BROTHERS SERIES

Coming soon!

Acknowledgments

I think I say this for each book, but it continues to be true… each time I start a new book, I assume the writing process will get easier. Somehow, it's always more difficult. Jules and Colt, in particular, were a challenge. These two were speaking to me big time while I wrote *Center Ice*—nagging at me to tell their story—but the minute I turned my full attention to them, and saw all their wounds, I knew they were going to be difficult. Good thing I like a challenge!

The way there were so many people out there asking for this story was what carried me through some of the tougher days of writing this book. I could not have finished this book if that enthusiasm wasn't already there, encouraging me to keep going—so, thank you to all the readers who reached out, who posted about my books, and whose reviews of *Center Ice* specifically mentioned needing Jules and Colt's story.

This book was finished during the most difficult time I've ever had in my personal life. I could not have done it without these amazing people in my corner:

Melissa – Thank you for working with me on draft after draft, until this story felt like the best version of what I had envisioned. Your honest feedback always pushes me to be better.

Rachel, Sarah, Kait, and Autumn – Your insights and feedback during the beta-reading process helped me immensely. I'm forever grateful for your time and your efforts to help me write the best book possible.

Emily – Without our almost-daily writing sprints, this book would not have gotten done even close to on-time.

Daphne – Our in-person meet-ups and writing time have been such a joy in a really dark time in my life…thank you!

Victoria, Harlow, and Danielle – For cheering me on from afar, to blurb help, to constant texts, voice messages, phone calls, and video chats…your friendships have sustained me!

Kait and Autumn – Thank you for keeping me on track. I'm not sure what I'd do without you both!

Amy and Elizabeth – Thank you squeezing in my project, and for your attention to detail and your responses to my *many* questions when I had a last minute crisis of confidence about this book.

Mandy – Thanks for suggesting the Neon Cactus as the bar the Rebels go to after games.

HEA Babes and Steamy KU Harlots – I don't know where I'd be without our group chats. Thanks for being amazing author friends!

And thanks to everyone else who has helped and supported me along the way, especially other author friends, my promo and ARC teams, and my family. And the hugest thank you to my readers, because without you I would not be able to do any of this!

Afterword

Thank you so much for reading! If you enjoyed the book, please consider leaving an honest review. Reader reviews mean so much to authors, and your time and feedback are appreciated.

Sign up for Julia's newsletter to stay up to date on the latest news and be the first to know about sales, audiobooks, and new releases!

www.juliaconnors.com/newsletter

About the Author

Julia Connors grew up in California, but her first decision as an adult was to trade her flip-flops for snow boots and move to Boston. She's been enjoying everything that New England has to offer for over two decades, and now that she's acclimated to the snowy winters and finally found all the places to get good sushi and tacos, she has zero regrets. You can usually find her in front of her computer, but when she stops writing she's most likely to be found outdoors, preferably with a pair of skis or snowshoes strapped to her feet in winter, or on a paddleboard in the summer.

goodreads.com/julia_connors

amazon.com/author/juliaconnors

instagram.com/juliaconnorsauthor

tiktok.com/@juliaconnorsauthor

facebook.com/juliaconnorsauthor

pinterest.com/juliaconnorsauthor